The Gift

A Supernatural Hint to what Peter is...

By
Doug White

Bookman
Publishing & Marketing
Providing Quality, Professional Author Services
www.bookmanmarketing.com

This book is a work of fiction. Any resemblances to any persons, living or dead, are completely coincidental.

© Copyright 2005, Doug White

All Rights Reserved.

No part of this book may be reproduced, stored in a retrieval system, or transmitted by any means, electronic, mechanical, photocopying, recording, or otherwise, without written permission from the author.

ISBN: 1-59453-649-X

DEDICATION

In the early 1980's while working as a camp counselor, I had a seven-year-old boy in my cabin with a chronic bedwetting problem; a result of neglect and emotional abuse. If ever there was a child that needed Jake Winters' type of TLC, this was the one. Because of my own ignorance, I failed him. I've never forgotten that boy, or my own shortcomings. I'd like to dedicate this book to him.

ACKNOWLEDGEMENT

In *The Gift*, Peter has many new experiences. One of those is a physical exam. In reality, I don't think this would be possible; but in fiction anything is possible. I have to thank both my niece, Renee Birdlingmaier, a nurse and the mother of three small children, and my doctor, Mark Swetz, for helping me understand what's involved in the exam of a young child. Ultimately I had to imagine myself in the shoes of a doctor who is about to examine a proven ghost in a mortal body and let my imagination go: Thus my fictional Dr. Bruce's sudden interest in neurology.

In the past when I visited a doctor's office, I scanned through sports and outdoor magazines. Since starting this series, I find myself reading child-rearing material.

A few years ago while heading home for Christmas on I-71 in Ohio, I pulled into a truck stop thirty miles north of Columbus and called Doug Denbow. Doug, a retired English teacher and I have been friends since teaming up as scoutmasters of a Salvation Army Troop, in the mid 1960's. Over a cup of coffee I chanced to mention I'd written a book. He asked if I'd send him a copy of the manuscript. Five weeks later he returned the first five chapters, edited. He's been my editor ever since.

As we worked together on the series, there was more than once we were both in tears since it deals with a neglected and abused six-year-old boy. However, as the series moves further away from the traumatic experiences Peter suffered through as a living child, Peter develops into a normal, fun-loving, active six-year-old boy with mischief in his eyes at times. As a result, Doug and I chuckled often over some of his antics. Many were the antics of children I'd worked with over the years, some were my own as a young child and a few are a product of my imagination. Thanks Doug.

In my second book, *The Editorial,* I asked Cathy Hardy if she would proofread it for me. I explained a time problem I had and gave her three days. She promised she'd do her best. Between a full time job and family responsibilities, she managed 374 pages in three days. She found a lot of mistakes, but didn't find them all. Who would expect her to in three days?

With this book, I gave her two months and two other proofreaders. Again Cathy, thanks much.

The other three proofreaders are also longtime friends; Jim Preston (after whom I modeled the character Bill Early, introduced in *The Editorial*); Jackie Pawlicki, our camp nurse going back twenty-five years, and the mother of Cindy who provided me with the inspiration for *The Load*; and Shelly Sellepack, my minister's wife.

Henry "Hank" Helton, (the character model for Hank Hamilton in the series) is a long-time truck driver (now retired) and friend. Both he and his wife, Julie, have served as critics for me. Thanks guys.

Wendy Mills, mother of three small children, home schooler and an independent representative of Usborne Books, a company out of Tulsa, Oklahoma that works with home schoolers, is also an artist. Wendy is the designer of the cover. Thanks Wendy.

Karen Smith is a friend that goes back to our elementary school days. She's a hard-hitting critic of mine. In both *The Editorial* and *The Gift,* I listened to what she had to say, reread portions of the books, decided she was right and rewrote portions of both. Thanks Karen.

Again, I must thank my brother-in-law, Harry "Bud" Yount, for being my continuous sounding board. He's listened to many of my ideas over the years and expressed his opinions. Thanks Bud.

I'd also like to thank my sister, Sue Yount, for also assisting with the proofreading of the text. Whenever I had a question pertaining to grammar, she was there. Thanks Sue.

I want to thank my growing base of followers for their support. I hope you continue to enjoy the antics of Peter and the adventures of the unique trucking team of Winters and Stevenson.

Finally, I have to thank my family and friends for not abandoning me yet and for their continued encouragement and input.

INTRODUCTION
And Background

Summary of *The Load* and *The Editorial*, two books leading up to *The Gift*, follows:

"A passenger! In my truck? I don't think so. I'm too independent for a passenger. I like my independence and the freedom that goes with it. Not on your life! Besides, who would sign his liability form?"

"He doesn't need a liability form," Jane said. "He's dead."

And that's how I ended up with a 106 year-old ghost as a passenger in my big rig. Peter Stevenson took on the form of the most charming six-year-old boy you'd ever hope to meet. In the short time we've been moving around the country together, we've been involved in some pretty wild things – some involving the law. Peter began to work his magic on me.

I'm Jake Winters, an over-the-road, bachelor trucker who'd just begun to dream of retirement and some serious fishing up north when Peter...

It all began on June 29, 2001. As a cross-country truck driver, I delivered a load of paper to a company in Butte, Montana. After unloading, I was dispatched to a small mining town some forty miles north of Butte. There I picked up a small piece of machinery at the J. and J. Mines in Slippery Gulch bound for a firm in Reno, Nevada, putting a secure seal on the trailer in accordance with shipping protocol.

Before leaving town with my load, I befriended a small waif, Peter Stevenson. He was the most severely neglected child I'd ever seen; and I have worked with a lot of kids years ago as a classroom science teacher and camp counselor and director. This boy's body and clothes were filthy dirty. His clothes, what were left of them, were rotting away with age. When he begged me to take him along, I asked why. He said his father was going to kill him.

Now, as a young child I often said the same thing. But I refused, explaining that a passenger had to be at least twelve. At Basin, the nearest little town eight miles south of Slippery Gulch, I stopped at the Silver Dollar Saloon and talked to some nice folks I'd met on the way in. Asking them to try and get some help for Peter, I left for Reno to deliver the load.

Once I reached Reno, I discovered the company that ordered the machinery had gone out of business exactly 100 years ago. As a result, the Nevada Department of Transportation (DOT) got involved. They broke the seal, opened the trailer door and discovered, much to my surprise, that the load (a two ton crusher) was gone.

Since this was the disappearance of interstate freight, the DOT notified the FBI. This also meant that as the driver, I was in deep doodoo. I hired an attorney, with the help of a Professional Trucker's Legal Association. Frank Krandell, a federal attorney, thought the case sounded fascinating. As he delved into the case, he received help from three key people in Basin: George Swansen (half-owner of the Silver Dollar Saloon in Basin); Jane Dowdy (George's sister and owner of the other half); and Jane's husband, Mike. Frank would learn a great deal about Slippery Gulch and Jeremiah Peabody, the owner of the J. and J. Mines. Oh, and Peter Stevenson! But when Frank visited Slippery Gulch and the mine he discovered that nothing was as I had described it.

At the mine, the archaic piece of machinery used to load the crusher into my truck was on its side, the wood rotting and the metal working parts frozen in rust. And he found no trace of the few people I'd seen in the town a few days earlier. The only visible footprints besides my own were the small barefoot tracks of Peter, overlapping mine as they did on my earlier visit.

Just as disturbing was the road into Slippery Gulch. Twenty feet of the road had been washed out by the spring melt, and that had happened several months earlier. It was impossible for me to have driven into Slippery Gulch when I did, yet my tire tracks were clearly visible going through town, up to the mine and then departing.

One week later, I found myself back in Slippery Gulch accompanied by two FBI agents, my attorney, the three folks from Basin, and Tasha, a parapsychologist. It was then that I received a devastating blow: I was informed that Peter Stevenson had been brutally murdered by his father on June 30th. I felt personally responsible for his murder; Peter had warned me and begged to leave town with me.

I was then informed there was nothing I or anyone else could have done. As a matter of public record, Peter was murdered by his father, June 30, 1901. This meant that Peter had to be a ghost; but I did not believe in their existence. One week earlier, I had talked to him, touched him and photographed him. For some reason, I had a brief encounter with the supernatural. Nevertheless, it was Peter that led us to the missing crusher.

A few days after the mystery of the missing equipment was solved, an editorial was discovered in the archives of Jefferson County, Montana. The publisher of the Slippery

Gulch Gazette, a one-sheet tabloid, had penned it four days after Peter's death. His editorial described the terrible life and brutal death of a little boy in Slippery Gulch – Peter Stevenson. It quoted Peter's last mortal words: "Please Lord, give me a friend." His funeral was also described as a travesty of a Christian burial, "bearing no respect by any parties present – save your faithful scribe – save the innocent deceased."

Four days after the crusher had been found, I was back in Basin. I was going back to Slippery Gulch alone to make one last contact with Peter. However, before returning, my new acquaintances, Jane, George, Mike and I decided to give Peter the Christian funeral he deserved. We planned the funeral for June 30, 2002, 101 years after his death. We would place his bones in a modern casket under a granite stone engraved with words of respect.

I was able to spend a day with Peter, learning just how special he was. He spoke of many horrid things he'd endured as a child while trying to survive in this frontier mining town – events not mentioned in the editorial. But he also raised a number of questions in my mind – mysteries pertaining to his life a century ago.

The most shocking disclosure was Peter's conviction that I was the answer to his prayer for a friend – at long last, I must add. For that reason, when Jane suggested I take Peter as my passenger in my truck, I balked at the idea but knew it was something I was destined to do. My Presbyterian background informed me that our friendship was foreordained in God. And so Peter came on the road with me.

Over the next three weeks on the road, Peter's worst fears came out in the form of nightmares. Ghosts sleep, you ask? I don't know, but mortals do. And for all intents and purposes, Peter seemed mortal to me – well…most of the time. It seemed that his terribly damaged, mortal body was returned to him by God in perfectly restored condition, as though he'd never been beaten – or dead! As a result, he was able to receive the love and affection he had been denied as a living child.

I humbly say this: Because of the love the two of us shared, his worst fears were faced down and defeated.

Once in New Mexico, Peter saved me from being involved in a serious accident. He foresaw it in his mind and told me to slow down. In the accident that I was able to avoid, a little girl was seriously injured and pinned in her parent's van. While sitting in my truck, Peter was able to see the child's injuries and knew she was dying from the loss of blood from a severe head wound. I gave him part of a sheet. Invisible to everyone but me, Peter entered the damaged mini-van and stopped the bleeding, thus saving the child's life. The news releases deemed the save "a miracle rescue on I-40." As a result, my new friends in Basin privately declared Peter an angel, rather than a ghost. Knowing Peter better than anybody else, I had to reject that notion. After all, I lived with him 24-7.

Four weeks after leaving Slippery Gulch, Peter and I were camping with friends of mine in Adirondack State Park in upstate New York. My friend of thirty-five years, Bill Early, brought along his teen-aged son, Danny, who was good for Peter. The first night in the park, Peter was asleep on my lap before a campfire when Danny asked if Peter could show us what his body looked like at his death, after his father murdered him.

Danny could not fathom what the reader might be able to understand. Peter's mother died shortly after Peter's birth. My friends and I believe that Peter's father became mentally unstable and blamed his wife's death on Peter. Whatever his thinking, this loss drove him over the edge. The older Peter grew, the more his father resented him. To paraphrase the biblical book of *Job*, his father cursed the day Peter was born. The day of Peter's murder, his father went berserk. It had not been a clean murder by gunshot. His father delivered a furious, fatal punch to the face. For Danny's comfort I speculated Peter likely died from the punch before he hit the ground. His father then knifed Peter over thirty times with a large blade. After the stabbing, his tiny body must have resembled a slab of raw meat on a butcher's block. I then had Danny look closely at Peter, peaceful and content on my lap. I asked if he was certain he wanted Peter to change his appearance. Danny looked at Peter with tearful eyes before he turned away and dashed into the woods, unloading his stomach on the way.

While Danny was gone, Bill asked if I'd thought that perhaps Peter wasn't a ghost at all. I thought he was suggesting that Peter might be an angel. However, his thoughts were in the opposite direction. He said he wanted me to consider something: Since Peter could change his appearance, could it be possible that he might have demonic powers?

At first I was stunned, but realized I couldn't give him a definitive answer one way or the other. Bill really set me thinking that night. Could the miracle rescue on I-40 have been a demonic ruse intended to set me and others up?

I didn't sleep very well that night, but I felt certain we'd all receive the proof we needed. As it turned out, we didn't have long to wait.

CHAPTER ONE

The next morning, I was up by six with a fire going, enjoying my first cup of coffee. Bill joined me at 6:30. I looked at him with droopy eyelids. "You didn't do much for my sleep last night, Bill."

He looked up from his cup, guiltily. "I'm really sorry about that, Jake. I should have kept my thoughts to myself. In fact, I'm not really certain where those thoughts originated. There's no way Peter's the devil. I'm sure that will be clear to us today. We dare not view Peter any differently today."

"I've thought about that all night. I know I won't." About 7:30, Danny joined us and at 8:15, sleepy-eyed Peter crawled out of the tent and walked toward me. I looked at him, masking my suspicions. When he climbed onto my lap, I melted. "Boy, are you ugly."

He giggled. "I am not, but I am sleepy." He stretched his arms up behind my neck.

"I bet you need some help waking up, right?" He nodded. I explained to the other two, "Peter and I have developed some traditions over the last few weeks. One of them is how I help him get awake in the morning." Over Peter's laughing I yelled, "Go ahead and cover your ears."

Soon my fingers were playing Peter's armpits, ribcage and stomach like timpani in an orchestra. We were merrily carrying on when suddenly Peter stopped. He stared off at nothing in particular. He slid off my lap without looking down. I'd never seen Peter act this way.

Finally I said, "Peter, what's going on?"

He came around a bit and said, "I'll be back in a couple of minutes, Jake."

And vanished.

When he disappeared, we all jumped as if a firecracker had gone off. "What's going on, Jake?" Bill gasped.

"I don't have a clue. He's never done anything like this before." We sat there waiting; for what, none of us knew. After maybe three or four minutes, Peter returned to my lap and shot his arms up in the air for me to continue where we left off.

"Peter, what happened just then?"

"Oh, I just had to do something. Could you wake me up just a little more?"

Not knowing what else to do, I did – figuring sooner or later I'd get an explanation. After he got his breath back, I said, "Are you awake now?"

"Yeah. That was a good one. Thanks." He turned around and gave me a hug. Of course, I returned the favor.

"Look, go get dressed. When you come out, I'll have a pancake ready for you."

"Okay." Into the tent he went.

"Jake," Bill fairly whispered, "it's a wonderful thing you're doing. But I don't understand what I think I saw. Is it, well, possible that…"

"Join the club. I think we'll find out."

A couple of minutes later, Peter rejoined us. The pancake was the color of his skin. I placed it on his aluminum camp plate. "Careful, it's hot." We froze, quietly watching him devour it as if that act were somehow supernatural. He was a kid enjoying each crowded bite, one after another. To prove it, he asked for another one. He watched me cook this one in fascination. He thrilled at my flipping it. So I did it once without the spatula – a true flapjack. He thought that was great and insisted I do it again. In the middle of that one, he asked for a third. These were not small pancakes, but they were the size of the frying pan. "Okay, but where are you going to put it?"

He pulled up his shirt and said, "Right here," rubbing his belly.

And he did, miraculously. It was then time to wash the dishes. I explained how everybody had to do their fair share and wash his own. I told him to come down to the lake and I'd show him how. Peter never complained. He happily accepted his responsibility.

Afterwards, he declared, "I have to poop. Where's the toilet?"

Having forgotten to tell him about the outhouse, I pointed toward it. He studied it and turned to me for help. "That's an outhouse, isn't it?" He had never used one when alive because of the fear of being trapped by his enemies. I recalled that upon sitting on his first toilet seat back in Basin, his tiny body nearly fell in. But he soon learned how to hold himself up. Now the thought of slipping into the dark, smelly pit below was too much. I understood where he was coming from. I felt certain he would soon conquer this fear as he conquered his earlier fears.

After the rest of us took our turns, we talked about the day. Bill came up with an idea: "Jake, you've been down on the far lake, haven't you?" I nodded. "Any fish down there?"

"Supposed to be bass and muskie, but you couldn't prove it by me."

"Are there any cabins on it?"

"None. In fact I've never seen anybody on it."

"By any chance is there a place to swim?"

I thought for a minute. "You know, I think there is. One corner looks like there may even be some sand in it."

"Well, why don't we make a day of it? We can fix a lunch, go down there and fish for a while, then eat lunch. After lunch, we can swim for a while, then fish some more."

Peter got so excited he started to flap his arms like a loon.

Just as we were ready to leave, Ranger Casey pulled up and got out of his government-issue, 4x4 pick-up. "Jake, could I talk to you for a minute?"

I walked up to him. "Sure, what's up?"

"I'm on my way back from Blue Mountain. Something happened over there about an hour ago so I drove over to check things out. I've never seen anything like it. I thought I'd talk to you, being a truck driver." I looked at my watch. Peter had disappeared exactly one hour ago. "If a fully loaded semi loses its brakes on a steep hill, how could it stop midway down?"

"Short of a thick, concrete wall, it couldn't. Why?"

"I didn't think so. A big truck loaded with 45,000 pounds of freight was coming down the hill into Blue Mountain from Long Lake, when it lost its brakes. As it came around the bend, a fifteen-passenger van was making its turn into the entrance to the museum. Twelve small kids were in the van, with three adults! They were in his direct path, the trucker says. But the truck pulled to a stop ten feet from the van! And no skid marks! The driver was at a loss as to how he stopped. He kept repeating, 'Praise the Lord.' Jake, how could that happen?"

I was speechless. I looked over at Peter, impatiently waiting in the canoe to get going, playing with the bottom of his shirt. "I don't know, but I firmly believe in miracles. I'd say Blue Mountain was the recipient of one."

"I've never believed in God or miracles and such, Jake."

"You have sixteen people in Blue Mountain that should be dead. But they're not. Do you have a better explanation?"

He stood there looking at the ground, shaking his head and kicking stones aimlessly. He stopped and bent over. He then reached down and picked up one to examine it closer. Then he stuck it out to me. It was a small piece of gray granite. In the middle were two black lines of feldspar. They roughly formed the shape of a cross. He looked at me, confused. I think he felt the same chill I felt. "No! I don't." He looked down at the rock, pocketed it and turned to go. "Well, good luck, Jake. Have a good day."

I walked over to the canoes. "What was that all about?" Bill asked.

I relayed the situation as the ranger explained it to me. I didn't mention the stone. We all looked at Peter. He put his head down, as if embarrassed. "Kiddo, that was you, wasn't it?"

He looked up slightly and nodded. Before I could say anything he said, "Jake, I couldn't let those kids die. Some of them were smaller than me."

I got down on my knees and gave him a hug. "I'm very proud of you, Little One, but how did you know?"

"I don't know. You were tickling me when all of a sudden, I saw everything in my head. I had to do something. When I got there, the truck was only 100 feet away from the van."

"How did you stop it?"

He thought about this. "I don't know, I just did. Jake, are you mad at me?"

"Are you kidding? How could I be? You just saved the lives of sixteen people, including the truck driver; most of those people were children. But why didn't you tell us when you came back?"

Again he put his head down and shrugged his shoulders. "I don't know." I knew. He never talked about saving the little girl on I-40. He wasn't a bragger. I looked at Bill with a question in my eyes: Now do you think he's the devil? He smiled and shook his head, no.

Both Bill and Danny came out of their canoe and shook Peter's hand. "You're a hero, Peter," Bill said. Then Danny shocked Peter by picking him up and giving him a hug. A hug from a teenager was almost enough to bowl him over.

"Keep one thing in mind, folks. Unfortunately, this will have to remain our secret," I said. They all agreed. "Well, let's get going."

It took about two hours to get to the second lake because Peter didn't have the strength to paddle any harder. But Bill and Danny were great and took it easy. Peter never knew they could have gone much faster.

Once we got to the lake, Peter and I pulled into shore for some fishing lessons. I showed him how to bait a hook with a worm. I put a bobber on the line and explained how and why to use it, then threw it out a ways. I showed him how the reel worked and handed the pole to Peter. I explained how to set the line if he got a bite. After a couple of minutes, he got one. He was so excited, he yanked the hook right out of the mouth of the fish and for that matter, out of the lake, too. "I think you set it a little too hard," I said trying not to laugh.

A few minutes later he got another bite and was much gentler with it. As a result, he landed it. It was a six-inch smallmouth bass, but to Peter, it was a small whale. Thank God, I brought a small camera for a few pictures. He wanted to save it and show it to Bill and Danny, but I explained that by then the fish would die. Disappointed, he agreed. As I showed him how to unhook and release the fish, I'm sure he reflected on the word die that I'd just spoken. He knew death!

From then on he baited the hook himself. He caught a half-dozen more that morning before lunch, releasing all but

The Gift

one. That one had swallowed the hook. After I yanked the hook out, the fish died. Peter's body slumped. I threw it as far out into the lake as I could. Almost immediately, a seagull swooped in and gulped it down. I explained that though the fish died, it became food for the seagull. And that's the way it is, the law of nature. He took everything in and seemed to understand.

We all compared notes over lunch. Since Peter caught several more than Danny, he was voted fisherman of the morning. He looked at me and said, "But you didn't fish at all, Jake."

"Kiddo, my fun was watching you." We chewed on PB & J's (more commonly known as peanut butter and jelly sandwiches) without saying much. We devoured small bags of potato chips, chocolate pudding and bug juice – the camper's term for Kool-aid. While we ate, a chipmunk came up to Peter for a handout. He reached out a small piece of bread. In a flash, it was gone.

After lunch, Peter asked when we could go swimming.

"How 'bout right now?" I reached into my small backpack and pulled out a pair of jockey swim trunks for Peter. He had been with me when I bought them and thought they were neat. I helped him get into them. Then it was off to the lake.

We spent the next hour boyishly playing and dunking and splashing in the water. Peter once gulped too much water and reached for my neck. Once his air passage was free, I threw him out from me as far as I could, much to his delight.

Bill and I got dried off while the kids stayed in a while longer. When the boys came out, I expected Peter to come to me to be dried. Instead, he stood in the sand moving his bare feet through it. As he watched the sand sift between his toes, he giggled. I was going to call to him but realized this was

Peter's introduction to sand. I sat down and watched, fascinated. Realizing what was happening, Bill and Danny quietly joined me.

Next, Peter himself sat down in the sand and watched it sift through his fingers. Now he poured it over his legs.

Bill grabbed my arm whispering, "This is fascinating."

Peter continued pouring sand over his body, experiencing the feel of it. He got up on his knees to dig holes. He was transfixed and so were we, watching him. Now he stood up and poured the sand over his head. He giggled with the feel of it sliding over his sun-dried shoulders and down his back and stomach.

Now it was back to the lake. Now back to the dry sand to roll in it 'til he was completely covered. He drew a circle on his sandy chest as water dripped from his hair onto his chest taking sand particles with it down to his stomach and beyond. He was totally oblivious of our eyes. Here was an infant six-year-old in discovery mode. Right now, he didn't need any of us. He was consumed with himself and the sand. And completely free!

It occurred to me that during his entire life, he had to depend solely on himself for entertainment. Out of his imagination he had to create whatever fun he could enjoy, like throwing rocks at objects. Others had taught him nothing along those lines. Granted, most of his time likely had been spent coming up with ways to avoid his worst enemies while finding enough food to stay alive. I doubt if the word "play" was in his vocabulary often.

He was up running from one side of the beach to the other, arms out from his side like wings, and his lips making the noise of a plane. On the way back he ran through ankle-deep water. He made the turn and did a belly flop in the sand as if landing, all the time giggling.

Next it was back in the lake then into the sand again. He rolled, did somersaults and attempted a headstand. This was completely unlike anything he could possibly do in Slippery Gulch. And the difference was not the sandy beach. Here with us, he was free and safe to be the child he was never given a chance to be.

Finally Peter had had enough and the three of us had been given a wonderful display of pristine childhood. The best part for us was that it was handed to us from a child who had never had a childhood.

But Peter was tired. He finally came to me, covered in sand and asked if he could lie out in the sun for a while. "Better hop in the lake and get the sand off. Don't forget your hair."

Soon he was back to be dried, his hair still a little gritty, but passable. "Can I?"

"I don't see why not." He rolled down the trunks as far as possible and lay down on the towel. "Why did you do that?"

"I want to get a tan every place." He giggled. "Well, almost every place."

I applied extra lotion to those areas not well tanned, namely his armpits and lower abdomen, but he was asleep before I finished. Danny lay down with him while Bill and I relocated under a tree.

"Jake, watching Peter play in the sand a few minutes ago: That was one of the greatest displays of exploration on the part of a small child I've ever witnessed. Is this the type of experience you've been having with Peter all along?"

"Ever since we hit the road together! Let me tell you some of his monumental discoveries; like the time he learned to blow bubbles with his butt while in a bathtub." Bill chortled at that. "Or the time at the end of the same bath, he feared being sucked down the tub drain." Bill cracked up, rolling away from the tree holding his side.

After Bill got his composure back I got serious and gave him several examples like planes, trains and buildings taller than two stories. I rolled Peter over and applied more lotion, explaining to Bill, "No sense in having him well done on only one side."

"Who's learned the most in your month together, you or Peter?"

"That's a good question, Bill. Peter has learned a lot, but I have too. It's just different. I've learned some things about myself that I never saw in me. I thought from my teaching and my camping days with kids that I knew children pretty well. Well, I don't. I've never had to actually raise one on a daily basis, and nurture him into overcoming his particular fears! I've had to learn what I've only taught to others: Learn to expect the unexpected."

Bill remained quiet so I went on. "I've learned how to answer some questions I didn't want to answer; some I thought I'd never have to address, never having had a family. I've learned how to do things I never even dreamed of doing before. Like teaching him how to blow his nose and wipe his own butt. I had to be the one to get down and dirty and give the help he needed."

"What's the one biggest change this has made on you, old friend?"

"I've come to accept the fact that I'm no longer number one." I reflected on that as Bill kept silent. "I've learned that my independence isn't as important as I once thought it was. And I've learned how to deal with some pretty rough emotions – both Peter's and mine. I sure can't control Peter's, and I've found that I can't control all of mine either."

"You mean you've cried or gotten real angry at times?"

"Right on both counts."

"How did he react to your tears?"

"He once told me he sees me as the father he always wanted but never had. When he saw another man cry, he thought it was strange. But when he saw me cry he figured it was normal."

"Wow! That's a helluva breakthrough. And a compliment to you."

"Don't I know it."

"Jake, with Peter's help, you're learning how to be a father. Isn't that true?"

"Yep!" I bit my lip.

"I'd say Peter's a pretty good teacher."

I burst out in a sudden laugh. "You know, I never looked at it that way. I guess I love Peter like a son. Look, as Peter's star pupil, I think I'd better get him out of the sun." I picked him up and sat down with him on my lap in the shade.

"True confession: I always thought that with Jake Winters, God was number one," Bill commented.

I looked up at Bill. Then back down at Peter. Then at Bill again. "I've tried. But plenty of times I forget and see myself acting like I'm above God – *the* most important thing behind the wheel – you know? But now I'm forced down to become number three." I looked at Peter again. "This little guy, without saying a word, is constantly reminding me that God is number one for both of us. After all, if it weren't for Him, Peter wouldn't be on my lap right now."

The three of us sat there quietly looking at the little miracle on my lap.

Finally Danny broke the silence. "You know, it was fun playing with him in the water. He's so light. He's so easy to throw around that you forget that he's...you know, dead, but he's just like us. He's...he's even warm." Danny rubbed a finger down Peter's cheek, affectionately.

I smiled. "I know. Took a lot of convincing for me to get the facts straight too."

"Earlier when he was discovering the feel of sand, I'm glad you let him enjoy his freedom and his childhood," Bill said. "It was obvious he wasn't the least bit concerned about us. He was too busy discovering."

Just then Peter stirred. After his eyes had focused on my face, I said, "Man, are you ever ugly." He started giggling at once. "You need some help waking up?" His giggles turned to laughter, and we all started laughing.

Once he got his breath back, I said, "Let's swim a little longer then gather our stuff together. We'll try fishing over there from the canoes for a few minutes; then we should start heading back."

While walking through the sand to the water, Peter slowed down, then stopped. We all stopped with him and watched the sand sift through his toes. "Jake, could you bury me?"

"Sure, I guess. In fact the three of us will work together."

We buried him in no time, everything but his sweet, trusting face.

"How does it feel in there?"

"Kind of neat. It's warm in here."

"I wonder what would happen if I poked a hole in the sand, right about here."

At first he giggled then squealed as my finger made contact with his ribs just below his right arm. In response, he exploded out of his sandy grave.

Then it was off to the lake for all of us. Peter was thrown, tossed, passed, pitched and spun to his heart's delight. When

The Gift

it was time to go fishing, the sand was totally out of his hair, and mind.

On the way over to our fishing spot, I explained to Peter how he'd have to behave in the canoe if he got a fish, so he wouldn't flip us over. We all fished with a bobber and a worm. Within five minutes, Danny got a nice bite. He played it well. Peter watched intently. I explained just what Danny was doing, and why. Finally Danny landed it. It was a five-pound smallmouth bass.

"Wow!" Peter exclaimed. "Look at the size of that thing. I didn't know a fish could get that big."

Moments later, Peter got a nice bite. He set it well and the fight was on. It was also a good one. "Jake, help. What should I do?"

"You're on your own, Kiddo. You know what to do. If he wants to run, let him; but keep some tension on the line. That's it, you're doing fine. Don't turn around; lead him to Bill's canoe."

At one point the bass jumped completely out of the water. Peter was ecstatic. He held on as Bill grabbed the line to bring him in. They wrestled it to the bottom of the canoe. Once on the scale hook, Bill called out, "It's a four-pounder!" We both had a bucket in our canoe for just that purpose, so Bill put it in his. But Peter wanted it in ours. We transferred it to our canoe. It was all Peter's now.

He studied it a long moment and then baited his hook and swung it back into the water. In a couple of minutes, Peter had another. Again, he played it well and brought in another four-pounder. We all laughed and were thrilled for him.

Then Danny got a three-pounder. And as suddenly as it started, it stopped. Often when the action suddenly stops, it indicates that something big is out there. If there was something, it wasn't interested in what we had to offer. We sat for another twenty minutes with no action whatsoever. Finally it was time to go. "Do we have to?" Peter whined.

"Yeah, it's getting late, Kiddo, and we have a long way to go." Bill and I had both been skunked and the kids made the most of it. We both acted disgusted and came up with several limp excuses for our lack of luck.

It was a new experience for me to be joining Bill as if we were two proud fathers putting our boys on a bit.

Danny pointed out that although he caught the biggest fish, Peter caught the most. "That makes Peter the fisherman of the day!" he asserted.

I felt a father's pride. For the first time, really.

In spite of his nap, Peter was dragging. He wasn't going to make it to ten tonight. What a day he had! He wanted to know if we could do it again tomorrow. We pretended that he had to talk us into it.

Bill got some pictures I'll always treasure. (They ended up on the visor over my steering wheel.) Danny and I worked on the fire while Bill cleaned the fish: Peter watched with a great deal of interest. He had plenty of questions.

Peter was so tired! He was barely able to get into his PJ's without help. He went to sleep on my lap so fast that we didn't have a chance to talk about the day's catch.

Danny, after a while, and with a touch of embarrassment, asked hesitantly if he could hold Peter for a little while.

"Sure, why not?" I gently put Peter on his lap.

Danny looked down at Peter affectionately. "He is so little and neat. And cute...and funny. How could anybody have hated him, especially his own father?"

"Danny, the day before he was murdered, three teenage boys caught him in an alley and beat him unmercifully. He suffered terrible internal injuries. The next morning a man found him nearly dead and carried him to his father. So that was why he was scared of you at first. You are a teenager."

Tears came to Danny's eyes. "I don't understand it. How could anybody not love this kid?" He thought for a minute. "He's not afraid of me now, is he? I mean, he knows I'd never hurt him, doesn't he?"

"He does. He thinks you're great!" In the background, Bill drew deep breaths of fatherly pride.

We both went for our cameras. Peter sat across Danny's lap with his head resting comfortably against Danny's chest. The pose made for many cute pictures.

After taking Peter back, I said, "Well, I'm beat!" I'm turning in."

"Yep, we're right behind you," Bill said. Bill and I stood up but Danny remained seated. "Danny, you coming?" Bill asked his son. Danny was deep in thought.

Danny looked up at me and out of the blue said, "Jake, have you ever thought that Peter…well, that maybe…he isn't a ghost?"

Did Danny think Peter could be the devil also? Bill and I sat back down. "What else could he be, son?" his dad asked.

"He's just such a nice person. He's so polite. And kind! You know, he saved you in New Mexico, Jake." (I had told them about the miracle rescue on I-40 earlier.) "And then this morning…I thought that, well maybe…oh, this is going to sound stupid."

"No, go ahead, Danny," I encouraged.

"Well, maybe…well, do you think he…Peter, could be a, an angel?"

"Actually Danny, you're not the first one to suggest that. But I personally don't think so. If he is an angel, would he have stolen candy – even though he was putting me to a test?

Would an angel have such evil nightmares? Would an angel be so lacking in self-confidence?"

"You said that most of the time, he's as mortal as the rest of us. Those are all things any kid might do, right?" asked Danny.

"I suppose so, but if he were an angel...I don't know, I just don't think he is."

"It sure beats speculating he's a demon, Jake," Bill said.

Danny was aghast! "Who said that?"

Bill looked a little embarrassed. "It was something I mentioned to Jake last night – as just something else to consider."

"There is no way Peter's evil," Danny said, troubled. "I don't think he has an evil bone in his body." He looked at Peter. "The devil could never appear as good as Peter. The devil isn't interested in saving people from death. Besides, Jake would know by now. Dad, I can't believe you even said it."

"It was just a passing thought last night. But after watching Peter today, that thought is gone. If anything, I now agree with you, Danny. I think there's a chance he might be an angel, an angel on a mission."

"I don't see how it could even have been a passing thought," Danny said to his father. "Peter is the neatest kid I've ever met and that includes my cousins. I don't think he's a ghost, and I know he's not the devil."

"Look, I don't want to get in the middle of a family feud, but Danny, your dad brought it up not because he believed it, but just something to think about. And I have thought a lot about it. In fact, I spent most of last night thinking about it. I also prayed about it. No, I didn't hear any voice in answer. But I feel very comfortable that Peter is not a demon. At the same time, I'm quite certain he's no angel either. He has said he's a ghost. If he were an angel, especially my guardian angel let's say, don't you think he'd know it? And so would I."

"Have you ever asked him?" I shook my head no. "But it dawns on me: If he were from the dark side, he wouldn't have seen his dying prayer answered."

"He was a terrific little kid who had a horrible life that ended in brutal death. Maybe the powers-that-be felt sorry for him. I got my prayer answered too, but I'm no angel."

They had no idea what I was talking about. I hadn't told them about the prayer that I said before leaving Slippery Gulch the first time. After relating the whole story, Danny said, "Wow, that's really spooky. I suppose you're right. Maybe it was the combination of both your prayers working together that brought him back."

I realized it couldn't be; after all, I met Peter before I said my prayer, but I was tired so just said, "Could be."

"Angel or no angel, he is pretty special," Bill interjected.

"I'm not going to argue with you there. Well, I'll keep an open mind. In the meantime, I'm beat and I'm going to bed." This time they both agreed.

CHAPTER TWO

The next morning Bill, Danny and I were out at the fire when Peter came out. He crawled up on my lap and patiently waited for a few minutes while the three of us continued our conversation. He finally lost his patience, looked at me and said, "Well?"

"Well, what?" I responded.

"Are you going to wake me up, or not?" he asked with a little disgust in his voice.

"Oh yeah. I forgot."

"You did not," he said with a giggle.

"You're right, I didn't." After he regained his breath from being tickled, I said, "Hey, let's see your pits."

"Oh yeah, I forgot." Stretching up both arms, he said, "Am I tan?"

He had a light golden tan, but not as dark as the rest of his body. "They're getting there, Kiddo. Well fisherman, why don't you go in and get dressed, so we can get moving?" With that he was gone and back in less than a minute, ready to eat and face another new and exciting day. He rushed for me and dove across my lap.

I put my hand on his back and said, "You're a darn good fisherman. You going to catch more today?"

Leaning down toward the ground and examining my bootlace he said, "I hope so, but I want you to catch something." With a little snicker he added, "I don't think you know how."

Bill and Danny started laughing. "Is that so! Well I'll show you, you little turkey." I dug my fingers into both sides of his ribs as he squirmed like a snake and squealed in delight.

After breakfast and cleanup, we were on our way. Peter, better rested than the day before and getting the hang of the canoe and the paddle, was paddling more proficiently. We made better time.

That morning we had no luck whatsoever. We decided to call it and go swimming. After swimming for a while, I got an idea. "Hey you guys, let's show Peter how to build a sand castle."

"A what?" Peter asked.

"That's a great idea, Jake," Danny said. "Come on, Peter. I'll show you."

I didn't know where to begin, but Danny jumped right in. He grabbed our empty fish buckets and construction was underway. With Danny as the construction engineer and Peter as the lone labor manager, the structure began to take shape. Bill and I were the token sidewalk observers.

For Peter, this was all brand new. Though Danny was building the traditional sand castle, Peter had no picture in his mind of what one looked like. So he often put in his own ideas.

Danny was patient with his little friend. Meanwhile, we two observers sat in total fascination as Peter's discoveries mounted in number. Miraculously, and partly because the sun was not drying it out, the castle grew ever larger up until lunchtime.

Over lunch, we men bragged on the job our boys had done, and they bragged on it too. During one of Peter's animated descriptions of how they fashioned the balconies, he dropped a large blob of grape jelly on his belly. He paused to get it off, but only managed to smear it around. Then smearing itself began to absorb him. It was soon all over his belly. Laughing he said, "Look, my belly button's purple."

He stood up and posed like something out of *National Geographic.*

At that point we decided we could all use a bath. Fortunately, that day we brought soap and shampoo. I had him remove his trunks. I scrubbed the jelly from the band of his trunks while he washed his belly. He worked on the sticky glob in his belly button now mixed with sand and found it was no longer fun. He finally asked for help.

I worked and got most of it. However, the sticky purple mess in the wrinkles of his belly button would have to wait for warm water and a Q-tip back at camp. After washing his hair, I helped him put his trunks on, then tossed him into deeper water. He immediately swam back. I threw him to Danny, who passed him to Bill, who then passed him back to me. He was a happy kid. After an hour, Bill and I got out and let the kids play a while longer.

Danny was doing an outstanding job of helping Peter's confidence grow. Peter could use a "big brother" on this outing. He needed to become weaned from me in some real ways. So we let our boys play a while longer outside of our immediate supervision.

When they came out, Peter lay a towel in the sun, rolled his trunks as low as possible and lay in the sun, spread eagle with arms stretched over his head. Today I had him apply the lotion.

Bill and I moved into the shade under a tree. After relaxing for a few minutes in silence I said, "You know, Bill, a couple of weeks ago, Peter asked why I never tickled him between his legs. After a couple of sessions, I think I finally got the lesson across. Most children Peter's age have a good understanding of things like that. But Peter never had a teacher – a friend he could turn to. Nobody ever talked to him except to call him names. In the last four weeks, it's been like dealing with an infant six-year-old. Everything we assume a six-year-old would know had to be taught, like how to use toilet paper. But this kid is extremely intelligent and learns fast. And he's appreciative.

"Over those four weeks he's become more independent. He is capable of drying himself and his hair, but that's become one of our traditions. He loves being wrapped up in that big soft towel and cuddled. Heavens, what kid doesn't like to be loved? He experienced no mother's love because she was dead. So I'm doubling as both mother and father. He needs affection...I give it to him." I managed to conclude with a tight-chested, "He knows I'm there for him."

After a minute or two Bill replied, "The more I see of Peter, the greater my admiration is for you. You're doing a terrific thing. Few orphans should be so lucky. And we're talking twenty-first century adjustments."

I gave Peter forty-five minutes on one side then had him roll over. Bill and I walked back to the shade of the tree where we continued our conversation. "Were you uncomfortable with those early demands Peter made on you?"

"No, but over the last few weeks, there were times I had to roll up my sleeves and do what a parent has to do. Like any real parent, I gradually got used to diapers and Band-Aids and lotions. I guess I'm a Mr. Mom, if you think about it."

"What was your worst experience, Mom?"

"That would be his first bath in the creek below Slippery Gulch. When he removed his clothes and I got my first look at his body, I was appalled. Almost sick to my stomach! And fighting tears of anger! Bill, he'd never had a bath in his life. The neglect was obvious everywhere. Where body parts came together, there was caked grit. Stinking filth!"

I paused to gain control of my emotions. I looked over at Peter, laying in the sun, clean, safe and enjoying himself. Bill sat patiently as I fought my emotions. "I've seen kids cover themselves with mud but Peter was painfully different. Though he's covered with fine peach fuzz, his body was too caked up for the hair to show.

"Anyway, we got down in the stream. I never use a washcloth myself so I didn't think to bring one. I had to use my hands. In retrospect, I think a washcloth would have been too harsh for his tender skin during his first bath anyway. I figured I'd wash his hair and he'd wash the rest, but he didn't know how. He'd never been taught. Not only that, I think he needed that human touch...to know that finally someone cares. You see, in some ways it was my worst experience, but it was our first tender moment. I will always treasure it.

"As I washed my little unwanted waif, I had to fight the tears. Peter noticed but said nothing. I was so disturbed over the neglect, I wasn't nervous about the job."

"Was Peter embarrassed?"

"No. He knew I cared: That I was there to help him. We talked as I washed his arms and I'd say, 'Wow, look at that. It's clean!' When I got to his belly button, I said, 'Hey, look what I found. What is that?' He looked at me, uncertain what to say.

"'Your belly button,' I said incredulously.

"'Belly button!' he repeated several times, examining it with his tiny fingers.

"As I worked my way down and around his body, I constantly came up with something to keep him laughing while keeping back my tears."

"Has he asked many questions about the body?"

"Lord, you won't believe. That's what I meant yesterday. I've already had a lot of questions I wasn't prepared for.

Never thought I'd have to address! I can't imagine them getting more difficult."

"Trust me! You ain't seen nothin' yet. It's amazing what uncomplicated, innocent minds can come up with to fluster adults."

"I'm sure you're right. When I left Basin with Peter, I was looking forward to a fun ride with a six-year-old. I wasn't expecting anything like what I got."

Bill laughed. "Welcome to fatherhood."

"Thanks! But you know Bill, I'm having a great time."

"I can tell." He looked out at Peter just now examining his purple, sticky belly button. "That's one happy little boy over there, thanks to you."

"If ever a kid deserves this, it's Peter. Let's go fishing."

I sat down next to Peter and put my hand on his chest. I brushed my hand across the fine peach fuzz and remembered. His skin was hot. "Hey, Little One, you ready to go fishing?" I picked him up and hugged him. As I did, Bill was smiling and nodding.

"Hey, what was that for?"

"It looked to me as if you needed one."

"I always need one," he said smiling. I then brought his belly up to my face and ran my beard across he bare center among squeals of joy.

I looked at Bill. "And I always need that. Hey, let's go fishing." Bill smiled in a knowing way as we headed for the canoes. Peter stayed in his trunks that afternoon. It seemed in no time we four were back out on our beloved lake, our lines in the water.

That afternoon, only one person had any success at all and that was me. I was casting with a surface lure while the others were fishing with bobbers when, suddenly, I got a hard hit. This was not a bass. I had everybody pull their lines in, and the fight was on.

Peter turned around, grabbed the sides of the canoe and watched in awe. After minutes of being pulled around the lake, the muskie finally jumped. It appeared to be thirty to thirty-five inches long – not huge as far as muskies go, but good enough, especially from a fourteen-foot canoe. Peter's eyes bulged like horse eyes when he saw its size. "Holy moley!" was all he said. In fact those were the last two words he'd say at all until we were on our way back to the campsite. He wasn't sure whether to laugh or cry. I wish I could have plucked him out of the canoe at that point, but that was impossible now.

Meanwhile, Bill and Danny circled our canoe – well out of the way – yelling words of encouragement. Peter held on white-knuckled. Unfortunately, I could only give Peter a few glances. He was okay. He did just what I wanted him to without a word from me.

After almost 90 minutes, the battle was over and I was able to land the vanquished creature. Only one of the lures three treble hooks was in him, so he wasn't injured, just mad; hence, the fight. However, I was determined and I won. I realized how lucky I was not to lose him. Once the exhausted monster was next to the canoe, I quickly snatched it by the gills and hoisted it into the boat. At that point, I thought Peter was going to bail out. He just looked at the muskie, eyes bulging as it lay on its side, struggling to breath. Peter couldn't take his eyes off its unbelievable teeth. We made it to shore without a word between us. Once on shore I killed the muskie with a good, solid blow to the head. It was larger than I originally thought. It was forty-two inches long and twenty-three pounds, seven pounds less than Peter.

We had Peter lay on the ground next to the monster for several pictures. He was eight inches shorter, which made the catch seem all the more impressive. We took a number of funny pictures; one with Peter and the muskie lying on their bellies looking at each other. It was a toss-up as to whose eyes were bulging more. Then a couple of shots of Danny holding the muskie between Peter and himself followed by Bill catching one of me standing behind Peter and holding the muskie in front of him. The muskie almost buried him. Meanwhile, Peter hadn't said a word. He just looked at the catch with awe and occasionally at me with admiring smiles.

I came up with one more idea. I had Peter remove his shirt. Danny held the fish between himself and Peter again. There was Peter with his purple belly button, staring bugged-eyed at the monster. It should make for a great picture.

We loaded the canoe and headed back to the campsite. My arms and shoulders were sore and I was beat. I apologized to everyone for being a little sluggish. They all understood. Somehow, Peter seemed to pick up the slack and pulled harder on his paddle than before.

"Jake," he finally spoke up, "how did you do that?"

"Do what?"

"How did you catch that thing?"

Before I could come up with a kidding reply, Bill said, "Peter, I've known Jake for thirty-five years and although he can't do everything well, he's a darn good fisherman. I had no doubt he was going to land that fish. And you were one brave little man. Took lots of courage to sit there in that canoe, not knowing what to expect. But then, what could you do? One panicky move and you could have tipped the canoe over. Instead, you were a big help to Jake by letting him give his full attention to what he had on the other end of the line."

Bill had a way of putting things just right, and in a way, Peter understood. I think Peter's chest expanded an inch or two with this latest congratulation. I added my praise to Bill's. Peter turned around and smiled a smile that is indelibly marked in my heart to this day – clearer than any photo of him.

Once back at the campsite, Bill, Danny and Peter cleaned the fish while I worked on the fire.

Thank goodness for Bill: He likes cleaning fish and is darn good at it. (I hate it and mess it up every time.) Bill was teaching Peter a lot and it was good for Peter to be looking to someone else for a change. I leaned back, closed my eyes and listened to Bill answer Peter's questions about one fish organ after another. Suddenly I realized I was jealous of Bill.

When they had finished their task, I called Peter to the table. "Kiddo, it's time to perform a navelectomy on you."

He looked at me with concern. "A what?"

I held up a Q-tip. "In other words, Funny Face, it's time to clean out your belly button. Take off your shirt and lay on the table. This shouldn't take too long."

He started giggling. As he lay on the table he asked, "Is it going to tickle?"

"I haven't lied to you yet. This could be a rough one, Funny Face, if I have to use the Q-tip. I'll try warm water and a washcloth first." As it turned out, that was all that was needed. After a minute of soaking with warm, soapy water, his purple belly button was back to normal.

Afterwards, Peter complained that the sunburn on his abdomen bothered him. He had worn his rolled-down trunks all the way back to the campsite. As a result, the burn was a good one. I gave him some salve to apply.

We had another unbelievable dinner that night. I ate so much I had a problem moving.

After clean up, I sat in my camp chair. Peter was over by the tent when I called him to come over. "Hey you little turkey, get yourself over here, now." I could tell he wasn't sure if he was in trouble. He stood before me. I took him by the arms. "So you didn't think I knew how to catch a fish. Are you sure now?"

He giggled with relief. "I am now. Wow, Jake, I'm so proud of you, I could spit."

After a good laugh, I explained to Bill and Danny that Peter was stealing what I normally said to him. He once told me I spit a lot. "Hey, let's all take a walk." Bill sensed this should be our private time, so he declined for Danny and himself.

Enthusiastically Peter said, "Okay! Could I put some more salve on before we go?"

"Sure, go ahead." I suggested he put his pajamas on since they were more comfortable for his burn. "But put your sneakers on too."

As we walked along, I found a round stone in the road to kick. I looked at Peter as we got up to it. "Your turn." He gave it a small boot as we walked on, kicking the stone until one of us kicked it into the weeds next to the road and lost it.

I found some Touch-Me-Nots where the stone disappeared and pointed them out to Peter. I explained that in late summer and early fall they develop a pod with seeds. When touched, they pop open, sending out seeds in all directions for the next season. It was a little early, but we found a few pods. I picked a stem of the plant and squeezed out some sap onto an insect bite on my arm. "The Indians believed it helps the itching go away."

I watched for his expression to fall when I mentioned "Indians," but it didn't. If anything, his expression reflected respect. It was only a few days ago he had overcome his hatred of Indians and in the process, made a number of new friends.

I mentioned that the plant was also known as Jewelweed. The Indians also claimed it was a remedy for Poison Ivy, and the two plants were often found growing in the same area.

We walked close enough to a swamp on our left to scare up a few ducks that startled us. We heard loons on the lake. We both laughed. Peter tried to duplicate their calls, but with little success. I suggested more practice.

I spotted a Great Blue Heron in the swamp, but from Peter's low vantage point, he couldn't see it. I lifted him to my shoulders. He was struck by its size. Only a few steps later, we heard a deep voice. It was a Bullfrog. Although we didn't see it jump, we heard the splash.

On the way back, Peter practiced his loon call again. He was improving, but he didn't get an answer. Perhaps it was because he sounded like a loon with a soprano voice.

"Jake, how come you know so much about the woods?"

I put him on the ground. He took my hand. "I've spent my whole life in the woods, Kiddo, and always kept my eyes and ears open. And I read about life in the woods."

Enjoying our stroll together I asked, "How do you think the campout is going?"

He squeezed my hand. I learned weeks earlier this was a short-form hug. We had that understanding between us. "I love it. I love everything like fishing and swimming. And the sand castle Danny and I built was really neat. I love the campfires and stories. I love the food." He thought for a minute. "I don't like the outhouse much." I laughed. "I love Bill and Danny, and I love you the most of all."

"I love you too, Kiddo, and I love having you with me." He squeezed my hand again.

The Gift

As we walked back into the campsite, Bill and Danny wanted to know how the walk went. Peter went over everything in detail.

That night, as we sat around the campfire, we had plenty to talk about. Although I was the only one who caught anything that day, they all had fun helping me. Peter wanted to go back tomorrow. We all agreed. About 8:45 he wanted to cuddle, but before he did I had him apply more salve to his sunburn. He was asleep in two minutes.

In the dim light of the sunset and fire, Danny brought up a question that must have been bugging him. "Jake, couldn't it have been any driver going into Slippery Gulch? Why was it you? And how did Peter know you were the one he prayed for?"

I told them of Peter and me looking at the clouds, only days earlier, in Chestnut Ridge Park. While letting our imaginations go and seeing pictures in the clouds, he explained to me how, while living in Slippery Gulch, he saw the same face on three different occasions. The last time he saw the face was the same day the boys beat him so badly in the alley; the day before he was murdered. He said it was clearly my face, so he knew who he was praying for. That was in 1901."

"Good Lord, Jake," Bill shot back immediately. "You really are dealing with the supernatural, aren't you?"

"So he knew you were the answer to his prayer when he first saw you?" Danny continued, in a way that reminded me of his dad.

"Yes, but he wasn't ready yet. He'd never been able to trust anybody and he wasn't about to put any trust in me either, a stranger. So he tested me many times to see how I would respond. While I didn't know I was being tested, I guess I passed everything he sent my way."

Danny paused, lawyer-like: "Did you know you loved him right away?"

"No, not at all." I looked at Bill. "I was wrapped up in...other things and didn't want to get involved. I could see he was a neglected child, and I wanted to get him some help, if possible. If things worked out for him, great! If not, so be it. I knew that once I left Slippery Gulch, I'd never see him again. It was somebody else's problem. Of course, Peter had other plans."

Danny looked at me hard. "How could you feel that way?"

I looked down at my right boot busily digging a hole in the ground without my realizing it. I looked up, watching the smoke from the fire slowly rise to the heavens, then at Bill. I could feel my emotions surfacing. I looked back to my busy right boot then at Peter. "I was a different person then, Danny. Peter has taught me a lot."

Bill knew where I was coming from and rescued me. "Well, I don't know how it happened, but I think both of you are very fortunate. I can see you are having the time of your life and it's obvious Peter is too. You look younger and you're acting younger. And I think we're very lucky to be sharing this experience with you." Danny agreed completely.

Gaining control of my emotions, I said. "I have to agree. I am thoroughly enjoying myself and Peter, but it hasn't all been easy." I reminded them about the stealing and how difficult it was to spank him. I also told them of some of the funny things that had happened. They were both rolling in the dirt, figuratively speaking. I also told them of the great satisfaction both of us felt in his learning how to read, write, do math and swim.

I also informed them of my most recent discovery, namely his hatred of Indians. They were shocked. It was so uncharacteristic of Peter, it was hard for them to believe it. So I explained how I remedied the situation. They thought it was great.

"How long is he going to be with you?" Bill asked.

"That is the million dollar question. I don't know. He can stay as long as he wants, as far as I'm concerned. He's such an easy kid to like, love and live with. He's a joy to have."

"Yeah, I can see that." Bill said.

"But I don't understand how the whole town could reject him," Danny stated. "He's so neat and cute. It just doesn't add up."

I hesitated. "There's a couple of things I haven't told you guys yet. First of all, as it turns out, Peter's father, Peter Sr., was a religious nut. He was also insane. Of course, any parent who murders his or her child must be. He was convinced Peter had murdered his mother at birth and that he had to be punished. He punished his son with beatings, which became more severe as the boy grew and as Mr. Stevenson's insanity intensified. But he perceived that God was punishing the boy, too. All indications are that Peter entered this world as a normal child, but then contracted a terrible disease. At age two, Peter's left hand was beginning to wither and his nose was already deformed. At that time, a doctor in Butte diagnosed Peter's illness as leprosy." Bill and Danny gasped.

"When Peter was three-and-a-half, the doctor amputated his left arm above the elbow, hoping to slow the progress of the disease. His nose became more and more deformed. At that time, his father had Peter circumcised, convinced it would drive the devil out of his body. But that didn't work.

"At four, Peter's father increased the beatings. He hung Peter by his legs from a beam in his cabin, naked, and beat him with a rope. When Peter escaped, his body and face had been severely deformed by the beatings and the leprosy.

Peter's appearance grew more and more hideous, and he became the freak of the town. That he lived to the age of six is a miracle in itself. I'm not trying to justify the actions of the town, but it is easier to understand."

"How did you find all this out?" Bill asked.

"The other day I told you Peter showed me his body after his last beating. The damage from the rope was horrendous. But I could see that his nose was deformed and part of his left arm was missing. I asked him what happened, but he couldn't remember. I talked to George in Basin and explained the situation. He assured me he'd do some investigating, but didn't promise anything. The only reason he unearthed what he did was because a hundred years ago a Dr. Goldstein, in Butte, kept fantastic records. They ended up as part of the history of the town."

"Why didn't the editor mention Peter's leprosy, his missing arm and his deformed nose in his article?" Danny questioned.

I thought about this. "Time to speculate, Danny. Leprosy has been a dreaded disease for thousands of years. It's been known as a disease of the devil. Lepers have been thrown into leper colonies, locked away and forgotten, and never talked of again. Sometimes they were just stoned to death or put to death in other ways. In some countries they still are. It's possible it wasn't talked about in Slippery Gulch. The thing that is amazing to me is that Peter lived to the age of six. Perhaps Peter's circumcision saved his life. Maybe his father promised the town that the operation would drive the devil from his body." I paused. "I really don't know."

They were both sickened. "But why is his body perfect now?" they both wanted to know.

"I don't know that either. Perhaps it's a heavenly reward for the great kid he was, in spite of the miserable life he was forced to lead and for the body he had to live with. His final prayer was answered. Perhaps that's a reward too."

"Didn't you say the editor mentioned that Peter was a little gentleman during his entire life?" Bill asked.

"Yes. He never called people the names he was being called. He was always polite. He never did anything to 'get even' with those who abused him. He just tried to live and let live."

We all were silent for some time. Finally, Danny broke the silence. "Jake, I'm more convinced than ever that Peter's an angel. I think he was born an angel. Look at everything! His mother died shortly after he was born. Then he contracted leprosy. His nose was rotting away and his left arm was amputated. During all that, his father was destroying his body with rope beatings, yet it sounds as if he kept his smile, so to speak. Those are not the actions of a normal human. I would have killed someone or maybe killed myself."

Danny presented a strong argument. But I couldn't get over or beyond the nightmares. He urinated on me and had a bowel movement in my truck. Was that appropriate behavior for an angel? Somehow I didn't think so. When I mentioned this to Bill and Danny, they both tended to agree with me…I think. Yet we all agreed that Peter was an outstanding youngster and a joy to have on our trip. "Well, I don't know about anybody else, but I'm beat. I'm going to bed." Both Bill and Danny agreed and we headed for the tent.

CHAPTER THREE

The next morning, Peter was up by 7:15. "Hi there, Funny Face. How are you this morning?"

He perched on my lap. After going through our morning ritual, I suggested he get dressed so we could eat and go fishing.

Small bass was all we got that morning, but we all had fun anyway. However, while we were out on the lake a problem developed. Peter suddenly said, "Uh-oh!" I asked what was wrong. He was already crying. Then I got the odor. Peter had an accident.

I told Bill and Danny that we were going into shore for a while. They followed, having no idea yet that we had a problem. Peter was terribly embarrassed. Through sobs he said, "I'm sorry, Jake. I thought I could hold it until we got to shore, but it just came out."

"Don't worry about it, Kiddo. We'll take care of it." As we were approaching shore, I told Bill I was going to need his help. "Could you very carefully lift Peter out of the canoe?" He then understood the nature of the problem.

The cleanup was not the problem. That went smooth enough. The real problem was dealing with Peter's psyche; but Danny was great. As I was working on Peter, Danny said, "Don't worry about it, Peter. Things like that happen. The same thing happened to me two years ago, when I was thirteen."

Peter looked at Danny in total amazement. "It did?"

"Yeah," he said matter-of-factly. "Sometimes it catches you by surprise and you can't control it."

"Wow!" I knew he was thinking, if it can happen to a teenager, I can't be that bad. His fear of teenagers was being replaced by respect.

After Peter and I did the best job we could with Kleenex, it was time for water and soap. I handed him the soap and told him to go swim, but reminded him that if he really needed my help, I was there. Although he was not growing physically, he was maturing. He was able to wash himself without any help from me. He did come to me to be inspected. That taken care of, I moved on to his shorts. They were the real mess. My inclination was to throw them out, but after a while, I got them to where they were wearable.

After lunch, we headed for the water to swim again. Peter was being thrown by all of us, loving every minute of it. Peter caught a few more rays. After rolling down his trunks he applied the lotion to his abdomen and armpits without being reminded.

Afterwards, he wanted to fish instead of swim. I guess he was hoping for another muskie.

Before fishing, he wandered off to pee. A minute later he came racing back with a stick in his right hand and something small in his left. "Jake, look what I found!" he yelled excitedly.

Before I had a chance to tell him not to run with the stick in his hand, he fell. He landed on his belly and screamed in pain. We all ran to him, afraid of what we'd find. Upon turning him over, he had a one-inch long, deep scratch to the right of his navel. It was bleeding and painful, but nothing like what we were fearful of finding.

My first-aid kit was back at the campsite, but I was able to wash out the wound and stop the bleeding. The pain was still there, but he was excited about what he'd found. He walked to where he'd fallen and picked up a mussel. He brought the clam shell to show us and said, "You guys have to see this." He took my hand pulling me in the direction he'd come. "There were real little human tracks by it. Someone is out here that's even smaller than me."

We all followed him to the location of his discovery. Sure enough, there were fresh raccoon tracks. I told him what it was. "A picture of the animal is in your new book. When we get back to the tent, I'll show it to you. By the way, how's your belly?"

He'd been so excited about showing us the tiny "human tracks," he'd forgotten about his pain. Now it was sore again. He decided to keep his trunks on rather than change into his shorts.

Paddling across to our fishing hole was painful for Peter, but he didn't complain once. We had no luck at all and took a late day dip. The water was soothing to Peter's scratch. This time he was not thrown around. We headed back to the campsite, with no fish for dinner.

I suggested Peter not paddle, but he wouldn't hear of it. "We're a team, Jake. I have to do my share of the work." I was not the only one impressed.

All in all, it was a good day. Peter had a lot of fun except for two minor accidents, and as far as we were concerned, the first one wasn't important. Peter found another pair of shorts to put on and the book with the raccoon, while I found the first-aid kit. While I cleaned his scratch, I told him about the raccoon. He thought it sounded like a pretty neat animal.

After dinner, we all went out fishing for a while, with no success, and finally went back to the campsite for a snack and story. I had Peter get into his bottoms first. One thing I found interesting was that he was never bothered by insects. How nice it must be. He made a gallant attempt to stay awake for the whole story, but didn't make it.

After he fell asleep, I looked at Danny. "After Peter's accident in the canoe this morning, do you still think Peter's an angel?"

Danny thought for a minute. "I never thought about that. Probably not! I suppose you're right." We soon turned in.

That night Peter woke us up with terrible screams. I held my breath, but all for naught. He remained dry. It was a typical little boy dream. He was being attacked by a giant muskie. He apologized for waking us up. The next morning he remembered nothing.

Peter was up by seven. He wandered out to the fire and groggily climbed up on my lap. After waking him up, I had Bill and Danny look at his stomach. There was no sign of the scratch. They were amazed.

"Peter, today is Bill and Danny's last day, so we decided we're going to do something special."

Enthusiastically, he jumped off my lap, smiling. "Great! What?"

Bill and Danny had no idea what was coming, but they both knew me. "We decided to go to the opera."

"What's the opera?" he asked, his smile waning.

"It's where you sit in a theater while watching and listening to a number of young ladies sing and dance."

I wasn't sure whether Peter was going to pass out or vomit. Bill and Danny were practically splitting a gut trying not to laugh. "We're going to sit around all day watching a bunch of dumb girls sing and dance?" He was so disgusted, I was surprised he used the word "dumb".

Bill and Danny could no longer control themselves. Peter looked at both of them then back at me. Now I was laughing too. "You guys are kidding me, aren't you?" We all laughed harder. "Jake, sometimes you can be a real pain." He looked at Bill and Danny. "You two must be taking lessons from Jake." His smile had not returned.

Suddenly I jumped up, grabbed Peter, and picked him up. "I'm a pretty good teacher, aren't I?" I threw him into the air, caught him and rubbed my beard across his bare belly amongst squeals of joy. Then I pitched him to Bill. He tickled Peter for a few seconds then pitched him to Danny who did the same before pitching Peter back to me.

"Well, everybody ready to go fishing?" I put Peter down.

He looked up sternly at me. "Jake, you are so mean to me." Turing to the other two he said, "You're all mean. Let's go!"

We laughed all the way to our lake. We caught nothing that morning and called it off early for swimming.

After lunch, Peter worked on his tan again, then it was off to fish. We had a little more luck this time and came up with enough for dinner, but nothing like our luck on the first two days.

Once back at camp and after dinner, we took a number of pictures. At one point, I set the big camera on the tripod and took a few group pictures. Peter was amazed that the camera could take pictures by itself. He then asked if he could take a couple of pictures of the rest of us. I'd forgotten he had never taken a picture before. I showed him how to do it. Again, another completely new experience. He thought it was awesome. Awesome? He must have picked that up from Danny.

Bill assured both of us that when we got home we would be invited over for dinner. Peter had really become attached to these two guys during the last four days and vice versa. It did his confidence a world of good.

I started a story earlier that night. Peter made it all the way through. Before he cuddled, Danny asked if he could hold Peter for a while. I agreed.

He started to cuddle in Danny's lap, but it wasn't the same. Both Peter and I could feel it. Bill finally sensed it too. He suggested Peter go back to my lap. Danny was disappointed but understood. Within a minute, Peter was asleep. Danny looked at me and said, "He wouldn't have gone to sleep on my lap, would he?"

"Danny, I know he thinks the world and all of both of you. He may have eventually fallen asleep, but I'm his security blanket. It's nothing against you."

"Remember, Danny," his father said, "Jake is the reason he came back."

"I know. I just don't know why he has to be dead. He's so neat and fun."

"If he wasn't dead," I said, "none of us would know him now. Keep one thing in mind, through the years, Peter will always be six. If we do this again next year, he'll still be six."

"Oh yeah, I forgot about that." Then he added sadly, "But that means he can never grow up, doesn't it?"

"Yes, it does. He'll always be a little boy and perhaps I'll always be his security blanket. Next June, his bones are going to be reburied and he will be given a proper funeral. I have no idea what will happen. At that time, he may go to wherever little ghosts are supposed to go or he may stay with me. I just don't know."

"You mean, you could lose him?" Danny asked sadly.

"I could. I just don't know."

He looked at his father and said, "Dad, could we go to his funeral?"

"It's way out in Montana, son."

"So what," he said as if to say, this is Peter we're talking about. "He's special."

"We'll talk about it, okay? Jake, thanks for inviting us. This was really a special trip, one that neither Danny or I will forget, and that little guy has a lot to do with it. But, watching you land that muskie was a real joy. I knew you'd do it all along."

"Thanks for your confidence. This was a great experience for Peter in many ways, and I really appreciate the interest you both took in him, not to mention the friendship you gave him. Not to slight you Bill, but Danny was the critical one this week. As I told you before, it was teenagers that gave him the most trouble in Slippery Gulch. When we went over to your house a few days ago, Peter was trembling. When you looked at his picture, Danny, and said 'disgusting', I thought for a minute he was going to bolt. He was terrified. Later, when you stumbled all over yourself apologizing, he relaxed a little, but when you said you thought he was neat, that did it, for the most part. That made him realize that he had been accepted by you.

"The rest of the time went as smooth as butter. You are the primary reason this week was so enjoyable for Peter, and for that matter, for me too."

"Why didn't you tell me this before we left?" Danny wanted to know.

"I thought about that for about five seconds and I chose not to. I was worried that if you knew the success of these four days fell on your shoulders, you'd get nervous. I suspected if you just acted like yourself, you and Peter would get alone fine. Obviously, I was right."

"I think you handled it just right, Jake," Bill said. "Knowing what you just told us would have made me nervous for Danny."

The Gift

"Yeah, I agree. Now that I think about it, I wouldn't have known how to act around him. Not knowing what you just said, I just had fun with him." Danny thought for a minute. "I just don't understand how you can't love him. He's so neat and fun to be with. And he's funny without really trying to be. When he told you he didn't think you knew how to catch fish, I was laughing so hard, I almost puked. And this morning when you brought up the opera, I just about died over his reaction to it. I'm not too excited about the opera either, but as a six-year-old boy, forget it!" We all had a good laugh over the many memories of the past four days.

"I know for a fact he thoroughly enjoys you. One of the other things that meant so much to him was your comment after fishing the first day. Although you caught the biggest fish, he caught the most and you were quick to point that out. You're the one that gave him the designation as being the fisherman of the day. Coming from Bill or me would have been great, but coming from you was truly special.

"The other thing that was important was when you told him you had an accident in your pants, too. It doesn't make any difference whether it happened or not, the important thing was hearing that it happened to a teenager. His fear of teenagers has decreased and his respect for them has increased.

"Well, look Danny, I just wanted to let you and your dad know how important you were to both Peter and me these last four days and, I thank you."

"Thanks for inviting us, Jake," Danny said. "And thanks for the other night, too. I want to remember Peter the way he is."

"Yeah, me too," Bill said. "You know Jake, in watching you work and play with Peter and listening to you talk to him, I'm amazed. I don't know where you learned to do all this."

I was puzzled. "What do you mean?"

"Peter's tiny. There's no getting around that. When I first saw him at the house last week, I was going to address him the way I would a three-year-old. But in listening to you talk to him, I realized you were addressing him as an adult. Better yet, he was talking to all of us as an adult. He even speaks clearly."

"I've never talked down to young children. How can you expect them to mature if you talk to them in an immature manner?"

"Good point!" He paused. "Jake, are you familiar with 1 Corinthians 11:11?"

"I think so. Isn't that the one that says, 'When I was a child, I spoke as a child, I understood as a child, I thought as a child'?"

He smiled. "That's the one. You know, Jake, in some ways Peter is as normal a six-year-old boy as you can get. He loves to run and play and have fun. At the end of the day, he has as many scratches and bruises as any other boy that age would have. If he wore long pants, he'd have holes in each knee in no time at all.

"He's loving and affectionate. He craves everyone's love and gives it back ten-fold. He has a charming personality, a sense of humor, a pleasant disposition and a wonderful outlook on life. He's intelligent and inquisitive.

"But, Jake, he doesn't speak like a child. In fact, Peter is unique in all areas. In one respect he's similar to an infant with the discoveries he's made since he's been with you... discoveries that go so far back in my past, it's impossible for me to remember making them.

The Gift

"In other ways he's a typical three-year-old. Sometimes he's consumed with himself, as he was the other day on the beach. In some ways I was surprised he didn't removed his trunks. That's a three-year-old characteristic, at least it was with mine. When naked, a three-year-old boy touches himself often. Even when he's not naked a boy will very often reach down inside his pants and play with himself. A six-year-old is beyond that, as Peter is.

"His strength and coordination are that of a nine- or ten-year-old. He demonstrated that on the beach the other day, too.

"Then again he often speaks as an adult and often has the uncanny understanding of an individual well into adulthood. Sometimes I think he has a better understanding of human nature than I do and often his thought processes are far beyond his six years.

"When you were teaching him to wipe his butt, blow his nose and do other basic essentials, he was an infant. You've brought him far beyond that. As a six-year-old, he loves to be tickled. He craves your attention. He loves to wrestle and rough-house. Yet he loves the affection and security your lap represents. He will do anything for your approval and praise.

"From time to time he shows the mentality of a nine-year-old. You may find he enjoys team sports now and then and the challenge they present.

"I noticed he has a lot of energy, but he seems to need a time to relax every afternoon. He may have some physical abilities of an older child, but he still has the body of a toddler. So he must have the internal organs of a toddler: I mean his heart and lungs. His energy isn't going to last as long as it would with an older child. His kidneys, his bladder and his intestines are small, too. His accident in the canoe the other day was probably a result of that. It may happen again."

I looked at Bill with respect. "Where did you learn all of this?"

Looking at his son, he smiled and said, "I've had first-hand experience."

Changing gears slightly he continued. "When you're playing with him, often it looks as if you're being too rough. Yet when I watch more closely, it becomes obvious just how gentle you are.

"Then the other day when you put lotion on him, I was watching both of you closely. You were putting lotion on his extreme lower abdomen. He had his trunks on but had they been down a half-inch farther, he would have been exposed. It was as if you were putting lotion on his face and he was responding to it in the same manner. It wasn't a big deal to either one of you. I would have been uncomfortable."

"I told you about his first bath, Bill. I was so disgusted about the level of neglect I was observing, I just rolled up my sleeves and jumped in. It just had to be done. He was incapable of taking care of himself at that time in his life.

"The first three weeks Peter was with me, he was having terrible nightmares. Every night I had to clean him. Sometimes he was awake and sometimes he wasn't. Most of the time he was in between. When we were in motels, I used a wash cloth. In the truck, I used paper towels. But the point is, it became part of our normal daily routine. It became so normal he came up with the question, 'why don't you ever tickle me down here?' At that point I told him that was his private area.

"The other day when he needed lotion applied, it was just a natural thing for both of us. Now he does it himself."

"The relationship you two have is unique. In fact, the trust you have for one another is incredible."

"I know the trust he has in me is fantastic, but what do you mean the trust I have in him?"

"He demonstrated to all of us the other morning, he can disappear anytime he wants. He could disappear from you and have all kinds of fun at your expense."

"Yes, he could, but I know he'd never do that any more than he knows I would never deliberately hurt him."

"That's trust," Bill said.

I thought about that. "Yeah, I guess it is. I never thought about it quite that way. Well, as both you and Danny now know, Peter is quite a kid. Knowing the life he had to endure, he had to grow up fast. He lived for six years with the darker side of human nature and now he's learning the better side. He learned how to survive without a single friend and now he's learning what it's like to have many. I'm going to enjoy his company, his friendship and his love as long as I can."

I paused. "Hey, it's getting late. I think it's time to get to bed."

CHAPTER FOUR

The next morning, after breakfast, it was time to help Bill and Danny pack. Both Peter and I were sorry to see them leave. "What are you guys going to do for the next six days?" Bill asked.

"We're still going to fish and swim, but I've got a few surprises up my sleeve."

Peter looked at me with excitement. "Really? Like what?"

"If I told you, it wouldn't be a surprise, would it?"

"Oh come on, Jake."

Both Bill and Danny laughed. "Well it sounds like you two have six full days coming up, so we better not keep you from it any longer," Bill said. We shook hands, then Danny came up to me, shook my hand and said to me quietly, "Thanks again for the other night. I love Peter just the way he is." He then went to Peter, picked him up and gave him a hug. "Thanks for being here, Peter. You're really a neat kid."

Peter was so overwhelmed, he didn't know what to say. Finally he said, "Thanks, you're pretty neat yourself." I gave Danny a big, double-thumbs up. Without the talk last night, I'm not sure if Danny would have caught the full significance of Peter's compliment, but I could see he did now. They climbed into their car, blew the horn, waved and were gone.

Peter and I stood there for a long moment watching our good friends disappear. This was new for both of us. Usually we were driving out of other people's lives, not waving them good-bye and staying behind. Then he turned to me and said, "Jake, why aren't all older kids like Danny?"

I knelt down next to him and put my hand on his shoulder. Looking into his eyes I asked, "Tell me. Are all

Indians alike?" He shook his head no. "Are all teenagers alike?" He paused a moment and shook his head no. "There are a whole truckload of teenagers everywhere just as nice as Danny, wherever a person goes in America. But let's face it, Danny's special. He loves you and anybody that loves your ugly mug in the morning has to be special."

He made a funny face and pulled away from me. Then he lunged and pushed me over in a hail of laughter. We rolled around on the ground, laughing together.

"Come on, let's get going."

"Okay," he said excitedly. "Where?"

I grabbed my camera and a few other things and said, "You'll see." We got in the car and headed for the hamlet of Long Lake. Once we got to the area where the seaplanes were moored, I said, "Now Peter, I want you to watch a couple of these planes take off and land." After a half-hour, I said, "Well, what do you think? Would you like to go for a ride in one?"

With eyes bulging, he said, "Really? We can do that?"

"If you really want to, but once we get into a plane, you won't be able to sit on my lap. You'll be in your own seat."

Suddenly, he wasn't so sure. "Why?" he asked with concern.

"Because that's the way it is. That's the way it is in a car and truck too, isn't it?"

"Oh, yeah. I forgot." We stood there for another twenty minutes and watched two more planes take off and one more land. Finally he said, "Yeah, I really want to."

"Okay, let's go." We walked into a small office where an older woman was sitting behind a desk. As soon as she saw Peter, she said, "Oh, what a cute little boy." She stood and walked over to greet us.

"Thank you," he said smiling.

"A child with manners. That's a rarity today. Do you want to fly in one of our planes?"

"Yes, please." She was so thrilled with Peter's good manners, she was beside herself.

"Have you ever flown before, honey?"

"No, ma'am."

"Are you scared?"

He looked at me then back at her and said, "I guess, a little."

"Is this your grandpa?" she asked looking at me and smiling.

"Yes, ma'am."

"Well I'm sure he'll take good care of you. My son will be taking you up in a few minutes. He's a real good pilot." She leaned down toward Peter. "I'm going to tell him to take you for a longer ride than usual, just because you're such a fine young man."

A few minutes later, a man in his late twenties walked in. A clean-shaven, handsome, six footer was introduced to us as Sam. "Sam, this little boy has never been in a plane before. I want you to give him an extra fifteen minutes if he wants, because he's such a polite child."

Peter was all smiles. Sam bent over and shook Peter's hand. On our walk out to the plane, Peter said, "Wait, I have to pee," and took off running.

I called after him. He stopped dead in his tracks. "Where are you going?"

"To the bathroom!" He yelled and turned around to run off.

"Do you know where it is?"

He looked around confused. "Oh yeah. I didn't think of that." Both Sam and I started laughing.

"Go into the office, Peter. My mother will let you use ours." He was off running again. "He's a little on the excited side, isn't he?" Sam said.

"Now that's the understatement of the day," I said, introducing myself and shaking Sam's hand.

"Cute kid. Your son?"

"Grandson," I said. Just then Peter came bounding back.

"Hey, little man," Sam said, "you set to do some serious flying?"

"You bet," he said with a huge smile, taking his security blanket in his hand at the same time. As we got closer to the plane, Peter said, "Wow! Look at that, Jake."

Sam opened the door. I said, "How do you want to work this, Sam?"

"He's so little he should sit in the back, but if he does, he won't see much."

"Okay," I said. "How about if he starts out in the back then once we get airborne, he moves up on my lap. Then he can move back before we land."

Sam thought for a minute and said, "He's not really supposed to do that, liability and all, but okay."

Of course, Sam had no way of knowing that liability was no problem with Peter. We got Peter strapped in, then Sam and I put our seat belts on. "You all set, little man?" Sam asked. Peter nodded as Sam started the plane. I looked back at Peter and could see immediately, the noise terrified him.

"Just a minute, Sam," I said then went back and knelt in front of him. "You okay?"

"It's so loud."

"Yeah, I know, and it's going to get louder as we take off; but once we get in the air, it will quiet down a little. Trust me, you're going to love this. You'll be okay. I haven't lied to you yet, have I?" He shook his head. "As soon as we get into the air, you can come up on my lap, okay?" He nodded. I moved back to my seat and put my seat belt on. "Okay, Sam, let's do it."

He nudged the throttle forward and we picked up speed bouncing over the small waves. I looked back at Peter. He was trembling with tears in his eyes. He was terrified and there wasn't a thing I could do about it. Once again he put his trust in me. Finally we were airborne. I looked at Sam. He nodded. I motioned for Peter to come up on my lap. He hurriedly undid his seat belt and awkwardly scurried through the small cabin to my lap.

He was still trembling, but once he looked out the window, his fear was forgotten. "Wow! We're really flying, just like a bird," he said swiping at the tears. From then on it was nonstop chatter. "Look at the trees, they're so little. Are those people down there? Is that a boat? Look at how little the lakes look. Can we fly over our lake? This is really neat. Are those clouds up there? That mountain doesn't look so big anymore. Why is everything so small? What's that dial for? Is that a house?" Sam and I were both laughing. I was thrilled he was having such a great time.

I told Sam the name of the lake we were camped on. He flew no more than twenty feet over Lake Durant. As we passed our campsite, Peter yelled out, "Wow! It went by so fast we must be flying a million miles an hour."

Sam laughed. "Pretty close, I'd say." When we flew over the lake where we caught the fish, Peter pointed to the small sandy beach. "That's where we went swimming, Sam."

"I bet you had fun," he replied.

"And that's where I caught a bass this big." He motioned with his arm. "And Jake caught a Muskie bigger than me."

With that Sam looked at me and said, "You did?"

The Gift

"Yeah. It was forty-two inches long and twenty-three pounds."

"Wow! That's quite a fish. That's not a very big lake. What kind of a boat were you in?"

"A fourteen foot canoe."

"You got that from a canoe? Good grief." He was amazed.

"I would never have gotten it if it weren't for Peter. He was in the canoe with me and he behaved perfectly."

Looking at Peter, Sam said, "You were? Weren't you scared?"

Peter was too proud to remember just how scared he was. "I guess a little," he said nonchalantly as if it really wasn't anything. Then remembering he said, "You should have seen the mouth and teeth on that thing, Sam. That thing was so big, Jake could have used me for bait."

We both laughed. Our flight was supposed to be twenty minutes. After fifty, I said, "Sam, we're way over the time even your mother said. You'd better get us down."

"Don't worry about it. We're not that busy today." About five minutes later he said, "Okay, little man, you'd better get to the back seat and buckle in. We'll be landing soon."

"Okay, Sam," no longer the least bit fearful. Peter moved to the back seat and did as requested. Soon we were back at the dock. After getting out of the plane, I thanked Sam for the personalized flight and his kindness and the interest he took in Peter. The flight cost $10 for Peter and $20 for me, so I offered Sam an extra forty. He refused but finally accepted twenty. He shook Peter's hand, ruffled his hair and told him to enjoy his stay in the park. I walked away with a very happy little boy.

"You were right again, Jake," he said with a smile. "I was really scared when we first took off, but you said I'd love it and I did. Thanks! You're the greatest, Jake. You're awesome!"

I couldn't let that pass. Feeling proud, humbled and completely at a loss for words, I swung him up on my shoulders. "Come on, we're going to eat. There's a restaurant right across the street in the hotel."

We ordered and while he played with the ashtray, the paper napkin holder and the silverware, I sat and watched him. I had to face it, humbly face it: I was succeeding pretty well in what I'd been handed. I was giving Peter the childhood God wanted him to have. And it was happening without any voices from heaven, any fireworks, anything too unusual. Nothing too much out of the ordinary.

And through me – a plain trucker with no kids to call my own.

'Til now!

Our order came and we dug in like we had just come back from outer space.

After finishing our meal and cleaning up a little, I suggested we go to the public beach next to the seaplane company. Peter had been so excited with the anticipation of flying that he never noticed it.

The beach was good sized, and it had a dock and two other attractions. One was a trampoline. You jump off the dock, come down on the trampoline and spring into the water. Then, too, at the end of the dock was a rope to swing out with. Peter had never experienced either but was ready for both as a junior Tarzan.

Once back at the car, I grabbed our towels, trunks and a folding chair. After changing in a small beach house, Peter wanted to try the trampoline first. He watched several kids jump off the dock, onto the trampoline and bound into the water. Then it was his turn. After bouncing off the trampoline in a most ungainly manner, he landed in the water mostly butt first, with arms and legs going in all directions. He climbed back on the dock laughing and said, "That's not what I meant to do."

The next time, he hit the water feet first; the time after that, head first in a dive. He was getting the hang of it. Several kids were doing flips. So he tried one. He did a flip and then some. He came down flat on his stomach with a smack. No tears! Rubbing his stomach he said to the other kids, "Man, is this water ever hard." I had to laugh to myself and keep my safe distance. The other kids were fascinated with what they must have viewed as a four-year-old at most.

He was quickly turning red from his thighs to his face. I had him sit on the dock for a couple of minutes; then it was off to the ropes. He swung out and let go. I winced as he sailed out and came down on his back, ker-smack. I came quickly to his side. Holding his back he said, "Jake, I think I'm ready to take a break." I picked him up and carried him to the beach. He was now completely red, both front and back.

I unfolded my chair and dried both of us off. Peter settled into my lap and we watched the others perform for a while. After five minutes of TLC, he was on the beach playing with some other kids in the sand. I was left to strike up a conversation with some of the adults. One of the women asked if he was my son.

"Grandson," I explained, somewhat elated over her misperception.

"He's beautiful. He's going to be a real ladies' man someday. How old is he?"

"Six. Both of his parents are small," I added before she had a chance to comment on his small stature. Suddenly we heard angry yelling coming from the direction of the beach. I looked up, concerned. Two boys were pushing and shoving each other, arguing over the possession of a community bucket. Finally one hit the other with a plastic shovel causing tears but no injury. He went off crying. The mother of the other boy went down and bawled her son out, then returned. Meanwhile, Peter was playing peacefully, ignoring the entire conflict.

A few minutes later he came up and sat on my lap. "You having fun?" I asked.

"Yeah, but that one boy wasn't very nice," he said. The boy's mother was the one sitting next to me. She looked at him.

"Oh? Why do you say that?" she asked.

"He wouldn't share the bucket. It wasn't even his. He shouldn't have hit the other boy."

"You're right. He shouldn't have," the mother said. "You are a nice boy," she said.

"Thank you," he said. "You want to go in the lake again?" he asked me.

"Sure, let's go." I hit the water as Peter tried a flip off the trampoline again with more success, then it was on to the rope. That was improving too. At one point, he let go of the rope far out on the swing and went in headfirst. His form was good. I was impressed.

As he swam to the dock, I became aware of a presence standing on my right. It was a little girl of about seven. I looked for a parent. The mother was coming up on my left, and what a mother she was. Like her daughter, she had blond hair, but more conspicuous was her near bikini. Or should I say, hardly conspicuous near bikini. Unlike her daughter, she filled hers out in full. "That was quite a dive. Cute kid! Your son?"

"Grandson," I said trying with little success to avert my eyes from her figure.

"He's so little. How old is he?"

"Sixteen! He's small for his age, but a terrific athlete."

"Sixteen. Oh, that's fun! My daughter is seven, going on sixteen too."

I let my nervous, unintended humor stand.

As the two kids approached the dock, they exchanged names. Paula, Darlene's mother and I did the same. Little Darlene asked Peter if he would teach her how to do the dive he'd just performed.

He explained to her carefully how he did it. Paula and I watched.

"Now watch," Peter said.

Peter swung out, let go at just the right time and went into another dive. He talked Darlene through her dive like a seasoned coach. At the right time he yelled, "Now!" She let go and dove in. How did he know when to tell her that? It dawned on me this was Peter's first teaching experience. He'd done a darn good job at it.

Darlene swam over and thanked him. Paula was amazed at her daughter's success.

"Come on over here, Kiddo," I said to him while he was still in the water. "There's someone I want you to meet." Paula and I pulled the kids from the water.

After the two children were introduced to the two adults, the kids went off to dive some more. Darlene went first and did a near-perfect dive. I looked into Paula's eyes. "Darlene is a pretty good athlete herself."

"Thank you. Did you teach Peter how to do that?"

I laughed. "Not me. If I tried that, I'd have to see my chiropractor. He came up with it himself."

"Really?" she marveled.

Just then Peter shouted, "Watch this, grandpa."

Peter was in his show-off mode. I had no idea what he was going to try or what the outcome would be. "Be careful, Peter."

Holding the rope, he raced off the dock, flew high and let go. This time he did a back flip, landing on the back of his head and shoulders. "That had to hurt," I stated.

I ran out and dove in after him. When I got to him he shook his head. I grabbed his arm. "You okay?"

"Yeah. I didn't hit right. But I was close, wasn't I?"

"You were. I think it's time to take a break."

We swam to the dock, had a seat and talked to Darlene and her mother. Darlene was regarding Peter as a bit of a hero. And Peter was soaking it up.

Finally Peter had talked enough and was ready for more action.

He headed for the rope. He flew out over the water, let go at the right time and shot into the water. His form couldn't have been better. His arms, body and legs were perfectly straight. As he surfaced, we all clapped. "Peter, that was your best one yet."

I noticed that when Paula laughed, her body laughed with her, making a lot of things move. "He's a cute kid. He has a wonderful personality. He's a little charmer," she said.

"That he is. Darlene is no slouch in looks and personality herself. They make for a cute couple." Peter joined us wearing his trunks dangerously low. I adjusted them then invited Paula and Darlene to join Peter and me on the beach.

Paula set her chair up next to mine. As Peter climbed onto my lap, Darlene climbed onto her mother's. We enjoyed small talk for a few minutes before Peter was ready for action again. He got involved in hitting a ball against a wall with a couple of other boys. Both boys were older and larger than he, but he held his own. The father of the older boy, watching with great interest finally asked, "How old did you say your grandson is?"

"Six."

"My son is eight but he sure doesn't have anything over your grandson. I've never seen such a well-coordinated six-year-old. And he's no bigger than a toddler."

"Both his parents were very athletic."

Several of the parents looked at me, including Paula. The father said, "Were?"

Uh-oh, I thought to myself. I blew it. "Both his parents are deceased. I'm raising him now."

"Oh, what a shame," the mother of the fighter said, "but you're certainly doing a wonderful job. He seems to be very well adjusted and a happy child." All agreed.

"Thank you again. He's a good kid and very easy to live with." Just then Peter came back to my lap. "Well Kiddo, I think it's about time we head to the campsite. Would you mind if we stop off for an ice cream cone on the way back?"

He smiled. "Okay."

"Are you sure, because we don't have to?"

He stretched his arms behind my head in his characteristic way and said with a big smile, "I want to."

I stuck a finger between two ribs, for instant giggles, which produced laughter in the adults. "Jake, could Darlene and I dive one more time?"

I looked at Paula, which was not difficult. She nodded. "Okay! One more dive, but no dare-devil stunts." He chuckled and agreed as the two ran to the rope and then decided who would go first.

Darlene pulled off one impressive dive. Peter followed her with his own impressive dive.

After we changed into dry clothes, Paula and Darlene walked to my car with us to say good-bye.

As the ladies retired to the beach, Peter and I drove off. "Peter, I'm proud of you. The coaching you gave Darlene was, well, awesome."

He smiled. "You think so?"

Just then we pulled into the ice cream parlor. "Absolutely! You were outstanding."

Ice cream cones were a challenge to Peter. Since we were outside, I had him remove his shirt. When he finished, a small stream was running down his chin and neck and was well on its way to his stomach. I asked the woman to dampen a napkin for me and got him cleaned up.

Once back at the campsite, our first priority was replenishing our wood supply. I cut down a small, dead tree and started cutting it up into smaller sections. After I had cut a couple of logs, Peter wanted to try. "Okay, but put your gloves on."

"I don't need them, Jake. I can do it better without them."

"You either put your gloves on or you don't cut."

In a disgusted, know-it-all tone he said, "Oh, Jake!"

"Yeah, I know. I'm a real pain in the neck, aren't I?"

I handed him his gloves. He disgustedly put them on. He sawed the way I taught him. On the third stroke back, the saw jumped out of the cut and the blade sliced across the top of his left hand, ripping open the leather for about an inch. He stood there in shocked disbelief. He looked at me. "How did you know?"

"I didn't. It's just something that could happen, so you protect yourself in advance. It's why we wear gloves around the truck; to protect us from the things that could happen."

"How did you get to be so smart?"

I smiled. "I'm not so smart. But I've gained wisdom over the years, through experience and listening to others who have more knowledge than me. Let's get this wood cut. Finish what you started but take it a little slower." He finished the one he started, then decided to stack instead.

After dinner, instead of going out in the canoe, we walked along the shore. I taught him how to skip stones; something every boy should know. He had a good arm and was getting the hang of it quickly.

At 7:30 we returned to the campsite. He went into the tent and put his bottoms on while I built up the fire. Then we settled back and roasted some marshmallows. We were enjoying our treats. After roasting a few more marshmallows, we sat quietly for a few minutes enjoying the serenity of the campsite, when he finally said, "Thanks, Jake."

I wasn't sure what he was thanking me for. "For what?"

"For taking me places and doing things with me. For teaching and showing me things. For taking me up in the airplane today! For helping me and protecting me and always being there for me. You're the friend I always wanted. Maybe when people ask if you are my grandpa, maybe I should say no. He's not my grandpa, he's my friend."

"That would be perfectly accurate, yes. But there's one thing wrong with saying that."

"What?"

"I'm your friend and more. I am for all practical purposes, your grandpa. And when you say somebody is your grandpa, it's just assumed he's your friend too."

"Thanks for your love, Grandpa."

I was fighting tears again. It wasn't always easy having Peter along, Lord knows, but the rewards were unbeatable. If ever there were a more charming and lovable kid than Peter, I'd love to meet him. "Kiddo, you are an absolute joy to have along. You thank me for all I've done for you, but I have to thank you for all the things you've done for me. No doubt you and I were meant for one another. I'm still not sure why we ever met or why God picked me, but I'm glad he did."

We were a happy pair. Suddenly, we heard a car approaching. It was Paula and Darlene. I had told them earlier where we were camped and invited them over some evening.

As they got out of their car, Peter and I walked over to say hello. "We were just roasting marshmallows. Care for some?" Peter asked. I suggested he put a shirt on first.

Darlene showed immediate interest and walked to the fire with Peter. Meanwhile, her mother looked around the campsite. "Isn't this…quaint." She said.

I looked at the tent, the fire pit, the table, then the outhouse. Maybe in one way it was quaint, but to Peter and me, for now it was home. I gave Paula a three-minute tour. As we walked by the fire pit, Peter was instructing Darlene on fire safety and how to roast marshmallows in a safe manner. After showing Paula the tent, I retrieved another chair and we joined the kids at the fire. Peter offered me a marshmallow ready to eat while Darlene did the same with her mother.

After one more marshmallow, I told Peter that was enough. Paula told Darlene the same. Peter put his stick down but Darlene stuck hers in the fire. Soon the end was burning and she was waving it through the air. Paula said nothing, so I was debating how to handle the situation when Peter said, "Darlene, that's not a safe thing to do. Somebody could get burned. You could even start a fire. The best thing to do is stick the end in the dirt until it's out, then put it down." Darlene did as Peter suggested, then both kids came up on our laps, but not for long.

Peter explained what we'd done during our stay. In the dying light of early dusk, he led us to the canoe and with help, turned it over. Proudly he pointed out his seat and paddle and showed Darlene how to use it. (What a good big brother he would have made some little sister!) He showed them his fishing pole and explained how to bait the hook and how to set a fish. He told of us swimming on the other lake.

From there he led us down the road and pointed out the plants I'd shown him a few days earlier. He even explained what the Indians used them for. His memory was fantastic. He explained what some of the noises were we heard, including a loon. I looked at Paula from time to time, hoping she wasn't bored. Instead I detected fascination on her face. She had likely not raised a boy of her own.

We returned to the fire and the chairs. Darlene returned to her mother's lap. Peter carefully placed two logs on the fire then came on my lap. "Peter, your knowledge of the woods is fantastic," Paula said. "Where did you learn all that?"

Peter reached his hands behind my neck. Proudly he said, "Grandpa!"

"Well, your grandpa is an amazing teacher and you're pretty good yourself," Paula said.

I gently rubbed my hands up and down his ribs. "Peter is an amazing student. His memory is incredible."

Enough praise for one night. Peter turned sideways on my lap facing Paula and her daughter. "Jake, could you tell us a story?"

I looked at Darlene and her mother. They both nodded. I told a short story. All enjoyed it.

"Jake, I'm really impressed with everything you're doing for your grandson. The fishing and canoeing – the camping. Just watching him around the fire…he certainly understands the dangers and knows the safety rules. The knowledge he's gaining of the woods is impressive."

As Paula talked, I became aware of Peter's pajamas and tucked them in. She laughed then turned serious. "Don't worry about his pajamas, Jake. They're cute…they're him. My son…he was a year younger than Darlene. He would be six." Tears welled up in her eyes. This was going to be tough. I gave Peter a slight hug. "He died of leukemia six months ago," she choked out. Now Darlene was in tears, too.

"I'm sorry!"

"Darlene and Teddy shared everything, including bath time. That's why Darlene is so comfortable about Peter." Peter was now in tears.

"Peter reminds both of us of Teddy; his good looks, intelligence, personality, sense of humor. And he could care less about clothes. I'm guessing Peter's the same." She gave us a difficult giggle. I hugged Peter a little harder. "I'm sorry. I didn't mean to spill out my grief like this."

"Sometimes it helps," I volunteered. I'm not good at times like this. I don't know anybody that is. "If Teddy was anything like Peter, he must have been a wonderful child."

She sniffled, nodded then looked longingly at Peter. I knew what she wanted and needed. Without checking with Peter, I said, "Paula, would you like to hold this guy for a minute?"

"Oh, may I?"

I hugged him. "Peter, would you mind?"

He slid off my lap. Darlene stood before her mother awkwardly as Paula lifted Peter to her lap. "Darlene," I said stretching out my arms to her. She came onto my lap willingly.

Paula's tears increased as she pulled Peter to her breast. Suddenly Peter said, in an alto voice, "Mommy, I love you."

The Gift

He looked at Darlene. "I love you too, big sister. I will be with you always. Please don't worry about me. I'm fine. I'm free of pain." The chills raced down my spine. Darlene got off my lap and hugged Peter, who looked a little bewildered.

After being hugged by both Darlene and Paula, Peter looked around, confused. Uncomfortably, Peter said in his soprano voice, "I have to go." Peter slipped off Paula's lap and returned to mine.

Paula looked at Peter as confused as he appeared to be. Darlene said, "Mommy, that was Teddy. He always called me big sister. Peter didn't know that."

We all looked at Peter. Finally Paula asked Peter how that had happened. Peter said he didn't know.

"However it happened, thank you for helping Teddy contact us. You truly are a wonderful child." She hugged her daughter, then wiped away her tears. Paula rose and touched Peter, then me, softly on my left shoulder.

"We should be going." With that she kissed me on my forehead. As they approached their car, they thanked us for the evening, and then they were gone, leaving Peter and me alone in a haunting atmosphere.

Peter was back on my lap facing me playing with his pajamas, when he broke the silence. "Jake, why do kids have to die?" I rubbed his back with both hands.

"It doesn't seem fair, does it?" He shook his head. "God has a plan for all of us. It's not up to us to know what that plan is."

"Does he have a plan for me, too?"

"Oh yes. I'm sure you're living his plan right now."

"I am?"

"You've done some wonderful things already. You saved me from being involved in a serious accident in New Mexico, and saved that little girl's life. You saved all those people in

Blue Mountain, and tonight you made two people very happy."

He thought about this. "If they were so happy, why were they crying so much?"

I smiled. "They learned that their son and brother was safe, happy and with them."

"Does God have a plan for you, too?"

"I think he does, Kiddo. He returned your six-year-old body to you in perfect form then returned you to earth. A little kid needs a guardian. I guess I'm it."

He stopped playing with his pajamas and gave me a hug. "I'm glad you are."

"Me too. Peter, was Teddy here the whole time?"

"No. Just when Darlene's mother started talking about him."

"You could see him at that time?" He nodded. "Does he look like you?"

"A little. He has blond hair and blue eyes. He's bigger than me. His hair is shorter. He's a real nice kid." Then with a devilish twinkle in his eyes, he added, "But he's not as cute as me."

I took his head by the chin and shook it slightly. "You're a little snot, and you know it." He giggled. "Hey, you never thanked me for allowing you to show off for Darlene today." He blushed, so I went on. "Of course, she was a fine looking lass."

"What's a lass?"

"Lass is a Scottish word for girl. Scottish people live in Scotland, and Scotland is a country in Europe. That's a long way from here. The point is, she was cute as a button. I don't blame you for showing off. And that bikini she had on sure didn't cover much."

His blush didn't decrease any.

"But Jake, I saw the way you were looking at Darlene's mother. She was a good looking lass, too. She sure had a pair of…I mean, she sure filled out her…I mean, she was real big…oh you know what I mean."

Now we were both blushing. "You're not supposed to notice things like that."

"Why not? You do."

"Yeah, but I'm older. I'm supposed to notice things like that. You're just a little kid. You're not."

He laughed as he leaned back over my knees so his head and arms were heading close to the ground. His ribs looked like little twigs. With difficulty he said, "Right, Jake."

"You're a little peanut." I stuck my finger in his bellybutton. "I think it's time for you to go to sleep."

He chuckled from down near the ground. I pulled him up then we walked into the tent.

After lying down, he said, "Jake, could I die again?"

I rolled on my side and put my hand on his chest. "I don't see how, Kiddo, but if you keep looking at older women the way you were looking at Darlene's mother today, I might kill you myself."

He laughed hard at that one. "You've taught me everything I know, Jake."

Now I was laughing with him. "Not only are you a little snot, you're a wise guy, too. Now go to sleep." That only increased his laughter. After several minutes I said, "Peter, I love the sound of your laughter. It's like the voice of God himself."

With that he rolled over and put his head on my chest. "And I love the sound of your voice. It's loving and kind, even when you're pretending to be mad at me."

I chuckled then put my hand on his back. "Who said I'm pretending?" I never got an answer. He was asleep. I rolled him back into his sleeping bag, put my hand on his chest and felt his strong heart beating, the same one that not too many weeks ago had been silent for the past one hundred years. Why was I privileged to participate in such a miracle? I didn't know and probably never would. I fell asleep as content as he was.

During my stint as a summer camp counselor working with younger children, I noticed that at night, I could be in a sound sleep, yet if one of the kids quietly stated my name, I was instantly awake. In fact it was as if I were never asleep. That night Peter quietly said, "Jake."

I was sound asleep but instantly came awake. I was lying on my back. "Yes, Kiddo."

"Do you really love me?"

There was a half moon providing some off light as it shone through the trees. I smiled as I rolled toward him. I put my hand on the far side of his face, resting my arm on his chest and left shoulder. He took it. "Yes, Little One, I really love you."

He hugged my hand and arm with his left arm as he hugged his teddy bear with his right. The contented smile reappeared on his face. I was certain he never woke.

CHAPTER FIVE

The next morning I was drinking coffee by 6:30. At 7:15, Peter joined me, rubbing his eyes as he climbed onto my lap. "Well, hi there, Funny Face. How are you?"

"Tired," he said while yawning and stretching. I allowed him to finish stretching then I woke him in our traditional way. I waited for him to regain his breath then asked, "Peter, how did Teddy come to speak to his family through you last night?"

"After I went to his mother, I asked him if he'd like to borrow me for a minute. When Darlene's mother asked me how that happened, I told her I didn't know, but I did. I didn't think I should tell her." He looked at me. "Was I right?"

"I think you were. You really are a wonderful little kid."

"You mean I'm no longer a little snot?"

We both laughed. "Well, not right now anyway. Hey, what do you want to do today?"

"Can we go back to the other lake and do some more fishing and swimming?"

"I don't see why not." We had a quick breakfast and headed for our canoe. A little way down the lake, he stopped paddling and turned around to me with a sparkle in his eyes.

"Jake, I've got an idea." Looking to the right side of the canoe he said, "Do you think we could climb Blue Mountain today?"

I knew of a well-marked trail going all the way to the top. Why not? "Kiddo, I'm game if you are. We'll have to turn around right now though." He instantly started paddling with no regard for direction. "Hey, slow down. And save that energy to make it up the mountain. Now let's turn this canoe around and get back to camp before you change your mind."

We gathered what we needed and headed for town. After an early lunch, we drove to the entrance of the trail. We had two one-quart canteens and a small backpack. I put one of the canteens on my belt and one on the elastic band of Peter's shorts. When I let go, the canteen hit the ground with a thump, taking his shorts with it. We both laughed. If only he had some hips!

Before starting, I cautioned him on several things. He was off and soon disappeared around a bend. Within a couple of minutes, he was back, and that's the way his cockiness went until carelessness and disobedience caught up to him.

About halfway up the mountain, I came around a bend to find him on a large log. He was walking across it like a tightrope walker. The top was stripped but some peeling bark remained on the sides. I knew it was slick. I'd warned him about this very thing before we started. The log was about four feet off the ground. As soon as I saw Peter, I took off running.

The next four seconds are etched in my memory forever. His right foot slipped off the right edge, then his left foot followed. With his feet gone, he did a belly flop crosswise on the log, then slipped off the far side into the undergrowth. As he did, my heart skipped a beat as I saw his head bounce violently backwards. He had caught his chin on the log on the way down.

I got to him in seconds. He lay on his back in the middle of a large blackberry patch, unconscious. He was brush-burned from his knees to the top of his chest with a nasty mark developing on his chin. He also had several scrapes and scratches running up both thighs, his stomach and chest. What I was looking at was shades of the past and I was sickened.

Suddenly there was someone next to me. "Looks like you could use some help. My wife and I saw him fall." Crawling under the log, he checked Peter's pulse, then each eye. As he was doing so, the young man introduced himself and his wife as Jack and Becky. He was a paramedic. As he probed, he said, "His breathing is regular. His heart is strong. His chin and both jaws are fine. No broken ribs; fortunately, his bones are rubbery enough that they spring right back to normal configuration. His shirt probably slid up his chest and collected under his chin. That saved him from serious injury, but he's going to have a lot of puncture wounds in his back and legs."

"Should we bring him back to Planet Earth?" I asked.

"Not yet. Becky, could you lay a towel on the ground?" Looking to me he said, "You pick him up so I can get the thorns out of him. Then we'll lay him on the towel."

I handed him over the log to Jack. Then I crawled under it as Peter was placed gently on the towel. I noticed they were both looking at me. I realized I hadn't introduced Peter, or myself.

After doing so, Jack said, "I think we'd better check what damage was done under his shorts. I'll lift up his back and you lower his shorts." There was one deep scratch on his left leg that went almost to his hip. Both hips were badly bruised, but that's about it. His shorts served him well.

Peter started to stir. He gradually focused on me and started crying. He looked at me with pleading eyes, begging me to make it stop hurting. He started to move, but I held him in place. I put my hand on the side of his face. "Not yet, Kiddo."

Our new friend said, "I know the brush burns and scratches are extremely painful, but it looks and feels worse than it is. When you get back to where you're staying, wash his brush burns with soap and warm water. Put some antibiotic salve on them and keep them clean. Get some ice on his hips and chin. Other than that, there's not much you can do. Check and make sure I got out the entire pricker. Then wash the puncture wounds. He's going to be a pretty sore kid for two or three days, but he should be fine." I knew Peter would be fine tomorrow.

Jack walked over to the log, then called me. Two feet from where Peter fell off was the three-inch remains of a sharp, small branch. If he had gone two more feet, he would have been ripped open from his belly button to his breastbone. I looked up through the forest canopy of foliage and gave a word of thanks.

As other hikers arrived from their walk up or down the mountain, Jack and I prepared to head down the trail. Six of the hikers joined hands in such a way as to make a flat stretcher, for Peter's stomach needed to remain flat. We managed to keep Peter as comfortable as possible. I held his hand all the way. Whimpering now and then as his body was jostled on the uneven trail, Peter cried, "Grandpa, I'm sorry I didn't listen to you. Now I've ruined our whole day."

"Don't worry about it, Kiddo. I'm more concerned about your wounds." Once to the car, the group got him on the back seat rather painlessly. I thanked everybody for their help and concern, then headed to a store with ice for sale.

Back at the campsite, I got a hand under his bottom and the other under his upper back. I got him to the picnic table rather painlessly. Fearful of my answer, he asked, "Jake, are you going to spank me?"

"Do you think I should?"

Tears forming again, he said, "Yes. You told me to stay off logs and why. I didn't listen." In a whisper he said, "I ruined everything."

I wrapped ice in three small towels then gently slipped his shorts off. I applied the ice to his hips and chin. I padded the deep scratch on his left thigh. I hoped that would stop the oozing. After enough effective silence, I said, "Peter, I guess a spanking is justified. But you've suffered more than enough pain for one day. Besides, I can't lay you over my lap. No, I'm not going to spank you." I lay a small towel from one hip to the other. "Now you stay put."

I was working on the fire when I heard him groan. I turned around to find him sitting straight up with his feet hanging from the table toward the bench. "Hey, what do you think you're doing?"

"I want to help." I could tell he was in a lot of pain.

I couldn't help but smile. "You little pumpkin. You're still not listening to me. Now let me help you ease back down."

"I like working with you. I want to help. We're a team."

"Peter, I love it when we work together. You're a very good worker. These injuries are darn serious, though not deep. You don't realize it, but your skin is your biggest organ. And when any organ is injured, it's not to be taken lightly. Now you stay put or I may spank you yet." I replaced the ice packs and the towel.

I started to walk back to the fire. "Jake, I promise. I will never disobey you again."

I walked back to him. "Peter, don't make promises you can't keep. You're a six-year-old boy and of course you will. I did, and so does every other six-year-old. This time you were seriously injured. Now lie there quietly and let this be a lesson. Pain and disappointment have a way of making us mature." I gently stroked his cheek then went to the fire.

Before long I had warm water. It was time to clean the brush burns.

"Is it going to hurt?"

"I sure wish I could say no, Kiddo, but I'm afraid I can't. This is probably going to sting like crazy, especially when I use the soap." He whimpered. "I'll be as gentle as I can."

Fighting my tears, I put warm water on his belly and chest. He whimpered and winced. Then came the soap. Although he cried, he didn't scream out. After getting it clean and dry, I applied the salve. That he found soothing.

I wiped away one of his tears; he wiped away one of mine. "I'm sorry Jake, for hurting you so bad."

What a great kid! He was more concerned about my emotional pain than his physical pain.

When I finished treating his brush-burned legs and scratch, I sat with him for a few minutes and stroked his cheek again. "Ready for the next round?"

He looked at me, concerned. "What's that?"

"I've got to make sure Jack got the entire pricker out of each wound before I wash them."

"Is that going to hurt, too?"

"Maybe not as bad." I rolled him on his side, inflicting as little pain as possible. I inspected his entire backside head to toes. I couldn't believe it. Jack had every one of them out. And none were broken off. Then it was on to washing him.

In a few minutes he was in a restless slumber. I was free to start working on dinner. After a while he asked how he was going to eat. I hadn't thought about that. Because of his stomach, he couldn't sit up. "We'll figure out something. In the mean time, you stay put."

"I will Jake, I promise."

He closed his eyes and drifted off again. After a half-hour, I was back with dinner. I put a couple of pillows under his head to raise it a little but not bend his stomach, then I fed him.

After a few bites he said, "When are you going to eat?"

"Will you stop worrying about me so I can concentrate on worrying about you? I'm not going to starve and I don't want you to either." He giggled then winced in pain.

Just then Ranger Casey pulled up. As he approached us he said, "Hi guys." Once he was upon us, he exclaimed, "Oh, my God! What happened?"

I explained Peter's fall. I pulled back the towel on either side and removed the ice from his left hip. An ugly bruise was visible. I assured him Peter would be fine. But our ranger friend was extremely concerned. He offered to rush him to the hospital. Peter looked worried. It was time for one more person to find out about Peter.

"Tom, I know Peter looks pretty bad right now, but tomorrow morning there will be no sign of his injuries. They will be gone." He looked at me incredulously. "Peter misbehaves now and then and doesn't always listen the way he should, but what six-year-old boy does?" Tom and I laughed at Peter's expense. "The point is, Tom, Peter is a terrific little kid, but he's…different." Peter and I looked at him. "You see, Peter is actually dead."

The ranger looked at me in disgust for what sounded like sick humor. "What did you say?"

"Peter, if it's okay with you, let's show Ranger Tom our proof."

Peter smiled real big and disappeared before our eyes.

Tom jumped back. He almost fell over. His eyes grew as big as his silver badge. Then Peter reappeared. Tom went for a chair to support himself. He was shaking. But I took up the job of feeding Peter again, explaining that we do not ordinarily share our secret with people. But as a friend and a ranger who'd seen everything, and who had not figured out how a runaway truck had averted hitting the van the past week, he needed to be in the loop.

I outlined Peter's past and how we were brought together and what redemptive purpose we seemed to be serving in each other's lives. He relaxed enough to ask some very good questions. Tom was one smart ranger, and it was a pleasure for both of us to address his excellent questions. Of course we asked him to keep these things confidential.

Finally, Tom sat with me as I ate and Peter dozed off. (Tom was not hungry.) Then he accompanied me to the lake where I cleaned the dishes and continued Peter's story.

Walking back from the lake, I concluded, "So that's why he doesn't need to see a doctor for his injuries." I sat on the table and stroked Peter's upper ribs. Tom was speechless now. He stood there staring up and down Peter's little battered body. "Tom, do you still have that strange rock your foot kicked up the other day?"

He reached in his pocket. "This one? The one with the cross on it!"

I nodded. "I suggested to you that day that you'd seen a miracle. Do you believe me now?"

Tom nodded back.

"There are sixteen people out there and alive today that shouldn't be. I'd be willing to bet they realize that what happened was a miracle. I know I do." I looked down at Peter and rubbed his cheek with the back of my fingers.

"Tom, close your mouth before the mosquitoes find it."

"How do you expect me to keep this to myself?"

"Easy. Who will believe you? You let it out and you will end up out of a job."

"You're right. Can I tell my wife?"

"If you want to ruin your marriage."

The Gift

"You don't understand. I have seen a miracle. With my own eyes. And I never in my life ever, ever believed in them. I've called the Bible a pack of fairy tales. I've been wrong, dead wrong."

"Just try to express your new-found awareness in new ways that leave Peter out of it. You do that and you'll get plenty of questions that you'll have a hard time answering. You can bet your badge on that. By the way Tom, you said you've seen a miracle. I would suggest you've seen two." He looked at me, confused. I looked down at Peter. Tom nodded his understanding.

Tom stood up and moved nervously like he was not in his woods but in a strange cathedral someplace. He said he had to be going. "Not that I don't believe you two; if you don't mind, I'd like to stop back tomorrow morning and check in on your patient."

"No problem. I'll have the camp coffee on." Tom and I shook hands and he left.

I looked at Peter. "So how did I handle that, Funny Tummy?"

He laughed over the new name but instantly tears appeared. He couldn't laugh without a lot of pain. I forgot, felt terrible and apologized.

"It's okay. That's a neat name. Can we go on your chair for a story?"

"No, I'm sorry but we can't. You can't bend that belly of yours. That's okay though. I can tell it right here. How do you feel?"

"Everything is still pretty sore."

All kids think they're invincible. The problem with Peter was that he is and he knew it. "Peter, you think of yourself as a ghost too much. But most of the time you're a six-year-old boy. Therefore, you can suffer just as much pain as anybody.

"Sometimes you've got the devil in your eyes. In other words, you misbehave and disobey me once in a while. You're no angel and I'm glad you're not. If you were, I wouldn't want to have anything to do with you. You'd be boring. Today you made a poor decision and got hurt, but I love you anyway. How about that story?" He smiled slightly and nodded.

The story I told was about a little boy who disobeyed his father often. As a result he was always in trouble or getting hurt. I stretched it out to about twenty minutes by giving several examples. About halfway through he put his right hand on mine. When finished he said, "That was a good story." He thought for a minute. "I was the little boy and you were the daddy, right?"

I smiled. "Could be. Hey, we're both beat. Let's go to bed."

It was only 7:45 but both of us were exhausted. Once in the tent, I replaced the ice and put my arm under his head. I stroked his side gently. It was a warm night so we didn't need to be covered. Because of his brush burns, that was good. "Jake, aren't you going to put my bottoms on me?"

"No. I'm afraid your bottoms would aggravate your injuries. You can stay the way you are for tonight, but only for tonight."

He smiled. "I like sleeping this way. It's comfortable."

I asked him a question but he was asleep. Later that night he had a nightmare. He dreamed he fell off the log again.

CHAPTER SIX

I lay in our tent beside Peter. Here was the only person that I have been close to in a dynamic, interactive way in the last half-century. Since my own childhood, really. As I lay there I could isolate one central emotion that morning – gratitude.

I was grateful for the relationship I was enjoying with Peter. He was making physical demands, sure. And his emotional demands were even greater. But I was grateful for having these demands in my life now.

But for what reason? I asked myself. I pondered that question a long time. Being a red-blooded male, I posed a little side question along the same line. What if...just what if I were lying wide awake beside someone as sweet and attractive as Paula? And now would get up and go our separate ways? What would all of that have meant to me in the long run?

Would I be lying here with the same deep sense of gratitude that I was feeling that morning with Peter beside me?

The difference had to do with one word – meaning. So I imagine myself saying over breakfast, "Peter, you have brought a lot of meaning to my life in our short time together."

Peter, I realize, would probably ask me, "What does 'meaning' mean?" I reflected a while on just how I would answer him.

Finally, I came up with this: Peter, take that tree that you were walking on against my better advice: That tree's purpose was not to make little disobedient boys fall and painfully skin themselves. The tree was meant to grow strong and tall and provide shade and a place for animals and birds to enjoy themselves. But now it is old, fallen down and decaying. Its new purpose is to nurture the soil where it lies rotting away. That is the final purpose or meaning of that tree in the grand scheme of things.

But Peter might ask, "And so what's the meaning in your life that I've given you?"

Now I was stumped for an answer. So I was glad Peter was still asleep. I knew what I was not going to say to him when he woke up.

Very seldom have things from my college psychology and English courses come back to my mind; things from my professors in science and history is another matter. So it was strange to have something from English literature pop up in my reflections that morning. But here it is, a quote from Samuel Johnson that had impressed me as a nineteen-year-old punk kid. The quote angered me at the time. I took sharp issue with it at the time. And that is maybe why it got lodged in my mind nearly four decades ago:

The end of all human ambition is to find satisfaction at home.

That may not be the exact wording, but it's painfully close.

The emotions of gratitude gripped me that morning there beside Peter. And held me for the better part of an hour. At times tears rolled out of the corners of my eyes for no apparent reason. That emotion of gratefulness seems to be heightened with an intense sense of coming home again. (I've always been most at home with the words anyway.) I was glad to be at home with Peter. I was feeling very at home

The Gift

with myself that morning. Or was it feeling at home with God who…with a God who answered Peter's dying prayer?

I quietly got up, got dressed and built a fire. In the process, I was thinking about the meaning of fire. It can be for cooking a meal or for wiping out thousands of acres of crops or timber. I knew how to build and regard a cooking fire. I was passing the meaning of fire for cooking onto Peter. He would be wise and not arrogant like the man in the Jack London classic *To Build A Fire*. That young man was foolish. He would not listen to wisdom and it cost him his life.

So while I made coffee, I pondered on the high cost of following foolishness – my own and Peter following his own. I thought of the wisdom of Paula with her daughter and how properly she handled our acquaintance. She was a classy lady, a good mom, and friendly enough to open up a bit of her life to me. Maybe she was a little foolish wearing her bikini to a beach and talking to a stranger whom she mistook for Peter's grandpa. But then, maybe she just wanted a thorough tan. Maybe this was her first real vacation since her son's death. After all, who was I to judge! For the first time I wondered about her husband. Perhaps he could not get off work. On the other hand, I have known of couples breaking up after losing a child in death. Likely breaking up for lack of ever coming to an agreement on just what the death was supposed to mean.

My morning was getting too serious, so I poured a second cup of coffee and was about to head for the tent when Peter emerged. I sat back down and got ready. I should have put his pajamas on him before leaving the tent, but I guess I was preoccupied in my own thoughts. "Hey, there's Mr. Bare Butt with a funny tummy. How are you this morning?" He stopped in his tracks, started laughing so hard he almost fell on the ground at the names, then charged for my lap and dove, landing belly down.

"I guess this means your belly's okay this morning."

"Yep, it's perfect." With effort he rolled over to show me his belly, bending his back like a pretzel. "And my hips are okay too, I think, aren't they?"

I put my hand on his strained belly and stroked him gently. It never ceased to amaze me how his wounds could heal so quickly. "Yeah, they're healed, too."

Then I let my fingers do the walking from one rib to the next all the way to his armpits. Because of the position he was in, he couldn't get up on his own, therefore he was at the mercy of my fingers. Before long he was laughing hysterically.

I sat him up. "Go in and put some shorts on, then we'll eat."

Then his sweet voice came from the tent, "Thank you, Jake, for everything you do for me. I love you."

That was new. To just say, "I love you" without any particular reason following that expression was new. And I savored it dearly. Then it dawned on me that because of all I was doing for him, I'd come to love him as a grandfather would love his grandson. At first I pitied him. It was pity that had drawn me to him. But the job of taking care of him was another thing.

"Peter, I love you, too." I realized that all the demands he put on me had grown this love for him that I was feeling. This gratitude for him! Without him, I still would have been an independent, over-the-road trucker, a curmudgeon without much meaning beyond getting my truck from point A to point B safely and on time. "Did you hear me, Peter. I love you, too."

Suddenly he burst from the tent, toothless smile and all, once again heading for my lap. He gave me a hug, which was my answer. That's all I needed to make my day.

After breakfast and while washing our dishes, Ranger Casey drove up. We both turned around to greet him. Looking at Peter standing in only his shorts, Tom said, "That's amazing. Completely healed. I would never have believed it if I hadn't seen it with my own eyes."

Peter flashed Tom his beautiful smile, lowered his shorts and said, "See, my hips are as good as new, too." Tom laughed and shook his head.

Walking back to the fire I poured Tom a cup of coffee. "Jake, I did a lot of soul searching last night." He looked at Peter. "How can I not believe in miracles when I have one sitting in front of me? And how can I not believe in God if I believe in miracles? That would be illogical, wouldn't it?" He looked from Peter to me then back to Peter. Peter smiled.

All of a sudden, as if he was not used to being God-conscious, he tipped up his cup and drank his coffee down, just like that. "Well guys, I've got to get to work."

After saying good-bye to Tom, we headed for our lake. Both of us caught several bass, but no keepers; nevertheless we had fun.

After lunch Peter asked if he could swim naked then lay in the sun naked for a while. I wasn't too excited about letting him do either, but then came up with an idea. "Peter, take your trunks off and put your life preserver on." He looked at me questioningly but did as I said. We got in to the canoe, Peter still confused. On the way to the middle of the lake I asked, "Peter, do you remember everything I told you to do if the canoe flipped?" He answered yes. "Good!"

At that point I flipped the canoe watching Peter carefully. He yelled "Jake" as he went under, but he held on to his paddle. When he bobbed to the surface, he still had it. Trying to flip his hair out of his eyes, he looked at me angrily and said, "Why did you do that?"

I laughed. "I wanted to see how well you remembered what I'd told you. You did it perfectly. You held onto your paddle and you came right back to the canoe."

He was still angry. "Well you could have warned me."

"It wouldn't have been the same. When a canoe flips for whatever reason, it doesn't say, 'Get ready, Peter. I'm going to flip in one minute.'"

He started laughing and his anger was over. I told him to hang on to his paddle, then we both swam under the canoe to discover a huge air supply. He thought that was pretty neat. I also showed him how to get back into the canoe. This was Peter's skinny-dipping time with a lesson attached.

While playing around in the middle of the lake, we heard someone say, "You boys having fun?" I looked up to see a man and his wife in another canoe, not twenty feet away.

"Yeah, my grandpa and I are having a great time. My grandpa showed me how to save myself if my canoe ever flips." Peter then pulled himself up and over into the water-filled canoe. "Come on up, grandpa."

The woman chuckled. "That's okay, grandpa. Why don't you stay where you are?"

I let out with an embarrassed laugh. "I do have trunks on but thank you, I think I'll do that."

"Sorry about invading your private time with your grandson," she said. "We'll try fishing on the other side."

After they left, we went back to our swimming area. He wanted to stay in the raw. He enjoyed his freedom from clothes. Who could blame him? But I said, "Peter, if you were to get burned in the wrong place, you'd be very sore for the rest of the day."

He looked down at himself and giggled. "I'll be careful."

"Like you were on the log?"

He gave me an embarrassed smile and put his trunks on. He hopped, skipped and jumped in the sand. He did somersaults, cartwheels and headstands with my help. Then he asked me how to do a back flip. I didn't have a clue but I helped him. When he was ready to try one on his own, he came down flat on his belly. He didn't give up. That wasn't the only time he landed on his belly but with persistence, he finally got it. Then it was on to a front flip. Again I helped him. When he tried it on his own he landed on his back and knocked the wind out of himself. After a few minutes and a couple of tears he was up and trying it again. After a few minutes he had the front flip too. He was happy with himself and I was proud of his tenacity.

He enjoyed the sand for a half-hour until we finally walked along the shoreline skipping stones and looking at things that interest little boys and big boys, too. As we walked, we came to a muddy area. I saw a chance for some fun and couldn't resist. I picked up a huge, flat rock, tossed it in the mud just right and totally plastered Peter. He saw it coming and tried to turn away but all he managed to do was close his eyes.

He turned toward me slowly, laughing hysterically. Spitting some mud out of his mouth, he said, "Oh Jake, you got me." He was covered with mud from ankles to face. I stood there laughing but then he lunged into the mud and crawled around like a worm. When he came out, there were two little white patches where his eyes were and that was it. I was laughing so hard I was almost sick. I told him he looked like a swamp monster, whereupon he played the part well. He walked along the shoreline, arms out in front of him dripping mud, legs stiff and moaning, groaning and growling. Of course his voice was so high, his growls sounded cute instead of threatening.

When we got back to our swimming area, it was time to get cleaned up. He dove under the surface and when he came up, he looked pretty good, but he still had some mud in his ears, nostrils and hair. While washing his hair I got some soap in his ears and his nose, which made him sneeze. As a result, he blew everything out. After drying him I said, "The monster is gone and the beautiful, little boy is back."

With the compliments I was constantly giving him along with everyone else, it would have been easy for him to have developed a swelled head and turned into a real brat. I mentioned that and added, "If you ever do, I'd tan your hide but good."

Worriedly he put his head down. "That's what my daddy always said before he beat me."

"Don't worry about that. What I mean is, if you act like a brat, I'll spank you."

He relaxed. "I won't. And if I do, I hope you do spank me."

We both lay in the sun for about twenty minutes. I was beginning to realize how important a short, quiet time was for him, even though he didn't. Bill was right. I put my hand on his chest while he slept for fifteen minutes.

We decided to fish near the other canoe. "Any luck?" I asked as we approached.

"Not much," the woman answered. "Look, we're really sorry coming up on you the way we did, but when we first saw you, we thought you were in trouble."

"No problem. It was Peter's first skinny dipping experience. I took the opportunity to teach him how to save himself if the canoe ever flipped."

"That's a good thing to know. He sure is a cutie."

We both smiled. He thanked her for her compliment. "Hey Kiddo, why don't you show them how to do it?"

He took out his rod, baited the hook and threw it in as the couple looked on with interest. Within three minutes he had a bass. He played it masterfully and landed it by himself. It weighed about two pounds. With the two people looking on in awe, he took it by the lower lip, removed the hook and was about to release it when the man said, "You're going to let it go?"

"My grandpa says, 'If you keep the little ones, there'll never be big ones.'" With that he gently returned it to the lake. I was so proud of him I could spit. Meanwhile the people in the other canoe were speechless. Finally the woman said, "Your grandpa's right." Then she removed two bass from their bucket, both smaller than the one Peter just caught, and released them.

The man looked at me and said, "Sir, you can be proud of your grandson. I'm amazed such a small child can handle a rod so proficiently. And bait his own hook, too! But to see him fight that bass and land it was too much. Then to take it off the hook and release it, well! He is quite a young man."

"Thank you. I'm very proud of him. It may help to know he's six, just small for his age."

"It doesn't make any difference. I've never seen a six-year-old that could do all that. What's your name, son?" Peter told him, somewhat embarrassed but very proud. "Well, Peter, it's nice to meet you. Good luck in your fishing."

We both thanked him and headed back to our campsite. On the way, I let Peter troll for a while with a floater. This was another new experience for him. He didn't know what trolling was, but he was excited anyway. We stopped paddling in the middle of the lake and put our paddles down. I had him turn around so he was facing me. Taking his fishing pole, I put a floating, muskie lure on it. Casting it out twenty feet from the canoe, I demonstrated how to play it for a little more action then returned his pole to him. Peter was so excited, he had a problem sitting still.

"Peter, if you get something, it's not going to be a bite like a bass. A muskie will come through fast, hit your lure, and won't even slow down to wink at you. That's why they call it a strike. You have to be ready all the time."

He turned deadly serious. I had him let the line out another twenty feet then started paddling. I was hoping he'd get something but praying he wouldn't get a monster like mine. A fish that size could yank his thirty pounds right out of the canoe.

Ten minutes later he got a strike. I moved up to him to offer my help if he needed it. He fought the muskie for about fifteen minutes. An adult could have landed it in two or three minutes, but that was okay. It was a good experience for him and he did it without my help.

When the exhausted muskie was pulled to the side of the canoe, I lifted it in. It was twenty-six inches and almost six pounds; the largest fish he ever caught, but it was not a keeper. It didn't matter. Peter was thrilled. To him it was his monster. I got several pictures of Peter and his muskie before returning it to his watery home. My proud little fisherman put his pole down and paddled the rest of the way in. Now we both had pictures of our own monsters.

That night after dinner, we read together for over an hour, but suddenly he realized that I wasn't listening. He put the book down concerned. "Jake, did I do something wrong?"

"What? Huh? Oh, no, Kiddo. I was just thinking. When you were alive, you wanted to go to school, right?" He nodded. In Slippery Gulch he was told by the schoolmaster he couldn't go to school because he was too stupid. "Well, now you know you're not stupid, right?"

"I guess."

"What do you mean, you guess? You're brilliant. The thing I was thinking about was…if I could arrange it, would you be interested in going to a real school? Sitting in a real classroom with other kids and a teacher."

His instant smile changed to a frown. "They probably wouldn't let me."

"If they didn't, it wouldn't be because you're stupid. The point is Kiddo, if I could arrange it, would you like to try it?"

Again, he smiled, but once again the frown returned. He said nothing. "Peter, what's wrong?"

The wheels were turning. He was troubled. Finally he said, "Would you put me in school, then go back on the road?" The tears were forming and his lower lip started to tremble. He'd come a long way in the weeks we'd been together, but he was still very insecure in many areas.

I turned him all the way around on my lap. "Peter, you thought this was my way of getting rid of you?" He lowered his head. I raised it. "Peter, you and I are a team. I don't know what I'd do without you anymore. What I had in mind was having you go to school for one week, just to see what it's like. Then the two of us would go back on the road, together. Hey, Funny Tummy, I wouldn't go anyplace without you."

"I'm sorry, Jake."

"You don't have anything to apologize for. I understand." He still couldn't rest in the fact of my solid commitment to him. "I don't know if I can arrange it, but I wanted to see if you'd be interested before I tried."

"If I go to school, could you go with me?"

"No. None of the parents or grandparents go to school with their children. However, the first day I would take you. Then I will come and pick you up at the end of the day. After that first day you can ride the bus to school with Nate."

Suddenly his eyes lit up. "I can ride a school bus?"

"Sure!" After traveling around the country in a big truck, this guy was excited over a school bus.

Now sullenly he asked, "Jake, what if the kids beat me up?"

His old fears resurfaced. "Kiddo, I know it's hard to get over past fears. If I thought for one minute that could happen, I'd never let you go."

"What if I'm dumber than all the other kids?"

"The way you've been picking up everything? There's not a chance they'll see you as dumb. You may find that you're the smartest kid in the class."

"Really?"

"Really! Do you want to try it for a week?"

He thought a few minutes. "Do you think I'd have fun?"

"I think you'll have a blast. Why, you will learn some very valuable things. And you'd have a chance to spend some time with kids your own age."

He giggled. "Jake, no kids are my age."

I laughed. "Okay, smartypants. You know what I mean."

He laughed. "I know. I think I'd like to try it."

"Okay. When we get home, I'll call a friend of mine and see what I can do. No promises though." He nodded.

I sat there thinking until I blurted out, "Peter, I don't understand you."

He looked at me, confused. I put both hands against his bare back supporting his slight weight. He said nothing, waiting. "Peter, I love you dearly. You know that. From what I know of your horribly brief, bad upbringing, you have every right to be a hateful, mean little boy. But you are loving, kind and wonderful in every way. Why? Can you explain this to me?"

He thought for a moment then responded with the wisdom of Solomon. "It's not that you don't understand me, it's that you don't understand yourself. You've taught me everything. You started teaching me when I first bumped into you in Slippery Gulch. You asked if I was okay. You showed concern. You cared. Nobody cared before. I was confused. You were kind. Then you taught me what love looks like. If it weren't for you, I think I would be mean."

He studied me as I pondered this. He could be partly right, yet I didn't think there had ever been a mean bone in his body. So I said, "I think your mother was quite a wonderful woman. I think you take after her even though you never knew her. It's for darn sure you don't take after your father, thank God."

"I think my mother talked to me once," he said quietly.

"What?' I asked, shocked. "I thought your mother died at your birth?"

"She did, but I think it was her." I kept quiet and let him continue. He looked at me long and hard. He wasn't angry but definitely worried. I had no idea what the problem was. Finally he said, "It was the first day you came to Slippery Gulch."

Something critical was coming. I kept prodding "It was she that talked to you?"

"Yes."

"Peter, did she tell you I was coming?"

"Yes."

"Did she tell you anything else?"

He hesitated then finally said, "Yes."

During this entire exchange, I was rubbing his back. "What did she say?"

He sat quietly for several minutes. Finally he said, "She told me 'the friend you prayed for' would be coming into town that day. She said you'd be real nice, but wouldn't be that interested in me and would finally leave. But she said you'd be back. She said, 'be patient.' She said that when you came back you would love me, but wouldn't know it yet. I didn't understand and she didn't explain. I never heard her again, but I think she was there anyway."

So it was this ghostly woman, more than likely his mother, who set everything up. "Why didn't you tell me about this before?"

He lowered his head. "I was afraid. I thought if you knew I knew you were coming, you might leave and never come back. I was also afraid if you found out I had talked to a ghost, you might think I was crazy."

I raised his head and looked at him to see if he was serious. He was. I started laughing. "Peter, do you have any idea how ridiculous that is?"

"What does redicilas mean?"

"Well, it refers to something that is laughable and unbelievable at the same time. You said you were worried that I'd think you were crazy if I knew you were talking to a ghost?" He nodded but failed to see the humor in what he'd said.

"Peter, for the last month, I've been traveling around the country with a little ghost. I eat and sleep with him. Lately, I've been fishing, canoeing and swimming with that same little ghost. I touch, talk to and tickle this little ghost. I love this little ghost. And right now the little ghost is sitting on my lap. And he's telling me that I might think he's crazy? What do you think I wondered about myself at times?"

Suddenly he got it and started laughing. "Yeah, but when I'm with you, I don't think of myself as a ghost. I don't even feel like a ghost."

"I know. That's why I take your hand when we cross a street. That's why I just naturally try to protect you in other ways, like any father or grandfather would. And the crazy thing is I don't really have to. In fact, if push came to shove, you would protect me."

"But you do, Jake." He touched his belly where the brush burn was. "You took care of me like nobody else ever did. Do you know how good it feels to have you for my best friend ever?"

I couldn't speak so I nodded my head yes and pulled the little guy to my chest till I could get my voice again.

"I have a question for you. As a ghost, you can never age. Does that bother you?"

He thought about this. "I never thought about it before. You are probably right. As long as I'm with you, will you always treat me as a six-year-old?"

"Do you want me to?"

"I like it when you hold my hand. I like it when you give me rides on your shoulder and let me sit on your lap. I like falling asleep on your lap. I love it when you hug, kiss and tickle me. I like knowing you're close when I have a nightmare or hurt myself. I like it when you tease me. I like it when you wash my hair and dry me off in a big soft towel. I even love it when you punish me because I know you love me and worry about me. If those are all things that people are supposed to do for six-year-olds, I want to stay a six-year-old."

"Good, because I like treating you that way." I sat thinking for a minute while he studied me. "Peter, you were told before I ever came to town, I was the answer to your prayer. But you didn't really settle for that. When did you really know for sure that I was...that I am?"

"When you asked me to leave town with you."

"If you knew I was your answer, but I didn't take you, what would you have done?"

Matter-of-factly he said, "Waited. You would have come back. Are you mad?"

"Are you kidding? No way! I don't know why I'm the one, but I thank God it is me."

"Could I tell you one more thing?"

"Sure! Go ahead."

Collecting his thoughts he hesitated for several minutes then said, "I don't know when it was, but you were leaving Dallas, on I-30 going to Paris, Texas, to pick up a load. It was raining real hard." The hairs on my neck began to stand on end. "You looked at the routing the company gave you. You looked at the map and found a short cut. You were debating on whether to take it. There was a slow truck in your lane, so you moved into the fast lane to pass. Just then there was the exit to your shortcut." The familiar chill had returned.

"You moved back into the slow lane to get to the exit. Just as you did, a big truck going west jack knifed into the median, bounced out and ended up in the fast lane, right where you would have been. It would have hit you in the driver's door. You would have been..." His voice trailed off. "Somebody else made that decision for you, Jake."

I was speechless for several minutes. Suddenly I was freezing. The chills were running up and down my spine so fast, they were passing each other. When I got my composure back, I said, "Peter, that was you?"

He shook his head. "I just heard about it."

"From your mother?"

The Gift

"No…It was just kind of a voice in my head. I don't know who it was or where it came from. I don't even know when I heard it." He seemed really confused on time. "The voice was so kind and clear. I heard the same voice just after you left Slippery Gulch the first time. The voice said, 'As the answer to your dying prayer, he shall return.'"

Now I was collecting my own thoughts. The incident Peter mentioned took place over four years ago. That meant he was not aware of past or future – just the event. That also meant I'd been picked as the answer to Peter's prayer, years earlier. Not only that, I now knew I had a guardian angel. I also knew Peter was not that angel.

I wanted to put Peter down and take a long walk to be by myself. But I did neither. I sat there seeing myself driving cross-country alone. There I was, an average trucker, an average Joe. Why not Hank or some other family men I knew? Then I saw myself driving along with Peter in the other seat. I had a smile on my face. I was thinking, 'I love this little guy. We're a good team.'

"Peter, do you have any idea why I am the one that was picked."

"Sure. We love each other."

That was right, but four years ago we didn't even know each other. It was probably the best answer I'd ever have. And to Peter, it was all that was needed. Maybe that's all I needed too. I smiled. "Yeah, we sure do, don't we?" I gave him a hug.

"Hey, it's 9:00. Time for you to go to sleep. But we had a good read and a good talk."

"I know. Could I run down the road a ways and back before I go to sleep?"

"I guess, but why?"

"I don't know. I just really feel good. I'm in the mood for it."

Now that I thought about it, I was too. "I'll tell you what. I feel good, too. I'll run with you. Put your sneakers on first. How about if we run down to the curve and back?"

As soon as his sneakers were tied, we were off. The air was clear between us and the run was just what the doctor ordered.

Once back he removed his sneakers, then came up on my lap to cuddle. I put my hand on his chest. He was asleep in seconds, a content smile on his face.

CHAPTER SEVEN

The next morning was rainy, as predicted. As I was getting dressed, Peter woke up. This was very uncharacteristic of him since it wasn't quite 6:30. "Hey, Funny Tummy, got an idea. It's raining out. Before waking up, how'd you like to take a walk in the rain?" Now what six-year-old boy could resist that?

He was up in a jiffy. "Do I have to put my rain coat on?"

"Nope. It's warm out. Go as you are. Maybe I should take a bar of soap along."

He wrinkled his nose. "Jake, that would ruin it."

I started laughing. "Okay, I'll leave the soap here."

As we walked down the road, Peter jumped in every puddle he could find. We were only gone for twenty minutes, but that was long enough. Peter was drenched; however I was dry. Since I wasn't a six-year-old boy, I wore a raincoat.

I had him remove his bottoms before entering the tent and rung them out. When I walked in, he'd dried most of himself but left his hair for me. "Get dressed Kiddo, while I get a fire going."

Twenty minutes later and well into my first cup of coffee, it occurred to me Peter still had not emerged from the tent. I called to him but didn't get a reply. I put my mug down and went to investigate. Peter was in a dry pair of shorts and sound asleep on his sleeping bag. I smiled, went out for another cup of coffee, then went back into the tent and waited.

At 7:45, he started to move. I pounced before he ever opened his eyes. At first, I thought he was going to cry, but then he realized what was going on and started laughing and squealing. Totally out of breath, he said, "Wow, you really got me that time, Jake."

I lay down next to him, put my arm under his head and gently stroked his ribs with my thumb. "I'm sorry, Kiddo. Maybe I am too mean. You didn't even have your eyes open yet. I'll tell you what. To make it up to you I'll treat you to a warm breakfast in a dry restaurant in town."

Tears began to well up in Peter's eyes. Concerned I asked, "Peter, what's wrong?"

Wiping at a tear he said, "You feed me all the time. They never even put food out for me. You rub and tickle my ribs; they broke them. You wipe my tears away; they made me cry. You rub my belly; they punched me there. You treat my cuts and bruises; they caused them. You ruffle my hair and wash it; they pulled and yanked it. You kiss my face; they punched and slapped it. You love me; they hated me. Everything you do to me and with me is out of love. You can be as mean to me as you want."

I choked back my emotions and hugged him. "Just remember, Little One, I will never, ever be mean in such a way as to hurt you."

"I know, Grandpa." He then seemed to return my hug and love ten-fold.

After a few minutes, I broke the silence. "This morning we are going to go into town for breakfast, but before we do, we're going to stop over at the park and take hot showers."

He wrinkled his nose as he sat up. "Do we have too?"

"Yes, we both do. We've been bathing in the lake, but we both need a hot shower."

"Okay. I guess you're right. Can we go to the museum then?"

"You bet, after we wash some clothes." While he got dressed, I put clean clothes and towels in my shoe bag.

The shower cost fifty cents, which gives you five minutes of water. You'd think with such a tiny body, he'd be able to wash in one or two minutes, but it took him almost five. Just as I got his hair completely lathered, the time ran out. Inserting another two quarters, we finally got his hair washed and rinsed, then got out and dried off. I gave him two quarters then showed him how to activate the shower in case I ran out of time, but I made it.

From there we went into the town of Indian Lake, for a breakfast of bacon and eggs and fresh orange juice. After I paid for the meal and gave him two dollars to put on the table for the waitress, we headed for the local laundromat. Then with clean clothes we moved on down to the general store.

While deciding what kind of cookies we desperately needed, we were both distracted by a little boy at the end of our aisle not much bigger than Peter. He decided he wanted a particular type of cookie, but his mother said no. He started screaming, even falling to the floor in protest. Finally his mother relented.

Peter was watching with great interest. I picked him up and said, "DON'T EVEN THINK ABOUT IT." He looked at me puzzled. "I told you if you ever acted like a brat, I'd tan your hide but good." The mother stiffened and stared at me. "You also wondered if I'd relent the way she did." The expression on Peter's face went from puzzlement to amazement while the woman appeared angry.

"The answer is, absolutely not. If you want something, you ask me in a civil way. Then we'll discuss it; but if I say no, end of subject."

The woman took her flailing son by the arm and stormed out of the store, the shocked boy in tow. After paying for our few items, we went to the car. Once inside, Peter said, "Jake, how did you know?"

I started laughing. "Just yesterday I told you, if you ever acted like a little brat, I'd spank you. You knew I would, so that wasn't the test. The test was just as I said; you were wondering if I'd relent. Now you know. I understand you. But Peter, please, no more tests. You know me well enough now."

He looked at me. "Jake, could you do me a favor?"

Well, I guess that was that. "Sure, Kiddo. What do you want?"

"Could you come around to my side of the car for a minute?"

"What?"

"Please?"

I walked to his side of the car. Without warning, he leaped into my arms and gave me a big hug. "Thanks, Jake. You got everything right. I was pretty sure you wouldn't give in, but I wanted to see if I was right. I'm glad you won't. I'd hate to have a grandpa who always gave me my way."

I was laughing. "You're a little pumpkin, you know that?" I ruffled his hair. "Did you ever think about asking? It would be a lot easier and may be a lot less painful, for both of us."

He thought for a minute then produced a silly chuckle. "I never thought of that."

I started laughing again. "You little peanut. Just ask from now on, okay?" He nodded. "Come on. Let's go to the museum."

CHAPTER EIGHT

The Adirondack Museum, in the hamlet of Blue Mountain, is large and beautifully laid out. We spent the day. It is based on the history, both natural and human, of the region. There were a lot of displays on both the mining and timber industries of the area. As we went through the different areas, I read some of the signs to Peter but let him struggle through others. I was amazed at his knowledge of the nineteenth century mining industry; of course he was the son of a miner of that time period.

At one point, we walked through a classroom from the 1800's. He was silent for a moment. I understood. The closest he ever came to going to school was to look through a window after everyone had left. Hopefully that would change soon.

There is a display of watercraft used by humans throughout history. It includes everything from dugouts to steamboats. We found that one most interesting. We talked to a lot of different people during the day. Peter was a hit with everyone. It was a long, tiring day for both of us, but a good one.

The day was typical for August, hot and humid. At times the sun was out fully and at other times it was raining. Once in the afternoon, we both heard a loud continuous roar. We looked at each other, confused, then I thought I understood. I'd only witnessed it once before in Northern Canada. I grabbed Peter's hand and charged up a flight of stairs to the observation deck. The sky above us was a beautiful, summer blue.

The deck was crowded. Everyone was looking to the northwest across the large lake at the natural spectacle bearing down on us. I lifted Peter to my shoulders. Together with many others, we viewed the awesome sight and the source of the roar. Covering the entire northwest portion of the lake was a massive dark cloud made much darker by the brilliant sunlight directly over our heads. It was a gully-washer or cloudburst. The roar was created by the billions of raindrops slamming into the surface of the lake. As the natural phenomenon grew closer to our vantage point, the roar increased to the point that I could not hear Peter without him yelling. With a hundred feet to spare, Peter and I made a mad dash to a nearby coffee shop.

Once safely inside, we watched the wall of water sweep over our position with an intensity that we in the northeast seldom witness. The stone wall around the observation deck, less than one-hundred feet away, vanished from our view. Within three or four minutes, the worst of the rain was over, but Mother Nature wasn't done dazzling us yet. I grabbed Peter's hand as we ran out the door and back up to the observation deck. The sun was returning, leaving the walkways steaming in the August heat. As we looked across the lake, we saw the most beautiful double rainbow I've ever seen. The brightest part of the rainbow dipped into the lake.

"Wow!" Peter exclaimed. "Do you think there's a pot of gold at the bottom of the lake?"

"You want to go find out?"

"Yeah! Can I?"

Then I remembered who and what I was talking to. "No!"

He looked a little disappointed then asked to be picked up. Looking at the rainbow he asked, "There really is a God isn't there?"

"There sure is, Kiddo."

"Why does God sometimes scare us a little then make us happy again like now?"

"He likes to remind us who's in charge, but then he always lets us know he still loves us."

He thought about this. "That's what you do to me, Jake. When you get mad at me you scare me a little, but you always tell me you love me."

I smiled. "I don't mean to scare you but I do mean to love you."

God's display was over...for now. We ate our dinner in town. As we headed back to our campsite, it began raining again.

In our tent, I went right for my chair, expecting Peter to join me as usual. Instead he sat on the floor with his back to me drawing imaginary figures. Something was up, so I waited. After ten minutes, nothing had changed. I asked if he'd like to come up on my lap. He responded with a sharp, "No!"

"Well in that case, put on your PJ's?" Again he responded with a sharp, "No!"

"Why not?"

"Because I don't want to, okay?"

I had no idea what was going on, but I couldn't allow this kind of response to go unanswered. I knelt down in front of him and took him by the arms, ready to lay into him verbally, when I realized his arms were hot. He had a high fever. I gently lifted up his chin. The tears were forming. "You don't feel good, do you?" He put his head back down and shook it. I helped him stretch out on his sleeping bag and then went for the thermometer. "Why didn't you say something?"

Without looking at me he said, "I don't know."

"Oh come on, Funny Face, you can do better than that." He didn't say anything. I sat next to him, wiped away a tear and slipped my hand under his shirt. His stomach was on fire. He was starting to shiver. "So why didn't you tell me?"

He was quiet for a couple of minutes then said, "We were having so much fun, Jake. I didn't want to spoil it." I smiled. The old Peter was back. He was typically either more concerned about me or about us as a team than about himself. He was not a typical six-year-old. I slipped the thermometer under his tongue.

"Peter, since we've been home, we've been going a mile a minute and in some cases, three. You're dealing with a mortal body for the first time in 100 years, and you're not used to it. Plus, for the first time in your life, you're safe and having fun. Once in a while, this little body of yours is going to send you a message. You know what it's going to say?" He shook his head. In falsetto, I said, "Peter, please slow down. I'm wearing out."

Peter giggled. A good sign. "I think it's sending you a message, Kiddo. Let's see, your temp' is 105. Wow! Now tell me, where don't you feel good?"

"I don't know."

Okay, so it was time for twenty questions. "Do you have a stomach ache?" He did so I did some prodding. It was tender just above his belly button. He thought he might have to go to the bathroom and felt like he could get sick to his stomach. This could be a rough night. He also had a sore throat and a headache. Deciding I'd deal with his headache and sore throat later, I carried him to the outhouse. He didn't do much. Before he had a chance to clean himself, he announced he was going to throw up. I grabbed him and got him outside and next to the structure. I got him on his knees and from behind, put gentle pressure on his stomach. With my other hand resting on his forehead, we just made it.

After cleaning him both top and bottom, I had him rinse out his mouth then gave him a half an adult aspirin, hoping I wasn't making a mistake. I had never thought about getting

The Gift

baby aspirin until now. I lay him on his sleeping bag and slipped the thermometer under his tongue again. It was 105.5. He was shivering violently. I crawled in next to him and pulled him close.

"What if my temperature keeps going up?"

"Then I'll take you out to the table and give you a sponge bath."

"Jake, I'm too much trouble. Maybe I should just go back…"

I cut him off. "You know, I was just thinking. Maybe after you go to sleep, I'll go into town for a few hours tonight."

He looked at me with fear in his eyes. "You, you wouldn't leave me alone would you?"

"Why not? You're thinking about leaving me alone." I paused to let him ponder this. "I'll tell you what. I'll promise you right now, I will not leave your side for the whole night, if you promise me you won't go back to Slippery Gulch."

He managed to give me the best smile he could muster under the circumstances, then took my hand and squeezed it gently. "I promise."

"Actually, I could go to town tonight and know you'd be fine in the morning."

"I know, but Jake, that's all part of it."

I was lost. "Part of what? What do you mean."

"It's all part of my prayer." He paused working out his explanation. "The other day when I fell off the log and hurt myself real bad, you didn't have to do anything except touch me. I would have been fine the next day anyway. But my pain caused you pain. You hurt in here." He put his hand on his chest. "You washed my wounds and put salve on them. You treated me like a normal kid. You cared. You always take care of me. I could have turned into a ghost until the next morning. Then it wouldn't have hurt but I would have been cheating and you couldn't have taken care of me.

"You see, Jake, I like to see your love for me.

"And what you're saying shows your love for me, too.

"When I was living in Slippery Gulch and got hurt, people laughed. When I was sick, no one was worried. No one took my temperature or was ready to give me a sponge bath if it went too high. No one cared.

"You wouldn't have to do anything. You wouldn't have to worry. I'd be okay if you went into town, but you won't because you care and you love me. You see, Jake, that's all part of it and I love you for it."

"You're right: I do care and I do love you. I'll watch your temperature and if it doesn't come down soon, I'll give you a sponge bath. You're a mortal now and I'll always treat you as a mortal." I put my hand on his chest and smiled into his watery eyes. "If you think you're going to get sick during the night, try and give me a couple of seconds to get one of these plastic bags up to your mouth, okay?"

"I'll do my best. Thanks, Jake."

"Ya know Kiddo, this is my fault. I saw you were starting to drag this afternoon. I should have put you on my lap and let you sleep for a while."

"I don't like taking naps."

"I know you don't but although you have a lot of energy it doesn't last as long as it would if you were bigger. Unfortunately you have a little body with a small heart and small lungs. When your energy's gone you have to get it back or you're in trouble, like now. The best way to get it back is through sleep. Even sleeping for fifteen or twenty minutes this afternoon may have been enough to prevent this." I started to remove my hand but he grabbed it back. "Hey,

Kiddo, give me chance to get ready for bed. Then I'm going to wrap my arms around you. You're freezing."

"Promise?"

"I promise, if you promise not to fall asleep first."

He giggled just a little. "I promise."

I soon had him wrapped in my arms and pulled close. "Are you still awake?"

"Yeah. I promised I would be."

"We sure made a lot of promises to each other tonight, didn't we?"

He chuckled. "Yeah. Jake, I wouldn't really have gone back to Slippery Gulch."

I chuckled. "I know and I wouldn't have gone into town either."

"I know. We really do understand each other, don't we."

"That we do, Little One, that we do." I kissed him on the back of his head. Just like that, he was asleep.

Fifteen minutes later I could tell his temperature was dropping. Peter was right; I could ignore him. It would be much less trouble. But I'd promised Peter I'd take care of him. Before ever leaving Slippery Gulch, I demonstrated to him I'd take care of him. I accepted the responsibility and I wasn't about to shrug it off now. I once said making a promise to a ghost was like making a promise to the wind. In Peter's case, I was wrong. Making a promise to Peter was like making a promise to God. After all, if it weren't for God, Peter wouldn't be here now. I kept my hand on his chest and fell asleep.

The plastic bags were not necessary, but that night we had a terrific thunderstorm – the first one I had experienced with Peter. As it approached, I wasn't sure what was going to happen. My hand was still on his chest. He still had a mild fever. He slept through the first part of the storm. Then we had a fantastic flash of lightning. An immediate clash of thunder reverberated through the very earth we were sleeping on. That did it. He let out a scream, which startled me. With one mighty bound, he made it out of his sleeping bag and into mine, all in the dark. I was impressed. He wrapped his small arms around me, trembling, and was not about to let go for the world. One storm followed another for the next two hours. Neither one of us slept. It seemed like he tightened his grip with every massive blast. Finally it ended and we both drifted off.

The next morning was dry and sunny, although the ground was saturated. I was drinking coffee when Peter finally walked out of the tent around eight. He crawled onto my lap, muddy feet and all, but didn't say a word. I soon noticed the tears. "Where don't you feel good, Kiddo?"

He just said "Jake," then started crying harder and buried his face in my shoulder. I wasn't sure what to do so I held him and rubbed his back. After five minutes, he said, "Jake, I feel terrible." When I asked him where, he pointed to his chest. I wasn't sure what he meant or what to do, but then he continued. "I was so mean to you last night, but you were so nice to me. I'm sorry, Jake."

I turned him all the way around on my lap so he was facing me. "Peter, I understood. That was your fever talking. You really felt rotten, but you didn't want to spoil the fun. From now on, Kiddo, when you don't feel good, let me know and we'll deal with it."

He gave me a hug. "Okay, I will." He smiled broadly. "Thanks Jake, for understanding everything."

"Hey, no problem. By the way, how do you feel this morning?"

"Fine and I didn't puke last night. I'm sure glad of that."

The Gift

I laughed. "You and me both!" I then woke him up in our traditional way.

After he regained his breath, he wanted to know what we were going to do that day. I gave him a few choices. He decided he wanted to go fishing and swimming again.

After breakfast and cleanup, we loaded the canoe.

As we paddled off, I complimented him for his improved ability with the paddle.

Luck was not with us that morning so after a couple of hours, we set the poles aside and went swimming. After lunch, I got an idea. We walked along the lake. Together we caught five small frogs and put them in our bucket. He wanted to know what we were going to do with them. My only answer was, "You'll see. Time to take it easy for a few minutes." Although he didn't sleep, sitting in the shade of a tree talking quietly is a good break. Peter was then ready to find out what we were going to do with the frogs.

Once back to our fishing spot, I showed him how to hook a frog and our luck changed. He didn't have his line in the water more than a minute when he got a bite. He set it perfectly and was in for a fight. After five minutes, the bass jumped out of the water. It had to be five pounds. He laughed with excitement but wanted my help. I moved up behind ready to take the pole if necessary, but he played it well.

After fifteen minutes, we landed it together.

"Jake, you take it off the hook."

"Okay, but not until you try it first."

He reluctantly grabbed hold of its lower lip but couldn't apply sufficient pressure. As a result, the fish bit down hard. Peter's tiny thumb disappeared in its mouth. Bass don't have teeth, but their jaws are bony. The larger the fish, the harder its bite. He yanked his thumb out with a yelp and looked at the blood from his new wound.

While I got the hook out of the bass, I said, "Kiddo, you set that bass perfectly! Terrific job of playing it, too! I couldn't have done better myself."

Remembering how I landed the muskie a few days earlier, it appeared that he took this compliment as if it were coming from a true professional. (So what if some of it was luck.) He beamed. "Really? Thanks Jake."

After depositing the huge fish in our bucket, I looked at Peter's face again. The expression and smile I saw were ones I had seen many times during this camping trip, but failed to recognize it until now. Suddenly I knew who I was in real life. I wasn't the onboard expert. I was his coach. I had a little epiphany at that moment:

That's what a good dad is: He's his kids dearest fan and best coach all at once.

For the first time in my life, I saw myself as a father – and the father of this boy. I went from being a father type to being this boy's only father. The boy's need was redefining me to myself. In my mind I'd known who his real father was. But in my heart I knew that man had been merely the man who sired him and who became his arch enemy – a living, breathing demon in Peter's formative years of life. This poor waif had no frame of reference from which to understand the very word father. I was commissioned to define that word for him. And for some supernatural reason I couldn't figure out in a million years!

Once again I was choked up. How long had Peter seen me as the father I now recognized myself to be? I continued looking at him until he brought me out of myself.

"Jake, is something wrong?"

"Yes and no. Let me put it this way. If you talk to a soccer or a football coach – I suppose even basketball coaches do this too, but I never asked one: Coaches cry a lot

The Gift

during big games. Sometimes they cry out of pride. Sometimes anger. Sometimes to relieve great tension."

"What's a coach?"

With the bass safely in the bucket, Peter and I kicked back and I explained all the things a coach does to build a team. And how he and they never lose what they build between them.

To my utter astonishment, Peter said, "A coach is like what you are to me, isn't he? He's sort of like a father and a grandpa put together."

My overriding joy was that this little guy sitting in front of me got it…maybe even before I did.

"Let me see that thumb."

Peter let out with an "Oh," and held it out. I think he'd forgotten about it. It still amazed me how a ghost could bleed in the first place.

"If we catch any more fish, we should throw them back. There's no sense in keeping more than we can eat; besides, I hate cleaning fish and I'm not very good at it."

"Really? I watched Bill clean all those fish the other day. Could I try?"

"Why not. You can't do a worse job than I do. Bait your hook and let's keep fishing." We caught several more bass that afternoon. One he caught was four pounds. He also caught one small muskie that he gladly let go. He was moving from being a fisherboy to a sportsman, and I told him so.

"Thanks coach." I smiled.

On the way back to the campsite, I noticed he produced his strongest strokes yet.

Once back at the campsite he was anxious to begin his grisly task. I supervised only because it was his first time working with a knife. As he sliced open the belly, I noticed a tear form in one eye. I was puzzled. He hadn't cut himself. "Peter, are you okay?"

"Yeah. It's kind of stupid. For a minute, it reminded me of what my father did to me." He wiped the tear from his eye leaving a smudge of blood in its place. I remained silent as he worked and lost himself in thoughts of his own.

As I watched him work, I became aware of how often people scratch themselves; or at least little boys. He removed his hair from his forehead several times and scratched his head often. He scratched his stomach and chest, both legs and arms and even his back twice. Each time he left a new deposit of blood. I could help but chuckle. When he finished we had two large fillets, sort of.

He did a much better job than I could have done. However, he was covered in blood, fish guts and scales from head to toe. He wore only shorts while cleaning his fish. I realized after the fact that may have been a mistake. I now had fish-smelling shorts and a fish-smelling boy.

I had to get him and his shorts clean and free of the fish odor before going into the tent that night or we could expect to be visited by a host of animals. Although the animals didn't bother me, the prospect of them creating a back door in my tent did.

We had a problem. One foot out from shore the weeds started. It was not the ideal situation for a bath but we were stuck with it. We put the fish in a frying pan, covered it with a plate and a heavy rock on top to protect it from the seagulls then walked down along the shore for about two hundred feet. I had soap, shampoo, a large cooking bucket, a towel and a washcloth. He wasn't too happy with the bathing arrangements but when I explained why it was important, he understood. He removed his shorts and stepped into the lake.

I poured a bucket of water over his head. After getting his hair totally lathered, I poured another bucket over his head slowly as he rinsed the shampoo from it.

"You know, every place you had an itch while you were cleaning that fish, you have a blood smear."

He giggled. "Even my butt?"

"No. You had your shorts on. While you work on your body, I'm going to work on your shorts."

He washed the rest of his body. I poured another bucket of water over him and had him start over again. We repeated the process one more time, but he still smelled like fish. His shorts did too.

Just as he was rinsing the last of the soap off, a canoe drifted by with a man and woman in it, fishing just off shore. "Bath time?" she asked.

Peter, unfazed by his nudity, turned toward them, smiled broadly and said, "Yeah. I cleaned my fish and got blood and guts all over myself."

Skeptically, she laughed. "And now your daddy's cleaning you, right?"

He looked at me and smiled then corrected her. "My grandpa. Do you want to see it?"

"Sure."

He went racing along the shoreline to the frying pan and held up the halves. "See?"

Obviously both impressed, she said, "Wow, that's quite a fish. You caught that?" He nodded proudly. "And you cleaned that yourself?" Again he nodded proudly. She looked at me with raised eyebrows for confirmation.

I wrapped a towel around him. "That's right. He set it, caught it and cleaned it. I hate cleaning fish but he doesn't mind and does a darn good job at it."

The woman looked and me and said, "Well aren't you proud!"

I nodded. I felt like the proud coach on the sidelines watching the credit pass from the crowd to the kid, as it should be in any sport.

They continued down the lake as I dried Peter and talked about how good his fresh catch was going to taste.

And it did. Peter had managed to get out most of the bones.

After dinner and dishes, Peter still smelled like fish. I got an idea. While in his fish-smelling shorts, I sprayed him up one side and down the other with deodorant. It worked but tomorrow was definitely a day for hot showers. To be safe, Peter's shorts went into a Zip-Lock bag, and into the trunk of the car.

That evening we stayed in camp, read and talked. He stayed on my lap the entire time. His reading was continuing to improve by leaps and bounds but he finally closed the book. He was troubled about something.

I sat there and waited while he fidgeted with his bottoms. Finally he said, "Jake, I'm tired. Can I go to bed a little early?"

"Now you're catching on. This is called 'reading your body,' Kiddo. You're learning what your body needs and letting it have it. Right now it said, 'I'm tired. Put me to bed, Peter.'" Of course I said it in falsetto.

Peter giggled at that. We walked into the tent together. He crawled into his sleeping bag while I lay on top of mine. I put my hand on his chest then he put his hand on top of mine. "This was fun today, Jake. But it's fun everyday with you."

"It was fun today. It's always fun with you, too."

He smiled in the off light. "Good night, coach!"

"Good night, little Sportsman."

CHAPTER NINE

The next morning after going through our ritual and breakfast, I announced we'd fish around Lake Durant for a while. Then we'd leave.
"Where are we going?"
"You'll see."
At 8:30, the morning was quiet and peaceful. The lake was glass smooth. The temperature had not yet reached 65 degrees. All was well with the world. Peter in his own little world and I in mine, both with fishing poles in hand anxiously awaiting our next nibble, I was reminded of a phrase Bill used to throw out every so often: This is the life.
Suddenly my emotional tranquillity was shattered. "Jake, could I ask you a question?"
"Sure! Go ahead, Kiddo."
"My mother died when I was born." I was looking forward to a bite so I never saw what was coming. I was completely blind-sided. I nodded.
"What did she have to do with it?"
I was lost. I gave my pole a slight jerk. "With what?"
"What did she have to do with my birth? Why did she die just because I was born?"
Oh boy! The birds and the bees! Isn't this supposed to come up around nine or ten, unless you grow up on a farm? Before, I was hoping Peter would get a nice bass; now I was praying for one. I swallowed while Peter waited for an answer. I held onto my pole for security.
"Peter, you know where you were born, right? Do you know where you were born from?"
"What do you mean?"
"Birds come from eggs, but where did you come from?"

He pondered a long while. "I don't know."

That's what I was afraid of. "You came from inside your mother."

His head jerked back, his eyes bugged. Then they looked at me in doubt. "How did I get inside her?"

Oh boy! With Peter's eyes on me, I did not look up. I watched the end of my pole hoping...praying. I just asked silently, "Lord, what are you doing to me?"

For the next ten minutes I went over the birds and the bees. I told him no more than he requested but more than what I was ready for. His reactions varied during our little talk. Sometimes it was, "Wow!" Other times I got a "Really?" Once I got a, "You're kidding me!" It ended with, "That's disgusting." Just then he got a bite. It was a small sunfish. I didn't care. At that point I would have taken seaweed. We were finished with the birds and the bees, I hoped.

After lunch I had Peter grab his baseball glove then we headed for Inlet and Arrowhead Park. I found what I was looking for. On the ball diamond were six young boys and two adults. The boys all appeared to be six- to nine-years-old. They were taking turns playing the field then batting. The smallest was at least five inches taller than Peter. We got out of the car and walked to the diamond. Two weeks ago, Peter wouldn't have been ready for this, but his confidence was growing by leaps and bounds. He was slightly hesitant as we walked to the diamond together, his glove in his left hand and my hand in his other. "Could he join in for a while?" I asked.

The man on the mound looked at Peter. "How old is he?"

"Six. He's small for his age."

He sized up Peter again, shrugging his shoulders like a pitcher throws off a sign from his catcher. "Sure, why not?

Go out in the field son. If you catch any, throw them back to me, if you can throw that far." If Peter caught the belittling remark, he showed no indication of it. Unfazed, he dropped my hand and ran to the outfield. The first ball hit to him bounced off the ground in front of him, then off his chest knocking him to the ground. Before I could react, Peter was up. Another boy picked up the ball and threw it back to the pitcher. The man on the mound snickered along with the kids.

A few minutes later, a fly ball was hit to Peter. He misjudged it and missed. Again I heard the snickers. I watched him carefully for signs of a rescue, but didn't see any. Again, another boy returned the ball to the pitcher. I was beginning to think this was a poor idea. The next hit sent the ball elsewhere. Peter watched the kid in left field run forward with his glove over his head, pocket pointing up, and catch it on the fly.

The next ball was to short center field. Peter stuck his glove up, pocket up and ran forward. But the ball dropped behind him. He picked it up and winged it all the way in to the pitcher's mound and the pitcher's glove. The guy didn't have to leave the mound to get it. He stared at Peter a long moment. "Okay, son!"

The next hit was a grounder to Peter's left. He studied how the right fielder scooped it up. He took a moment to imitate what he'd just seen. This kid was cool, to say the least.

The next hit was a fly ball heading towards Peter. He moved up, glove in the right position and caught it. Then came a grounder to Peter's right. He moved over, scooped it up and tossed it in.

At that point the pitcher said, "Let's let the little kid have a turn at batting."

Peter was smiling as he ran to the batter's box. He threw me the glove and picked up the bat. He swung it tentatively a few times. I could tell it was heavy for him.

The first ball was high but Peter swung anyway, putting everything into it. Not only did he miss, the weight of the bat took him around in a circle. Peter lost his balance and landed in the dirt in a small cloud of dust. Some of the boys in the field were laughing so hard, they were on the ground. The pitcher and catcher both tried to keep from laughing but neither succeeded.

Once up, Peter kicked the dirt, threw the bat on the ground and stormed away. I intercepted him. "Where are you going?"

Tears were in his eyes. "I can't do this, Jake. Everybody's laughing at me."

"Yep, they sure are and if you keep walking, they'll keep laughing: Except then they'll be laughing at a loser and a quitter." I could see the deep hurt in his eyes. I had to build him up quick. I knelt down in front of him and took his arms gently. "Peter, I guarantee you, most of those boys out there have done the same thing you just did. They're laughing at themselves as much as they are at you. They're relieved to see someone do what they've already done.

"That bat's too big for you. You forgot to choke up. You also swung at a pitch you knew you couldn't hit. When you go back to the mound, choke-up on the bat and make the pitcher pitch to you. If it's too high or too low, don't swing."

He looked at me though his tears. "Do you think I can hit it?"

"I think so, but you're not going to find out by standing here or walking away, are you?"

He looked at the pitcher then at the boys and realized none were laughing. Hesitantly he said, "Okay, I'll try again."

As I wiped a tear off his cheek I said, "The most important thing to remember, Little One, is no matter what happens, I love you." He gave me a hug then slowly walked back to the batter's box. Lord, I was proud of him. It took real guts to face that pitcher again. "Peter," I called after him. "Remember, keep your eye on the ball." I detected respect on the pitcher's face.

Peter picked up the bat, choked up on it and stepped up to the mound. The next two pitches were high. He didn't swing at either one. He looked at me. I winked. With each pitch, I noticed the boys in the field move in closer. The man on the mound was getting aggravated and said, "Where do you want it, kid?"

"Right here," Peter said with determination, leveling the bat waist high.

"You're so puny, you don't give me much of a target," the pitcher said laughing at his own joke. All the kids laughed with him and moved in a little closer. All were now inside the baseline. I was about to say something, but decided to keep my mouth shut and see what happened. I'm glad I did. The next pitch was perfect and had Peter's name all over it. I kept my fingers crossed. He stepped into it swinging and connected. The ball flew forty feet beyond the boys; one of the better hits of the afternoon. Several of the boys yelled, "Wow!" One ran after it while the pitcher was left standing on the mound with his mouth open. I smiled at Peter and gave him a thumbs up. He gave me a smile mixed with love.

"Do you think you can do that again, Little One?" the pitcher called out.

Peter looked at me and cringed. Little One was a name I used for him during our tenderest of moments. It was the first time someone else called him that and obviously, he didn't like it. I shrugged my shoulders and smiled. He looked at the pitcher. "If you throw it right." He snapped back without a smile and full of confidence. I realized none of the comments the pitcher had said had gone over his head.

The pitcher threw the next ball in the right spot but noticeably harder. He had a smirk on his face knowing what to expect, but didn't get it. Peter connected again and hit it almost to the fence in center field. The catcher said, "Good grief, can that kid hit. There's not a kid in the field that could have hit that."

"His coordination is fantastic. He must have gotten it from his mother," I volunteered.

He laughed but the pitcher was speechless. I walked up to Peter and said, "Hey, Kiddo, why don't you let one of the other boys hit for a while?"

"Okay," he said. He was satisfied. He made his point and proved himself. He lay the bat down and was about to walk to the outfield when the pitcher said, "How about one more?"

Peter looked at me for my approval. I nodded so he picked up the bat again, stepped up into the batter's box ready to kill the ball. All the kids were much farther back. Everybody took him seriously now. He stood there more determined than ever. The pitcher threw the ball harder. Peter nailed it but not quite as far. One of the kids managed to catch it and Peter was out, but not before he gained the admiration of all.

The pitcher, a large man of over six feet, walked up to Peter, bent way over and said, "Hey, little man. You can play on my team anytime." He stuck out his hand, shook Peter's and ruffled his hair with the other. Both had big smiles on their faces. He then walked over to me and said, "You've got one great little kid here. I thought sure he was going to quit for a minute and frankly, I wouldn't have blamed him."

"He's not a quitter. He just has to be reminded of that once in a while."

I put my hand on Peter's shoulder. "What do you think, Kiddo? You want to play a little longer or do something else?" There was a public beach nearby.

He thought for a minute. "Could I play for a few minutes longer?"

"Sure! Go ahead." He smiled and headed for the field. Immediately all the kids surrounded and congratulated him. I was really proud of him. We stayed for another hour. Many balls were hit to him and although he didn't catch them all, he did catch most of them. He also had a chance to bat twice more. That time he caught no one by surprise. Finally he was ready. As he jogged off the field, several of the boys came with him. Both men came over to us. They all wanted to know if we could come back tomorrow. I explained where we were camping and that tomorrow was our last day. It would be Peter's choice.

While Peter talked to some of the kids, the pitcher said to me, "You sure have one outstanding little athlete here. How old did you say he is?"

"Six. He's small for his age but he makes up for it with heart and spirit."

"And determination," the pitcher said. "I could tell he was mad at me when he returned to the plate, but he was determined he was going to hit that ball. He did! He had a chance to stuff it down my throat." He looked over at Peter, smiled and said, "There aren't many kids that wouldn't have jumped at the opportunity. I'm impressed." He was looking for a name.

"Jake Winters," I said and shook his hand.

"Fred Thomas. That's my boy over there," he said pointing to a tall eight- or nine-year-old talking to Peter. "He can hit and throw pretty good but not much better than that boy of yours. When your boy gets to be my son's age, he's going to be something else." Little did he know!

We said our good-byes and headed for the bathhouse, Peter with a whole new group of friends.

We swam and played in the sand for two hours, took a short nap and then headed into town for dinner.

Once back at the campsite with a fire going, we roasted marshmallows.

"Thanks for today, Jake. It was really fun."

"Hey, speaking of today, I was so proud of you at the park, I could hardly contain myself."

"Thanks," he said smiling. "I hit the ball pretty good, didn't I?"

"You sure did but that's not why I was proud of you." He looked at me puzzled. "Oh, I was proud of the way you hit the ball, but that pitcher and the kids were giving you a rough time because you were so small. He didn't think you could hit it and he said a few things that weren't very nice. I almost stepped in but decided to let you handle it. You did it just right. You made a believer and friend out of him and the kids and you did it without help from me.

"Then you could have rubbed the whole thing in their faces; in other words, you could have become a little brat. Under the circumstances, I wouldn't have blamed you but you didn't. That's why I was so proud of you. The pitcher realized you could have responded that way too, but was extremely impressed when you didn't. That's what I meant last night when I said you're beautiful in here." I put my hand on his chest. "Now you have more friends than ever."

He raised his head from my chest and looked at me without smiling. "That's just me, Jake," he said in all seriousness. "I don't know how else to behave."

"I know and I love you for it."

He smiled. "But Jake, I didn't handle it on my own. You talked me into going back and trying it again."

"You're not a quitter Peter, and you're not a loser. You proved that in Slippery Gulch. But when a lot of people are laughing at you because of a mistake you make, it's tough on anybody. It's harder on you. Remember, I understand."

He put his head back on my chest. "Jake, when you called me a quitter and a loser, I felt so bad I wanted to sit down and cry. I thought you stopped loving me. But you kept talking. You said to choke up and keep my eye on the ball. But when you said, 'the most important thing to remember is no matter what happens, I love you,' I felt so good, I felt like I could hit anything."

"Never forget that, Kiddo. I know I was hard on you today but I will always love you. If I had let you walk away, you would have felt bad about it for weeks and you would never have known if you could have done it. As a result, you faced down the pitcher, all of those kids and gained temporary control of a powerful fear."

"What do you mean temporary?"

"The fear of being laughed at is a normal, human fear. It's a fear almost everybody has. Most people have it well under control. Yours is out of control. However, you were able to gain temporary control of it today and that was encouraging."

"Yeah, but I couldn't have done it without you."

"Peter, you wanted somebody that was caring and understanding, among other things. When you were battling your nightmares, I told you we'd beat them together and we did. But the fight isn't over yet. You still have many fears to conquer or gain control of and I'm going to help you all the way, whether you like it or not. I made you feel bad today. You may have even been mad at me for a moment. It may happen again. Just remember, Kiddo, I love you and whatever I do I'm doing it because I think it's best for you. I will never make you do something I know you can't, but if I feel you're capable of it, I'll push and push hard."

"Did you know I was going to hit that ball?"

"Yep, sure did. I just didn't know you were going to hit it that far. That was fantastic."

"Thanks for believing in me, Jake."

"Hey, what can I say? We're a team. Tomorrow's our last day, Kiddo. What would you like to do?"

He thought for a minute. "I guess go back to our lake."

"Okay. That's what we'll do. Why don't you go in and put your PJ's on?" He was soon back on my lap.

We talked for a while longer but he was fading. "Hey slugger. How about turning around and getting ready to go to sleep?" Once around I asked him another couple of questions but I was too late. My little slugger was asleep. And with a look on his face I still cherish in my heart and mind. One I could never have caught on film if I tried. But one I could paint if I were an artist.

CHAPTER TEN

The next morning after our morning ritual he said, "Jake, tomorrow it will be time to leave but it seems like we just got here. How come the time went so fast? It never used to."

"When you lived in Slippery Gulch, your life was miserable. Everything you did was to stay alive and it wasn't very much fun, was it?" He shook his head. "Now everything you're doing is fun and when you're having fun, time flies."

"Well, I sure am having fun and I'm learning a lot too." He gave me a big hug. I grabbed him by the armpits and threw him into the air, both of us laughing. I caught him, gave him a quick hug. "How about breakfast?"

As we were getting ready to leave he said, "Jake, do you think I could try the back of the canoe today?"

I should have thought of this earlier. The sternman, for the most part, controls the direction of the canoe with the sweep and jay strokes. "I'll tell you what. When we start out today, you sit in the front seat but face me. I'll show you what I am doing, how I'm doing it and why. Then after a while we'll pull into shore and switch and you can try it for a while."

He was excited. He sat in the front seat facing me as we headed down the lake. I showed him how to do the jay stroke. This turns the canoe to the side you're paddling. I showed him how to turn the canoe in the opposite direction by using the sweep. I kept going from one to the other thus keeping the canoe going in a straight line without changing sides. After covering about half the lake I said, "Well, Kiddo, you ready to try it?"

"Yeah," he said excitedly. We pulled into shore and he jumped out, holding the canoe for me. Then he climbed back in proudly occupying the 'captain's chair.' I pushed us out and got ready. When we finally got to the other lake we'd paddled about twice as far as necessary. By the time we got there he was angry, frustrated and tired.

We meandered our way to our swimming hole and pulled in. We never stopped to fish. He grabbed a towel, threw it on the ground, and lay down. He was not in a good mood. I pulled the canoe up and walked over to him. "Hey, Funny Face, move over a little." I thought I'd get a little smile from him, but didn't. He hadn't said a word for twenty minutes. He spent an hour and a half in the stern and just couldn't do it. I really felt bad for him but decided it was best to remain silent until he was ready to talk.

After five minutes, he put his hands under his head and one leg over mine. I knew he was getting ready. After another three minutes, he said, "I really stink at stern, don't I?"

I rolled over and faced him putting my left hand under his neck and wiped away a tear with my right. "Peter, not everybody can handle the stern. That's nothing against you. Your size is working against you so in order to succeed, your style has to be perfect. You haven't been in the stern long enough to develop a good style."

"Do you think I ever will?"

"Do you remember the first day we came down to this lake?" He nodded. "It seemed as if we kept up with Bill and Danny, but we didn't. They slowed down for us. Your style was poor. Going back it was the same way." The tears were increasing so I started stroking his chest with my thumb. "The next day they didn't ease up as much because they didn't have to. Your style was improving and your strength was increasing. The third day they didn't ease off at all."

"They didn't?"

"No. Although you're not as strong as Bill or Danny, your style improved dramatically."

"You're not just saying that to make me feel better are you?"

"No, I'm not. Now as far as your ability to handle the stern in the future goes, maybe, maybe not. You have the coordination to succeed but I can't really answer that. Your style is outstanding in the bow but the style is totally different in the stern. The thing of it is, you need a lot more practice before we decide whether you can or can't do it. I should have gotten you in the stern several days ago, but I never thought about it."

"So you think I might be able to do it?"

"I don't know but it's way too early to decide you're a failure. Remember, you're not a quitter. If we do this again next year, I'll get you in the stern more."

He lay there digesting everything. After a couple of minutes, he turned his head to me, smiled and said, "Thanks, Jake." He closed his eyes and was soon asleep. He only slept for twenty minutes.

When he woke, we went swimming again. It was our last day and we made the most of it.

While heading back to the campsite after catching a few small ones, he said, "Jake, I'm kind of sore."

"In your arms?"

"Yeah. How did you know?"

"You use a whole different set of muscles in the stern than in the bow. I bet your shoulders and chest are a little sore too, right?"

He was amazed. "Yeah. How did you know that?"

"I've been canoeing for over thirty-five years, Kiddo. I've seen a lot of kids get sore in the same place when they first worked the stern. It can be a lot of work back there and you were working a lot harder than I ever do."

"I was? Why?"

"As I said before, it all has to do with style and practice. Your size doesn't help either."

"Is there anything I can do for my sore muscles?"

"Not much. When we get back to camp, I'll rub them a little."

Back at our camp, I was rubbing his arms and shoulders when we heard a car approach. It was Fred Thomas and his son.

"Sorry for barging in, but we were both curious as to exactly where you guys are camping and how you're getting along," Fred said. I could see Fred was not the least bit excited with the campsite, and I suspected the whole thing was beneath him. Bobby and Peter were smiling broadly.

Fred suggested he and I take a walk and give the boys a chance to get to know one another a little better. I told Peter that we'd be back in a few minutes. Peter looked a little worried but nodded in agreement. As Fred and I were leaving the campsite, I looked back to see Peter taking Bobby to the tent. He'd be fine.

As we walked, Fred said, "You know, Bobby sure is impressed with Peter. He's a terrific kid and one hell of an athlete. He's a good loser and a better winner. And that's unusual to find in a young boy. My son is eight. He doesn't get along with younger boys, but he thinks so much of Peter, he wants to see more of him. Bobby's a good athlete, but he could see right away that your boy is much better at that age than he was."

"Thank you for the compliment. I'll be sure to pass it on."

"You know, the scary thing is, if he's this good at six, what's he going to be like at eighteen?"

The Gift

We walked into the campsite to find both boys sitting on the table with their shirts off. Peter was talking about the fish we both caught.

"Hey, would you guys be interested in staying for dinner? It's not going to be anything special but we have enough." I looked at Peter for his reaction. His smile told me I guessed right.

Bobby said, "Wow, can we dad?"

I could tell Fred wasn't nearly as excited about it as his son and said, "You're mother was expecting us home for dinner." He was going to leave it at that but noticed the disappointment on his son's face and continued; "but let me call her and see what she says." He walked over to the car and called his wife. He returned saying, "Well, it looks like were staying for dinner."

Both boys jumped up and down yelling. Then Bobby jumped into his father's arms and said, "Thanks, Dad!"

"What's gotten into you, Bobby? I don't think I've ever seen you like this before."

"Peter's a neat kid and Mr. Winter's a truck driver and they drive all over the country and Peter's a real ghost."

Peter looked at me right away. He knew he goofed and was concerned.

Fred looked at his son. "What was that last one?" Fred asked.

"Yeah, Peter's a ghost. He was born in a little town in Montana, in 1894 and was murdered by his father in 1901. He can disappear, too."

"Well that's a pretty good story, Peter. I can see you've got my son convinced."

"But he is dead. I saw him disappear."

Fred looked at his son, then at Peter, then at me, then back to his son and finally back to me. "Jake?"

Before I could say anything, Peter looked at me with a tear in his eye and said, "I'm sorry, Jake. I shouldn't have said anything."

"Oh, come off it." Fred said looking at me.

I moved over to Peter and ruffled his hair. I knew he thought he was going to be punished, but I wanted to encourage him. "It's true. I'll tell you Peter's story if you'd like." Both Fred and Bobby anxiously agreed. I pulled a chair out of the tent for Fred. After both boys were comfortably situated on our respective laps, I began.

"Peter was born in the town of Slippery Gulch, Montana, in 1894. On June 29th of this year, I drove into Slippery Gulch to pick up a load at the mine in town. For all practical purposes, it was a ghost town so when I got there, I stopped to look around before going to the mine. As I was walking around, a little boy ran out from an alley and right into me. He was a cute little kid but the filthiest child I'd ever seen – obviously severely neglected. When I asked his name he said in a small, weak and frightened voice, 'Peter Stevenson.'"

I handed them the three pictures. Bobby looked at all three and said, "Is this really you?" Peter just nodded. As he passed them to his father, I continued.

"I felt sorry for him and decided I wanted to try and get him some help, but that's as far as it went. I didn't want to get involved."

Peter looked at me. "You didn't?"

I smiled at him just a little. "No. In fact I figured once I left the town, I'd never see you again, and that was fine with me."

"You...you...it was?" Peter asked. I gave him a reassuring hug. I spent the next hour going over Peter's abbreviated story leaving out most of the gore for Bobby's sake. Nevertheless we were all in tears when I finished that part of the story.

"During my third trip to Slippery Gulch, my friends in Basin tried to talk me into taking Peter with me in my truck. I came up with every excuse I could think of why I couldn't. However one of those friends got me to understand how much I love him." Peter snuggled closer. "I went back to the town the next day, gave Peter a bath and that's the last either one of us has seen of Slippery Gulch."

When I finished, Fred just sat there for several minutes. Finally, he looked at Peter, then at me. "I'm sorry. This is just too much to believe. If you really are a ghost, could you disappear for me?" Peter looked at me and I nodded. Suddenly Fred breathed, "Oh my God!" as Bobby said over him, "See, I told you he's a ghost."

Both he and Bobby had a lot of questions. Many I had to answer with speculations.

Finally, I said, "Why don't we start working on dinner?" I did the cooking as Fred looked on with interest. Peter soaped the pots and pans with Bobby's help, explaining competently how to do it and why.

After dinner, Peter asked if he and Bobby could wash the dishes. I could tell Bobby was not exactly thrilled he'd been volunteered for this job, but agreed. I looked at Fred and he nodded. Reluctantly I gave the okay and the two boys grabbed everything with two Brillo Pads and headed for the lake. "If you need any help, let us know."

"Wow, wait until my wife hears about this. She's not going to believe it."

"I'm sure she won't, but are you prepared to give your son a good scrubbing?"

He looked at me. "What do you mean?"

"Just wait. You'll see." I hesitated. "Look, Fred, Peter shouldn't have said anything to Bobby. Now that you both know, I strongly suggest you both keep it to yourselves."

"Don't worry, we will. Who'd believe us anyway? But I don't understand how this is possible."

"Peter was granted his final prayer. His mortal body was returned to him in perfect condition." Looking up to the sky, I said, "I believe that can come from only one source. I'm a mere mortal. It's not up to me to understand. And now Peter's a mortal too, 99.9% of the time. I believe I'm living with a miracle and I fully intend to enjoy it as long as I can."

"How long will he be with you?"

"I don't know." I explained the upcoming funeral in June 2002 and the uncertainties involved. Just then the boys returned and proudly set the clean pots, pans and plates down where they were supposed to be. Then Fred started laughing. "I see what you mean."

Both boys looked at him, confused and a little disappointed. Peter said slowly, "Didn't we do a good job?"

"You both did a fine job," I said, "but why don't you look at each other?"

They did, then started laughing themselves. Their stomachs, chests, arms, shoulders, necks and faces were covered with grease, carbon from the pots and pans and dirty soap from the Brillo Pads.

Soon the four of us were on our way back to the lake armed with soap, towels and washcloths. Fred washed his son from the waist up while I washed Peter, but we were all laughing the entire time. As I was drying Peter off, he asked if Bobby could stay overnight with us.

I explained it wouldn't work since Peter and I were to leave the next day. Although Peter and Bobby looked disappointed, they both understood. Fred looked relieved.

The Gift

The four of us sat around the fire talking for the next hour. About 8:30 Fred said that he thought they should get going. They both thanked us for dinner and a great evening. Then Fred added, "Jake, I don't remember when I have enjoyed the company of my son more than tonight or have appreciated him more, and it is all because of you and Peter." He hugged Bobby. "Thanks for a great time."

I looked at his son. "Bobby is a terrific kid. He's soon going to be a young man. Enjoy his childhood while you can. Let tonight be the start."

"Thanks, Jake. I admire the way you and Peter get along. Well, I'd better get Bobby home before he falls asleep on me."

"Yeah," I said. "This one's about ready to fall asleep too."

Fred looked at me and said, "Ghosts sleep?"

I laughed. "This one does but remember, he's a mortal now." We all shook hands. I looked at Bobby and said, "I hope you realize you have a pretty outstanding dad."

He smiled and looked at Fred. "I know. Thanks, Mr. Winters and Peter."

"Thanks for being so nice to Peter. We both really appreciated it."

They both smiled. "He's a great kid, Jake," Fred said. "It was good to get to know Peter. Maybe if you guys come back next year, we can do it again." As an afterthought he said, "At least I hope we can." Both Peter and Bobby were all smiles.

I smiled and agreed. But who really knew what the future would bring? Too many questions were still unanswered. Would Peter still be mortal after the funeral? Would he still be with me? If he were, would Bobby still be interested?

After all, Bobby would be bigger and Peter would be unchanged.

As they pulled out, I noticed it was 9:00. "Peter, why don't put on your PJ's and come back to my lap." Without saying a word, he dragged himself to the tent and put his PJ's on. As he staggered toward me, I went to his rescue. I picked him up and carried him back to my chair and lap.

Once on my lap, he said, "Bobby's a nice kid, isn't he?"

"Yes, he is."

He looked at me with concern. "Do you love him more than me?" He played with his bottoms nervously.

I turned him around so he was facing me. "I don't love him at all. He's a real nice kid and I like him a lot, but he's no Peter Stevenson." I kissed his forehead.

"Peter, I know you're tired but there's one more thing we have to discuss before you go to sleep."

He put his head down. "I know. I should never have told Bobby, should I?"

"There wasn't any reason for them to know."

His head was still down. "Jake, are you going to spank me?"

I lifted his head. "No way, Little One. We've never talked about this before. In fact, I never thought about it before. Now we have to talk about it. In the past you've only vanished for those individuals who had a reason to know your status, such as Betty and Jerry, the Earlies, Hank and Jason. Ranger Casey had to know only because of your injuries. But there was no reason for Bobby or his dad to find out."

"I know. I don't know why I said anything."

I thought about that. "Peter, Bobby is your first kid friend close to your age. I think more than anything, you wanted to impress him. What better way to do it than to do something no other kid in the world can do? But Bobby was already impressed with you. You're a good ballplayer and he knows it, as does his dad. You're also a good sportsman. Let's make a rule, Kiddo. You never disappear unless it's an emergency like the other day to save the people in the van. Other than that, the only time you disappear is when I give the okay. How does that sound?"

"Yeah! The rest of the time I'm just a normal kid like Bobby, right?"

"Right. Do we have a deal?"

He smiled. "Deal!" His smile left his face. "Jake, are you mad at me?"

"Not this time." He knew what I meant. He hugged me and stayed in that position. After a couple of minutes I said, "Hey, Funny Face, how about going to bed?" After getting no reply, I leaned him back a little. He had a pleasant smile on his face but was sound asleep. I carried him into the tent where I joined him in sleep.

CHAPTER ELEVEN

Around midnight, Peter's heel came down hard on my hip, his arms were thrashing over his head and he was screaming, "Jake, Jake, help!"

I grabbed his ankles with my left hand, assuring I wouldn't get kicked in the hip again or in a more sensitive area, then held his arms down with my right. He continued screaming my name, struggling against my grip. Finally he relaxed and said my name in a normal voice. "Hey, Kiddo, you okay?"

"Yeah. I just dreamed I was being chased by a giant muskie."

I guess that muskie affected him more than what I thought. I laughed a little. "Well, I think you won the race." With that I ran a finger lightly between two ribs. He chuckled a little and just like that was asleep, if, in fact, he was ever really awake.

The next morning I woke up at six as planned. I had to get Peter moving quickly. We had to be at my niece's house near Rochester by 1:00 for a birthday party and there was a lot to do. Trying to wake him up before he was ready was like trying to start a car without a battery. I finally gave up, rolled up my own sleeping bag and got a fire going for coffee.

After one cup, I went back into the tent and moved everything out, including Peter. Then I took the tent down and rolled it. I had completed most of the packing when Peter began to stir. He was on the table and in his sleeping bag. I hid below the table and waited. I heard him finally sit up worried: "Jake?"

I growled a little. In a more concerned voice he yelled. "Jake, where are you?"

I jumped up from below the table. He screamed in shock, then smiled. "You scared me so bad, I almost peed."

I bent over and kissed him on the forehead. "I'm sorry. Maybe I am too mean."

"No, you're not. That was funny, but I really have to pee bad." I carried him to the woods. I made the mistake of asking him how his muscles felt, before he was finished.

"Fine! See." He turned around before finishing, flexing his arms. I jumped back barely missing getting hit. He started laughing so hard he couldn't stop. He tried to apologize but couldn't. I was laughing also. I grabbed him, threw him on the table and dug in. After a minute he said still panting, "If you ever stop being mean to me, I'll think you stopped loving me."

"In that case Kiddo, I'll be mean to you forever." With that I got the most beautiful smile you'd ever hope to see.

He looked around. "Hey, where's the tent?"

"That's why you're out here. I took it down."

"Why didn't you wake me up?"

"You've got to be kidding me. When you're asleep nothing can wake you." He giggled. "Why don't you get dressed? We still have some packing to do, then it'll be time to leave and take a shower. We have to be over at my niece's house this afternoon."

"Oh yeah, I forgot about that." Worriedly he asked, "What if they don't like me?"

"Peter, I really don't think you have to worry. Everybody loves you. Let's finish packing and take our showers."

We finished packing. I put the canoe on the car, and lifted him up. He pulled on the rack straps as tight as he could. I gave them a last tug.

Just then Ranger Casey pulled up to our vacated campsite. "I was hoping to catch you two before you pulled out. I won't take very much time." He pulled out the special rock from his pocket. "As an official of the park, I'd like to thank both of you for being here this year. I haven't said a word to anyone but I now know the hamlet of Blue Mountain has been visited by a miracle in more ways than one this year. Peter, I'd like to thank you for all those people who would now be dead if it hadn't been for you."

He bent over and picked Peter up. "Peter, you are the miracle. And now I want to thank God for you." While holding Peter in his arms he looked up and said, "Lord, thank you for this little boy. Because of him sixteen people are still alive and I now believe. Thank you, Lord." He hugged Peter.

I walked over and put my arms around both of them. "Amen," I added. The ranger had tears in his eyes. "See you next year, Tom." I looked at his hand. "Hang on to that stone and remember." He put Peter down and we wordlessly shook hands. Peter and I walked to the car, waved and drove off in silence toward the showers.

An hour later we reached Inlet to return the canoe. The same young man that fixed us up with the canoe was again in the canoe rental section. I doubted he remembered us from two weeks ago. "Well, little sport, how was the fishing?"

That's all Peter needed. He talked about the big bass he caught and my muskie and how it was longer than he was tall. I could tell the man was impressed. Peter would have kept talking about it but to the man's credit he said, "Ah, your grandpa probably does that all the time." He winked at me. "Tell me about some of the other fish you caught."

Peter mentioned, in a matter of fact way, the bass he released because we didn't need them for dinner. This really caught the man's attention. "You threw a trophy back?" Peter nodded. "Son, you are not only a good fisherman, you are a great sportsman. I'd like to shake your hand." The man held out his large hand, and Peter took it, unbelievably proud of himself.

"Well, Kiddo, I think we'd better hit the road."

"Thanks for doing business with us. Keep up the good work."

I took Peter's hand and squeezed it gently as we walked to the car. He didn't say anything. He just squeezed back and smiled up at me. That was all I needed to make my day.

After breakfast he slept for an hour. As we drove, I thought about this afternoon. My sister was going to fill in my niece and nephew on Peter's situation. I hoped things would go well.

When he woke up, I looked back at him and said, "Hi there, Sleepyhead. I hope you feel better than you look."

He chuckled and said, "Jake, are Sleepyhead and Funny Face and Funny Tummy and Mr. Bare Butt...efactanate names?"

I chuckled as I pronounced it correctly. After a couple of tries he almost had it. "They sure are. When you were constipated a couple of weeks ago, I could have called you Stinkbomb. That would have been affectionate too and very fitting."

He laughed. "Yeah, it sure would. Why didn't you?"

"I didn't think of it."

"Is Little One the most affectionate of all?"

"Yes, Little One. It is."

After a long pause came, "Are we almost there yet?"

"In a few minutes. Betty and Jerry are going to be there, too. Everybody will be fishermen so you'll have a lot to talk about. My niece and nephew also have two children. I can't remember if I told you that or not. They're both girls."

"Girls?" he said in a disgusted tone wrinkling his nose.

"Yeah," I said chuckling. "I know they're not your most favorite animal but they're not bad, as far as girls go. One is two and the other is four."

He thought about this for a minute. "Do you love them?"

I knew where this was going. "Of course I love them. Why do you ask?"

He looked at me and hesitated for a minute. "Do you love them more than me?"

I believe he was thinking, Two more children that Jake loves. Will I have to compete for his love? "Peter, it's possible for a person to love more than one child at the same time. I love them as much as I love you, but I love you in a very special way. I'm responsible and caring for you. I'm not responsible for them."

He thought about this for several minutes. I kept my mouth shut letting the wheels turn. Love may be a familiar mystery with most people, but to Peter, it was just now becoming familiar. It's something he always wanted but never had, yet now that he had it he wasn't sure why or how it worked. He knew only that love felt good. Now he feared competition. I realized I was going to be walking a tightrope between my nieces and him. This day was not going to be easy.

"So in a way you love me more than them?"

"In the most important way, I do. I get to do more acts of love for you. I am responsible before God for you in a way that I am not to them. Does that help?"

I paused for a minute. "Don't worry about it too much, Little One. I will always love you no matter what."

A few minutes later we pulled into their driveway. We walked around to the backyard to find the girls in the pool with their father, Randy. The rest came up to greet us. We

The Gift

both said hello to Betty and Jerry. Then I gave my niece, Connie, a big hug. I turned to Peter and introduced him. She looked at Peter then at Betty and said, "He's even cuter than you described." Peter gave her a big, toothless smile.

"Do you want to go swimming with the others?" He shook his head. I knew he wanted to but he wasn't ready yet.

Soon Randy and the girls came out to meet us. Randy, shaking Peter's hand said, "It's nice meeting you. We've heard so much about you." The girls looked Peter up one side and down the other while he did the same. I gave the girls a big hug as Peter looked on with clear jealousy. I picked up Lori, the older one. "How is my birthday-girl today?" Her answer included more information than what I asked for but that was fine.

We all settled into yard chairs around an umbrella table near their above ground pool. Before Peter had a chance for my lap, Lori was on it – wet bathing suit and all. Peter sulked into the only chair left, one next to Randy, sullenly looking at me. He was a portrait of jealousy.

Connie, who has always been more aware of personal emotions than anyone else in the family, picked up on it immediately and called Lori over to her. I looked at her as if to say thanks. She winked back. I called Peter over to fill the vacancy and the tension dropped instantly.

"How was the fishing?" Randy asked Peter.

"Okay," he mumbled.

"Oh, come on, Kiddo, it was a little better than just okay."

Silence!

"I hope you took some pictures," Connie said.

"I sure did." I described the pictures of Peter and my muskie and built up to Peter's muskie and bass.

Again, silence.

"You know, Peter was perfect in the canoe. One wrong move by him and we could have had a real disaster."

Peter took the bait. "I didn't know what to do. I was scared stiff. You should have seen the size of its mouth." Peter slid off my lap. "Jake could have used me for bait. It was bigger than me," he said dramatically using his arms to illustrate. Everybody roared in relief.

"Well, Peter," Jerry said, "I can hardly wait to see the pictures."

Excitedly he said, "I know." He returned to my lap before one of the girls could claim it.

"You know," I added recalling the memory, "the thing I was proudest of was Peter throwing back the bass we didn't need for dinner. One of those babies was over four pounds."

Betty whistled. "Peter, that's the mark of a darn good fisherman. Jake has every right to be proud of you." Everybody agreed.

Peter was trying to keep his pride in check. "Thank you," he said beaming.

"Hey everybody," Connie said. "I think it's time to eat. Maybe Lori would be willing to open some birthday presents." Lori nodded but she was studying Peter – two years older but smaller than herself…where did this kid come from?

I thought about Peter's birthday, December 2nd. I would celebrate it with him wherever we were, but would it be his 7th birthday or his 107th birthday? Or his 6th birthday again? This was going to take some thought.

After lunch we sang happy birthday to Lori. Peter sat on the ground with his head down. He didn't know the song. This was the first birthday party he'd ever been to. He never had one of his own.

The Gift

Everybody looked at Lori but made sideways glances at Peter, who was emotionally withdrawn again. They looked at me as if saying, Come on Jake, do something. I was at a loss.

As Lori received her first present, Peter looked up at me with eyes I hadn't seen since Slippery Gulch. He was begging for my lap but wouldn't come over on his own. Maybe he didn't want to draw my attention from Lori.

I motioned for him. He came over slowly, wiping his eyes with the back of his little hands. I lifted him onto my lap. He said very quietly, "I never..." But he couldn't finish. I hugged him and said, "I know," and wiped new tears away. Knowing I understood helped a lot.

After the cake, we all went swimming for a few minutes. Now it was time to head home.

Peter and I said good-bye to all and agreed to meet Jerry and Betty at our favorite restaurant in Orchard Park, New York, for a light meal. At the restaurant, I ordered chicken wings for Peter and me, knowing that it was a mistake.

He got a child's potion of medium and I got adult hot. These were the original Buffalo-area chicken wings. We dug in. As if my mess wasn't enough, trying to keep up with his too was nearly impossible. Eating chicken wings without front teeth didn't help. He had to attack each wing with either the right or left side of his mouth, which meant his face was a mess. Betty helped, but the juice ran down his chin and neck and quickly disappeared under his shirt.

Once home and back in the house, Peter took his shirt off.

When Betty, Jerry and I reacted with laugher, Peter grew puzzled. So I lifted him up to a mirror. Then he laughed too. His shirt absorbed the greasy streams. But an amber river made it all the way to his belly button where it collected in a gooey mess. We decided it best to have him sit in the tub for a while and soak. Eventually, all of it came out but his belly button bore a pinkish-orange stain for a few days.

While he was soaking, Betty motioned for me to join her out in the hall. "Jake, Peter's birthday is December 2nd, right?"

"Yeah. Why?"

"Today we noticed how sad he was while Lori was opening her presents. He's never had a birthday party, has he?"

"No, I doubt anybody ever wished him happy birthday."

"It just about broke my heart to see that. We all agreed that we want to have a surprise party for him. We'll invite Bill and Danny, too. But can you get home on December second?"

I was speechless.

She gave me a hug.

"December 2nd we'll be here, come hell or high water."

We both heard a deep laugh and a high laugh coming from the bathroom. We walked back into the bathroom to find Peter and Jerry involved in a splashing war. It looked as if the bathroom was losing.

Betty, with hands on her hips, said, "Hey, what's going on in here?"

Peter slid down as far as he could go. Jerry said, smiling at Peter, "Uh-oh, I think we got caught." Peter wasn't sure if it was safe to smile or not.

"Boys will be boys," she said giving her husband a stern look but with a twinkle in her eye. "Both of you, get this bathroom cleaned up. Peter, out of that tub, now." He jumped out so fast, he slipped on the floor and almost fell. All of us were trying to keep from laughing, but I was still thinking about the party. Before I ever got the towel around him, I gave him a big hug.

"Hey, what was that for? You're going to get soaked."
"I felt like it. Is that okay?"
"Sure, anytime." Behind Peter's back, Betty gave Jerry the thumbs-up sign. After getting Peter dried, he and Jerry cleaned up the bathroom. Betty and I walked out in the hall again. "Don't worry about a thing, we'll make all the arrangements. One question though; how old should we say he is?"
"I was thinking about that earlier. Actually he'd be the same age he is now unless you take his ghostly age. How about if we have a party for him but don't say his age?"
"That doesn't seem quite right either if it's a birthday party and it has to be, or it will be meaningless to him. Hey, does he even know when his birthday is?"
"Oh, yeah. His father would remind him every year that that's the day he should have died instead of his mother. His father also told him that Peter had murdered her."
"Oh, what a rotten S.O.B."
"His father didn't wait for December second to tell him that. He just stressed it then."
"Lord, that man was one sick puppy, wasn't he? It's just a shame he never realized what he had in Peter."
Just then Peter came out of the bathroom. "That was fun."
"You mean, cleaning up the bathroom?" Betty asked.
"Well, no, that wasn't fun. But the water fight was."
"Oh darn," she said. "I was hoping you had fun cleaning up. Because if you did, I'd ask you to do it again."
"I'd do it again, if you really wanted me to."
She winked at me. "I'll keep that offer in mind."
"You know Peter, you're standing in the hall wrapped in a towel that's ready to drop to the floor, talking to a lady. Why don't you put your PJ's on."

He chuckled. "Oh, yeah. Sorry. Can I put just my bottoms on?"

"Sure. Go ahead." Peter dashed off. Halfway to our room, his towel landed on the floor. He didn't stop to pick it up.

Betty just shook her head as we moved downstairs. Peter soon joined us in the family room.

After Peter settled on my lap, I said, "You know, Betty and Jerry, I've been thinking about taking Peter to a doctor for a complete physical." Peter looked at me not comprehending. "I'd like to make sure he's as healthy as he appears. But can you imagine how a doctor will respond when he discovers his new patient is already dead?" We all laughed at that. "I also thought that it would be a good idea for Peter to get all his childhood shots; not so much to protect him as to protect me. If he came down with the chicken pox, he'd shake it in a day but could pass shingles, the adult version, on to me."

"I never thought about that. That's a good idea. What about your doctor? You've known him for years."

"I guess I'll call him. But I've got another call to make too." I told her about my idea of getting Peter into school for a week.

Another good idea, she thought. The four of us talked about the camping trip, Lori's birthday party and chicken wings and laughed at Peter's orange belly button until he fell asleep. We all went to bed shortly after.

CHAPTER TWELVE

The next morning after breakfast, Peter returned to our room to straighten it up while I called Dr. Bruce for an appointment. Due to a last minute cancellation there was a 10:00 opening that very morning. I said I wanted a physical for a schoolboy, age six. I described him as being in my temporary custody.

Next I called Lance Turner, superintendent of schools. I asked his secretary if I might speak to him. I referred to him as Lance to portray our friendship, one reaching back to our grade school days. "I want to discuss placing my grandson in an elementary classroom for a brief time." Lance knew I never married. The mention of grandson brought a quick response.

"Jake, how you doing?" Before I could reply, he added, "And what's with suddenly having a grandson?"

"Relax. It was meant to get your attention, and it worked." We chuckled but I detected a slight annoyance. I explained, "He's a little boy I picked up in Montana a few weeks ago. I want you to meet him. Any chance of coming to your office in the next few days?"

After a hesitation, he said, "You've sure got my curiosity up. How about tomorrow at nine?"

"Great! We'll see you then."

Peter came down as I hung up the phone. "Peter, you have a doctor's appointment this morning at ten o'clock."

He looked a little worried. "You're coming with me, aren't you?"

"You darn right I am. But first it's bath time. You'll be as clean as a whistle for the doctor."

"I just took a bath last night, remember?"

"No. Your belly button took one last night. This morning we'll wash everything."

He chuckled. "Oh yeah. Okay."

While drying him after his bath, I said, "I want you to wear your underpants today."

"Why?"

"Doctors are used to seeing little boys in underpants. We don't want to let him down."

"Is he going to make me take my clothes off?"

"Probably. At least most of them anyway."

"Why?"

"In order to examine your body properly, he has to see it."

He looked down at himself, then at me. "All of it?"

Peter was a little boy who'd never been to a doctor for this purpose. The two times he'd seen a doctor in Butte, Montana, was pertaining to his illness – leprosy. The last time Peter saw the doctor at age three, his withered left arm was amputated just above the elbow. This was to be a whole new experience. He had no idea what to expect. "Probably."

He wanted to know what else to expect. I thought about that. I've never been present during the examination of a child since I was a child myself. More than likely things have changed since then. Of course I was assuming the doctor would feel comfortable examining a ghost in the first place. I may have been assuming a lot. Chances were he had never examined a ghost before.

As we were leaving, Peter became nervous. "Wait a minute. I have to pee again." He started for the bathroom, but I stopped him. "You can't. The doctor will want you to pee in his office for him."

He looked startled. As we headed for the car he said, "You mean like I did for Mike?" I nodded. Nervously he asked, "Is he going to prick my finger for blood, too?"

"He won't take it from your finger, Kiddo." I showed him on my arm where he'd insert the needle. Of course he wanted to know if it would hurt. "Peter, I've never lied to you and I'm not going to now. It is going to hurt but I'll keep a hand on you at all times, okay?"

He nodded as we pulled into the parking lot. His nervousness was increasing but there was no trembling. I was proud of him.

After checking in with registration, I was asked if the child had ever been here before. When I answered no, I was given several forms to fill out pertaining to Peter's health and family history and the medical plan he was covered under. I walked to a chair with Peter in tow and read over the forms. The only space I could fill out honestly and without concern was Peter's name. D.O.B. – no way. Mother and father's first name – I didn't know. Address: Boot Hill, Slippery Gulch, Montana: That just wouldn't work.

I returned to the window. "If you don't mind I'm going to go over these forms with the doctor. There are some things I have to discuss with him."

"Perhaps I can answer your questions."

I looked at her. "Well okay, but first, are you a doctor?"

"No, of course not."

"I apologize if I sound rude but there are some medical concerns I have. Dr. Bruce has been my doctor for over twenty years. I'm sure he won't mind." I turned around and went back to Peter before she could object. We only had to wait a couple of minutes before we were ushered to an inner office. Two or three minutes later, Dr. Bruce walked in.

"Hello, Jake. Long time, no see! You look well. And who do we have here?"

"This is Peter Stevenson, Dr. Bruce." The doctor stuck out his hand and Peter cooperated after a slight hesitation and a glancing check at me.

"Doctor Bruce, for starters we're here for a school physical."

"Is he related to you?"

"No. I sort of adopted him."

His right eyebrow went up. "How do you sort of adopt a child?"

I ignored the question. "This has to be kept confidential."

"Unless this is legal, Jacob, I can not..."

"Legal, yes. A little strange would be a better description. Nothing is illegal. Strange, yes, but not illegal. That's why it must be confidential."

"I'm sorry, Jake, but I can't promise anything until I know your authority over this child. Do you have written permission, say, from a parent? Or some agency?"

"I don't think so. Look, this is going to sound crazy." I sat Peter on the table. "Peter is dead!" Both eyebrows raised at this news. "He's a ghost and I can prove it. Listen to his heart."

At that point Peter pulled his shirt up. The doctor looked at Peter's small chest, then at me as if I was nuts. I smiled and nodded. Slowly he raised his scope to Peter's chest and listened.

"What do you hear?"

With relief and confidence, he said, "A very strong, healthy, young heart." His eyebrows went down.

"Okay, Kiddo, now." (Peter and I prearranged everything.) "Listen to his heart again." The doctor tried frantically moving the stethoscope around Peter's chest.

"Forget it Doc. It isn't there and it won't be until I tell Peter to start it again."

The doctor fairly fell into a chair. "This is impossible."

"You're right, it is. Unless, however, Peter is actually dead." The man's face blanched as I continued. "Would you like additional proof?"

Slowly he nodded, his eyes fixed on the patient he'd not yet officially accepted. Maybe he was going to consider this an emergency situation.

"Peter, vanish please." Instantly, he was gone. I thought the doctor was going to have a stroke as he used his arms to lift himself out of his chair and steady himself.

"Okay, Peter, that's enough and start your heart again." Instantly Peter was back and the good doctor sighed in relief.

Weakly the doctor asked, "What do you want?"

"I want you to keep this confidential. I also want you to give him a complete physical."

He was shaking. "If he's dead…"

"Peter has taken on all the characteristics of a living child. I want to make sure that child is completely healthy. If there is a problem, I want to know about it."

The proof was there. This child before the doctor was dead. Suddenly it occurred to me he was looking at me with suspicion. I removed a folded copy of the editorial from my wallet. "Read this doctor. It should help answer some of your questions." As he read, I had a seat while Peter came on my lap.

Putting the paper aside after reading it and dabbing at a tear, he looked at both of us. "This is incredible. Am I to assume Peter's final prayer was answered?" Peter and I smiled and nodded. "And, Jacob, you are the answer?" Again both Peter and I smiled and nodded. The doctor looked at us. "How?"

"I don't know how and I don't know why me."

Peter turned around on my lap. "Yes you do. Because we love each other."

I kissed his forehead. "You're right, we do."

I could see the fear abating and the compassion in this man I'd known for over twenty years, replacing it. "Do you want all the lab...well I guess there's no sense in trying to take his blood."

"Peter's as mortal as you and me right now. Yes, I want the lab work, plus x-rays."

"That's impossible. How can you x-ray a ghost?"

"As I said doctor, right now he's a mortal."

Somehow, right then I was humbly reminded that I was a plain old trucker talking to a physician like I knew more about his work than he did. I wanted to laugh, but didn't dare. I thought, what if Mike and Jane could see us now. George would either be laughing his guts out or dragging me out of the room by my shirt.

It was good that the doctor knew me. And my family! And that he could remember me as a responsible science teacher – I guess.

"Well, all right. Is it okay if I have an assistant work with me?"

"Sure, just don't mention Peter's condition."

Peter broke in. "Jake, I have to pee, bad.

The doctor's eyebrows shot up.

"I told him to hold it until we got here. Can we do that first?"

Peter and I walked across the hall where he filled a cup and then some. Upon returning, Dr. Bruce introduced us to nurse Michelle. She was in her early thirties, not beautiful but attractive, friendly and warm. "Jake, would you like to help him get out of his clothes?" Dr. Bruce asked.

The Gift

"Do I have to take everything off?" Peter asked. This is the first time he demonstrated any form of modesty. However, he was nervous. Dr. Bruce was too.

"You can keep your underpants on for now." I noticed the doctor never spoke to Peter, directly. I guess he wasn't accustomed to speaking to ghosts. At that point the doctor exited the room perhaps relieved he had other patients to attend to.

Once out of his clothes, Peter submitted to nurse Michelle, being weighed and measured. He was thirty-four and one-half inches tall and weighed thirty pounds.

"You're a little one, but you sure are cute," Michelle intoned. "Jake, could you sit him on the table for me?" She took his blood pressure and pulse. Both were excellent. "You must be an athlete," she commented.

He had no idea what that was. "Peter likes playing baseball and soccer. His coordination is unbelievable. He can hit the ball a mile and he has a heck of an arm. Not only that, he's fast. He's also a tumbler. He can stand on his head and hands and he can do forward and back flips."

"You're kidding? There isn't enough room in here to do a flip but could you stand on your hands?"

He smiled broadly. "Sure." He jumped off the table and was soon on his hands.

Michelle clapped as Peter jumped back on the table. "Peter, you're amazing." She put her hand on his right thigh and squeezed it gently in several different places as Peter giggled. "Well, I can certainly see why he's so fast. He's skinny but this leg is all muscle." She then felt his arms and shoulders. "Why you're all muscle." Again Peter smiled. "Could you lay down on you back for me?"

He did and immediately arched his back. "It's cold," he complained.

"Your body will warm it up quick. My goodness, what happened to your belly button? It's orange." She examined it closely.

Both Peter and I laughed and Peter explained what happened. She thought that was great. "His belly button has been taking a beating. When we were camping, he dropped some grape jelly in it. Then it was purple for a while." We all laughed.

"Now Peter, I'm going to take just a little of your blood."

Instantly a tear replaced the smile. "It's going to hurt, isn't it?"

"Just a little, honey, but Jake will be right here." As she prepared his right arm, I put my hand on his chest and stroked him gently. He put his left hand on mine for double security. As she inserted the needle, Peter squeezed my hand. Although the tears increased, he never cried out once. Then it was over.

The tears continued. "Michelle, I'm worried about something and since you're a nurse, you may be able to check it out." Both Peter and Michelle looked at me with concern. "It seems to me there's a little to much space between these two ribs." I stuck my finger between two ribs. Peter flinched and squealed at the same time. Michelle got the hint.

"Right here?" she asked sticking her finger between the same two ribs. Again Peter squealed and the loss of blood and the pain was instantly forgotten. "I think they're just the way they should be." We all laughed. She looked at me. "I'll have to remember that for future patients."

She turned to Peter. "Peter, you are a brave young man. A lot of children older than you scream terribly when I take their blood. Although you cried, you never made a peep." Peter gave her his best smile.

The Gift

After taking his temperature she proclaimed it to be a perfect 98.6.

She moved on to the eye exam. She was amazed at the results so she went through it again (with the same results). His eyesight was 20/10, the best the exam registered but she suspected it was even better.

She then explained the hearing test to Peter and me, then inserted a probe into Peter's right ear, then the left. After the test she again was amazed and repeated it. She'd never seen a test so high. Just then the doctor walked in.

"Peter is the perfect patient, doctor, and everything is normal or above average." She showed Dr. Bruce the results of the eye and hearing tests.

He looked at her findings. "Are you sure of this, Michelle?"

"Yes doctor. I repeated both and checked the equipment. The results are correct." He continued to study the findings. "Doctor, if you don't need me for anything else, I'll get his blood and urine to the lab." She looked at Peter and said, "It was nice meeting you, Peter." He gave her a nice smile. Little did she know she had ghostly samples in the vials she held in her hands.

The doctor had Peter sit on the table again. He hesitantly put the stethoscope against Peter's chest. The doctor smiled with relief as he listened to Peter's strong, young 107-year-old heart. He listened to Peter's heart then changed the scope to his back and had Peter take several deep breaths. He looked into Peter's eyes, ears, nose and throat. When he inserted the tongue depressor, Peter didn't like that at all and gagged as tears came to his eyes.

The doctor inspected his scalp and hair, I suppose looking for lice. He felt the glands on both sides of his neck.

The doctor had Peter watch his finger without moving his head as he moved it from one side of Peter's face to the other then up and down. He had Peter squeeze his finger with one hand then the other. The doctor had Peter stick his right leg out straight and keep it straight while the doctor pushed down slightly on it. He did the same with the left leg.

He checked Peter's reflexes by tapping his knee with a small rubber mallet, then had him lie back down. He moved the stethoscope around Peter's stomach and abdomen. He prodded and tapped the same area. Noticing Peter's strange orange belly button, he waited for an explanation. Upon hearing it, he laughed for the first time. He was beginning to relax.

The doctor lowered Peter's underpants and checked for a hernia and inspected his genitalia.

He had Peter do several sit-ups and leg lifts. As Peter did so the doctor felt the muscles in his stomach and abdomen. I wondered if this was normal.

The doctor had Peter roll over, put his arms over his head and spread his legs slightly. I was wondering what this was all about. After having him rest his chin on the mat and look forward, the doctor ran his fingers from the base of Peter's skull to his tailbone. He felt each rib as it moved away from the spinal column. He put some pressure on each kidney and asked if there was any pain. There wasn't.

The doctor shook his head. Suddenly I was worried.

When finished on the table, the doctor had Peter walk a straight line, one foot in front of the other. Peter hopped on one foot for him several times, then the other. He had Peter bend over and touch his toes. Again the doctor studied Peter's backbone. I thought he was looking for signs of scoliosis. He ended by having Peter do several near-perfect push-ups.

The doctor looked at me, then down at Peter. "I don't believe any of this. Peter is dead, yet he's the healthiest child I've ever examined. He's slender but all muscle. His reflexes are quick and his coordination is better than most nine-year-olds. It's impossible and yet, here he is."

Peter came over to me and sat on my lap. "Doctor Bruce, I noticed you looked at his spine and shook your head. Is there a problem?"

"Yes! It's perfect. Everything's perfect. I don't understand it. That's the problem."

I chuckled. "Don't feel bad, Doc. I've been living with Peter for six weeks now, and there are things about him I cannot believe. Here's something else. When hurt, injured or sick, he's able to repair or heal himself within twelve to twenty-four hours, but initially he feels the normal pain and discomfort. He takes care of himself very well." I explained the several different minor wounds he suffered and that by morning, there was no trace of anything. Dr. Bruce was amazed.

I also mentioned Peter's bout with constipation and how that threw him. "He wasn't able to correct that himself for some reason. I had him living on fruit for almost five days and finally got a child's enema. I was just ready to give it to him, when at the end of the seventh day, the dam broke. But Peter was in agony for days."

"If that happens again, don't let it go beyond four days." Then the doctor thought about Peter's constipation. "You always eat in truck stops?" I nodded. "And often in different states on the same day?" Again I nodded. "So the food you're both eating is prepared in different ways?"

"I suppose. What are you getting at?"

"Constipation is not caused by a bug. The way you're both eating would be hard on anybody's system and Peter seems to have all the systems everybody has. I would guess Peter's digestive system was adjusting to the changes he was experiencing. Your system long ago adjusted." It certainly sounded reasonable to me.

"Now let's do the x-rays. The cost is on me. They may satisfy some of my questions. Anything you want besides the chest x-rays?"

"Yes. From the bottom of the pelvic region to the chin in front and from the tailbone to the base of his skull in back. I would also like several taken of his skull in front and on the left side."

He looked at me questioningly. His eyebrows rose. "I assume there's a reason for that?"

"There is. I think that will be evident once you see the x-rays."

"That is if they're not all blank," the doctor added.

I shrugged my shoulders. "It could be interesting, but I don't think they will be." I looked at Peter. "Peter, an x-ray is like a camera except instead of taking pictures of your outsides, it takes pictures of your bones under your skin. It doesn't hurt a bit."

He looked at his arm. "You mean it can see my bones without my skin?" I smiled and nodded.

Worriedly he asked, "What does that machine do with my skin? Does it take it off?"

"No. It looks right through your skin, like you look through a window and see trees."

"Can I see the pictures, too?"

I looked at Dr. Bruce. "We'll see," the doctor said. He handed me a tiny gown for Peter.

We walked down the hall, Peter's gown dragging on the ground. At radiology, a good-looking, red head was waiting for us. While I was studying the radiologist, Peter was looking at the huge equipment. Interrupting my thoughts he said, "Are you sure this isn't going to hurt?"

The radiologist, whose eyes were not taken off Peter since we'd entered, assured him it wasn't going to hurt at all, "Just like having your handsome face photographed!"

I was jealous.

"Michelle told me you were darling, but I didn't think you'd be so darling. I'm Linda." They shook hands. He gave her a smile without taking his eyes off the equipment. I could tell he wasn't sure about this at all.

She led him to a plate that was in a stand against the wall and adjusted it to his size. "Peter, I'm going to have you stand against this wall several different ways. Stand very still, while I take the pictures. Can you do that for me?"

He nodded then asked, "Well Jake be in here with me?"

She looked at me, really for the first time. "You must be Jake." We shook hands. "Cute kid. Jake will be in here with me every time I change your position. But when I snap the picture, he'll be in that little room right over there. Is that okay with you?"

"I guess," he mumbled.

"Dr. Bruce told me what he wants. I think Peter's small enough we can get everything on one frontal shot and one rear shot. Then I'll take the shots of his skull. Peter, why don't you give your gown to Jake."

She had Peter stand against the wall facing her with his arms stretched over his head. As the huge machine slowly approached him, he looked small, vulnerable and petrified. He was trembling as a single tear coursed down his right cheek. Another tear was ready to well out of his left eye. Both eyes were on me now.

"Wait a minute," I said. I went up to Peter and knelt on the floor. I put my hands on either side of his chest and gently stroked him. "Kiddo, you've overcome a lot of fears in the last six weeks. I've been so proud of you, I could spit." He smiled a little. "Now you have a new fear – fear of the unknown. True, this is not like taking your picture with your muskie. But don't let this machine bother you. It's not big and noisy like the Babes. So relax. Trust me, you'll feel nothing and you'll be fine."

"Okay. But, Jake, could I put my arms down for a minute? They're tired."

"Only if you promise to give me a big hug, Funny Tummy."

I got the promised hug. "You okay now?"

"Yeah. Thanks, Jake."

"You bet. Now stretch up those arms and let's see those ribs." He put his arms over his head again. I immediately poked a finger in each side of his ribcage.

He brought both arms down quick with a squeal and said, "Hey, that wasn't fair."

"I know. I'm being mean again. I'm sorry."

He laughed. "You are mean but I really needed it."

"I know. Now get those arms up again. I promise I won't tickle you." He did as he was told. I walked over to the radiologist. "He's ready now." As we left the room, she reminded him to stand very still. From the other room she told him to take a deep breath. He did as he was told. Five seconds later we returned and told him to release his breath. "That wasn't so bad, was it?"

"You already took it?"

"Yep. That was it." She had him turn around, took the next one and over the next five minutes, finished her work. As Peter and I were leaving, she said, "Mr. Winters, you were a big help today. That was beautiful. But if you don't mind me asking, who is the Babes?"

Peter and I both chuckled. "The Babes is the name I use for my truck."

We found Michelle waiting for us. Looking at her, Peter asked, "Can I get dressed now?" Michelle approved. He then looked at me. "Jake, can I take these darn things off?" pulling at the crotch of his underpants.

I laughed and explained to Michelle that he hated wearing underpants. She laughed and mentioned she didn't think they looked very comfortable. Peter removed them without hesitation. Once off, I stuck them in my pocket.

Dr. Bruce stuck his head in the door. "May I see you for a few minutes, Jake? Michelle, will you please stay with Peter?"

She was already asking Peter about his camping trip as I made my exit.

After we were seated in his office Dr. Bruce said, "I know Peter's dead. I know he's a ghost, you proved that to me – but he's an above average…way above the average six-year-old. For me, that doesn't make sense. So I'm not charging you for the call. This has been the high point of my medical career…I tell you! And I've seen everything until today."

"Are you sure?"

"I'm sure. There is one thing though. He's very small for his age, however, that's comparing him to the average six-year-old today. That isn't fair since he wasn't born in 1994. That accounts for quite a bit of it. Kids were shorter back then. Do you know anything about his parents? Were they shorter than normal? I don't suppose you know anything about Peter's health while he was alive, do you?"

"Actually I know quite a bit. It appears Peter was born a healthy child but things went down hill rapidly from there." I went through Peter's brief medical history from birth to his last visit with the doctor in Butte, Montana, at age three. "That's when his medical history stops. From that point on his history is based on Peter's memory, the editorial and speculation."

The doctor's eyebrows went up when I mentioned leprosy. He was fascinated that Peter's arm had been amputated but now he had it. I also mentioned the doctor in Butte indicated in his records, Peter was small for his age. Then I remembered back. "Now that you mention it, Peter did tell me once he thought his father was shorter than me." I didn't mention I once saw his father in a vision.

"Was he ever sick as a child?"

"He mentioned a few weeks ago that most of his bowel movements were runny. However, most of the food he ate came from the town dump. He indicated a few days ago there were times he was sick. But there was no one to go to for help and no one cared anyway."

The doctor shook his head. "Lord, what a miserable life. No wonder his final prayer was answered." He paused in thought for a minute. How long is he going to be with you?"

I told him I didn't know and explained why. He understood, I think but said if he was still with me a year from now, he'd like to exam him again, on the house. I agreed.

I continued, "I've got two more questions for you. You said Peter has the coordination and strength of a nine- or ten-year-old." I told him about Peter playing baseball while on the camping trip. The doctor was not surprised. I went on. "His energy is unbelievable but it doesn't last. Eventually he needs a break. Is that normal?"

"He has the physical abilities of an older child. It stands to reason he'd have the energy to go along with it. However, he has the body of a toddler. His heart and lungs are the right size for his body so his energy is going to last accordingly. Does he take naps?"

"On active days I've gotten him to sit on my lap for twenty or thirty minutes. Sometimes he dozes for a few. But to lie down and sleep, forget it."

He laughed. "Sounds normal. That may be all it takes. Play that one by ear."

"Okay. Next question, but I doubt if you'll be able to answer it. It doesn't make sense. The first day I saw Peter, he was a pathetic little creature." I showed him the first picture I took of Peter. All Dr. Bruce could do was shake his head. "It looks as if he hadn't eaten for weeks. You look at him today and his legs, arms, chest, stomach and shoulders have all filled out. He's eating well and getting a lot of exercise. He's a picture of health – no longer pathetic. Yet I weighed him before ever leaving Basin. He weighed the same then as he does now. How can that be?"

He stared at me then slowly rose and walked over to the wall studying his diplomas. He returned to his chair, had a seat and rubbed his clean-shaven chin. "You're right. I can't answer that. It's illogical. If he's filling out and adding muscle to his frame, he should be adding weight. If you think about it though, adding muscle to his frame is illogical. He's dead. His body should have remained as it was at the time of his death. In fact, I can't even explain why he has a body."

"I explained that one to you earlier but that doesn't make it any easier for us mortals to understand. Let's face it, Doc., everything's illogical. You shouldn't have been able to hear a heartbeat or working lungs. You shouldn't have a sample of his blood and urine right now and you certainly shouldn't have photographs of his skeletal system."

"We're not sure yet that we do, but you're right! I think you've got a little miracle on you hands, Jake. I don't think there's any logical or scientific explanation for it. I'm just happy to be a part of it. Keep track of his size and weight."

"I intend to but I don't expect to see any change at all." I then mentioned the forms the front office wanted me to fill out with difficult questions such as date of birth.

"I'll take care of them...somehow."

I thanked him then thought of one more question. "During the exam you had him lay on his belly and ran your finger down his spinal column from his head to his tail bone. Is that part of a normal exam for a child?"

He looked a little embarrassed. "No! I'm not a neurologist but I was wondering if I'd feel any irregularities...anything that would feel different. I didn't. I don't think a neurologist would either. I did a few other things you'd experience in a neurological exam to satisfy my own curiosity. Peter is amazing, Jake, but I guess I don't have to tell you that."

There was a knock at the door. Doctor Bruce went to the door, opened it then excused himself. He went into the hall closing the door behind him. I sat in his office for seven or eight minutes wondering what this was about.

Returning, he apologized for his absence. He had a file in his hand. "Jake, that was Linda, the radiologist. She gave me Peter's x-rays and explained them. You asked for the x-rays you did because you knew what would be found, correct?"

"Actually I asked for them because I was hoping Peter was exaggerating. I was also hoping the editor of the Slippery Gulch Gazette would have described Peter's death inaccurately. Doctor, I was hoping the x-rays would reveal something else."

I sat waiting. The doctor sat down hard as if he was suddenly exhausted. "Jake, you love Peter. That's very obvious. He loves you too. When you asked for the x-rays you did, it never occurred to me the damage…" He cleared his throat. "Both Peter and the editor were right."

I choked as tears came to my eyes. "With the untrained eye the x-rays would be meaningless to you. I could describe the damage to you but I'm not sure if it matters now."

I looked down at the floor while I played nervously with my hands. "I want to know. I'm not sure why but I want to know."

He looked at me hard. "All right, I'll try." He paused struggling to contain his emotions. "Most of Peter's ribs had been shattered. Probably by a long, sharp instrument. Based on the editor's eyewitness account, it was a hunting knife. That would fit. The ones that had not been shattered had been broken. The editor said when the knife was plunged into the boy's breastbone, it sounded like a gunshot. Looking at the damage that initial thrust caused, I'm sure it did. It was thrown with such force, it severed Peter's spinal column."

The doctor paused to reclaim his emotions. "But that's not what killed him." I didn't think so but I looked at the doctor surprised anyway. He sighed and continued. "I'll get to that in a minute. When you told me Peter's left arm had been amputated, I doubted you but the x-rays confirm it.

"His pelvis was broken. That would indicate several hard punches or kicks to that region or perhaps even a hard instrument was used such as a stick or a rock. The editor didn't mention anything about that."

"He didn't know about that." I described the nature and severity of the beating Peter received from the three teenage boys in the alley the day before he was murdered. I lost control of my emotions. Wiping my eyes I said, "At the time he was dragged to his father, he was near death. He didn't have the strength or will to fight anymore. I suspect he barely had the strength to utter his final prayer."

I'd never cried in front of another adult before. But I had come close with Bill and Danny. It was over the same topic. Truckers aren't supposed to do that. We're supposed to be strong both physically and emotionally. At least that's what everybody thinks. I was embarrassed. But the doctor was wiping a few tears too. We were in the same emotional boat.

After a moment for both of us, he said, "Would you like me to continue?"

"Please, if you can."

He swallowed hard. "The punch to Peter's face the editor mentioned is verified too. That punch had to have been horrendous. The editor described it as a punch that would have leveled any adult. Peter's upper and lower jaws were broken and his left cheekbone was shattered. His neck was broken too. Jake, I'm sure Peter was dead before he ever hit the ground."

All this happened while the entire population of Slippery Gulch watched...doing nothing. I jumped out of my seat so fast the doctor almost fell over in his chair. "That rotten son of a bitch. That whole rotten town was full of nothing but damn..."

"Jacob!" The doctor yelled at me. He came over and put his hand firmly on my shoulder. "It happened one hundred years ago. There's nothing that can be done about Peter's father, or the people of Slippery Gulch. What can be done now is what you're already doing – giving Peter the childhood he deserves."

I slumped back into my seat. "I'm sorry for that outburst but it's so darn hard. I saw what Peter's body looked like after that last beating he received from his father. He told me in graphic detail about the beating he received from the teenagers. He was willing to show me what his body looked like after he'd been murdered, but I knew I couldn't take it.

The Gift

"The Indians have a saying: Don't judge a man until you've walked a mile in his moccasins. Well, Doc, I feel like I've walked many miles in Peter's moccasins and now we're walking together. When he's hurting, I'm hurting. When he's happy, I'm happy. But when his memory takes him back to one of those dark times in his life, it's as if he grabs hold of my memory and takes it back with him. Fortunately his recent good memories now appear more frequent than his distant bad memories."

Dr. Bruce looked down at his desk and picked up the picture of Peter. His sad eyes began to brighten. He looked at me and smiled. Well, Mr. Winters, I'd say you have a little boy...a very happy little boy walking with you in your moccasins now. Keep him with you in your moccasins, Jake. You're doing a fine job."

"Thanks." I continued to simmer. "Did Linda indicate when these injuries took place?"

"That really threw her. It appears most of the injuries took place within the last one to two months. The severe injuries to the head would certainly have killed the boy. If somehow he had survived that, he wouldn't have survived the severing of his spinal column. It was severed in five different places. Yet here he is. Not only that, the damage has been repaired perfectly. No human can do that. Let's face it Jake, you have a little miracle on your hands and I'm not convinced he's a ghost. I believe he could be an angel."

I watched him return to his chair. "Angels are supposed to be superior to humans. Peter's a great little kid, but he's got the devil in his eyes like every other six-year-old boy. I don't think he's an angel."

He thought about that and smiled. "You may be right. Initially Linda wanted to call the police. She suspected you were the cause of the injuries yet that didn't make sense. But I dealt with it."

"Good! I'm glad to hear that. Could we go back and join Peter?"

We walked across the hall to find Peter explaining to Michelle how to clean a fish. As we walked in, Peter gave me his radiant smile then turned serious. "Jake, are you okay?"

Doctor Bruce looked at Peter amazed. "Yeah, I'm fine, Little One, and you are too." He jumped into my arms and gave me a hug.

"One more thing, Doc. I know Peter can become constipated but could he get anything else like a cold or even worse, Chicken Pox or another childhood disease?"

"He has the body of a living child. He seems to have all the internal and external parts and they all seem to work perfectly. I would think he could come down with anything, but unlike the normal child, eventually he could destroy any bacteria or virus he gets. I'm more worried about you. Let's say he does develop Chicken Pox. Before he is able to destroy it, he could pass the adult version, shingles, on to you. You're in trouble and he's fine."

"That's what I was afraid of. Is it too late for him to get his childhood shots?"

"No. I could give him half of them today. I'd like you back in a week to discuss the lab work. We can take care of the rest then. As I said, this is more for your protection than Peter's."

Peter had no idea what we were talking about, so the doctor explained what a shot was. Peter didn't want to have anything to do with them. I explained how he could pass an illness on to me. By getting these shots, he was protecting me. He was then quite agreeable.

The Gift

When we left, I was assured that Peter's health and body was outstanding. The doctor reminded me there would be no charge for today because of the uniqueness of the situation. Next week would be on the house too. How could I beat that?

CHAPTER THIRTEEN

On the way home, Peter had several questions. The first one was not the one I was expecting; "Why were you crying while in the doctor's office? Are you sure you're okay?"

I looked at him in the rearview mirror. "How did you know I was?"

He answered me with a response I've often used with him. "I know you, Jake. I could tell."

I smiled at his response. "You're right, Kiddo. The doctor told me about your x-rays. The horror you lived through as a little boy in Slippery Gulch was verified. Just seeing the proof of the damage that was done to you while you were alive was too much. You know how I am."

He smiled. "You're okay now?"

I swallowed hard. "I'm okay."

"Good! Can I ask you some other questions?" I nodded.

"How come the doctor looked at and touched my things?"

"That's all part of the exam. He was just making sure you had all the right parts."

He chuckled. "I do, don't I?"

"Oh yeah. You've got everything you're supposed to and everything's right where it's supposed to be."

Again, he chuckled. "In my book about the doctor giving the boy an exam, why didn't he do that to him?"

"Perhaps he wasn't having a complete physical the way you were."

My answer was accepted and the questions continued. "Why did he stick that piece of wood down my throat? He almost made me puke. Why did he hit me in my knees with a hammer? Why did he look up my nose? Why did he look in my ears? Why did he shine a light in my eyes?" And on and on they went, all the way home.

Once we walked into the house, Betty wanted to know how it went. "It was neat, well some of it was anyway. They took pictures of my bones." Betty's look prompted my explanation. I explained the x-rays. "But he stuck needles in both my arms. I didn't think that was too neat."

For the rest of the day, he ran a low-grade fever and was rather listless. He got sick to his stomach once. His arms were sore for the rest of the day but by late afternoon, he was raring to go.

During dinner I noticed Peter was wolfing down his food. We were having a meal of roast beef, mashed potatoes and gravy and green beans. The only assistance he required was a little help with cutting his meat. Halfway though the meal, he looked at Betty and said, "Aunt Betty, you're a good cook. This is great!"

"Well, thank you, Peter. What brought that on?"

"I've been eating Jake's cooking for the last two weeks."

Everybody laughed. "You little stinker. Next time I'll let you starve."

Later, during our evening talk I said, "Peter, tomorrow morning you and I have another appointment."

"We do? Do we have to see another doctor?"

"Yes, but the doctor we'll see is a different type of doctor. He is a doctor of education. His name is Dr. Turner and he will say whether you can attend his school for a week. I think you'll like him, and I'm sure he'll like you too."

"Do you think he'll let me?"

"I don't know, Kiddo. I can't predict this one. We'll just have to wait and see."

He sat quietly for several minutes playing with his pajamas. I thought he was contemplating what I'd just said, however he completely changed the subject. "Jake, Doctor Bruce had fearful hands today."

He took me so totally by surprise, I didn't have a clue as to what he was talking about. I looked at him, puzzled. "What?"

"When the doctor found out I wasn't what he thought I was, he was afraid."

"How could you tell?"

"I could feel the fear in his hands. Everybody I've met since I've been with you has had friendly hands. When I shake their hand, I can feel their friendship. The people in Slippery Gulch had hateful hands. But you have loving hands. Every time you touch me, I feel your love. Even when you spanked me and it hurt, I still felt your love." Then he looked concerned. "Don't I have loving hands for you? When I take your hand, can't you feel it? Can't you feel my love?"

Now I knew what he meant. "Peter, that's a beautiful way of putting it. Now I understand what you mean. You bet I feel it. Did you only feel fear in the doctor's hands?"

He thought for a minute. "No. It changed. When I shook his hand, I felt friendship. Later it was fear, but near the end of the exam, they were caring hands."

"So does that mean you approve of Doctor Bruce?"

"Yeah. Once he got to know me, he was nice." He thought for a minute. "Well at least until he stuck all those needles in my arms." He started to cuddle and was soon asleep.

CHAPTER FOURTEEN

The next morning on the way to superintendent Turner's office, Peter was nervous as we discussed how I wanted to handle the appointment. Peter would remain invisible.

After mutual pleasantries in his office, Lance asked me where my grandson was. I said that I'd introduce him in a moment, but that he needed to hear some confidential background on the boy. I spent the next fifteen minutes giving Lance a summary of Peter's life and death. I could see from his snide smile that he thought I was playing the campfire storyteller, throwing in the part about death. I explained that Peter was prevented from attending school, partly because he was considered to be too stupid. I explained how I'd been working with Peter on reading, writing, spelling and arithmetic. He nodded, clearly impressed.

"When can I meet this…traveling little ghost?"

"How about right now?"

"Fine. Is he out in your car?"

"No! Actually he's been sitting on my lap listening to us. Lance, may I introduce to you, Peter Stevenson." Peter slowly faded in. For a moment, I was afraid Lance would pass out.

Peter got off my lap and walked over to Lance's chair, stuck out his hand and said, "Very nice to meet you, Dr. Turner."

Lance gaped at him. "Don't worry, Lance. He is now as mortal as you and I are." Lance cautiously took Peter's small hand, still in shock and speechless.

Finally he said, "This is incredible."

"Yes it is and so is he. But relax: Peter's a normal little kid who wants to go to school. Could we try it for one week?"

"Jake, I wish you would have given me some warning."

"Well now, what sort of warning would you have accepted?"

He looked between the two of us for a few minutes. "Never mind. We-e-e. I think I'm going to be all right. Now, how long did you say you've been working with him? And what is his name again. My mind has left me."

"Peter Stevenson."

"Five days you say." He thought about this. "If we did put him in a classroom for one week – creating the least amount of stir, I think it should be kindergarten. I imagine he's far behind our first graders."

I shook my head. "I disagree, Lance. You see, Peter is a dream student. Not only is he highly intelligent, he's also very motivated. He started teaching himself how to read before he was murdered. That was no small feat, considering he was in survival mode at the time. He was homeless. He lived in the woods for the most part."

Lance took all of this in before taking a small book off his shelf. "Can you read this for me, Peter?"

Peter took the book and started reading with no hesitation. Lance then handed him another. Again Peter read it but with more difficulty. Lance was taken aback. He then wrote some math problems. Peter worked most of them, but struggled with the last two. They involved carry-over numerals, something we were just getting into.

Lance just shook his head. "I guess you're right. The first book was a beginner first grade, the second was an advanced second grade."

The Gift

"Let me go on, Lance. Peter knows the name of most of the state capitals we've traveled through and that is twenty-two states. As we travel along, he's picking up some science, U.S. geography and history. He's learning how to read a road map, and he can tell time on a standard watch and a digital. He's gaining an understanding of time zones and why we have them. He's also learning about the ecosystems of the northeast. I could go on but I think you get the picture on this boy."

"Good Lord! He's exceptionally bright and he's got a good teacher."

"See, Funny Face," I said to Peter, now back on my lap, "I told you that you're smart." Peter started to beam so brightly that Lance and I began to laugh with delight. Peter was an educator's delight, no doubt about it.

Lance turned serious. "There is one thing that bothers me. Peter can vanish anytime he wants; that's obvious. If he were to vanish while in the classroom, we'd have real problems. My phone…"

"I'd never do that."

"Why?" Lance asked.

"As far back as I can remember, I wanted to go to school. Now I have a chance. If I disappeared, I'd mess everything up for myself. You'd never let me come back." He shook his head. "No, Dr. Turner, I'd never do that."

Lance studied Peter through a warm smile. "I believe you, Peter. Let me make a phone call. Pardon me, but would you two mind stepping out of my office for a minute."

For the next five minutes the suspense was raising fears in me. Then Lance opened his door to welcome us.

"Could you two be back here at 2:00, this afternoon?"

"Sure, what do you have in mind?"

"I just talked to Grace Pryor. She's a first-grade teacher and a real sweetheart with kids. She'll be here at 1:30. I'll explain a little to her then and leave the rest to you, Jake. Have Peter come in the way he is now, in other words, visible. I'll invite the building principal, Mr. Stewart, to join us." Lance shook his head and laughed. "I don't believe I'm doing this."

On the way home, I asked, "Well, what do you think?"

"He's nice. All your friends are nice."

"If they weren't, they wouldn't be my friend. How about a game of tag before lunch? Then a little nap before our appointment so you'll be real fresh."

Peter nodded, his face ablaze with his inimitable angelic expression.

That afternoon we were ushered into Lance's office and introduced to Mrs. Pryor and Mr. Stewart, who stood as we entered. Peter again proved to all to be the little gentleman he was.

Mrs. Pryor was a pleasing forty-year-old. It was obvious, the way she greeted Peter, she loved children. Peter picked up on it too. Lance wasted no time.

"Jake, Peter, I have explained to Mrs. Pryor and Mr. Stewart as best I could, your...situation, Peter. As you can imagine, they are having a difficult time believing me. Perhaps you and Jake can help them."

I looked at Lance. "I assume you told them what I told you?" He nodded. I looked at them. "It's true. His father murdered Peter in 1901. Therefore he can be a ghost, but right now he's as mortal as we are. He always wanted to go to school when he was alive but was told he was too stupid. As Dr. T. can attest to, he is anything but. It's been a painstaking road to get Peter to begin to accept that fact. After all, he has had a century of self-talk to the contrary."

"Mr. Winters, I apologize for interrupting, but I can't accept what Dr. T. told me about Peter," Mrs. Pryor said. "He's a charming child. But a ghost?"

"I don't blame you. That's one of the reasons we're here. Peter, why don't you fade out then back for these folks?"

So he did matter-of-factly. They gasped.

"Keep in mind, Peter is a mortal child 99.9% of the time. If he comes into your classroom for a week, he will be mortal 100% of the time."

All three sat transfixed. I decided to keep talking. "When he falls and scraps a knee, he bleeds and cries like any other little boy. He needs love and affection just as any child desires. Peter, however, returns the affection several fold."

Still they remained speechless, looking to Dr. T. as if for some professional explanation. Finally, Mrs. Pryor looked at Peter as if he were her student already. "Peter, you wouldn't disappear on me, would you?"

"No ma'am, I wouldn't. If I did, Jake would spank me and you would be mad and never let me come back."

Now there was a concerned look on her face. "Does Mr. Winters spank you often?"

"Just once, but I deserved it."

"Why didn't you just disappear?"

"I love Jake. I'd never disappear from him. Jake loves me, too. He's fair. When he finished spanking me, he hugged and kissed me and told me how much he loved me."

No one said a word, though Dr. T. and Mr. Stewart were looking at her to carry the ball. Mrs. Pryor broke the silence again. "I'll take Peter for the week." Peter excitedly broke out in a blue-ribbon smile.

She then looked at Lance. "I've got a feeling I'm going to miss him after he leaves."

I broke in with, "Oh, I guarantee you that, Mrs. Pryor."

"Not so fast everybody," Lance said. "It just dawned on me: We will need a record of his last physical and a record of his childhood shots. That may be impossible."

"He had a physical yesterday along with half of his shots. He gets the rest next week."

Lance exclaimed, "You actually found a doctor to examine him? Surely he didn't know what he had on his hands."

"Yes, he did. I wanted assurance that I was traveling around the country with a healthy ghost-turned-mortal. If he picked up certain childhood diseases, I might have some serious medical consequences."

Our joint laughter included Peter. Amazingly, we all parted in the good assurance that we were doing right by Peter.

As soon as we got home, I called Jason. Peter and I were planning to go back on the road August 28, but since Peter was going to school, we couldn't head out until September 10.

Once I had Jason on the phone, he was anxious to hear about our camping trip. I filled him in on everything. "You know Jason, this kid is like an infant. Every new experience is an adventure except that he can communicate his thoughts and feelings. And he's a fast learner. We're both having the time of our lives."

Jason laughed at my enthusiasm.

I explained the reason I was calling. Jason replied, "Take the time you need to enjoy yourselves and keep up the good work with Peter."

"Good! I'll keep you posted."

That afternoon was too hot and humid for anything. Betty and I were sitting on the back porch drinking iced tea and Peter, a soft drink, but he was bored. Then I got an idea. I got the sprinkler out and let Peter go. At one point he knelt over the sprinkler so it was shooting up the leg of his shorts. He was laughing then pulled out the waste band. The spray hit him square in the face knocking him on his butt from surprise. Betty and I both laughed.

Enough of that! Then it was jumping over the sprinkler. Once his shorts ended up around his ankles, and he ended up on his face. Again Betty and I roared! I called him over. I had him take his shorts off then dried him. "Run in and put your trunks on." He was in and out in a matter of seconds.

We continued to chuckle at Peter's antics. At one point he got up on his hands. Then he tried walking. He didn't get far but tried again. After several more tries he was able to take a few tentative steps. He was satisfied, for now.

Then it was time for flips but that didn't work out at all. Wet feet on wet grass didn't make it. His feet kept slipping out from under him. Nevertheless, Peter was becoming quite the acrobat.

That evening after Peter fell asleep, I told Betty and Jerry that since we had another month before going back on the road, I'd decided to buy Peter a bike. They both thought that was a great idea. Not yet though. There were too many things on the agenda for that week.

That week we went to the zoo and to two museums. We went to a couple of movies and spent a day in the park hiking. We visited Canada and the Welland Canal and watched a couple of huge ships move through the locks. The size of the ships about blew his mind. He had so many questions – they about blew mine.

We went out on Lake Erie for the day with a friend on his thirty-foot boat. Peter had a great time. We even fished a little but without luck.

We spent a day between Niagara Falls and Fort Niagara. He couldn't believe the size of the falls and loved the Maid of the Mist, the ship that goes under the falls.

He found the fort interesting, but seemed nervous. Finally he asked if we could leave. Once away from the fort, I asked him what was bothering him.

"There were too many people in there sort of like me. Some of them weren't very nice. They scared me."

I looked at him. "Do you mean, ghosts?"

"Yeah, but they weren't exactly like me. They were a little different but I'm not sure how. They all knew what I was, too. Most of them laughed at me. I don't like ghosts. Living people are nice, but ghosts scare me."

I chuckled to myself over the irony of his last statement. "Have you ever seen ghosts before?"

"A couple of times."

"I wish you would have said something. In the future, if you see any, tell me right away and we'll leave."

I had made arrangements several days earlier for Peter and me to go to the Indian Reservation for a visit and a game of soccer. Sara, a Seneca elder, called the morning of the game. It had rained that night and her back yard was a giant mud puddle. But the boys were excited about our visit and could care less about the mud. She asked if I thought Peter would mind playing in the mud. I looked at him and laughed. "This kid? You've got to be kidding."

She laughed and suggested that I bring along at least one change of clothes for him.

Peter had been looking forward to a reunion with his newfound Indian friends. I explained the condition of Sara's backyard because of the rain last night. "Peter, it's awful muddy. If you were to play soccer with the kids, you'd end up a mess. I don't suppose you'd want to do that, would you?"

His eyes lit up. "Yeah! That sounds great!" So the day and the game were on.

A couple of weeks ago, our trip to the reservation was cool at best. Peter's hatred for Indians was out of control, but Sara's love for children, and Peter in particular right from the get-go, won out. Peter had had a great time and quickly lost his baseless hatred for them.

Now he began chattering nonstop. He was so looking forward to seeing "Aunt" Sara and the Indian boys again.

As we pulled into her driveway, Sara came out to meet us with her great smile. Peter got out and gave Sara a hug, as did I. Suddenly a herd of little Indian boys came charging around the house, all smiles and caked with mud. The only boy that was missing from two weeks ago was the youngest who had come down with the chicken pox. However, the other four were there plus five new faces; two were eight, one was nine and two were ten. They all dwarfed little Peter. Their physical superiority was no issue with him: He was ecstatic over seeing his old friends again. The chance to make five more new friends while playing soccer thrilled him.

Bubba, a big six-year-old whom Peter befriended two weeks ago, walked up to Peter. With a muddy finger, he ran a three-inch line down each of Peter's cheeks and said, "Good seeing you again, Golden Hair. You ready to play?"

Peter smiled at his new nickname. He shook Bubba's muddy hand. Peter's team were the skins so he removed his shirt with one clean hand and one dirty hand, tossed it to me and headed for the muddy backyard with the rest. Sara and I sat on the porch, laughing and cheering.

All the boys spent a lot of time on the ground. When Peter wasn't on the ground, he sped around repeatedly, breaking away from the opposition. I was impressed with his toughness, but not with his recklessness. He had the coordination and speed of a nine-year-old but in a four-year-old body. When he crashed into someone, he tended to bounce off. When someone crashed into him, they sent him flying. More than once I held my breath. He always got up for more.

At one point, Peter and a ten-year-old on the opposing team went after the ball at the same time. The older boy was slightly ahead of Peter. As the other boy went to kick it, Peter dove feet first, sliding between the boy's legs and kicking the ball to his right, right to Bubba. Bubba managed to take the ball to the goal. But in his scoring kick, his feet went out from under him. The ball went wide left of the goal but Bubba was a perfect shot. He slid into the goal taking the goal and the goalie with him as he slid into and through it.

Meanwhile the ten-year-old lost his footing and landed on his rear end, inches from Peter's head. Both stood up quickly. "You can't do that!" The older boy yelled, glowering down at Peter.

Peter put his hands defiantly on his hips and looked up. "Why not? I didn't touch it with my hands."

The ten-year-old on Peter's team came up and joined in the argument. "Yeah, why not? Who says he can't?"

The older boy on the opposing side thought about this. "You never see that in professional games."

"They don't play in mud and besides, they don't have anybody as small as Golden Hair," the other ten-year-old argued.

"Yeah, I guess you're right." The argument was over. The three turned to the end of the field and laughed. They ran to retrieve Bubba, the goal, the goalie and the ball. That's how the whole game went.

When Sara later called half time, Peter came over, panting. All the boys were totally coated in mud. "Peter, you're getting killed out there. Do you want to continue?"

"Oh yeah, Jake. This is great!"

I could tell all the boys had a lot of respect for Peter. As a result, none treated him according to his size. The game continued along with the slipping and sliding through the mud. Peter finally got a good breakaway and took it in for the score. However, as he kicked it, his feet went out from under him and he went down. The opposing ten-year-old tried to stop when Peter went down but lost his footing. He slid into Peter and they both slid into the goalie. All continued sliding for another ten feet taking the net with them. While they all got up laughing, Peter was limping. The older boy was concerned, but Peter seemed to walk it off.

Finally the game was over – much to my relief. All the boys ran over to Sara, who was waiting for them with a hose. Each boy was sprayed semi-clean. They walked to the far end of the deck, which served as the make-shift locker room, removed their muddy clothes and dried themselves with the towels that Sara had passed out. Peter started to come to me to be dried. But he realized the other boys were drying themselves. So he did as well.

Sara produced a first-aid kit. Between the two of us we cleaned and dressed a few cuts and scratches. If Peter wasn't in the worst shape, he was a close second. He was cut, scratched and bruised from head to toe, but happy and proud.

After lunch, Sara asked Peter how the camping trip went. That took care of the next half-hour. He had us all in stitches. The boys were most attentive to his description of the plane ride.

Bubba changed the subject and asked what it was like to ride around the country in a big truck. Peter killed another half-hour.

Finally it was time to go.

On the way home, his excitement kept him awake. At home, it was serious bath time and off to a nap.

One hour later, he wandered downstairs sore and limping, but calling me for a game of tag. I had to help him realize that his left leg needed more rest.

That evening during our talk I said, "You know, Golden Hair, you are one tough kid."

"You think so?"

"I know so. That ten-year old weighed at least 40 pounds more than you, yet you didn't seem to be the least bit intimidated. In fact, all the boys were much bigger than you, yet it didn't seem to faze you a bit, did it?"

"Jake, I lived with wolves. And I learned something that came back to me this morning. A wolf must not think of his little size when he attacked a much larger animal. They are fearless. I want to be fearless too."

I laughed. "Well, you sure were this morning. Maybe I worried enough for both of us."

Out of nowhere he asked, "Jake, were you mad at me when I dried myself off?"

"Not at all! I was proud of you. All the other boys were drying themselves, so why shouldn't you? Did it bother you a little?"

"Yeah, kind of. It's one of our traditions."

"True. But several weeks ago when I had you learn how to take care of yourself, I had something like this in mind. I think you made the right decision."

"Thanks, Jake. You always know what is best for me."

"I try. It's hard for a man like me who's never been a father."

I was collecting my thoughts to review some things that I wished I'd handled better with him, but when I looked down he was fast asleep.

CHAPTER FIFTEEN

The next morning he was all healed. At breakfast, I announced that he and I had something to do today. He wanted to know what it was, but I told him he'd see.

Later we said good-bye to Betty. During the hour drive, he said little. When we pulled into a huge amusement park, Peter's eyes opened wide with excitement. "What are we doing here?"

"This is the thing I said we had to do today. I hope this place won't bore you."

He gave me an angry look. "You're mean! I've been worried about this since breakfast. Can we stay all day?"

I winked.

He laughed. "I love your kind of meanness."

"Peter, there are some rules you must follow." As I went through them, I knew he wasn't listening. He was too busy looking at the sights. I got down on my knees, put my hands on either side of his face as blinders and said, "Ground to Peter, now hear this." I turned his head one way then the other, sticking my little finger in each ear just enough to cause a giggle. Your ears are nice and clean now, so listen."

He giggled again. "Most important rule of all is: When not on Jake's shoulders, hold his hand. Got it?"

"I've got it, Jake. I'll behave."

"I'm not worried about your behavior; I'm worried about you not listening."

"I know. I'll listen this time. I remember the tree," he said with a sheepish grin, rubbing his stomach.

The two of us had a great day, for the most part. Lucky for me, Peter was too short for many of the bigger and faster rides, especially the Stomach Churner – the giant roller coaster with loops that looked terrifying. As we stood and watched it go through its three loops, I gave a silent prayer of thanks. We did ride a smaller roller coaster. As it turned out, it was just right for the both of us. So were our other rides designed for smaller kids accompanied by older adults.

For lunch, Peter had two-and-a-half hot dogs, French fries, root beer and an ice cream cone. Then I made a mistake. After eating and cleaning the ice cream from his stomach and chest, we went on a fast, twisting and spinning ride. He was enthralled until he suddenly turned peaked. Once off the ride, he dropped my hand to run for the nearest grass where he deposited his two-and-one-half hot dogs, French fries, ice cream cone and root beer.

Not long afterwards, I noticed him dragging. "Peter, remember how lousy you were feeling after the museum?" He nodded. "It was all because you were exhausted. You ran out of energy – remember?" Again he nodded. "Let's take twenty or thirty minutes right now and get your energy back." I lifted him on my lap. For the next half-hour, he sat on my lap as I rubbed his stomach. He apologized for dropping my hand earlier. I assured him he did the right thing; after all, that was an emergency. With that he dozed off for a catnap.

That afternoon, we went through a fun house. Standing in front of one scene where people were screaming, I looked at Peter, concerned. I saw a snide little grin on his face and the devil in his eyes. I squeezed his hand slightly harder and said, "Don't even think about it." He looked at me, surprised.

Once outside he asked me what I meant by that.

"I saw it in your eyes. You were thinking, boy could I ever have fun."

He started laughing. "I don't believe it. You know me too well. I was thinking that, but I wasn't going to do anything."

"Remember when we were camping and I said you were no angel, just a fun-loving little boy? I like that about you." We looked at each other and laughed.

Cotton candy was a hit, as was his cinnamon apple. If you've ever watched a child without front teeth trying to eat an apple, you know where this is going. Well, so did I. I had him remove his shirt for obvious reasons. I called it right. Cinnamon began running down his chin and neck to his chest and stomach. Needless to say we had to clean him up in the men's room before putting the shirt back on.

As I was completing the task, a young father came in accompanied by his toothless, shirtless son with gooey red lines running down his front. "Use warm water. It works well on cinnamon." The father and I both laughed as Peter and I walked out.

After a full day, we headed home. Neither of us had slowed down all day except for our rest break after lunch. It may have been that break that kept Peter from getting sick that night.

While waiting for dinner, Betty and Jerry asked Peter how the day went. For the next twenty minutes he talked nonstop with the enthusiasm we had come to love. He was left with barely enough energy to finish dinner. He was asleep before seven.

Later that night, I was awakened by Peter's bloodcurdling scream. But in the next moment he laughed hysterically. And in the next he began screaming again. It was so loud that Betty came into our bedroom. By then I had a light on, and Peter was laughing again. I was sitting on his bed with my hand on his chest, when again he screamed. From the expression on his face, I could see this last scream clearly was not of terror or fear. Betty and I looked at each other, perplexed. Now he was awake and laughing.

His eyes focused on my face. "Wow, Jake, that was neat."

The Gift

"What was neat, Kiddo?"

"I was riding a huge roller coaster. Every time I went up a loop, I laughed. Then going down, I screamed."

"Peter, have you ever had a fun dream before?"

He thought about this. "No."

I said to myself, what a shame. "Well, Peter, this will have been the first of many."

One afternoon when Jerry was off work, Betty, Jerry, Peter and I took a hike deep in the woods behind our home. Peter began to demonstrate what he knew about the woods, both from hiding in them early on and from my instructions. Betty and Jerry were duly impressed. But they – and I, as well – were flat out amazed with his little lecture on the touch-me-nots. Taking a pod in his little hands he said, "You guys see this pod? An animal walks by and touches it and seeds inside pop out and they go everywhere and that's how the plant moves around. And if I touch it like this the same thing happens. See?" With that he touched the pod and seeds shot out.

While walking along a dirt road, Peter spotted small puddles. Being a small boy, he made the most of each one. Most of the time he only got himself wet. Occasionally he got the rest of us too.

We finally had enough of his antics and I told him to stop. But it was too late. He was having too much fun annoying us. Then I saw it – a big puddle just ahead beside the road. Down on my knees I whispered, "Wait until Jerry and Betty are right next to that puddle, then jump in with both feet."

He gave me a nasty smile. "Should I?"

"Sure. Why not?"

I caught up to Jerry and Betty enjoying the late August day. Suddenly, from behind us we heard an ear-splitting scream. We turned in time to see Peter leaping through the air, feet first into the huge puddle. He hit the surface screaming with the devil in his eyes as he slipped below the muddy surface. First his bubbles surfaced, then Peter himself, treading water.

He was madder than a ground hornet. "Hey, that wasn't fair. Jake, you knew it was deep."

"Yes, and now you do too," I said laughing. I walked over and reached down to take his hand. As I did, Jerry pushed me from behind. Now both Peter and I were looking up from this mini-pond. Peter was laughing so hard he couldn't breathe.

"You little stinker! This is all your fault." So I dunked him. He went down laughing hard and came up laughing harder.

We would periodically look at each other and giggle all the way back to the house.

In our yard, Betty grabbed the hose and sprayed us down. We were one muddy mess. "Now both of you go into the laundry room and leave your clothes there. Then run up to the shower." I stripped to my boxers as Peter stripped clean down to his birthday suit. Jerry handed us towels through the door.

Peter, scampering up the stairs ahead of me, said, "That was fun."

"That was fun. But you are still a little stinker."

Still laughing he asked, "Can we take a shower together?"

"Nope. I'll get the water running for you. While you're in the shower, I'll get clean clothes for us. When you step out, I'll step in."

We soon joined Betty and Jerry downstairs, all of us still laughing over our family walk in the woods.

CHAPTER SIXTEEN

There were several times I went out for the evening and left Peter with Betty. Although he never went into a sound sleep until I got home, I couldn't let it bother me. This was my only chance to do any socializing, and I have to admit, it was kind of nice once in a while, to get out with adult company.

Peter was disappointed on those few occasions when I left him with Betty. He seemed to understand and not complain. But I never went out two nights in a row.

Once, when I had a date with an old friend and Betty was not available, I left Peter with Danny. Carol knew Peter and his situation since we'd gotten together for breakfast several days earlier. She suggested I bring him along; but let's face it, a six-year-old on a date doesn't do a lot for the atmosphere.

I gave Danny my cell phone number in case of a problem. I wasn't expecting any since Danny and Peter enjoyed each other's company.

Following a late dinner, my cherished female friend and I were enjoying pleasant company and conversation when my cell phone rang. I had completely forgotten about the phone, Danny and Peter.

Danny informed me that Peter was trembling and appeared terrified. Peter either couldn't or wouldn't explain his problem. Danny felt I should come to his house ASAP.

I briefed Carol on the situation. She understood, yet we were both disappointed. I said, "I would prefer to forget Peter for another hour or two but I'm worried. I'll take you home first then pick up Peter."

"No, Jake, I insist. Your first obligation is to Peter."

Carol and I got to the Early's house at midnight. Peter was awake and trembling when I walked in. He flew into my arms and I gave him a hug and a kiss. "Peter, what's wrong?"

With tears in his eyes he whined, "I thought you left me forever, Jake."

"Peter, I never want to leave you." In a minute, he was sound asleep on my shoulder.

Three days later Bill, Sue and Danny invited us over for a cookout. After dinner we looked at the pictures of our camping trip.

Peter went on to tell the three of them in detail about his first airplane ride, his first experience at playing baseball, and so many more first experiences. He recalled details I forgot.

"You went up in a seaplane?" Danny asked with excitement.

"Yeah. It was really neat. Sam took us right past our campsite, really low."

"Wow, that's cool," Danny stated. They had a lot of other questions for Peter. He answered all enthusiastically, enjoying the fact that he was the center of attention.

He lasted until 9:30, then fell asleep. Peter and I left about 10:00.

When Bill Murphy, the executive vice president in charge of operations of the trucking company I drove for, called the afternoon of the 17th, Peter and I were out. Betty assured him we would be home the next morning at 10:00.

In early July when my load mysteriously disappeared from my trailer while in Reno, Nevada, Bill represented my company. It was mandatory that I attend a meeting at our terminal in Salt Lake City. Since I was the driver, I was expected to explain the disappearance of the freight. I couldn't. As a result I expected to be fired on the spot. The

The Gift

load is always the responsibility of the driver. But Bill, with the help of my attorney, Frank Krandell, understood there was more going on than met the eye.

A week later the missing freight was found with the help of Peter. Bill learned shortly afterwards that the freight had been located and was relieved, but didn't believe the child in question was a ghost.

In late July, Bill called my house to find both Peter and me at home. He'd heard of the miracle rescue on I-40 and knew I had been at the scene of the accident. At that time he suspected I had a mysterious and underage rider in my truck. Peter was scared to death Bill was going to send him back to Slippery Gulch. Instead Bill insisted Peter remain with me in my truck and showed a strong desire to meet Peter. Thus the meeting now!

Bill pulled into our driveway at 9:55 in his rental car. He looked nothing like a vice president of anything. He wore a faded plaid shirt tucked into his jeans. We shook hands. I introduced him to Betty and Peter.

After greeting Betty in a proper way, Bill dropped to one knee and said, "Peter, I've always wanted to meet a true hero. I'm honored."

Bill couldn't have picked better words if he had tried. Peter beamed from ear to ear.

"Are you as important to the company as Jake says you are?"

"I don't know how important Jake said I am, but I'm not as important as Jake."

Peter looked at me wide-eyed and back at Bill. "You're not?"

"Not on your life." I saw him wince on his choice of words, but when he saw no reaction from Peter, he continued.

"Jake and all the drivers are more important than me. Without them, I wouldn't have a job."

Peter thought about this. "If Jake is more important than you, does he get paid more than you?"

Bill was stymied. I jumped in to help. "Peter, what Bill means is that if suddenly every driver quit, the company would close down. Who would drive the trucks? If Bill quit, the company would go on. They would hire someone else to do his job. I, as a driver, am responsible for one truck and one load. I get paid accordingly. But Bill is responsible for all the loads, all the trucks and all their drivers. So Bill gets paid more than any one driver."

"Now I understand." Then he looked at me and said, "If he's responsible for you, is he responsible for me too?"

Bill interrupted, "Oh no. Jake alone is responsible for you and I think he's doing a darn good job."

In the family room, Peter sat on my lap. When Bill asked him how he was enjoying his vacation, Peter slipped off to tell Bill everything in his own animated, enthusiastic way. He dramatized the way he paddles a canoe and the way Sam's plane flies. Sometimes he was hopping or jumping with excitement and other times he was rolling on the floor. Most of the time he had us all in stitches.

He showed Bill all the pictures of our camping trip. When Bill saw my muskie, he asked how I was able to land it from a canoe. He smiled real big at the fish Peter caught, including Peter's own muskie.

"Bill, Peter doesn't fit the stereotype ghost, does he?"

"Absolutely not."

"How would you explain Peter to a stranger?"

"I…I…couldn't."

The Gift

"To be perfectly honest, I can't either. In fact I never really believed in ghosts before. But I do now. Peter, would you fade out slowly, then come back for Bill's benefit?"

"Sure." As he did his thing, Bill's eyes enlarged. "That's incredible!" He breathed aloud. I sat there letting his mind process what he'd just seen. Finally he looked at me. "Jake, what is it like driving around the country with a…a ghost?"

"The first few weeks, it was pretty rough on both of us, would you agree, Kiddo?"

Peter nodded in agreement. I decided not to mention his nightmares. "He's a product of the late 19th century. Suddenly he's riding around the country in a computerized big truck in the 21st century. Everything we take for granted had to be taught to Peter. For example, the first time in a bathroom he didn't know how to wash himself or brush his teeth. This boy had never seen silverware before. Then throw in interstate highways, cars, helicopters and planes. Everything was all new to Peter and it all had to be learned."

"I never thought of that," Bill said.

"Before Peter and I left Basin, I didn't either. But Peter has adjusted well and quickly. He's having the time of his life, and to be perfectly honest, I am too." Peter stretched up and put his hands on the back my neck.

Bill laughed. "I can see that. I can also see the great job you're doing with Peter."

I thanked him. I explained that Peter's physical and emotional needs are the same as those of every other six-year-old. "When he's scared or hurt he needs comforting. And when he's injured, he's healed by the next morning. But in the meantime, he feels pain like anyone else. Now when he's uncertain of himself, he needs encouragement. The one thing he seldom needs is discipline. Usually a simple reminder will do."

"This is all incredible."

"He's amazing Bill, and a great kid. I don't know what I'd do without him anymore." I affectionately ran my hands up and down Peter's ribs.

Peter turned around and gave me a hug. "I don't know what I'd do without you either, Jake."

"I can certainly see you two are more than a team. There's nothing in the company policy that says you can't have a ghost riding with you. Eventually, it's bound to leak out somehow. But until then, let's keep it our secret."

Bill rose to his feet. "In the meantime, Peter, it's been a distinct pleasure meeting you. You are certainly a wonderful little boy. And a charmer of a ghost."

Bill walked over and shook Peter's hand. Then he handed me his card. "Jake, if there's anything I can do for you and Peter, let me know."

Peter and I walked Bill to the door, saying our good-byes.

CHAPTER SEVENTEEN

The next morning Peter and I went back to Doctor Bruce for the lab results. Everything showed above average.

He gave Peter the rest of his shots. For his last one he had Peter pull down his pants and lie across my lap. Peter let the whole building hear his displeasure at being shot in the butt.

Peter got off my lap rubbing his butt, looked at the doctor angrily and asked, "Why did you do that?"

Fighting a laugh, he said, "Sorry, Peter, but that's the way that shot has to be given."

I looked at the doctor, winked and asked, "Does this mean I can't spank him today?"

Peter looked at me worriedly, then at the doctor waiting for his answer. "It may be best to wait until tomorrow for that, Jake. The right side of his rear end is likely to be tender for the rest of the day." Peter looked relieved.

On the way home, Peter had only one question. "Jake, were you thinking about spanking me today?"

"Have you given me a reason to spank you?"

"I don't think so."

"I assure you, you haven't. I was just joking with Doctor Bruce."

He looked at me relieved. "You *are* mean, Jake."

That evening after dinner, Jerry and I announced we were going out together, leaving Peter with Betty again. He wasn't very happy, but he understood.

We were back before 9:00. Peter was in his pajamas and thrilled over my early return. He was on my lap in seconds. While we talked, Peter fell asleep.

This was our chance. Jerry slipped to the garage and returned with a brand new bike. Tomorrow morning Peter would be in for the surprise of his life.

Betty said, "It's so small. Did you get training wheels?"

I replied, "They had them but I didn't get them. Peter won't need them. He got his balance down pretty good a few weeks ago on Nat's bike."

"But most children Peter's size haven't been weaned from tricycles yet," Betty insisted.

"Peter is six-and-a-half going on 107. He has the coordination of a nine-year-old. He'll be a little shaky at first, but he'll be okay."

The next morning we adults heard the toilet flush upstairs. The bathroom Peter and I used was directly over the kitchen nook, so we always knew when Peter was up. Peter staggered into the kitchen more asleep than awake. Since the bike was set up in the family room, he didn't see it. After waking him in our traditional way, I suggested we move to the family room for a moment. I carried him toward the rocking chair when he noticed the bike. His eyes popped nearly out of his head. He was speechless. I stood there holding him. He looked at Betty. He looked at Jerry. Then he looked at me. "Is that for me?"

"It doesn't fit any of us, Kiddo." I put him down. "It's all yours."

He slowly approached it in disbelief as if seeing a ghost. His eyes ran over the metallic crimson fenders. Then the chrome handlebars. He walked from one side to the other and back. His expression was not so much pleasure as outright awe. He felt the seat. He squeezed the brakes. Then he rubbed his small hands all over it like a blind man.

"Well, Kiddo, what do you think?"

"It's neat, Jake! It's really awesome...but why?"

The Gift

I walked over to him and knelt down. Putting an arm around his shoulders, I said, "Because you're worthy of it, Little One. And because every boy should have a bike."

"Did you have one when you were a boy?"

"I still do. This morning you and I are going for a ride together, if that's okay with you."

He stared at me. Finally he said, "You're too nice to me, Jake," and threw himself into my arms.

"Yeah, you're probably right. Maybe I should take it back."

He looked at me. "You're so mean to me. I love you, Grandpa. Thanks!"

I ruffled his hair. "Come on, let's go eat. Then we'll check your balance." I was hoping to buy a bike with gears for Peter but the smallest bike made with gears without special order was a twenty-inch. That was way too big for Peter's thirty-four inches.

He inhaled breakfast in record time. After he dressed in firefighter speed we followed him through the garage as he wheeled his bike beside him. First, we put on his helmet. "Why do I have to wear that?"

"Simple! If you fall off and hit your head, we don't want blood on the driveway."

He looked at me, uncertain how to take that.

Betty said, "Jake, you're disgusting. Peter, I don't understand what you see in this brother of mine." He chuckled. "The reason you wear a helmet is to protect that beautiful head of yours if you fall. The reason Jake wears a helmet is to protect his ugly mug."

Peter laughed. "You have to wear one, too?"

"You bet I do." Once I got the helmet on him, I had him sit on the seat while I held the bike upright. It was a little high, so I adjusted the height with a wrench.

To check out his balance, I had him ride in the grass. It was good enough. I looked at Betty and winked. She nodded and smiled. "How about the two of us riding around the court and back to the garage?" Coming back up the 200 foot long driveway, he had to walk the last fifty because he didn't get a good enough run at it and he had no gears.

We then left the court and headed up the street for a short distance. The farther we rode the less he wobbled. We turned around and headed for the driveway again. He got a better run but as the grade slowed him, he got up off his seat to pump harder.

"Peter, stay on your seat. One foot is liable to slip off a peddle. If that happens, you could hurt yourself."

"I won't slip, Jake. And even if I do it won't hurt any because the bar is covered with rubber padding."

I smiled knowingly. "Okay, Kiddo, but if you do, remember this conversation." He was going to have to learn the hard way, as I did. Of course the bar on my bike fifty years ago and even now wasn't covered by anything.

Upon reaching the top, he stood and exclaimed, "See, Jake, I made it."

"Well, you did this time."

"I can do it every time on this bike."

Betty came out to join us. "Well, Peter, what do you think?"

"I wish Uncle Jerry was here to see me."

I put in, "By now you know how it is with us truckers."

Rubbing one hand affectionately over the fender, he said, "This is awesome. Jake, you're the greatest! Can we ride around the neighborhood?"

"Let's do it. We'll be back in a while, Betty. Peter, let's watch for cars and you do as I say."

"Hold it, guys." Betty pulled up her camera and took several pictures of Peter. "Now be careful you two."

Minutes later we were climbing a hill at the back of the neighborhood. As it got steeper, Peter stood up for more power. I told him to sit but he insisted he was okay. While putting a hard thrust down on his right foot, it slipped off the peddle and he came down hard on the padded bar. He almost wiped out but regained control. He put the bike down and sat on a nearby lawn, hands between his legs. The tears were close but didn't quite form. I sat next to him, laughing.

He looked at me with anger. "You are mean. Why are you laughing?"

"Peter, remember the log I told you to stay off of a few weeks ago?" He nodded. "Remember a few minutes ago when I told you to sit back down. And why?"

He nodded and smiled with one corner of his mouth. "I did it again, didn't I?"

I smiled back. "Yeah, you did. How are you feeling?"

"Better. Thank goodness for the padding on the bar. But how did you know?"

"I did the same thing as a kid and there wasn't any padding on the bar back then." Peter winced. "In fact, I did it more than once before I learned. I was laughing, Kiddo, because what I predicted, happened."

"Why don't I listen, Jake?"

"I've told you before: You're no angel. You're a normal six-year-old boy. You'll do it again. But sooner or later, you'll learn."

"It wasn't nice of you to laugh."

"You're right. It wasn't." I rolled over and dug my fingers into his belly. "You ready to go?"

Both humbled, we both got on our bikes and rode off. We stopped at every creek and marsh we came to. We stopped and watched men build a new house for a while. Sometimes we stopped to give the older boy a break.

By the time we got home, he was as good a rider as Nat. We had had the time of our lives. I announced to Betty that Peter was a natural. He was proud of himself, but told Betty what happened; and that I tried to warn him, but he didn't listen.

"Did you learn your lesson?" she asked.

At the same time he answered yes, I said, "I doubt it." Peter and I looked at each other and laughed. "You know me too well, Jake."

"I don't like to see you get hurt, Kiddo, but sometimes that's the best way to learn."

"Can we ride this afternoon?"

"Aren't you getting a little tired?"

"No way!"

I winked at Betty and told Peter, "I was afraid you were going to say that. Hey, I've got an idea. How about we ride over to the school you'll be visiting in a couple of weeks?"

"Can we? Do you think we can go in? Will Mrs. Pryor be there? Will Mr. Stewart be there? Can I see my classroom? Do you think..."

I put my hand over his mouth as both Betty and I laughed. "The answer to your first question is yes. For the rest, we'll just have to wait until we get there. Shall we go or would you rather take a nap?"

The look I got in answer, I expected. Without answering my stupid question, he was up and on his way. "Guess he doesn't want to take a nap," I said to Betty, laughing. "See you later."

We rode from one side of the village to the other. I reminded him how the traffic signal worked and how we always walk our bikes across intersections. We passed the

The Gift

middle school and headed up to the primary school. It was smaller than the middle school but a whale of a lot bigger than the one-room school house he wanted to attend in Slippery Gulch. The cars in the parking lot told us it was open. We parked our bikes at the front door and walked in.

Upon entering the building, Peter stopped dead in his tracks. He'd been in large buildings before, but this one was different: It was kid friendly. Directly in front of him was a water fountain. He ran to it and got a drink without having to be lifted. He looked around for a long minute before turning to me. "Jake, this is really neat! Come on, let's keep looking."

I grabbed his hand. "We have to check in at the office."

I introduced Peter and myself to the secretary and explained that he would be coming to school here in September.

Before she could reply, Mr. Stewart emerged from his office. "Mr. Winters, Peter! You've come for a tour of the school?"

"Hadn't thought about that. We were out riding our bikes and decided to come over. Peter has never seen anything like this before. A tour would be great! Is Mrs. Pryor here?"

"Yes, she is. Come along. Peter, I'll show you the room you'll be in."

Peter was so excited he had to stop at the restroom first. When he came out, he said full of excitement, "Jake, you've got to come in here. You're not going to believe this." He took my hand and led me in with Mr. Stewart following us. "Look, the sinks and urinals are my size and look at this." He pushed a stall door open and said, "See, even the toilet fits me," where upon he sat down to demonstrate. For the first time, his toes touched the floor and he wouldn't have to worry about falling in.

"Wow, Kiddo. It's as if everything in here was built for you."

"I know. This is awesome!"

Back in the hall we turned to our right. As we walked down the hall, Peter took everything in with wide eyes. Mr. Stewart and I loved Peter's enthusiasm. When we got to the second room from the end on the left, Mr. Stewart stopped. "Peter, this will be your room."

Immediately, Mrs. Pryor walked out to join us. "Peter, Mr. Winters, so nice to see both of you again." She shook our hands, Peter's first. "Please, come in."

As we walked in, Peter's eyes opened even wider. "Jake, look, the chairs are my size, too! What's this?" he asked looking at a desk in front of the chair.

"That's a desk. The week you are here, you will have your very own. The students do their work on them," she said walking over to it. She lifted the top. "The students keep their supplies in here."

"I'll have my own desk, Mrs. Pryor?"

"That's right." Pulling out the chair, she added, "And chair. Here, have a seat."

He cautiously sat as if afraid he may break it. "Wow, Jake! This is really neat!" Suddenly he spotted the thirty-gallon aquarium in the back of the room. "Wow! What is that?"

Mrs. Pryor took his hand and led him to the aquarium as she slowly explained the tank. Pointing out the different fish, she said over her shoulder to me, "I wish all my students were this enthusiastic."

"As a former teacher – and a current one, now that I think about it, I understand where you're coming from. You have to remember though: This little guy has been waiting over a century to go to school. He's one motivated customer."

The Gift

After ten minutes Mr. Stewart led us down to the gym. Mr. Stewart explained the use of the huge room. Peter kept repeating one word – wow!

Two large ropes hung down from the ceiling, so I asked Peter if he could climb one of them to the ceiling?

"Sure!"

Mr. Stewart looked at him, and then told us that not many kids who've practiced for weeks could do that. Peter insisted that he could. I looked at the principal and nodded approval. Mr. Stewart was hesitant, but the two of us dragged a mat from the stack and placed it under the longer rope.

Peter put his hands on it to begin, but I stopped him. "Peter, listen to me. I know what I'm talking about. When you come down, go hand over hand just as you did going up. Don't slide down or you'll end up with very bad rope burns on your hands and on the inside of your thighs. Do you hear me?"

I looked at the principal. "He has excellent hearing, but at times I have to be sure he's listening."

Mr. Stewart chuckled. "What's new with boys?"

I nodded. "Okay, Kiddo, do it." Peter scampered to the top without even slowing. Now the principal whispered, "I'll be darned!" as he stared at the ceiling. I said, "Fantastic, Kiddo! Now remember, hand over hand coming down." He did that very thing until he was five feet from my reach. In his five-foot slide into my waiting arms, he turned his hands and thighs red and hot.

Shaking his hands and rubbing his thighs, close to tears, he said, "I see what you mean."

Mr. Stewart glanced at Peter's red hands and asked, "Peter, did you use your ghostly powers to do that?"

"No sir. I can't. That would be cheating."

"Mr. Stewart, the doctor said Peter has the strength and coordination of a nine- or ten-year-old, though he appears to be a toddler by today's standards. His weight is thirty pounds. Put that together with his strength and coordination and physically, he's surprising. But then he's surprising in many other ways, too."

He laughed, shook his head and agreed. I took Peter into the locker room where I had him hold his hands under cold water while I held cold, wet paper towels against his thighs. "I was proud of you the way you climbed that rope, Kiddo, but the only reason we're in here now is because you didn't listen to me again. It could have been worse though. At least you came down the correct way most of the way."

"Will I ever listen Jake, or will I always have to learn the hard way?"

I smiled. "Sometimes you'll listen, but sometimes you'll learn the hard way. How do your hands and legs feel?"

"Better. I'm sure glad I had my shorts on." I laughed as we rejoined Mr. Stewart. As Peter wandered around the gym looking at things, I assured Mr. Stewart he would not have to worry about Peter using his ghostly powers during his week in school. After some discussion, he brought up another concern. Hesitantly he said, "I couldn't help but notice that he's not wearing underwear. I think while he's in school, he should."

"I agree," I said. "While alive, he never wore them. In fact, he knew nothing about them. He's had trouble adjusting to them. But I assure you, he will be sporting underwear."

Mr. Stewart chuckled knowingly as he opened the door to let us out to the playground behind and to the right of the school.

As Peter and I walked out to the impressive playground, I was about to bring up the underwear problem. But he exclaimed, "Jake, this is really great! If I really like it, do you think I could go for another two or three weeks?"

"Well, there's a couple of problems with that, Kiddo. First, I don't think they'd let you."

Before I had a chance to explain, he put his head down and said softly, "Why? Because I'm too stupid?"

I stopped dead in my tracks, knelt down in front of him and exploded. I grabbed him by the arms and shook him. "No, damn it."

Immediately, I wished I could take back my words and actions. Once again I spoke and acted before I thought. Peter's lower lip was quivering and his tears were instantaneous. He was trembling. He had never heard me swear, especially at him. I picked him up and hugged him.

"Peter, I'm sorry. I didn't mean to lose my temper. It's just that I'm frustrated. You've been told your entire life you're too stupid to do this and that, but you're not. I – and others, have told you countless times how smart you are, yet you won't believe us. You were told you were ugly. You can look in a mirror and see you're not. Problem is, there is no magic mirror to look in to see yourself as intelligent."

"I'm sorry, Jake. I know I should believe you, but it's hard." Though crying, he was no longer trembling.

"I know. Look, the one-week idea is a favor to me. The other problem is that after that one week, I have to go back on the road. I have no doubt Betty and Jerry would be more than willing to keep you while I'm on the road, but it would mean we wouldn't be together for six or seven weeks."

He looked at me in shock, wiping at the tears. "I forgot about that. I don't care how much fun it is; we have to be together. We're meant to be together."

"Am I forgiven?"

He gave me a hug. "Yes." I stuck a finger between two ribs and put him down. He began to run around the playground, free as the wind.

A half-hour later we were back on our bikes. As we rode along, he asked, "Jake, what would you do if I swore at you?"

I looked at him. "You know what the answer should be, right?" He nodded. "However, if you ever became as frustrated with me as I got with you, I couldn't spank you and be fair. But don't test it."

He laughed. "I thought that would be your answer because you're fair, but I won't."

"Then again, if you were to test it, there is the old fashion soap cure that my mother used on me."

He chuckled. "What's the soap cure? Take a bath when you don't need one?"

"No, worse still. I think I'll just keep that one to myself for now. I got your attention."

When we got home, he talked non-stop about his latest experience. What would it be like after his first day in school?

CHAPTER EIGHTEEN

We went to church on Sunday. The first time Peter went to church with us shortly after we got home in July, he was frightened. The minister in Slippery Gulch would not allow Peter into the church because he said Peter was not good enough for God. Therefore Peter was afraid he would not be allowed in our church either. He discovered his fear was unfounded. Now he was not concerned. In fact he was looking forward to Sunday school for the promise that other children would be there. Unfortunately, the two scheduled teachers were absent, so the class was canceled.

After Peter got a nod from me, he went up to the front of the church for the children's sermon and sat with the rest of the kids. To set up his talk, our pastor asked how many children had traveled to states outside New York State. Ten hands and one voice spoke up – Peter's. "Jake and I have." Then to how many were born in another state, Peter confirmed this by raising his hand. When the minister opened his mouth to continue, a wee voice called out, "I was born in Montana." There were chuckles all across the congregation.

During the rest of the service, Peter remained silent but his behavior was far from composed. He was a typical six-year-old boy with pent-up, late morning energy. Sometimes just his arms or legs moved; at other times he moved all four at once. For a while he was first on my lap and then on Betty's. He knelt on the floor. Then he sat on the floor examining the texture of the rug.

He surprised me when after the minister's statement, "Jesus knew these people by their fruits," he asked in a whisper from the floor, "Were they fruit farmers?"

Now I realized he could listen regardless of his body configuration. We were seated near the center aisle. So when the acolyte passed by carrying the lit candle, Peter walked into the aisle and extinguished it with a huge blast of air. Those not in closed-eyes prayer saw it and either snickered or muffled their mouths to stifle outright guffaws. I let him know he was never to do that again.

The next two weeks went by quickly. On good days we went riding, swimming at the park or hiking in the woods. Rainy days we spent playing indoor games, reading, visiting friends and doing other indoor activities. I spent several nights out. During those times, I left Peter with Betty or Danny. Although he was better, he still was not completely comfortable.

The Friday before school began, Nat came over to invite Peter to ride bikes together. He needed to spend time with someone closer to his age, so I approved. Peter was at first excited; then a trace of worry came over him. I quickly added, "Now don't stay too long. And Peter, listen to Nat, okay?" He assured me he would and out the door they scrambled.

About forty-five minutes later, as I was reading about the new football season, I heard him call. "Oh, Peter must be home," I said to Betty. I went to the door and looked into the garage, but neither Peter nor his bike was there.

Betty gave me a strange look. "Did you hear him?" she asked.

"I thought I did." I looked out the back window to see if he was in the backyard. He wasn't.

"Didn't you hear him?"

"No! I never heard a thing."

Just then I heard his pleading voice, "Jake, help!"

I went running outside and yelled his name, but there was no answer. By now Betty had joined me. "You heard him that time, didn't you?"

Shaking her head no she said, "Jake, what's going on?"

I asked out loud, "Peter, where are you?"

He answered in a quivering voice, "In the woods off Hunters Creek Road."

I looked at Betty. "You didn't hear his answer, did you?"

She shook her head, looking at me as if I were nuts. "I've got to find him. He's hurt."

Quickly, she joined me in the van. We headed for the bike trails at the end of Hunters Creek Road. When I stopped, we yelled into the woods for both Peter and Nat. Nat yelled back from the trail. "Over here Mr. Winters. Peter's hurt." Nathan motioned us toward them.

Peter was lying on his right side. "I knew you'd come. I did it again, Jake. I didn't listen."

"Let's not worry about that now. Where do you hurt?"

Whimpering and holding his right wrist he said, "My right arm hurts real bad. I think it's broken."

I put him on his back and examined his arm. I suspected a hairline fracture as I gathered him up and headed for the van. Betty and Nat brought the two bikes. As we walked back to the road, Nat intoned tearfully. "It's all my fault, Mr. Winters. I should never have brought him over here."

"That's all right. I was going to bring him over here tomorrow myself. Did you see what happened?"

"Yeah. I showed him how to take the jump. I told him to stay in his seat going up the ramp, then stand when he got to the top, but he stood going up the ramp. His left foot slipped off the pedal and he lost it."

"I'm not surprised." I got Peter into the van, then the two bikes so Nat could go with us.

Once home in Betty's kitchen, I gingerly examined Peter's arm. It generated a lot of pain just above the wrist. Betty helped me wrap it in ice.

As we were doing so, I said, "Peter, you called me, didn't you." He nodded, afraid he might be in trouble. "How did you do that?"

"I don't know. I just called you in my mind. I knew you'd hear me. Then you asked me where I was and I told you. Are you mad?"

"No! Well, surely not for that." He put his head down. "So if we're separated and one of us is in trouble, we can contact each other?"

"I guess." He paused then got to the big question, "Jake, are you going to spank me?" His concern bordered on dread.

Betty looked at me too.

"Peter, you deserve it and you know it." He nodded and let his head down. "You don't like being spanked. And I hate to spank you. So, no!"

His head shot up. "You're not?"

"No!" I stood up and walked to the kitchen door. With my back to Peter, I said, "Many people have seen the first picture I took of you. In your eyes everybody saw sadness, loneliness and fright." I turned and walked to him and knelt down to be at eye level. "But I now believe that God let me see something deeper. I wasn't able to identify it until our camping trip. What I'd seen from the first was an appeal for hope in your eyes. That's the first picture I took of you but not the first picture that's permanently etched in my memory."

Both of them studied me, a bit confused. "During my first trip to Slippery Gulch, you ran out from the alley, bumped into me and fell to the ground. I turned and looked down at you. What I saw unnerved me. Sure, a filthy and neglected little boy. Sad, lonely and frightened eyes stared back at me. There was that subtle appeal to hope. It came across to me one other time – when I got ready to spank you in the truck – after you stole the candy to test me. You were begging me not to beat you. You were scared and desperate. I saw unabashed despair in your eyes. Hopelessness! I never spanked you again. That doesn't mean I won't. And it doesn't mean you're getting off scott-free this time. Your bike is off-limits for the rest of the weekend and outside is off-limits for the rest of the day. There'll be no spanking… this time"

Both Betty and I watched him closely. He was relieved. He knew he had it coming. He glanced out the door. Boyish disappointment took over, naturally. "That's fair. I'm sorry I disobeyed you again. I thought if I got a little more speed, I could jump farther than Nat. I think I finally learned my lesson."

I laughed. "I certainly hope so. At least you didn't tell me you thought you should go back to Slippery Gulch." As I studied him, he had dirt from his right shin to his right shoulder with a minor brush burn on his right knee. "You are a mess. Are you sore anyplace besides your arm?"

"My right knee, hip and shoulder are all a little sore, but not bad. I hit a rock with my head when I fell. I know why I'm supposed to wear a helmet now." He smiled his sheepish grin.

"Well, now you're growing up. Experience does have its way with us boys, especially."

After cleaning him, we took it easy for the rest of the day. Later I joined Betty to read the paper on the back porch. Suddenly Peter joined us, too. "What are you doing out here?"

He looked at me, puzzled. "Remember, outdoors is off-limits to you today." His expression went from puzzlement to sadness but he put his head down, turned around and walked back inside. I didn't have to see his face to know there were tears forming. I was rejecting him. The problem I had in punishing Peter is that often I felt as bad, if not worse, than he did. I was going to let him sit for one hour by himself. I only made it thirty minutes.

I found him right where I expected him to be – lying on the family room floor. He was sad and lonely. I lay down next to him and pulled him on top of me. He put his head down on my chest. My shirt was soon wet from tears. As I rubbed his back he asked, "Jake, why don't I listen?"

"We've been through this before, Little One. You're six, you're a boy and you're a fun-loving little kid with the devil in your eye." He bobbed up and down as I laughed. "And I love you for it. Nobody can say you're boring. Yet when you misbehave or don't listen, you have to understand there will be consequences."

"What does cons-a-gences mean?"

I gave him a chance to get it right. "When you misbehave or don't listen, something is going to happen. You may get into trouble or you may get hurt. Today both happened."

He thought about this. "But you love me anyway?"

"Peter, I will always love you. As I've said before, you're no angel and I'm glad you're not. But more than anyone else, I know about the suffering you went through in Slippery Gulch. As a result, I hate to see you suffer in any way. When you suffer, I suffer."

"I hate to see you suffer, too, Jake. I cause you to suffer more than anyone else. Maybe I should…"

I put my hand over his mouth. "Peter, most of the time you're smiling, laughing, jumping, skipping, hopping, and running. You only suffer because you're a normal boy and that is why I love you so much; but Peter, you're not going back to Slippery Gulch without me." I moved my hand to the back of his head then kissed it. He awkwardly tilted his head toward mine and gave me his beautiful smile. Then he put his head back on my chest.

After a minute I asked, "By the way, how's your arm?" I was too late; he was asleep.

As expected, the next morning his arm was fine. Of course there was no bike riding on Saturday or Sunday. I could have ridden my bike with Nathan on Saturday but that would have gone beyond mean to cruel. I just couldn't do that to Peter.

The evening before school started, he was extremely excited and a little nervous. During bath time he wanted me to wash his entire body to make sure he was really clean. I assured him he would do a fine job himself. I did wash his hair. I'd forgotten to bring up the underwear problem, so I mentioned it then. I told him it was the school's dress code. Although he wasn't happy about it, he accepted it.

After his bath, we went downstairs to visit Betty and Jerry. He talked non-stop until he ran out of steam and fell asleep. However, it didn't last. He was too wound up. Upon awaking, I suggested he sleep with me for the rest of the night. He was delighted. The two of us went back upstairs and he slept soundly for the rest of the night.

The next morning, he was strangely quiet as we pulled into the parking lot of the school. "Peter, are you okay?"

At first he didn't say a thing. Finally, came, "Jake, I'm scared…well, a little scared."

I smiled. "Good! That means you're normal." He gave me a funny look. "Every kid is nervous on his first day. If you weren't, I'd be worried. I was nervous my first day, too."

"You were? But you were a teacher."

"I wasn't when I was a little kid, but that brings up a good point. I was very nervous the first day of school every year I was a teacher, and I'm sure Mrs. Pryor is nervous today, too. A teacher never knows what he or she is going to end up with in his or her classroom. Maybe a room full of jerks! Think of it, Mrs. Pryor will have a little ghost to start her year off this year."

He chuckled. "Yeah, I see what you mean. Will you walk in with me?"

"You bet I will." As we did, children and adults were scurrying around in all different directions. We made our way through the congested halls to Peter's room.

About half the kids were there. As we walked in, Mrs. Pryor came right up to us. She shook my hand and ruffled Peter's hair, then called two little boys to the front of the room. "Peter, this is Craig and Jamie. They will be your guides for the week. They will make sure you get to every place you are supposed to be."

Greg was a chubby youngster with glasses, blond hair and brown eyes. He was at least six inches taller than Peter and outweighed him by thirty pounds.

Jamie was only two inches taller than Peter and weighed perhaps forty pounds. He was a handsome boy with dark brown hair and blue eyes.

The three sized each other up before Jamie said, "Is it true you ride around the country with your grandpa in an 18-wheeler?" Peter beamed with pride and nodded. "Cool! I wish I could do that. Come on. Got something to show you."

Halfway across the room, Peter turned around, waved with a big smile on his face and said as an afterthought, "Bye, Grandpa."

I waved to Peter weakly as he turned away. Mrs. Pryor looked at me sympathetically, patted my arm and said, "He'll be fine."

"Thanks for everything. I'll be back at three." I went home and became what I always thought only women were – a nervous wreck – for the rest of the day. I figured Peter was getting on better than I was. I went over and spent a couple of hours with a semi-retired friend of mine.

He knew about Peter and was aware it was Peter's first day at school. He couldn't help but laugh at me. "You're worst than my wife was the first day my oldest went to school. Peter will be fine."

I chuckled. "Yeah, but your daughter wasn't a ghost."

"You keep reminding us that Peter's as mortal as the rest of us. Maybe you should settle for that."

He was right, but it didn't help me much.

Finally it was time. I sat in the school parking lot, biting my nails for ten minutes before going in. I walked up to his room and waited outside with several mothers. Finally the door opened and kids filed out, all with smiles on their faces. Many wore sneakers with lights on them that lit in different patterns as they walked. Greg looked at me, smiled and waved but Jamie came over. "Peter's a really a neat kid, Mr. Winters. He's fun. Got to catch up to my mom. She's down at the office. See ya!" Jamie's perpetual motion never gave me a chance to respond. All I could do was laugh in relief. The important thing was I got the opinion from a child expert – Peter's a neat kid.

Peter was the last to come out and jumped into my arms with a huge smile on his face. "I guess you had a good day."

He was non-stop talk until Mrs. Pryor was free to turn her attention to us. She sent Peter back into the room and began. "Peter had a wonderful day. He got along well with the children, however I had a feeling he was bored at times. Is that possible?"

I thought about this. "Yes, I suppose it is. He was probably expecting to get right into reading and other subjects the first day. He's always eager to learn new things."

"Do you have any idea the level of his reading skills?"

"Lance had Peter read a couple books in his office two weeks ago. The second book he read was advanced second grade, but Lance didn't have him go on. We've been reading the last two weeks. He's showing steady improvement all along."

"But he couldn't pick up another grade level in just two weeks."

"Don't bet on it. He's a dream student. He's very motivated and highly intelligent."

She laughed skeptically. "Perhaps you're right. Give me a minute: I'll be right back."

In the classroom I found Peter standing by the aquarium nervously playing with his hands. "Am I in trouble?"

"Of course not. Where's your desk?"

"Over there," he pointed excitedly. "You want to see it?"

"I sure do." He proudly led me to one of the many miniature desks. He opened it and pointed to his variety of supplies: Some were his and some were school provisions. Just then Mrs. Pryor walked in carrying several books. She did not interrupt until she was certain Peter had proudly completed explaining things to me.

"Peter, would you be willing to read from a couple of books for me?"

Walking up to her desk he said, "sure", with a big smile on his face. Upon seeing the first book, he announced he'd already read it. She looked perplexed. "When?"

He looked at me.

"Four or five weeks ago, I think."

"Read the first page anyway." Looking slightly bored, he read the first page of what amounted to not much more than a picture book. She put that one away and went to the next one. "Have you read this one, too?" She asked. He shook his head. He read one page, again flawlessly. She took out the last book and had him read from it. He struggled but was able to sound out all hard words but one. Mrs. Pryor helped him and turned to me with lips minus sounds, communicated: "Amazing!"

"Mr. Winters, since you were able to teach Peter to read this well in just six weeks, you are a very fine reading teacher."

Peter smiled. I looked at Mrs. Pryor and said, "I wish I could take credit. I guess I can take some, but Peter is gifted with a good mind and a willing spirit."

"You deserve all the credit, Jake," Peter piped up. "It's true, Mrs. Pryor, I always wanted to read. But Jake bought me just the right books." He looked at me. "You always encouraged me. When I didn't want to read, you never made me. And when I wanted to read for two hours, you sat with me." Peter paused. "When I was discouraged and ready to give up, you wouldn't let me. You told me we'd do it together. And we did."

Mrs. Pryor was looking at me a bit misty-eyed.

I realized Peter was alluding to the dreams and other fears we'd fought through together. And won! Just as I had hoped, his success in conquering his fears flowed over to his success with reading.

"I appreciate that, Peter. But it was you who did the hard job. I was just there to guide and help you."

Peter and I were on the same page, so to speak, and we knew it. And I sensed Mrs. Pryor knew she'd been privy to a special interchange between Peter and me just now.

She spoke up. "I think you both deserve a lot of credit. The last book Peter read is advanced third grade. Academically, Peter should be in the third grade. He's very mature for his age and size, but due to his size, he wouldn't fit in there. Mr. Winters, what do you wish for Peter to get out of this week with me?"

"Well, for one thing, a little teacher-mothering. You know how female teachers have a special place in a boy's heart at this age. Peter, of course, never knew his mother."

Peter looked at me intently. "But more than anything, I want Peter to have a positive experience in here. Especially, in adapting to other supervised children his own age while I'm not around. Then, too, I want him to experience a modern public school, just as you and I did."

"Great! Then this week can be a success for Peter." Mrs. Pryor squatted down before her latest new student. "A lot is going to depend on you, Peter. You may be more advanced or ahead in some ways than the other children in this class. You could tease them and laugh at some of them making them feel stupid. But I observed today that you are not that kind of boy. You want to make friends with them. And they clearly want to make friends with you.

"As the week goes along, I will be asking the class a lot of questions. I suspect you will be able to answer most of them. If you raise your hand to answer all of them, it will build resentment among the other children. Do you understand what I'm saying?"

"Mrs. Pryor, I know what it's like to have enemies. That's all I ever had, until now." He looked at me and smiled.

"I know how it feels to be teased and hated. I would never do that to anybody. I understand what you're saying."

Mrs. Pryor could not resist. She gathered the little guy in her arms, and now I was fighting emotion. I also realized why I was drawn to this lady, who, after all, was wearing a wedding ring and was almost twenty years younger than I. It was her motherly way with Peter. My little boy! No wonder I wanted a small place for her in my heart, too.

Peter slowly put his arms around Mrs. Pryor's neck. Then he released them and came to me to be lifted. In my arms, he continued. "Jake knows how I used to be called stupid. And I believed them." Peter gave me a hug.

She looked at Peter with newfound respect and awe. She stroked the back of Peter's head and smiled. "Peter, are you really six or are you forty but trapped in a six-year-old body?"

I laughed. "I've asked that question more than once myself. Suffice to say, Mrs. Pryor, Peter never had a childhood. He had no time for one. He was too busy trying to survive in a hostile place. Now his childhood is beginning. The upside is, his rough past has matured him well beyond his years. And I need to tell you a secret about Peter." Peter's head shot off my shoulder and his eyes burned into mine. "He's cute right now, but you should see how ugly he is first thing in the morning." Peter banged his fist down on my shoulder.

"Ja-a-a-ke!"

He giggled and punched me lightly on the chest. "I am not!" I stuck a finger between two ribs. Peter's infectious laughter got both of us going.

"Peter, I think you'll get along fine this week," Mrs. Pryor said. She paused for a moment in thought. "Would you be willing, sometime this week, to tell the class what it's like to ride all over the country in a truck?"

Excitedly he said, "Sure! That'd be fun!" He looked around the room, wheels of his own turning in his mind. "Can I stand up there by your desk when I tell them?"

"May...I stand up there?" After her correction, Peter corrected himself. She said yes.

"Wow, Jake! I get to be a student in a real school this week, but I even get to be a teacher for a few minutes."

Both Mrs. Pryor and I laughed. I put him down. "Well, Funny Face, how about you and I head for home and ride for a while? Ma-a-aybe tonight you can practice your speech."

His excitement never ceased. "Yeah! Okay! Hey, Jake, may I ride the bus tomorrow?"

I'd already cleared that. "You bet!"

"Oh by the way, Mr. Winters," Mrs. Pryor added, "Wednesday the class has gym. Please send Peter in with an extra pair of shorts and another shirt."

"Sure, and do the children take showers?"

"That starts in the fourth grade."

"Why the fourth grade?" Peter shot back.

"Many of the children can't dry themselves properly yet. Can you?"

"Sure!" He answered proudly. "Jake taught me." He gave me a smile.

We said good-bye to Mrs. Pryor.

As we headed for the car, he said, "Jake, remember those goofy-looking shorts I tried on once?" He was referring to shorts that went down below his knees. He objected to them being to long. "May I get a pair of them?"

"Sure, but why the change of attitude toward them?"

"I don't know. Everybody thinks they're cool."

"Do you?"

The Gift

"Not really." He put his head down.

"But you want to be cool, too?"

He played with his hands. "I guess."

"Hey, Kiddo, there's nothing wrong with wanting to fit in as long as it doesn't change you in here." I put my hand on my chest. "Did some of the kids tease you about the shorts you were wearing today?"

"No, I just thought it would be neat to look more like them."

So Peter was beginning to pick up on the power of peer pressure. "Tell you what. Let's head for the store now."

He smiled.

We pulled into the parking lot. Once in the store, I asked if he wanted to ride in the cart. He looked around then shook his head. He loved riding. Maybe he thought he would meet up with one of the kids from school.

The type of shorts he was looking for were half-off because it was the end of the season. I had him look through them and pick out the pair he liked the best and head into the changing room. He put them on, looked at himself in the mirror and grunted, "I still think they look goofy. But everybody else thinks they're cool. I guess I better take them."

"You know, Kiddo, you don't have to look like everybody else. If you look like yourself, you could stand out as an individual."

"I stood out from everybody else in Slippery Gulch, and they laughed at me."

I was going to point out that nobody laughed at him here, but I knew his fear. "I understand. Why don't you pick out three more? You're going to be there all week."

"Are you sure?"

"Of course, I'm sure. Put your own shorts back on and leave the new ones in here." As he was changing back, I said, "By the way, how did you get along with your underpants today?"

"They drove me nuts. But I don't think I grabbed myself down there very much."

I chuckled. "Well that's good." I decided not to mention them for the rest of the week. Maybe he'd get used to them. He picked three more pair of shorts. "You'd better try those on."

From there we went over to the shoe department. "What are we doing over here?"

"You only have one pair of sneakers. If they get wet, you'd have to wear your hiking boots to school. That wouldn't look cool. I think we should get you another pair. You pick them out. I don't know what kids are wearing today."

We walked down a row of miniature sneakers until we got to Peter's size. He looked at several then removed a pair with lights on them. Inwardly I smiled. "I like these, Jake. Should I try them on?"

"Sure, go ahead."

He sat on the floor and put the new ones on. As he walked down the aisle I said, "Hey, something's wrong with those things. They light up as you walk."

He giggled. "They're supposed to. They have lights on them."

"Lights! Why do you need lights on your sneakers? If it's dark out, use a flashlight."

He started laughing. "Jake, they're not to see with. They just look neat when I walk. They're cool."

"Oh! Do all the kids have this kind of sneaker?"

"Not all, but a lot."

The Gift

"So these are the ones you want?" He smiled and nodded.

After paying for Peter's cool, new shorts and sneakers, we headed for home. In the parking lot, he looked at me and said, "Thanks, Grandpa. You understand everything so well."

"Sure, Kiddo. It wouldn't be right to have an uncool ghost in a cool first grade class."

That evening, Peter stood before Betty, Jerry and me to practice what he planned to say to his classmates later in the week. When he finished, we clapped and I said it was good.

However, an old fear surfaced. "Jake, what if the kids laugh at me?"

"Well, some of the things you just said were funny. We laughed and so will they. Just keep in mind, they will be laughing at what you say, not at you. I think you'll get along fine."

That night I woke up to hear Peter laughing. I turned on the light and watched the fruit of some wonderful dream unfolding. The dream ended and I went back to sleep.

CHAPTER NINETEEN

Tuesday morning, Peter walked out to the bus with Nat, unbelievably excited. It was his first ride in a school bus. Nat was his guide and felt as important as Peter was excited. Nat was also going to make sure Peter got on the right bus after school.

At one point, I noticed Nat look at Peter's shorts and sneakers. As I stood in the front window, I saw Peter touch his right thigh, then he turned around and gave me a smile and a thumbs-up. The shorts and sneakers were a hit.

That afternoon, I was at the bus stop waiting for him, hoping he got on the right one. He leaped from the last step of the bus into my arms. "I guess the day went pretty good, right?"

"Yeah, and tomorrow I give my speech! And we have gym!"

"That's great! You'd better practice again tonight." I looked at Nathan. "Nat, thank you. You're an excellent guide." He couldn't have felt more important.

When I put Peter down, I expected him to take my hand but instead he put both his hands in his pockets and swaggered toward the driveway. I noticed both sneakers were untied. I guess my first grade ghost was now cool. I managed to direct him onto the grass and once there, I stepped on his sneaker lace. He fell flat on his face. He rolled over, wiped some grass off his right knee and said with anger in his eyes, "Hey, you did that on purpose."

I sat down next to him. "You're right, I did. But if your sneakers had been tied, I couldn't have done that."

"Yeah, but Jake, you don't understand. Tied sneakers aren't cool."

Well, that's interesting. Yesterday I understood everything and today I don't understand a thing. "Peter, it isn't cool to do something that could cause you or someone else injury. If you would have fallen on the driveway, more than just your pride could have been hurt. That's why I directed you onto the grass. I wanted to point out something without hurting you. As you well know, us truckers never try and do anything that could hurt ourselves or someone else, because that isn't cool."

"Yeah, but having my sneakers untied isn't going to hurt anybody."

"Oh, really? All the kids walk around with their sneakers untied?" He nodded. "Well let me give you a hypothetical situation."

He looked at me. "A what?"

I laughed. "A hypothetical situation. In other words, I'm going to think of something that could happen." I thought for a moment. "Let's say you're all going to lunch. Jamie is at the head of the line, you're next and Greg is right behind you, with the rest of the class behind him. You have your sneakers untied. Greg accidentally steps on your untied lace and you fall into Jamie. Jamie falls down and you land on top of him. Greg trips over you and lands on both of you. Then the next ten kids in line trip and land on all of you. Poor Jamie is at the bottom of the pile. Do you think he'd get up laughing and praise you for being cool?"

He digested this whole scenario. "No. He'd be hurt and crying. Greg and I would probably be hurt too and maybe some others, too." After a pause he continued. "It would be my fault, wouldn't it?" I nodded. He brought one foot up then the other and tied his sneakers. Then he sat there thinking. "So being cool is okay sometimes, but not all the time?"

"Right! You have to think of all the ramifications. Sometimes that's hard to do."

"The what?"

Again I laughed. "In other words, you have to think of all the things that could happen. Remember when you were sawing the log when we were camping and I insisted you put your gloves on?" He nodded. "That's what I mean. It may have been cool to saw the log without gloves, but not very smart. You've got to think of what could happen and protect yourself and others in case it does."

"How come you're so smart?"

"It comes with age and experience, Kiddo and you're having some great experiences."

He smiled. "Could you say those two big words again?"

"You mean hypothetical and ramification?"

"Yeah." He tried both of them several times and finally got them both. He was developing quite an impressive vocabulary.

That evening, Peter practiced his speech again. He planned to take in a scale model of a company truck I had at home so he could explain a number of different things about the truck. He also planned to mention some of the CB lingo and what it meant. He was well prepared and confident. I was proud of him.

The next afternoon as he got off the bus, I immediately asked how it went. He shrugged his shoulders. "Okay, I guess," he said as he stuck his hands in his pockets and swaggered towards the house. At least his sneakers were tied. Since he was not a bragger, I took that as meaning, great! But I wasn't going to let him get away with that.

As we were walking up the driveway, I grabbed him, threw him gently into the grass, sat on his legs and held his arms above his head. "You little stinker. I want to know.

How did it go? Tell me now or I'm going to unbutton your belly button." I pulled his shirt up.

Laughing, he said, "Okay! Okay! They loved it. You were right again, Jake. The kids laughed a lot but they weren't laughing at me. They had a lot of questions, too. I could answer all of them. It was a lot of fun. They wanted to know if the next time we're home, we could drive the truck to school. Do you think we could?"

"I'll have to talk to Mrs. Pryor and Mr. Stewart about that, but it's possible."

I let go of his arms and started to get up. Lying with his arms still over his head, he said, "Wait a minute. Aren't you going to unbutton my belly button?"

"I don't have to now. You told me what I wanted to know." He looked genuinely disappointed and was about to say something, when I slipped my hands under his shirt and pretended to rearrange his ribs. The two of us rolled in the grass for the next five minutes, laughing together.

CHAPTER TWENTY

As Peter was preparing for bed that night, I noticed he still had his underpants on. This was the third day in a row he'd worn them the entire day. Maybe underpants were now cool. I decided to keep my mouth shut and see how the rest of the week went.

That night, Mrs. Pryor called shortly after Peter went to sleep. She gave Peter rave reviews on his speech. At times she said, he had the entire class, including herself, in stitches. "He told the class about Hank and how he got to talk to him on the CB. He also told about the relationship you and Hank have and how funny you both are.

"He mentioned some CB lingo and what it meant, including, 'squirt the dirt,' but I'll get back to that in a minute. He talked a great deal about you and what a great driver and grandpa you are. He certainly worships the ground you walk on. He pointed out on the U.S. map many of the places you've been. He also told about the important part you played in saving the little girl in that accident in New Mexico."

"Did he say anything about the part he played?"

"He just said you told him to wait in the truck."

"Good! I'm glad he said that. I did tell him that, but after that he played the major role in the rescue." I began to relate the story.

About halfway through she said, "Oh, my goodness! Is that what the news reported as the miracle rescue on I-40?"

"That's it and Peter was the miracle." I then finished Peter's story, not mine.

"Mr. Winters, I don't think you have a ghost on your hands, rather a bona fide angel. Maybe your guardian angel."

From what Peter said while camping, I do have a guardian angel but it's not Peter.

"Since I have you on the phone, how did gym go for him today?"

"He didn't tell you?"

"No, but based on your question, I'm going to assume it went well. Peter's not a bragger. He lets other people do that for him."

"I usually don't go to gym with the children, but today I did. I was concerned he may not be able to keep up with the others. My concerns were unwarranted. Today was physical fitness tests. He was the fastest child in the running test and the strongest child in the strength test such as push-ups. There wasn't anything he couldn't do. He is the best-coordinated child in my class. The other children were jealous of him until his after-gym speech."

"That little peanut. He just will not talk about himself. But none of what you're saying surprises me."

"He's a wonderful child, Mr. Winters. How long is he going to be with you?"

I told her about the upcoming funeral for Peter in June and why. I told her I could lose him at that point forever.

She hesitated. "I don't think you will. If I'm right, he's yours until the end."

"That would be nice, but I honestly believe he's a ghost. You said you'd get back to the term, 'squirt the dirt.' I hope he didn't demonstrate."

She laughed. "Oh no, nothing like that. In the afternoon, at different times, three boys raised their hands and asked if they could 'squirt the dirt.' The first time it was cute; but when the third boy asked, I became annoyed. Peter realized that I was about to say something, when suddenly he jumped up on his chair and said, 'I'll handle this, Mrs. Pryor.' I was flabbergasted. I've never had a child do anything like that before.

"I was debating on how to react to him when he said, 'You guys can't say that. I just said that to demonstrate trucker's lingo. You have to be a trucker to say that. If my grandpa found out I told you, he might spank me. You wouldn't want that would you?' In unison they all shook their heads. I was fighting to keep from laughing. The respect all the children have for Peter on the first three days of school, for heaven's sake, is unbelievable. I've never seen anything like it.

"I told my husband last night, I hope no two boys decide to beat up on Peter. Being as small as he is, he could be a prime target. If a boy in the upper grades started to lay a hand on Peter, why, I think even the girls would jump the kid."

"Do you have any theories as to why people love him almost on sight? Is it his cute appearance?"

"Peter is special. Every child and teacher can feel it, but the ones I've talked to can't explain why. I'm beginning to. Peter has an aura around him. Nobody can see it, but everybody feels it. Sure, he's a natural leader, but it goes beyond that. He has the looks, the intelligence and the athletic ability of a champion, yet he doesn't lord it over others. He treats even the slowest child with kindness and respect. And he gets it back in spades. He's a wonderful child, Mr. Winters." She hesitated for a minute. "Mark my word: He's an angel, Mr. Winters. Maybe yours."

I sat there stunned. Would any trucker's guardian angel poop in their truck? And urinate on him like Peter did me? Angels don't get constipated that I know of, never having read the Old Testament much.

The Gift

Mrs. Pryor continued, pulling me out of my ruminations and back to the present. "He also talked about the word 'cool' and what it means."

Seems he'd given them the same speech I gave him. He even used my words "hypothetical" and "ramification." And told them what they meant.

"Tell me. Did he pronounce them correctly?"

"Yes, for heaven's sake! I was, as I said, flabbergasted several times today. Get this: He said, 'truckers are cool and my grandpa is too, but never at the expense of our safety or someone else's. So tie your shoes so you or someone else doesn't trip over them.' Immediately, the kids went to work tying their sneakers. I've been trying to figure out for years how to get the children to keep their sneakers tied. Peter accomplished the impossible in one speech. Did you talk to him about his sneakers yesterday?"

"Yes, I did."

"Well, he heard everything you said. And the vocabulary he has is remarkable."

"I've never talked down to him, Mrs. Pryor. Once I realized how intelligent he was, I demanded he move toward my level and he's done that."

"He certainly has. Talking about vocabulary, during recess today I walked by five boys sitting on the ground talking. Peter was one of them. As I was moving away from the group, I heard one of the boys use the F word. I turned around to confront the boys, but before I could, Peter took charge: 'Toby, that's a bad word. There are a lot of bad words. But good people don't use them. My grandpa never uses bad words and I don't either. And you shouldn't either.' I doubt if Toby will ever swear again.

"But let me go to one other thing. Some of the girls have been eyeing him pretty good and he seems to be sweet on one of them."

I laughed. "Oh? What's her name?"

"Tammy. And she is a dear girl."

Giving her a nasty laugh, I said, "Well, I'll have to make the most of this."

She laughed. "Well, he's won my heart. I could take him home with me, if you…well, yes, you know exactly what I mean."

"Mrs. Pryor, you are just what the doctor ordered."

"Just before I called, I told my husband that I'm going to miss him dearly next week when you two go back on the road."

CHAPTER TWENTY-ONE

The next morning I sat on the side of Peter's bed, waiting for him to wake up. Upon telling him how ugly he was, I got that beautiful ray of sunshine in return. My tickles woke him up for the rest of the day.

I put my hand on his chest. "Peter, Mrs. Pryor called last night." He looked worried. "Don't worry. You're not in trouble." He relaxed and rested his hands behind his head. "She told me how your day went yesterday. You certainly had everybody's attention during your speech and you even talked about being cool. Kiddo, I'm so proud of you I could spit."

He put his pillow over his face and plopped back down in bed. Then he popped his face out: "Thanks, Jake, for being a good teacher to me. I know how to be a little proud of myself without looking down on somebody else. Or being bratty about it."

"That's called humility and you've got it. But Peter, you're intelligent and you have the desire and willingness to learn. Without those qualities, no teacher could teach you anything, no matter how good he or she is with other students."

I paused. He knew something was coming. "I understand Toby used the F word."

He gave me a puzzled look. "How did you know?"

"I know all, Kiddo. I also know that you set that offending kid straight. You told him good people don't use bad words. Peter, I'm so proud of you I…"

He flopped back and pulled the pillow over his face again.

"Hey, what's with this disappearing act all of a sudden?"

"I'm not disappearing. I just don't want to get spit on by you."

We both laughed and I ruffled his hair. "Come on. Let's get you moving and ready for school." He was ready to take on the world of first grade again.

That evening Peter reported an uneventful day. But I knew better. That night, while on my lap, I primed him with, "Peter, I understand you have your eye on a little tomato."

He looked at me blankly. "I didn't see any tomatoes today."

"What's this I hear about, Tammy?"

He turned beet red. "I don't like her. She's a girl," he said in artificial disgust.

"That's not what I hear." I then stated the old mocking child's verse, "Tammy and Peter, sitting in a tree, k-i-s-s-i-n-g." He was getting upset with me, so I changed my approach. "Peter I'm glad you're making friends with girls as well as boys – because they make up about half the world – the prettier half." His blush returned. "And if you think one is prettier than another, that's natural, too, for a boy. But tell me this: What do you like about her besides her cute face?"

Still flushing, he mumbled, "I don't know, Jake."

"Does she seem to like you?"

"I think so." He put his head down in the fold of his arm for a minute. Then he looked up at me with one smiling eye. "Jake, could you do me a favor?"

"I will if I can, Kiddo."

"It's okay if you tease me about her, but only do it when you and I are alone, okay?"

"You bet. In fact I won't tease you at all about her if you don't want me too."

"No, that's okay. It's kind of fun…but not too much fun."

"Why not?"

"Jake, you know I want to be with you forever."

Suddenly I remembered myself at that age. I'd told Mom the same thing.

The last day, I was asked if I could come into school one hour before dismissal. I had no idea why. I learned later that Peter had been called to the principal's office at 10:00 that morning, to run some errands for Mr. Stewart. While he was gone, Mrs. Pryor and the children planned Peter's going-away party. At 1:45 he was sent to the office again. During that time a cake arrived at the classroom door from Tammy's mom.

I knew nothing of any of this until I walked in at 2:00 during Peter's absence. When Mrs. Pryor told me what was afoot, I was barely able to control my emotions.

Jamie, the spokesman for the children, informed me what I was to say when Peter returned. Meanwhile the kids hid around the room. At 2:10 Peter returned, escorted by Mr. Stewart. He never had a chance to say a thing. Standing with my hands on my hips, I said in mock anger, "I understand you were sent to the principal's office, young man. Would you mind explaining why?"

Peter looked around, confused. His eyes were turning red and getting some tears ready to be released. "I...he..." was as far as he got. The children jumped out from their hiding places yelling, "Surprise!" Peter was speechless. He looked at each beaming face of his classmates. Then to me he let out with a long, "Ja-a-a-ke!" I hiked my shoulders in ignorance.

Meanwhile, the children had formed into a group around him. (I noticed all of them had their sneakers tied.) I had to sit down in one of those tiny chairs before I fell down. The kids began singing, "For He's a Jolly Good Fellow."

At the conclusion, Mrs. Pryor directed Peter and me to a back table where the cake, in the shape of a big truck was set out. I picked Peter up so he could see it from a bird's eye view. On the trailer was written, "We love Peter. Come back soon. Keep the sunny side up."

Peter turned around to face his classmates, his eyes shining. Mrs. Pryor snapped a picture. Peter's smile was radiant. As I put him down, Craig and Jamie came up to him, putting their arms around his shoulders. The kids got quiet to hear what Jamie would say. "Nice having you, little brother. Come back and see us anytime you and your grandpa are back in town."

Coming out of his shock, Peter found his voice. "Everybody's so nice to me! Thank you everybody."

"Hey, you're cool, Peter."

Peter was overwhelmed. This week was more than what I could possibly have hoped for him, and I told Mrs. Pryor so in a note that I left on her desk when she was not looking. Not only did he find out from a real teacher that he was intelligent, he found a large group of children that liked him just because he was Peter. They didn't know me and I wasn't around them at all.

I watched Peter with his classmates for a few minutes trying to determine who his favorite was. It appeared he liked them all. But Greg and Jamie were special to him. Eventually, I sensed the mutual attraction between Peter and the girl who turned out to be – you guessed it – Tammy. When I learned where the cake came from, I knew that certain news traveled in both homes.

I left him with his little buddies and went to Mrs. Pryor's side. "You have no idea what this whole week and especially today means to Peter. During his entire life he has known nothing but rejection and hate. He was told he was stupid and ugly. He was even told by the minister that he couldn't go to church because he wasn't good enough for God. Now all of this. It's almost too much. That's why he exclaimed, 'Everybody is so nice to me!'"

Wiping an eye with the back of her hand, she replied in a clutched voice, "Why didn't you tell me this?"

"I knew that you didn't need that burden on your mind. I could see that you would be just what Peter needs at this time. You have been a champion for both of us. Thank you, Mrs. Pryor. I could go on about his past abuse, but you would not be able to finish your day."

"Why would anyone treat such a wonderful child..."

"Maybe I'll explain it someday. I'll tell you, I could write a book about this child."

"I think you will, Mr. Winters."

As we were leaving, their smiles and good-byes followed us out the door. We made it to the parking lot and out of there before the dismissal bell. As we passed one car, Peter whispered, "That's Tammy's mom in that SUV over there."

"She's as pretty as her daughter, isn't she?"

"How do you know?"

"I know everything, Kiddo. Tammy was dressed in yellow today."

"Jake, you do know everything."

"You've got good taste in women."

When we got home, I called Lance, the superintendent of schools, to thank him and to tell him exactly what his school had done for my Peter that week. It was something that no parent and no grandparent could accomplish for a wounded, hurting little boy from another century.

CHAPTER TWENTY-TWO

The next morning I watched him dress with interest. He put his underpants on first. My curiosity got the better of me. "Peter, I haven't said a thing all week, but I've noticed you've been wearing your underpants all day since Monday. Why?"

"I'm kind of used to them now. I guess they're not too bad. All the other guys wear underpants so I decided I should too."

I didn't ask how he knew. "So underpants are now in?" He nodded. "That must mean they're cool, right?"

He giggled a little. "Yeah, I guess." He thought for a moment. "Jake, would you have forced me to wear underpants if I really didn't want to?"

"No! I figured sooner or later, you'd wear them on your own. And I was right."

That day was spent packing, doing laundry and shopping. Of course, we made time to throw the ball around, play tag, wrestle and ride our bikes together to the back of the neighborhood one last time.

That night after dinner, we went upstairs. He got into his pajamas, then sat on my lap. "Well, kiddo, what do you think? Tomorrow we go back on the road. Was this time spent here at home worth it?"

Excitedly he said, "Oh yeah, Jake. Even if I went back to Slippery Gulch today, what you've given me and done for me since we've been together...it's more than I could know back then to pray for. I never knew back then what a home and a family and friends were. But God knew! Jesus knows, too!"

"How do you know that?"

The Gift

"The minister said so. He said that Jesus knows our prayers before we ask them."

"Did he?"

"Jake, weren't you paying attention in church?"

"I was too busy paying attention to you, you peanut."

He was quiet for a moment. "Everything was great here in New York State except when the doctor stuck me in the butt."

I laughed. "Peter, I have a confession to make for you."

"What?"

"I don't remember when I've had so much fun coming off the road…and in all those years. I can hardly remember what I used to do to relax. I think I did just a bunch of little things: House repairs, a little fishing and camping – but nothing like the break I've enjoyed with you."

"Thank you, Jake."

"You bet. It's been work, but it's all been very relaxing. I love watching you run, play, smile and laugh knowing you're happy and safe and in good hands. You've learned a lot in the last two months. And you've matured a lot too. Now we're heading out and I'm refreshed and ready to go again."

"And I'll be with you." Turning concerned he asked, "Jake, you'd never think of sending me back, would you?"

"No way, Kiddo. We belong to each other. We're a team. Let's go down and spend some time with Betty and Jerry."

A couple of minutes later, I was in the rocking chair with Peter on my lap.

Jerry sighed. "Well, Peter, you two go back on the road tomorrow. Have you enjoyed your time here?"

He stretched his arms behind my head. "Oh yeah! It was great! Thanks for having me."

"You are welcome," Betty said. "I have to admit, when I found out a ghost was moving into our house for a while, I got concerned he'd never leave. They do tend to hang around in one place. Please come back for another visit."

"Thank you, Aunt Betty, Uncle Jerry. I love you both."

Jerry uncharacteristically put in his oar. "Peter, you are the nicest little boy I think I've ever met. We both hope you come back and see us."

I stroked Peter's ribs lightly. He gave me a reverse hug. He drifted off as one very happy and proud little boy.

Later that night, I had a terrible nightmare. I was parked on the side of the road somewhere and for some reason decided to send Peter back to Slippery Gulch. I told him to get out, but he was begging me to let him stay. I wouldn't listen, went around to his side of the truck and pulled him out. I threw him to the ground. All the time he was crying and begging me. As I drove off, I could hear him pleading, "Please Jake, don't leave me. Don't stop loving me."

I woke up shaking and in a cold sweat. It occurred to me that I was still hearing Peter begging me to let him stay. I turned on the light and looked over at him. He was thrashing and kicking, obviously in a bad dream of his own. But whose dream was it? Did I dream that because I heard Peter in my sleep or…

I grabbed a small towel I kept nearby. Peter and I sat in the chair with Peter on my lap facing me. Placing the towel inside his pajamas, I hugged him and waited. Just then he yelled, in a pleading voice, "Please Jake, don't leave me. Don't stop loving me." A chill ran down my spine. Then Peter woke up, crying. "Jake?"

"I've got you, Little One. You're okay."

"You're really here." He threw his small arms around me. "That was a bad one, my worst one yet."

"I know. It was rough on me too." I told him about his own dream. He was confused. "How did you know?"

"I don't know why, but I just had the same nightmare." I removed the towel to find it dry. As I did, Peter immediately started twisting the right leg of his pajamas. "Peter, what's wrong?"

His tears were an eyelash away again. "Jake, you, you wouldn't really do that, would you?"

"Kiddo, I wouldn't know what to do without you. I will never send you back, I promise."

He smiled and gave me a hug. "I know you won't, but I had to ask you again."

"Come on. Let's get back to bed."

"Can I sleep with you for the rest of the night?"

"You bet, under one condition. Stay out of my nightmares."

He laughed. "You stay out of mine, too."

I ruffled his hair, picked him up and carried him off to bed again.

The next morning, I told Betty and Jerry about our mutual dreams. They thought that was spooky. However we all agreed it was because of the unusually strong bond growing between Peter and me.

Soon we heard the upstairs toilet flush then a muffled thump, thump, thump. Peter was coming down the stairs on his butt again. He entered the kitchen more asleep than awake.

As he crawled onto my lap, Jerry said, "Jake told us about the dream you two had last night. That was weird."

"I know. That was the worst nightmare I ever had."

"I agree, Peter. It was the worse dream I ever had, too. I never want to have another dream like it. Well, Kiddo, let's wake you up and get moving."

After waking him, I kissed him on his head then wiped my mouth with my shirtsleeve.

"What's wrong?" he asked.

"Your hair stinks."

He giggled. "It does not."

"You're right it doesn't, but today we're leaving and we're both going to leave sparkling clean. Do you want to take your bath first or should I take my shower first?"

Lacking enthusiasm he asked, "May I take my bath first?"

"Yes, you may."

"May you come up with me?"

"I might and I may."

"Jake, you're funny sometimes."

He was off my lap and up the stairs before I could get moving.

By the time I got up there, Peter was already in the tub. While he washed himself, I trimmed my beard. "Jake, how come you keep trimming your beard?"

"If I didn't it would soon be all over the place. I'd look like a wild man."

He thought this was pretty funny. As I washed his hair he agreed that my beard looked neater trimmed. After I dried him, he slipped into his bottoms and headed for our room saying over his shoulder, "Jake, what should I wear?"

Before I could answer, Betty yelled up: "Peter, I have clean clothes for you down here. They're still warm from the dryer." He turned around and jumped down the stairs.

During breakfast, Betty mentioned that she noticed Peter was now wearing underpants. "Why the change?"

"At school, he discovered all the other boys wore underpants. Underpants are now cool."

"How did you discover that, Peter?" Jerry asked.

Without looking up from his cereal he said, "We had gym on Wednesday and had to change clothes." Without skipping a beat, he added, "Jake, may I get some underpants with designs on them?"

"Maybe. What do you have in mind?"

"Well, Jamie has Spiderman underpants. Greg has Superman underpants. Paul has Mickey Mouse underpants. Jeff has…"

"What did you do, go around checking out everybody's underpants?"

He giggled. "No. I saw everybody's during gym class and everybody saw mine too."

"Everybody's?"

He flushed slightly. "Well not everybody. Just the boys. Only one other kid wears white underpants."

"That's a problem?"

"White underpants aren't as cool."

"If that's important to you, we can do some underpants shopping."

He started laughing. "That sounds funny."

"It is funny." I looked at Betty and Jerry. "I never dreamed I'd go underpants shopping with Peter. Now go upstairs and brush your teeth. I'll be up in a few minutes."

"Jake, I'm honored," Betty said. "A few minutes ago, Peter came down here very comfortable with this house, Jerry and me. He's become a part of the family. I take that as a compliment."

"After the life he endured in Slippery Gulch, he has a right to enjoy who he's living with and feel comfortable with the arrangements," Jerry added.

"Thanks, you two. I needed that. I'm doing this fathering thing for the very first time in my life. Maybe I get too…"

"Over-fatherly. But on the other hand, Little Brother, I'm proud of the job you are doing. And so is Jerry. And so are some other people around the town and in church. Not many men your age would take on what you have – ghost or no ghost. We admire you."

"Thank you. Thank you both. I'm humbled." I was embarrassed, too. I realized I didn't have a choice in the whole matter. It was decided by God. It's a good thing. If it had been up to me, I would have made the wrong decision and Peter wouldn't be with me today. "Thank you, God," I said in a silent prayer.

CHAPTER TWENTY-THREE

After saying good-bye to Betty and Jerry, Peter and I were on our way to our company's truck yard in Ohio. That afternoon we went underpants shopping. We bought two packages of three underpants each; three with cartoon figures and three with super heroes. The ironic thing was that Peter was a real super hero, but he didn't see it that way. After moving into the truck that afternoon, he modeled each pair. "Which ones do you like the best, Jake?"

They were all tiny and cute. I really didn't care. "Gee, I'm not sure. They all look good on you. Which ones do you like the best?"

He held up the Spiderman underpants. "I think I like these the best."

I studied them carefully. "You know, I think I do too."

"Really?" He quickly replaced his Donald Duck underpants with the Spiderman pair and modeled them again.

As he turned around in circles making sure I could see all sides, I said, "Yep, those are my favorites." He beamed.

As he was putting his shorts on, I asked, "Peter, you made twenty-two new friends this week. Who's you favorite...I mean besides Tammy." I winked.

He giggled and punched me lightly on the shoulder. "She's not my favorite. Jamie is."

"Any idea why?"

He thought about it for a moment. "He's cool and he's nice and he's fun."

"I thought all the kids were cool, nice and fun."

"They are, but Jamie isn't too much bigger than me. He and I fool around and wrestle and play together but sometimes we just sit and talk. We don't have to goof around all the time but we still have fun."

I think he was trying to say that Jamie was more mature than the others. Then I looked at him with concern. "Peter, you didn't tell Jamie about yourself, did you?"

"No Jake, I promise. I didn't." He thought for a minute. "Do you like Jamie?"

"I don't know any of the kids very well, but right from the first day, Jamie seemed really nice and friendly. You took to each other quickly. So what do you two talk about?"

"I talk about you a lot. Jamie thinks you're pretty cool. I talk about where we've been and what we've done. I told him about camping and your muskie and things like that.

"He talks about his family and some of the vacations they've taken together. He also talks about his grandpa. Jamie really loved him but he died six months ago." He hesitated. "Jake, he also asked me about my parents."

"Oh! What did you tell him?"

"I told him my mommy died when I was born and daddy didn't want me. That's why I'm with you. I told him I didn't like daddy anyway but I love you and you love me."

"That was a pretty good answer. Was he satisfied?"

"At first he felt sorry for me. But when I told him how you and I love each other, he thought it was pretty neat."

"Good. I think you did a good job."

The next morning we picked up a short run to northern New Jersey. I would drop it in our yard Tuesday morning and wait for a local driver to bring in our next load. On our way to New Jersey, I got a message from Jason. "Jake, isn't the yard in New Jersey right across the river from Manhattan?"

Returning the message I said, "10-4. We will also be able to see the Statue of Liberty."

The Gift

"Great! That'll be quite an experience for Peter. Just be glad you don't have to go into the city. Let me know what he thinks."

"That's a big 10-4." Driving into New York City is not fun when navigating something that's 75 feet long, 102 inches wide and in two pieces. I thanked my lucky stars I didn't have to do it this time.

Monday evening we stayed at a rest area on the Jersey Turnpike, about ten miles from the yard. Tuesday morning I was awake by 6:00 and I went in for a cup of coffee.

Peter started stirring around 6:45. After our wake-up thing, we went in to eat. During breakfast, I filled him in on the day. "Yesterday I was telling you a little about New York City, right?" he nodded. "Well, today you'll see the entire city from the yard. New York City is one of the most spectacular cities of the world."

He looked at me. "Jake, where is the rest of the world?"

I looked at him. What a dynamite question, and one I'd never been asked before, or for that matter, ever thought about. Then again, Peter is the first person I'd ever met in the whole world from such a tiny little town. A ghost town at that! I would have to show him the globe we had at home, which, unfortunately, I had never thought about back then. "Peter, that's a fantastic question."

He smiled. "It is?"

"It sure is, but I can't answer it. The next time we're home, I'll show you a globe of the world and show you where the United States is, then you'll be able to see where the rest of the world is." Anticipating his next question I said, "A globe is like a ball."

An hour later we had eaten and taken care of our bathroom needs. It was a beautifully clear day as we headed for the yard.

We arrived at the drop yard at 8:30 and dropped the trailer we'd just brought in from Ohio. Taking my paperwork to the office while Peter remained in the truck, I learned our next trailer wasn't in yet. We strolled to the edge of the yard and looked across the Hudson River at New York City. Peter stared in awe.

"Are we going to go there someday?"

"Probably someday, but not today."

"What are those two real tall buildings?"

"They are called the World Trade Center, Or twin towers for short. Tens of thousands of people work in those two buildings. They come from many different countries spread all over the world."

"Wow. How tall are they?"

"They're 110 stories or floors high. Beauties, aren't they? Now over there is one of the most famous buildings in the world. It's called the Empire State Building. In the early 1940's a plane flew into it."

"Wow, and it didn't fall over?"

"No, it didn't." Next I pointed out the Statue of Liberty. I told him the history of the statue and of Ellis Island. He was fascinated. I took his hand. "Let's see if our load is in."

I started toward our truck when he pulled me hard. "Jake, what's that plane doing?"

I turned around and said, "What plane?" He pointed toward the city, but before I had a chance to react, the plane flew into the North Tower of the World Trade Center. There was a tremendous explosion and fireball. Instinctively I picked Peter up and held him close. I looked at the date on my watch. It was September 11, 2001.

We both stared in shock. Finally after several minutes of silence he said, "What happened, Jake?"

I just shook my head. "I don't know, Kiddo. The plane may have had engine trouble and the pilot may have lost control. But I'm really not sure."

I stood there at a total loss for words. I became aware that people some distance from us were starting to call out, "My God. That was a plane! It flew right into the damn thing." Truckers and yard workers were coming together to discuss their ignorance and yell out in protest that such a thing could happen on such a clear day as this one.

One lady from the office was crying into her fist held up to her mouth.

"Gee, look at that Peter. You can see small sections of the building falling off."

Peter said, "Is that a big video, Jake? Is that pretend?"

"Peter, this is real."

He looked on in fear, tears coming out of both eyes. He looked back to the building. In a sad, weak voice he said, "Those aren't parts of the building, Jake."

I was confused. That's what it looked like to me. "What are they?"

He sniffled hard and wiped away his tears. "Those are people jumping."

His eyes were better than mine. I didn't want to believe him.

Others were saying the same thing.

My eyes were filling with tears now. I could see nothing without wiping them.

I felt I needed to pull Peter away from this scene. I took his hand and headed toward the yard offices. I thought, the hell with my truck. We have bigger problems right now.

As we got to the building, I realized we had no reason to go in. Everybody was standing in the yard. Just then Peter pulled on my hand.

He shouted, "Jake!" and pointed just as someone else yelled out, "Oh my God!" I caught the movement just as another plane flew into the South Tower with another explosion and fireball.

It was clear to most of us that we were not witnessing two freak accidents. We were seeing the work of deliberate madmen.

Peter's sweet, innocent voice rang out in the midst of one of those silent pauses that shouting people have on occasion. It caused big men to turn and look for its childish source.

"Did they have engine trouble, Jake?"

"No, Peter, those were deliberate acts."

I picked Peter up and quietly tried to explain what might be going on. He kept staring at the towers in a fixed gaze I observed in the van accident on I-40.

Then he said, "Jake, I'll be back in a few minutes."

I squeezed him so hard he yelled. "No, Peter, you stay put." I said it in a tone and a low volume that he'd never heard. I didn't want a scene here in the yard. But I knew I couldn't keep him from vanishing, hard as I might try.

"But Jake, I…"

"Peter, you're not going anywhere. Trust me on this one, Kiddo. I don't want you going anywhere." Then in a pleading tone full of emotion, I said, "Please, Peter, stay with me."

"Okay. But Jake, could you stop squeezing me so hard? It hurts."

I put him back on the ground and just started to apologize when suddenly the South Tower collapsed. "Oh, God, help them!" I breathed as the tower went down slowly, and so did I. Peter looked down at me in fright. "I'm okay, Kiddo. My old knees just gave out."

I drew Peter down to me. "Kiddo, this is the worst thing I've ever seen in my whole life." I realized in his six-year-old mind, he had seen and experienced things much worse and much more personal. There was no way he could comprehend what was really going on and I doubted I would ever be able to explain it.

Suddenly it hit me. All those people stranded in that building have kids hearing and watching in front of TV's all over the globe.

Just then my cell phone rang. "Jake, this is Jason. Where are you?"

"In the yard."

"Can you see the city from where you are?"

"We have a horribly perfect view. Peter saw everything right from the first. I didn't see the first plane's impact but he did."

"Oh Lord! Look, Jake, your load is there. Hook up, get your paperwork and take off. If you don't leave now you won't get out for days. And get Peter out of there. He doesn't need this."

"Oh my God, Jason! There goes the second tower."

"Jake, grab that little boy and get the hell out of there… now. That's a company order."

"You're right. I'll call back in a couple of hours."

We hooked to the proper trailer. I ran to the fence at the edge of our property where everyone was watching the horror and found the office worker. She was holding the paperwork for my load. I signed the proper form, handed it back to her and ran for the truck. Peter was strapped in and ready to go.

We weren't going anywhere fast. The roads were jammed and everybody was moving at a snail's pace. I prayed one of those clutch prayers that men behind the steering wheels make sometimes. By the grace of God we finally reached the Jersey Turnpike. I didn't dare turn on the AM radio, just the CB. I learned that right behind us, all the ramps and bridges were being officially closed. We would not have gotten out until the next day, if then. After a couple of hours, we made it to I-80 heading west. It was hard to concentrate. Peter finally asked, "Why did we have to leave? That was neat."

My anger flared, but I quickly got it in check. "That was not neat. It was a deliberate act. Somebody flew those planes into those buildings on purpose and thousands of people were killed. It wasn't neat Peter, it was frightening and sad."

"Why would anybody do that? Wouldn't the pilot be killed, too?"

"Yes, he would. The people that flew those planes must have been terrorists." He didn't understand the term. I tried to explain that degree of hate but I don't understand it very well myself.

Eventually I turned on the AM radio. We leaned that the Pentagon was hit, and that a plane went down in Pennsylvania. Peter had a lot of questions, none of which I could answer. And I had more questions of my own.

Truckers have different ways of coping, I suppose. We spent the day listening to the radio, talking to each other, listening and talking on the CB and just listening to others talk; in this case talking about something they knew nothing about. But the sound of our chatter helped Peter and me.

We stopped at a truck stop on I-80 near Stroudsburg, Pennsylvania where I got two American flags, and taped them to the CB antennas. In the next few days more and more American flags would appear. They were on cars, trucks, heavy equipment, fire trucks and railroad engines. They were flying from large buildings and the porches of homes, homes of the rich and poor. They were flying from overpasses and underpasses. Patriotism was alive and well.

As time went along, dully, so did we. At one point we were at a truck stop. Peter was in the shower. I was trimming my beard when suddenly he started screaming, "Jake, help! Something's wrong."

I got to him so fast I almost fell. "Peter, what's wrong?"

"Jake, look at me. It's gone!" He was in tears and appeared to be in genuine pain.

I inspected him carefully but everything was there. "What's gone?"

In tears he said, "My tan. It's gone."

I backed up and flopped on a bench. Laughing so hard, I nearly doubled over. At first, he was mad at me.

"Peter," I finally said, "to keep your tan, you have to stay in the sun. If you don't, it fades away. Nothing's wrong. You're normal."

"You mean I'm going to have to start all over next year?"

"'Fraid so, kiddo." I apologized for laughing. "Let's get your hair washed and dried, then we'll eat."

Another time we were going along listening to an oldies station when I decided it was time to teach Peter how to sing. I thought it would be good therapy for both of us. I decided it would be best to start out humming. I demonstrated what I meant. Finally a song came on that he'd heard before. I turned the radio low enough so I could hear him hum. That's when I made a terrible discovery: Peter was tone deaf. Peter couldn't carry a tune in a bushel basket if he had to.

The worst time we had following the disaster was when Peter had a bout with diarrhea. I suspected it had to do with nerves. Again we moved into a motel. There were a lot of tears and a lot of messes to clean up; both on the bathroom floor and on Peter, but the next morning he was once again ready to go. During this I had one question: Could an angel get diarrhea? I didn't think so.

Traveling through Nebraska, we were approaching Kearney. "Peter, I've got a surprise for you." He looked at me wide-eyed. "In a few minutes, we're going to make a stop at a very special place. See that curve up ahead?" He nodded in anticipation. "Keep watching straight ahead."

As we rounded the curve, his eyes enlarged. Spanning I-80 was a huge arch. "Wow! What is that thing?"

"That is the Great Platte River Road Archway Monument."

He looked at me. "Say what?"

I chuckled. Who did he pick up that expression from? "It commemorates the brave men, women and children who traveled across the Oregon Trail in the 1800's; traveling to such places as California and Oregon. In your mother's and grandparents' case, they headed north to Montana out of Wyoming."

"Wow! What does co…comemberate mean?"

I gave him a chance to get it right then explained. We got off at the next exit and backtracked two miles on a side road. Walking into the structure, I gave him a chance to stand and stare. It was most impressive. I took his hand and smiled. I'd gone through it two or three years earlier. Because of my interest in the westward movement and history of the west, I found it fascinating. Peter squeezed my hand. Somehow I knew it was going to be far more meaningful today. I returned the squeeze.

We went to the ticket counter and bought our tickets. After I paid for them and moved away from the counter he asked, "Jake, why did you pay for me? Kids under five are free and I look like I'm only three or four. You wasted your money."

The Gift

We went to a bench where I sat him on my lap. "You're right. She thought you were younger than what you are and wasn't going to charge me, but would that have been right?"

He thought about this for a moment. "I see what you mean. It would have been cheating, wouldn't it?" How many parents fail their children in simple lessons of honesty like this? From my years in the classroom, I had a feel for the answer to that one. Too many!

I smiled. "'Cheating' is exactly what it would have been. Come on, let's go in."

We gave the man our tickets and proceeded to the next man. He gave us a set of earphones, showed us how to wear them and explained why they were important.

We proceeded to the long escalator that climbed what must have been two or three stories. Ahead of us and at the top of the escalator was a huge screen showing pioneers and their covered wagons heading in the same direction we were – west on the Oregon Trail. It was as if we were now part of their wagon train. As we rode higher we were climbing a hill to catch up to the last wagon. I kept a careful eye on Peter. He appeared to be in awe of everything.

Once at the top, we moved into a small room. At that point a man started talking into our headsets. Peter at first was startled. But he soon settled down. The room depicted Fort Kearney, the last form of civilization the pioneers would experience for weeks to come.

We saw and heard running buffalo. When it was mentioned that the pioneers used buffalo chips – that is dung – in place of firewood, Peter looked at me in surprise and disgust. "They cooked their food over that sh…stuff?"

I chuckled. "That was close." He let loose with an uncomfortable giggle. "There weren't any trees here at the time, Kiddo. I've heard that the white man planted every tree, directly or indirectly, except for those found on islands in the Platte River. This is the prairie and they had huge prairie fires back then. Trees never had a chance."

Although his grandparents probably took the Bozeman Trail to Montana, the cut off came in what is now the state of Wyoming. More than likely they traveled along this part of the road. I pointed that out to Peter. "They were right here…my mother and grandparents?"

"Yep. Pretty close to where we are right now." This time I noticed the effects of a chill go up and down his spine.

The suffering of the pioneers along the road was spelled out clearly. Peter listened with quiet interest. I knew he was thinking of his unknown mother and grandparents.

We heard of Peter McBride, a young boy who was the sole survivor of his family upon reaching California. Peter listened, troubled. Then he asked, "I'm the sole survivor of my family, aren't I?"

I knelt down to face him and put my hands on his little shoulders. "Yes you are, Kiddo, of that family. But now you're a part of my family."

He smiled as he took my hand and squeezed it. "My grandparents didn't survive. Were they weak?" His grandparents were killed during an Indian attack on the Bozeman trail. Exactly where, we don't know: probably near the Black Hills. Since the trail was open for only three or four years, their death probably happened in the mid 1860's.

"No! It's just that they were in the wrong place at the wrong time. They were very strong and very brave. If they had not been, they wouldn't have made it as far as they did. Remember though, your mother survived. Even though she was an infant at the time, she had to be very strong. She's where you get your strength and courage."

The Gift

We moved on. We learned about the mountain men; those courageous men who preceded the pioneers. The drawings of Jim "Old Gabe" Bridger and James Beckwourth were displayed.

We read about the tragedy of the Donner Party; the party that was caught in an early snowstorm in the Sierra Mountains. A large portion of the party died in the mountains and many of those that survived turned cannibalistic in order to live. Peter wanted to know what cannibalism was. "It's when one person eats another person."

He looked at me, aghast. "You mean for food? Why would they do that? That's disgusting."

"That's the only way they could survive, Kiddo. When a person died, his or her body was used for food. It is disgusting but because of that, some lived."

He wrinkled his nose and asked with concern. "Did they eat little kids, too?"

"Sure." I then took his arm, moved my hand across the peach fuzz slowly, and said, "Mmmmm, tender," as I moved it toward my mouth. He ripped his arm from my hands and said, "Jake, that isn't funny."

We were beginning to laugh like we used to. That day in New York City had left a cloud over our souls. Slowly, it was lifting.

We learned about the Pony Express. "Wow! It took three weeks to get the mail across the country? Now we can get across in five days."

"And a plane can do it in five hours," I reminded him.

We moved on to the building of the transcontinental railroad and learned about Promontory Point, where the west met the east. The last spike driven in was solid gold to commemorate the event. "Neat! Is it still there?" Peter wondered.

"No, it's in a museum somewhere." He found it interesting that the Chinese helped build the railroads too. He was aware that the Chinese worked in many of the mines of the west including the J. and J. Mines in Slippery Gulch.

We saw an overland stage. Peter said one came into Slippery Gulch once a week. It was always a big deal because he thought it brought mail and sometimes a new face to town. Sometimes someone got on it though and was never seen again. For that reason he was afraid of it. He was afraid that someday someone would put him on it and he'd never be seen again either. He didn't know where it went, but suspected it went straight to hell. In reality, he was already in hell.

Toward the end of the tour, we learned about the Lincoln Highway and watched a video about it. It appeared that most of it was mud. Everybody was driving through muddy ruts in old cars. He thought it was funny but glad we didn't have to drive through anything like that. I pointed out that a former president, Dwight D. Eisenhower, was responsible for the building of the modern interstate system we drive on today.

When we finished our tour, we both agreed it was a great way to spend an hour. Peter was fascinated with the history of the country and constantly amazed at how much things had changed since he was born. Of course in a small way, he was a part of that history.

As we drove through central Nebraska, Peter looked out the window with interest. The Platte River he found especially interesting, but I wasn't sure why. He often turned in his seat to look back at it as we crossed the river. Yet we went mile after mile in silence.

Finally he asked, "Jake, do you really think my mommy and grandparents came along here in a wagon train?"

"I think they did, Kiddo."

"Did they have bridges across the river back then?"

"No bridges back then."

Just then we crossed another bridge going over the Platte. Peter looked at the river carefully. "How did they get across then?"

"They didn't cross the river any more than necessary, Kiddo. They followed it. If they had to cross they looked for a ford or shallow place. However fords could be tricky. Some were permanent and remained year after year but some lasted only a week or two then changed as the river changed. If a ford wasn't available when they had to get to the other side for whatever reason, they had to drive their wagons across the river and hope it wasn't too deep or hope their wagons didn't get bogged down in the mud. If it was too deep the wagon could wash away and they could lose everything including the family. If the wagon got bogged down in mud it would be very difficult to free. If a young child fell off the wagon during the crossing, he or she could drown before being rescued."

Peter looked at the Platte to our north, all the time thinking about what I said. Finally he looked at me. "Jake, if they could lose everything, why did they even start out?"

"It was because of their pot of gold at the end of the rainbow, Kiddo."

His eyes widened. "What do you mean?"

"In some cases some people found actual gold at the end of their trip. In other cases what they found was just as valuable as gold to them. It may have been land to farm or raise livestock on. In other cases it was just a chance to start over. But whatever their pot of gold was, they all thought the risk was worth it."

Once again we rode in silence for several miles. Peter continued to watch the river and the surrounding countryside.

He broke the silence again. "Jake, if there was a real pot of gold at the end, maybe I'd try it, but for anything else, no way. It was too hard."

"It's a good thing your grandparents didn't feel the way you do. If they had, your mother would not have reached Montana, and you would never have existed."

I didn't give him time to think about this. "Peter, we've been together for almost nine weeks. Have you enjoyed yourself during that time more than you did in Slippery Gulch?"

"Of course, Jake. You know that."

"If you were to go back to Slippery Gulch right now, would you say you've reached your pot of gold?"

He looked at me worried. "Are you thinking about sending me back?"

"No way, Kiddo. I'm just trying to point out that a pot of gold for one person is not the same as for another. The love we share for one another is our pot of gold. Some pioneers turned around when the going got tough. During the first few weeks of our journey, the going got tough for both of us. Either one of us could have turned around and called it quits, but we didn't. We kept going. Now we both have our own pot of gold. The struggle was worth it."

Suddenly he burst into a beautiful smile. "Now I understand. You're my pot of gold and I'm your pot of gold."

"You've got it, Little One. And you're worth far more to me than some old real pot of gold."

The smile I got went from beautiful to radiant. "And you're worth more to me than a whole bunch of pots of gold. You're worth my whole life." He paused then continued. "Jake, when we were camping, I'm sure glad we didn't have to cook our food over buffalo...chips."

I laughed as we drove on.

The next day we stopped at a major truck stop in Rawlins, Wyoming, for ice cream. While we were enjoying our treat I said, "Peter, I've been thinking. I think it's time you get a haircut."

He looked at me, shocked. We talked about this once before. Shortly after starting our trip he was mistaken for a little girl. To a six-year-old boy, there is no greater insult. We talked about him getting a haircut at that time, but decided against it. After all, Peter was dead. If we didn't like it, we were stuck. It wouldn't grow back. He now questioned my decision.

"Your hair is beautiful, but uneven. On the right side it's down below your right shoulder. On your left it's not quite to your shoulder. And there are longer strands on your forehead and around your back. I'm thinking about just having it evened out – nothing off the top. What do you think?"

I saw his concern. He'd never had a haircut in his life. He couldn't picture what I was talking about, but his concerns went deeper. "How bad does it hurt?"

I smiled. "It doesn't hurt at all. Your hair is dead."

"The rest of me is too but when I skin my knee, it hurts."

I chuckled but he saw no humor in his statement. "Trust me, Funny Face, it doesn't hurt at all. I'll tell you what. Let's go in and take showers. We need them anyway. Then I'll show you what I've got in mind. I'll get my hair cut too. The barber is a friend of mine. I've been getting my hair cut here for years. She'll cut yours as I say."

He agreed with the shower but wasn't sure about the haircut. Once in the shower room, I had him remove his shirt and sat him on the counter so I could show him what I meant. He never noticed the uneveness before so reluctantly agreed with the haircut.

As soon as we walked in to the barbershop, the barber stopped her hair cutting. "Well, Jake Winters! Haven't seen you for a while."

"Sorry about that. I've gotten in too late at night or left too early in the morning. How have you been, Nancy?"

"Just fine!" Looking at Peter, she said, "Who do we have here?"

"Peter Stevenson, my grandson. Peter, this is Nancy."

Nancy came right over and shook his hand. "Wow! Your hair is beautiful. And so fine!" As she continued feeling his hair she said, "But Jake, I didn't know you had a grandson."

"Well, that just goes to show you don't know everything." We all laughed including the customer in the chair.

When it was my turn, Peter watched with a great deal of interest. I finally volunteered that Peter had never had a haircut or at least not one he could remember, so he was a little worried.

"Not to worry, honey. It doesn't hurt a bit," Nancy said. Finally it was Peter's turn. Nancy put a seat across the two arms for toddlers while I lifted Peter onto it. Nancy moved her hand through Peter's fine hair. "Jake, I hope you don't want me to cut all this off."

"No way!" I explained to her what we were looking for. "Nothing off the top."

"Good! It's so beautiful, I almost hate to cut any of it."

As Nancy began, Peter watched his hair fall to the apron with concern. He'd pick it up and inspect it. I watched Nancy carefully to make sure she cut only what I told her to. But she cut as if she were working on a masterpiece. Meanwhile, I could tell she had a lot of questions about Peter. I was hoping they'd go unasked.

The Gift

Finally she completed her task. She looked to me for my approval. As I walked around Peter, I was impressed. It looked good. I winked at her. She knew me well enough to know something was coming. "It looks pretty good Nancy, but what do we do about that bald spot?"

Peter jerked his head around and looked at me then at Nancy, waiting for an answer. He was close to tears. Nancy produced a mirror so he could see the back of his head. He was looking for the mystery bald spot. Nancy started laughing. "Peter, I assure you, there isn't any bald spot. Is your grandpa always this mean to you?"

Peter giggled. "Yeah. Sometimes even worse."

"Jake, you should be ashamed of yourself. Now look at your hair again Peter, but don't worry about some bald spot that isn't there."

He giggled some more then looked at the results of the cut. "Wow! It does look good. It's even everyplace."

I liked it better all the time. Not only was it clean, it now appeared well groomed. He was moving further away from the little boy nobody wanted. "Why, Peter, you're so handsome you may not be ugly in the morning when you first wake up anymore." He started laughing. "Well, on second thought, I don't think that will change."

He laughed harder looking at Nancy. "See what I mean? He's always mean."

Nancy was now laughing. "You two are quite a pair."

I paid Nancy for two haircuts then gave her a generous tip. "Thanks for two great haircuts. See you next time, but I don't know when that will be."

She sighed. "I know. Be careful out there, Jake. Nice meeting you, Peter. Take care of your grandpa for me."

Peter smiled. "I will. Thanks for the haircut."

As we were pulling up the ramp to I-80, I looked at Peter. "That wasn't so bad, was it?"

"No, but you about scared the life out of me when you mentioned the bald spot."

"Now Peter, you know I would never have allowed that to happen."

"I know, but you said it so seriously."

"That's just me, Kiddo. Sorry." He wasn't really that mad at me.

The next day we stopped at Fort Bridger, Wyoming. Fort Bridger is a State Historical Site originally built by Jim Bridger, (perhaps the most famous mountain man of all) in the 1840's. I had stopped there many times before and knew immediately where we were going first.

Not far from the entrance was a series of old buildings. Hand-in-hand, Peter and I walked towards them. As we approached one he dropped my hand and raced toward it. "That's it, Jake! That's what you were driving when I first saw you."

Inside was a huge freight wagon, known as a Pittsburgh Freighter. The front wheels were large, the back wheels larger. Peter only came up to the hub of the rear wheel. There was a railing protecting the wagon from the public, but before I could get to him, Peter was under it. He went to the front of the wagon, looked at it carefully then excitedly proclaimed, "This is the same one you were driving, Jake."

I was skeptical. "How do you know?"

"Remember when you were at the mine and Peabody called you to the office?" I nodded. "You and I said good-bye and I left. After you went into the office, I snuck back to the wagon. I found a sharp stone and carved my initials into the front of the wagon. Here they are right next to yours."

The Gift

I climbed over the railing certain he was mistaken. Putting my glasses on I looked at the wood. Barely legible but unmistakably written by a child were the initials PS. Less than a foot away were the initials JW carved into the wood, more than likely by a knife. Both were badly weathered. The child that carved these initials into this wagon, 100 years ago, was standing next to me. My familiar chill returned.

On my first visit to Slippery Gulch, I was driving a big truck, but Peter saw a freight wagon pulled by twenty horses. The teamster of that wagon, one hundred years ago, was also named Jake Winters. Peter was confusing June, 2001 with June,1901, but that's all he was confusing. I was stunned. When I got my voice back I said, "Come on. Got something else to show you." We went to what was a replica of the original fort.

I pointed out several things to him when I realized he wasn't listening. He was looking to his other side. Then he laughed and said, "No, he won't."

I looked at him puzzled. "Peter, what's going on?"

He looked at me with a smile on his face. He was about to say something, when he laughed again, looked in the other direction and said, "No, he won't. Jake's nice." He looked back to me and said, "Jake, somebody sort of like me is here and you know him. We both saw his picture two days ago."

I was startled. "I do? We did?"

"Wait a minute." He looked back the other way, paused, then turned back to me and said, "You don't know him but you know a lot about him. He's seen you here before."

I was confused and shaken. "Who is he?"

"His name is Mr. Bridger: You know, 'Old Gabe.'"

A mild breeze could have blown me over. "Jim Bridger?"

"Yeah!" Peter turned back the other way, paused then asked, "Will it hurt? Well, okay."

Suddenly Peter's voice changed. It was deep and masculine. "Well I'll be. I don't reckon I been this small since I was knee-high to one of them critters I used to shoot out of them Missoura trees. Jim Bridger, Jake! Glad to make your acquaintance." Peter's hand stuck out to be shaken.

I bit my lip to make sure I wasn't dreaming. It hurt. I tentatively stuck out my hand, taking Peter's small hand in mine and held on. In an accusing way I asked, "Is Peter okay?"

"You done got a fine youngun here, Jake. I'd never hurt him and I'd kill the man that tried. I'm just borrowing his body for a spell."

I released the small hand. "Mr. Bridger…"

"Jim!" he interrupted me.

"Jim, I've been reading about your life for decades. You and men like you performed a wonderful service for this country. If it hadn't been for you, the whole history of the country may have been different."

"Shucks, I done reckon we was just havin fun and tryin to earn enough to buy us a little whiskey at the next rendezvous."

"Maybe, but you men had more guts than most men today would know what to do with."

"I don't know about that. I done seen that rig you and Peter come in on today and it seems to me it'd take a powerful lot of guts just to get in that crazy thing."

"It took you all day to go fifteen miles. I can do that in twelve minutes." His eyes were wide but I didn't give him a chance to respond. "Peter said you were something like him. What did he mean?"

He thought about this. "We is both spirits but he ain't the same as me. He's special."

"What do you mean?"

The Gift

"He ain't stuck in one place like me. He can travel round the country with you. He also got his body back. I don't understand it. I ain't complaining mind ya, but he is special."

"Jim, do you know what an angel is?"

He looked to the northwest then back to me. "Marcus Wittman: You done ever heared tell ah him?"

"Yes. Dr. Wittman and his wife served as missionaries among the Indians in what was then the Territory of Oregon in the 1840's."

"You're right. They both done got themselves kilt by them red devils up there. Joe Meek's daughter, Helen, done got kilt at the same time. Mary Ann, my daughter, done got carried away. We never knowed what happened to her. Anyway, Marcus always said Mary Ann was an angel: I reckon because she was so precious to me. I know this youngun is precious too, so I reckon he's an angel to you. Ain't that what ya meant?" Certainly Peter was precious to me but that's not what I was getting at, however, I answered yes.

"A couple more questions, Jim. You were able to take over Peter's body easily. Could a demon do the same thing?"

"I weren't able to take over his body without his permission. No evil spirit could never do what I done. You're watchin over this little body but somebody else is watchin over his spirit. You ain't got no worry bout that, Jake. No bad spirit will ever get in here. This house belongs to God.

"Well, speakin of this little body, I better give it back to Peter. I enjoyed meetin both of ya. I'll watch for ya the next time."

"It was a real honor talking to you. Will Peter be okay?"

"He may be a might weak for a spell but he'll be fine. You two have fun. You done got a fine lad here, Jake."

Suddenly Peter slumped to the ground. I knelt down to him. "Are you okay?"

"Just a little weak." I picked him up and was about to say something when Peter looked the other way. "You're welcome, Mr. Bridger. I know. I love him too. Okay, bye."

"Peter, how did you know it was okay to lend him your body."

"The voice in my head said it was okay." So Jim was right. Something or someone was watching over Peter's spirit. If there was any doubt left, it was completely gone. Peter was not a demon and never could be.

As we wandered around the fort, I pointed out the ruts of wagons that long ago passed this way heading west. Some of the travelers no doubt found their pot of gold, but others found their hell instead. I pointed out that the Donner Party stopped here in 1846 and talked to "Old Gabe", just as we did. All he could say was, "Wow!"

We spent an hour in the museum. We both loved it, but both of us loved the west and the history of the pioneers. Of course, Peter was born in the late time period we were learning about, and sometimes I felt I should have been.

It was time to go. As we were leaving, Peter turned around, smiled, waved and said, "See you next time, Mr. Bridger." I decided to wave myself. We received strange looks from several tourists.

CHAPTER TWENTY-FOUR

When we got home in October, both Betty and Jerry complimented Peter on his haircut. We were home in time for Halloween. I explained the tradition of tricks and treats to Peter. He thought it sounded like fun. Tricks with him could have taken on a whole new meaning. We all talked about what he could go as. At one point, I suggested him going as the devil but he wasn't interested. He'd seen enough demons in his life. We finally agreed he should go as a ghost. Betty cut up an old sheet, put holes in it for his eyes and he was set. So, for Holloween, my little ghost was dressed as a little ghost. Not very original, but it worked and we had fun.

November 1st was an unusually warm and dry day for the Buffalo area. Peter and I spent much of the afternoon in the backyard playing catch, tag and spinning him until we were both dizzy. We lay down in the warm, fall sun. Peter lay down perpendicular to me with his head resting on my stomach. Neither of us said a word for quite some time. I was relaxing and thought he was too. At one point, I looked at him to find a tear slowly working it's way down the side of his face. "Peter, what's wrong?"

"I don't know."

"Ah, come on, Kiddo. We've been talking real good since we've been together. Let's not end it now."

He was silent for several minutes then said, "Jake, do… do you ever get tired of me?"

I was lost. Where was this coming from? "No! Why are you even asking?"

After a hesitation he asked, "You're going out tonight, aren't you?"

Now I understood. A female friend and I were meeting ten other people at a local bar at 5:00 for wings and beer. We'd all been associated with the Jaycees in the 1970's and had maintained a close friendship ever since. "Yes, I am, but not because I'm tired of you. I'm getting together with some friends I've known for thirty years."

"But you don't want me there, do you?"

"It's not that I don't want you there, Kiddo, but you'd be bored stiff. We'll be talking about some of the things we did years ago, politics, and other boring stuff like that. Plus the place we're going is for adults only."

"Do you ever talk about me?"

"Sometimes. You've met almost everybody that's going to be there tonight. Bill and Sue are going to be there too. I know they're going to want to know how you're doing."

He was silent for a moment. "When you're out with your friends, do you still love me?"

So, there it was. The thought of losing my love was never far from the surface. "Peter, except for the time when we're talking about you, I could go for hours and never think about you. But that doesn't mean I stop loving you. Let's say Betty called me at the bar at 7:30 to tell me you just fell down the stairs and broke an arm. Do you think I'd say, 'Betty, I'm right in the middle of a good discussion. I'll be home in a few hours.' No! I'd be heading for the car almost before I hung up. That's love, Kiddo."

"You would?"

"You're darn right I would. Let's put the shoe on the other foot for a minute. Let's say tomorrow afternoon, you're next door playing with Nat. You're over there for several hours and involved in a long game and you're winning, when Betty calls and tells you I just fell and I'm hurt. I don't think you'd tell Betty you'd be there as soon as you finish the game, would you?"

"No way! I'd be there instantly."

"That's love, Kiddo. You may not have thought of me for hours because you were concentrating on the game, but that doesn't mean you stopped loving me. Love isn't like a light bulb. You don't turn it on and off. You understand?"

"Yeah. So no matter what you're doing, even if I'm not there, you still love me."

"You bet I do. Peter, have you been worried about this since we were home in August? Is that why you didn't sleep when I went out?"

He shrugged his shoulders. "I guess."

"You were also worried I wouldn't come back, weren't you?" He looked a little embarrassed and nodded. "You know now I'll never leave you, don't you?" He finally smiled and again nodded. "Come on, Funny Face, I'll play tag for a few minutes then I've got to take a shower." We were once again up and running. After twenty minutes I grabbed and tickled him for the last time that afternoon. "Do you feel better about me going out tonight?"

"Yeah. Thanks, Jake. I just had to make sure."

"I understand. I just wish you would have asked me in August."

That night when I returned at midnight, Peter was asleep on Betty's lap. However he immediately woke up. "Hi, Jake! Did you have fun?"

"Yes, I did but I was thinking of you. How did it go?"

He enjoyed hearing I was thinking of him. "Aunt Betty and I had fun playing games."

"He even went to sleep right on time," Betty added.

"That's great!"

I took him off Betty's lap. He was soon fast asleep with his head resting on my shoulder. "I don't know what you said to him this afternoon, but whatever it was, it worked."

The next morning the roles were reversed. I didn't get up until 7:30. He was dressed and downstairs with Betty when they heard the toilet flush. As I walked into the kitchen, I smiled slightly and said, "I need help waking up bad this morning, Peter." Then I walked over and lightly sat down on his lap. He was laughing so hard he couldn't breathe. He thought that was great but it didn't last long. The roles were soon back to normal.

That morning we were scheduled to be at school at 10:00. Peter and I spent time the last three days spit-polishing the outside and cleaning the inside of our truck. It was beautiful. He took a bath and I took a shower. We left at nine to pick up the trailer. We pulled in front of the school at ten sharp. Peter's classroom was in the front of the building so when we pulled up, any semblance of control went out the window.

As Peter jumped into my arms, we could hear the yelling. The windows were filled with twenty-two beaming little faces and one big one. Peter waved as we walked to the building. Mr. Stewart met us at the door. He was happy to see both of us and escorted us down to the room. As we walked in, Peter was swamped. Jamie had a huge smile on his face. He was missing his two front teeth.

Mrs. Pryor walked up to me, beaming. She noticed Peter's haircut immediately and commented on it positively. "It's great to see both of you again. Ever since I told the children this morning the two of you would be here at ten, they've been bouncing off the wall. Peter made quite a hit."

"I can see that. It really was a great experience for him." I looked at him being mobbed by his little friends. "It still is."

"What great adventures have the two of you shared since we last saw you?" she asked.

"Unfortunately 9-11 immediately comes to mind."

Oh, I know. Wasn't that horrendous? Did you see it on TV?"

"No. At the time we were standing in our drop-yard in Northern New Jersey. I was pointing out the skyline of Manhattan to Peter when the first plane hit."

"Oh my God!" She put her hand to her mouth. "You saw the whole thing?"

"Saw and heard it from start to finish!"

"Lord! How did Peter take it?"

"At first he thought it was neat. However as the day went along, we talked a lot. He finally realized the disaster it truly was. It may have been best for him if I would have allowed him to think it was neat, but I couldn't. For a week he slept on my bunk. He had at least one nightmare a night and I had a few also. We comforted each other. But life goes on and we did too. We're both fine now."

"It sounds like you both provide strength for one another."

"We do. Sometimes Peter is going on forty."

She laughed. "Isn't that the truth." She turned and asked the children to take their seats including Peter. "Children, before we go out to the truck, Mr. Winters is going to explain the rules. Listen carefully, for we must all follow the rules about being close to the truck."

I rose to begin. Peter sat in the middle of the children flanked by Jamie and Greg. "I'd like to ask my driving partner to come forward." Peter's face lit up. He walked to me with a sense of importance about him – minus any smugness. A couple classmates touched his arms as if he were celebrity. "You see kids, Peter and I are a team. He knows the rules as well as I do. So I'll have him explain them. If he forgets something, I'll remind him. It's all yours, Kiddo." I took my seat.

This was totally unexpected. We had not discussed this at all. He looked at me with pure love. I noticed that Tammy watched her hero climb on a chair to see better. Every eye was on him now.

Peter and the class looked at each other with unadulterated respect. He rehearsed the rules as I'd given them to him months ago. Nobody moved. When it came to the subject of the air brake buttons on the dashboard, he warned, "if you touch those buttons, my grandpa may spank you." Despite my struggle to keep a straight face, I attempted to look my sternest. Mrs. Pryor was amused at Peter shaking his finger while making his point with the children. I knew the brakes would not be touched. He concluded, "So listen to my grandpa and me and do as we say. Are there any questions?"

There were several. Of course the first was, "Can we blow the air horns?" The answer was, "Yes, but only once per kid." That was Peter's rule, not mine.

Once at the truck, Peter gave them a walking tour around the truck. He was explaining the landing gears on the trailer when he noticed two boys talking. One was Jamie. Peter paused, got Jamie's attention and proceeded. I could see Jamie was embarrassed by Peter's silent reprimand. Peter didn't notice.

"Jake, can we look inside the truck now?"

"You're in charge. If you say so."

I lifted him and the first three children into the truck. Peter carried on like a pro. Mrs. Pryor and I stood side-by-side: She kept order while I lifted three down and three more up. With each new group, the air horn blew three times, never four. When all had their turn, Peter jumped into my arms. Once back on the ground, Peter asked if I would start the Babes.

I had no idea what he had in mind but I climbed in and did as he requested. At the initial roar, many children jumped back. Peter waited. Then as the air pressure rose to 150 PSI, the compressor let loose with a blast of air causing a small dust cloud. Again several children jumped and a few coughed. Peter climbed onto the second running board and yelled to the children over the noise of the engine. He explained the air system of the truck, thus the air brakes. I was impressed. When Peter finished, he motioned for me to cut the engine. Afterward, I joined him on the ground.

Greg raised his hand. "Can we see the engine?" I raised the hood. Childish wows went up. Peter exclaimed, "She's a monster, isn't she."

Tammy raised her hand. Peter looked at me with a smile. She asked, "Peter, why do you and your grandpa call it the Babes?"

"Most truckers have names for their trucks. Jake has always called his, the Babes."

Back in the classroom, Peter still presiding, Jamie asked the one question neither of us wanted to hear. "Where were you when they blew up the Twin Towers?"

Peter's face fell as he turned to me. I said simply that we'd seen it on television, which we had in one truck stop after another for several days on end. Neither one of us could tell the children what we saw and heard firsthand.

Mrs. Pryor moved in to rescue us. "Would anybody like to go out on the playground?" All was forgotten as a collective cheer filled the classroom. We walked to the playground in an orderly manner. I saw my first grader quickly revert back to a six-year-old. He jumped, skipped, hopped, slid, ran and played tag with the other boys. At no time did Jamie or the other boy show any animosity toward Peter for his earlier reprimand.

As we stood watching the children play, Mrs. Pryor said, "You have coached Peter well. He did an outstanding job." I told her it was totally impromptu on Peter's part. She was impressed but not surprised.

I spotted Peter hanging by his knees from the monkey bars while a tangle of girls talked to his upside down face. I know boys! He was showing off for Tammy. His shirt was down around his armpits while he scratched his protruding ribs, making the sound of an ape. He happened to catch Mrs. Pryor and me observing him. We both smiled and I winked. He was so embarrassed he almost fell.

After twenty minutes, we joined the class for lunch. I'd forgotten how loud a school cafeteria can be. It was a joy when lunch was over.

Back in the classroom all the kids lined up to say good-bye. Peter and I went down the line saying good-bye to each child. When Peter got to Tammy, she gave him a slight peck on the cheek. All the kids made a mocking noise while both Tammy and Peter looked at me and turned bright red. I winked at both of them.

Mrs. Pryor thanked us for coming, and we walked to the truck. As we pulled away, we waved and I blew the air horns. En route to the truck stop to drop the trailer, I said to Peter, "I was real proud of you today. You did a fantastic job. I couldn't have done it better myself. When you got the attention of Jamie and the other boy, I thought you used good manners and were careful to not embarrass them. No wonder the kids respect you.

"You see Kiddo, when we give friendship and respect freely, we get it back double. The only time you stumbled

The Gift

was when Jamie asked his question. I was glad you looked to me first before you answered."

"I didn't know what to say, Jake. I didn't want to talk about it."

"I didn't either. We both handled it just right." He was close to tears. The memories were too close.

"Hey, how about that peck on the cheek from Tammy!" Instead of tears, he turned bright red. "How about if we drop the trailer and go riding?"

We parked the truck at the curb in front of the house. Peter jumped into my arms. Before putting him down I turned his head to the side and said, "Look at that, lipstick. She planted a pretty good one on you." Once again he turned red and wiped his cheek. I laughed, so he punched me.

"Hey, Jake, can we ride our bikes together now?"

"Sure, partner." We rode our bikes for the rest of the afternoon.

During our evening talk, we discussed the day. Peter asked, "Jake, do you know what a sleepover is?"

I nodded. "But if you're thinking of asking Tammy, the answer is no."

He blushed. "Jake, that isn't funny. I was thinking of Jamie. Do you think I could invite him for a night?"

I thought about this. "When were you thinking of?"

"Tomorrow night. Maybe on Saturday we could go to the zoo or something like that."

Both Jamie and Greg were good friends of Peter's, but Jamie was his favorite. His personality was very similar to Peter's. He seemed to be a sensitive, fun loving little kid with a lot of energy, but controllable. "That doesn't give us very much time, Kiddo. I'll have to get permission from Aunt Betty first then call Jamie's parents tonight and ask them."

"Okay." Then he expressed concern. "Jake, what happens if I have a nightmare and pee?"

"Jamie is six like you. I'm sure he has nightmares too. Probably peed a time or two."

"Do you think so?"

"I'm sure of it. The question is, what would I do if you both had a nightmare at the same time?"

He giggled. "Hold us both I guess."

"I'll call his folks tonight and let you know what they say tomorrow."

Excitedly he added, "Maybe he could come over for dinner and we could go to that restaurant for chicken wings."

"Wait a minute. You remember what happened the last time we did that? You ended up with an orange bellybutton. I'm not sure if I want to deal with two orange bellybuttons."

He laughed. "Maybe it won't happen again."

"Maybe, but now neither one of you have front teeth. By the way, did any of the kids notice your haircut?"

"Yeah, several did. Tammy noticed it first. They all liked it."

After he went to sleep, I called the Rotundo's.

Peter and I met Mrs. Rotundo at Peter's going away party in September. She was quite agreeable to the sleepover but would not say anything to him until he returned home from school Friday afternoon.

I asked if Jamie liked chicken wings. He loves them. I asked if he'd eaten any since he'd lost his front teeth. The answer was no. I explained how Peter ended up with an orange bellybutton the last time he ate them. She laughed and thought that was cute. I would wait for her call Friday afternoon.

The Gift

That night, Peter had another nightmare about the Twin Towers, probably brought on by Jamie's question. It didn't last long and he remained dry.

The next morning, Peter woke up excited. When he heard Jamie's mother gave the okay, his excitement mounted. When the call came from Mrs. Rotundo, Peter could hardly contain himself. She said Jamie was in the same state of mind. She would bring him over in fifteen minutes.

When Peter's friend arrived, the two boys were so excited they danced around in typical six-year-old glee. Mrs. Rotundo kissed her son and reminded him to do as I say. Then she looked at me. "He has excellent hearing but sometimes he forgets to listen."

I looked at Peter and winked. "That sounds familiar," I said to her out the side of my mouth.

After taking Jamie's bag into the house, Peter asked, "Grandpa, can we teach Jamie our form of tag?" I wasn't expecting that kind of activity so fast. But knowing both boys, I should have.

In the garage, Peter removed his shirt. It was 70 degrees. Jamie looked at Peter then at me. "Should I take my shirt off too?"

"Peter likes playing with his shirt off but you don't have to. It's up to you. Play the way you're comfortable." He chose to keep his shirt on but that lasted only five minutes. I was soon chasing two boys around the back yard and running out of energy twice as fast. When I took a break, both boys lay down next to me until I was ready to go again.

It was finally time to eat. Peter and Jamie were looking forward to chicken wings, but Betty, Jerry and I were dreading it. The three adults had fish dinners so we could pay more attention to the boys. I sat between the two boys with

Betty next to Peter and Jerry next to Jamie. Among the three adults, we kept up with the messes pretty well.

Upon returning home, we had both boys remove their shirts. Although there were some gooey streams running down both chests, there were no orange bellybuttons tonight.

At eight, Peter, Jamie and I went into the bedroom where I had them change into their pajamas before our promised story. While changing, they checked each other out but apparently decided they were both normal.

"Grandpa," Peter asked, "Jamie's a guest. Should I wear my new pajamas?"

I hadn't thought about that. "Good idea! Wear your tops too." He wasn't happy about that, but offered no argument. It was then story time. I lay on the bed supported by pillows. Jamie lay on my left, Peter on my right. By 8:30 the story was over.

"If you guys would like to talk for a while, you may." I got up and left the room with the door ajar. There was some giggling as I heard Peter say something about his other pajama bottoms. With that, I went downstairs. At nine I returned.

Peter asked, "Grandpa, could you lay down between us for a while?" Jamie looked as hopeful as Peter. I slipped in between them, Peter resting his head on my right arm, Jamie on my left. Peter was soon asleep. Jamie asked Peter a question but there was no response.

"He's asleep, Jamie."

"He is? Already?" I smiled and nodded. "Grandpa, I mean Mr. Winters…"

"You can call me Grandpa if you'd like."

"I can? Okay. Thank you. Both of my grandpas are in heaven."

"Oh. I'm sorry to hear that."

"It's okay. Grandpa, could you stay here for a while, just you and me?"

"If you'd like."

He smiled and hesitated. "Grandpa, Peter's different isn't he?"

I looked at him. "How do you mean?"

"I don't know. He's not like the rest of us. He's smaller than us, but he seems…older. He understands things like a grownup does. He likes everybody and everybody likes him. There's one kid in another class everybody picks on but Peter doesn't. He even told us it isn't nice to pick on him because it makes him feel bad." He thought for a moment. "It's almost like he knows what it's like to be picked on but nobody picks on Peter. Everybody wants to be his friend. If the rest of the guys knew Peter invited me over, I think they might be jealous."

"Yesterday, when Peter got your attention, when you and Kenny were talking instead of paying attention, did you feel yourself get mad at him?"

"No! I was mad at myself for letting Peter down. When Peter talks, you feel you have to listen. He goofs around like the rest of us, but when he stands before us to talk, it's always important. He's like a grownup. He knows things the rest of us don't know. And he knows how to talk like a grownup."

He paused. "Like when he told us about traveling around with you in your truck. He made it feel as if we were all in the truck with him. When he told us it wasn't cool to walk around with our sneakers untied and why, we all understood. When he uses a big grown-up type word, he stops to explain them. That's something that grownups don't always do. They just keep talking."

"Jamie, were you one of the boys that asked your teacher that afternoon in September, if you could squirt the dirt?"

"Yeah," he said in a guilty tone. "I was the last one. I knew Mrs. Pryor was getting mad, but it was fun. Peter bawled us out for that but he didn't make us feel bad. He just...I don't know, made us think it was time to quit. He told us if you knew he told us about squirt the dirt, you'd spank him." He paused. "Would you?"

"Not for that."

"Would you have spanked us yesterday if one of us had touched those brake things on the dash board?"

"Do you think I would have?"

He studied me. "I'm not sure, but I don't think so."

"Hopefully you'll never find out."

"Have you ever spanked Peter?"

"Once. Have you ever been spanked?"

He put his head down in shame. "Once." He paused. "I got mad at my big sister and punched her in the stomach."

I looked at him amazed. "You?"

He giggled. "Yeah. She was teasing me real bad and I finally got mad. Daddy didn't see what she was doing but he walked in just as I punched her. He grabbed and spanked me. Why did you spank Peter?"

"He tested me one time, just to see how I would react."

"How did you?"

"That's the one time I spanked him."

"Did he cry?"

"He sure did. Didn't you?"

"Yeah. It hurt bad. Did you like spanking Peter?"

"No, I hated it. We both apologized to each other later. Do you think your daddy liked spanking you?"

"No! He apologized to me later and I promised I'd never punch my sister again. Grandpa, it's hard to believe Peter would ever do anything wrong."

"Peter is no angel, Jamie. He often gets into trouble because he doesn't always listen. Sometimes he gets hurt for the same reason. I bet you're the same way." He was embarrassed. "But I think you're both pretty special. How about going to sleep now?"

He smiled. "Okay. Thanks Grandpa. Will you stay here until I fall asleep?"

"I'll be happy to."

The next morning I was sitting on the side of their bed when both boys started to stir. Peter opened his eyes first then Jamie. "Well, look at this. Man are you two ever ugly."

They both giggled then Peter looked at Jamie. "He tells me I'm ugly every morning. Could you wake us both up this morning?"

"I think I can manage that." They were both squealing joyously when Peter announced he had to pee and Jamie agreed. After returning from the bathroom, they both dressed quickly.

After eating, Peter, Jamie and I left for the zoo. After an enjoyable day, we returned by mid-afternoon. The boys napped a bit on the drive back. I had Jamie home by four.

I told Jamie's folks what a joy he was to have around.

That night Peter and I talked about Jamie. "Peter, would you like to stay over at his house sometime?"

He looked worried. "Would you go over too?"

"No, that wouldn't be right. His parents didn't come over here, did they?"

He thought about this. "Jake, do I have to go over there if he asks me?"

He was so insecure he couldn't stand the thought of being separated from me for even one night. "Not if you don't want to." Someday I thought it would be good for him, but not yet. It would be too soon. I also suspected that if the sleepovers continued with Jamie, others would soon learn of Peter's status. Jamie already knew Peter was different.

Suddenly, Peter grew worried. "Do you like Jamie as much as Bobby?" I knew where this was going. I nodded. "Do you like Jamie as much as me?"

I knew it. "Peter, Jamie is a nice kid. He's smart, sharp and well behaved. He's polite and kind." Peter was becoming more concerned by the second. "He worships the ground you walk on. You pick good friends, Kiddo. Jamie's special but he's no Peter Stevenson. I like Jamie a lot but I love you. You're special to me in ways another child could never be. Remember, I'm the answer to your prayer. I'm not the answer to Jamie's or anybody else's. That alone makes you special. But you're special in other ways too. You need me and I need you. Jamie doesn't. He has his parents. We're a team, you and me."

"What did you mean 'he worships the ground I walk on'?"

"Jamie has called you 'Little Brother' hasn't he?" Peter nodded. "Jamie loves you, Kiddo. He loves you as he would a little brother."

"Wow! Can I love him like a big brother?"

I smiled. "I think you already do."

CHAPTER TWENTY-FIVE

After church, we went home and got ready for the Buffalo Bills football game on TV. During the game, Peter had a lot of questions, but also had us in stitches. I had a full-size football. During a break in the action, Peter decided to play center and hiked me the ball. When I said hike, he tried but he was so small and the ball was so big, he hiked it into his groin and went down in mock pain.

During another break in the action on TV, he decided he would play quarterback, but he soon found his hands were far too small to hold the ball. I also sacked him.

During the next commercial, he decided to play receiver. I threw him a five-foot pass. He caught it without a problem, turned around to run and immediately ran into the couch, bouncing back about three feet. After getting up and shaking his head, he asked what had happened.

"You made a good catch but got tackled and got your bell rung."

He looked at me confused. "I what?"

"In other words, you just got tackled hard."

Later he tried another position. He decided to play a defensive lineman and tackle the running back. I was the running back. Just as I was ready to run, he assumed a three point stance, made as nasty a face as he was capable of, snarled and in his meanest, high soprano voice said, "Come on sucker, make my day." I started laughing so hard I fell over. He got me in the backfield.

During a commercial break due to an injured player on the field, he decided he wanted to play that position again. I once again played running back. This time I didn't laugh. He almost got ground into the rug.

His next position was running back, but he got crunched.

We'd just seen the running back dive over the defensive line for a touchdown, so Peter decided to play running back again. But this time he wanted to try something different. He called Jerry off the bench (the couch) and had him play center. After a huddle, Jerry hiked the ball to Peter. Jerry immediately got on all fours and Peter climbed on his back. Using Jerry's back as a springboard producing an oomph from Uncle Jerry, Peter tried to dive over the defensive line ...me, but landed on my shoulder.

I stood up and spun him fifteen or twenty times then sat him on my shoulder. I ran from the family room through the kitchen to the dinning room. I continued my run through the living room to the front hall, back to the kitchen and ending back in the family room. My little victor appeared to be tipsy from the spins.

As I ran, I yelled "And the team from Slippery Gulch wins in the final moments of the game. His coach, the great Jake Winters, has him on his shoulders and runs around the stadium track." (Jerry and Betty joined right in with applause and cheers.) "Fans are shouting on both sides of the field. What a play. What a game. And what a dive Peter Stevenson made with just thirty seconds on the clock. Folks, today's family room football has come into its own as a major sport in New York State." I lay him across my shoulder and spun him again and flopped him gently to the floor. He rolled around in a drunken stupor, laughing hysterically.

When he gained control of himself he said, "Jake, you zad-gerate too much."

"The word, my good man, is exaggerate. And you, as usual, are right."

That night Peter and I broke with tradition. We had our talk in the family room. I began with a summary. "Peter, I'm so proud of you, I could…but I won't here in Betty's family room. Five months ago, in early June, you were a lonely, friendless little ghost. Look at you. Today you're in New York, a normal, mortal little boy with some wonderful friends – young and old, and a family that loves you. By God's grace, you've come an impossibly long way from being the Montana Funny Face I first met in a hostile mining ghost town. But one thing hasn't changed: You are still as ugly as sin when you first wake up in the morning – that is until I apply my tickling fingers." And with that I did it again.

After he quit laughing and we were getting on our feet, he asked, "Jake, what's 'God's grace?' You said, 'By God's grace I have come a long way.' We came here in your truck."

"So we did. Well now…God's grace is…let me think a …Jerry, you've been in church a-heck-of-lot more than I have in the last dozen years. You answer the boy for me."

Jerry stiffened up in his chair and pushed the Sunday paper off his lap as if it were too mundane to come between him and the little communicant staring at him, all ears and eyes. "I like what our Sunday school teacher said once: Grace is 'God's riches at Christ's expense.' See how the first letters spell out the word Grace: G-R-A-C-E! That says it for me."

"Does God's grace include Jake and his truck?"

Jerry paused. "Yes, yes it does. God gives us Jesus plus Jesus' people of faith; it all works in a mix. God seems to do it that way so if you don't have faith, you can thank somebody who's indirectly involved in the thing – like Jake. God's grace will let Jake get all the credit, if you don't want to credit God for anything. And even that is gracious of God, isn't it?"

I was flabbergasted. I'd never heard Jerry talk that way. But then maybe nobody ever asked him. Here he was, talking like a Sunday school teacher.

"Then God's grace gave you Jake, and Uncle Jerry and Aunt Betty."

I put in, "And Mrs. Pryor, Jamie, Bobby, Tammy, and on and on the list goes. All the way back to Jane, George and Mike. All the way back to that editor who was moved to proclaim to Slippery Gulch how disgusted he was with the treatment you got at the hands of everybody."

"Does God's grace include you dragging me up to the cemetery the first time you told me I'm special?"

I smiled and nodded.

"But I wouldn't listen. I was sure I wasn't special. I was nothin'. Remember, Jake, how I told you I felt that way?"

"I remember."

"But I know I'm special now. Not so much as a ghost. But as the little boy I am. But I know I'm not too special. Besides knowing lots of other things other kids haven't learned yet, I'm just like them. Except for seeing a lot of America out of our truck window, I'm pretty much like them."

"Peter," I began. Suddenly, I sensed a wisdom beyond me kick in. I really forgot what I was about to say and I heard myself say this: "Peter, we are all special, right off the bat. How? Why? Because God makes each of us special, but we get busy and tend to forget that fact."

"Am I special because I lived a hundred years in Slippery Gulch?"

"No, being special in God's eyes is a different thing. It's not what we can brag about. Or what good health or good looks we have. Or how we can have a perfect driving record – in my case, or climb a rope faster than the rest of the boys – as in your case, or turn Tammy's pretty little head, again, in your case. We are special to God simply because he made us. We have been created in his likeness and in his image. We are not like God himself. None of the animals can say that about themselves. And we are made for God. Notice, no dog or cat I ever met takes time out to worship like we humans do. Nor do they confess their faults to each other, like humans are able to do. We are the ones that need God's forgiveness, not the deer that steals the vegetation out of Betty's garden, nor their thieving buddies, the rabbits. Does that make any sense, Peter?"

"It helps, Jake. You know how I always tell people that I am what I am because of you?"

"Yes, and it gets a little embarrassing, frankly."

"Well, what I really tried to say, but didn't know how, is that by the grace of God, you are special too. But because you were never a ghost, I didn't think 'special' was the right word. Now, I do. Jake, thanks for being special."

"Yes, I guess I have to admit it. I'm as special to God as Jerry and everybody else who loves and trusts in God. Peter, as you know, when Jane suggested I take you with me in the truck, I came up with every excuse I could think of why I couldn't. Jane shot down every excuse. I told all of them I didn't even like you."

Peter gave me a hard look.

"Now stay with me. When Jane told me to look her in the eyes and tell her I didn't love you, I couldn't. I knew then that I was going to ask you to go with me. Kiddo, I never told you this before: At that moment back then, I was so scared, I was shaking."

"You were? Why?"

"Before Slippery Gulch, I didn't want anybody in my truck, ever. I was an independent old cuss that had no cares or responsibilities and that's just the way I liked it. And the last thing I wanted in my truck was a snot-nosed brat that didn't know a thing about the twenty-first century. Of course

I knew from day one that you weren't a little brat. And on our way to the swimming hole, you blew everything out of your nose so I knew then you weren't snot-nosed either." Peter chuckled. "The point is Kiddo, you taught me how to think of someone else other than myself. To accept responsibility for someone else! I taught you how to reach out and care, sure, but you taught me the same thing. I guess we taught each other a lot."

A certain quiet came over the family room. Betty, who had been waiting for the right moment, came in with a tray with hot chocolate and cookies for us.

I was glad we would change the subject. I was having a bit of a headache for some reason. But I slept well that night and it was gone in the morning.

We all slept well that night.

The next morning before going back on the road, Betty pulled me aside and asked if I was set for December 2nd.

I assured her that I was.

CHAPTER TWENTY-SIX

It was the third week in November. We had just started down Lookout Pass on I-90 in northern Idaho, when the air gauge started dropping. It was dark, 3:30 in the morning Pacific time, snowing hard with the roads covered. We had ten miles of down grade to go and no run-away truck ramps. I knew we were in serious trouble.

I looked over at Peter. I moved him up to his seat an hour earlier before we started driving that morning. He was in a sound sleep.

I knew I'd lose the brakes in one or two short miles. I needed an answer to my steering wheel prayer, "God, help us. We need your help badly."

Then it dawned on me: "Peter, I need you."

Suddenly, Peter was awake. He was wide-awake, as if he'd never been asleep. Before I had a chance to speak, he said, "I'll be right back," and vanished.

In seconds, he was back. "There's a tube hanging down from the right maxi brake on the front axle of the trailer. It's your airline. I'll try to reattach it. If I can, I'll be right back. If I can't, I'll hold it in place until we get to the bottom of the hill."

"Peter..." Before I could continue, he was gone. I watched the air gauge. Within seconds it started going up. I gave a sigh of relief. I was not concerned about Peter. He was not human at the moment.

Once at the bottom of the hill, I pulled over onto the shoulder and came to a safe stop. I said a prayer of thanks, grabbed my huge winter jacket, jumped down and ran to the rear of the trailer. Except for the bottoms of his pajamas, Peter was naked but before I could offer my coat he said,

"Don't worry about me, Jake. I'm a ghost now. Get some wire and I'll fix it."

I ran to the cab and got a clothes hanger, the only wire I had. As I headed for the trailer, I never thought about how thick a hanger is until I handed it to him. "Sorry, this is all I had."

He took it and said, "Perfect!" I then watched in disbelief. He pulled the hanger apart effortlessly. He instantly wrapped it around the tube as if it was a piece of string and said "we're ready to go."

"Sure. Okay, that ought to hold until we get to a shop, right?"

"Right." He headed back to the truck ahead of me, but turned around and looked at me still standing there, stunned. As I joined him, I reached for his hand but it wasn't there. This was the first time I was not able to touch him and that stung. He drifted into the truck as I climbed in. I started the truck and turned the heat on high.

I looked at him and said, "Are you a little boy now?"

"Yes, and I'm freezing."

I grabbed a heavy towel, wrapped it around him, sat him on my lap and hugged him for a long time. "Peter, how did you know the name of that brake?"

He thought for a minute. "I don't know, I just did."

"How could you bend that hanger?"

"I don't know, I just could."

"Well, ghost or little boy, I love you. You just saved my life. I'm in debt to you. Thank you."

"You're wrong. You saved me and I will always owe that to you."

"Well, that proves we're meant for each other. We both owe one another." I continued hugging him and kissed the back of his head. "That's why you weren't cold out there, right?"

"I guess. Could you help me wake up now?"

"You bet I can," and with that I removed the towel and dug in.

About one hundred miles down the road, I pulled into a Freightliner shop in Missoula, Montana. When a mechanic had a chance to look at it, he said, "How did you get that hanger wrapped around this so tight?"

"I had some help," I said winking at Peter.

I called the Silver Dollar Saloon in Basin from Missoula. George answered. I explained Peter and I would be passing through Butte in about two hours. Because of our schedule, we weren't able to make a side trip up to Basin, but would be glad to have a quick lunch with anyone that could make the trip to Butte.

Jane and Mike met us at the Flying J truck stop in Butte. We were thrilled to see one another. Jane noticed Peter's haircut at once and liked it.

Peter talked so much, he hardly ate anything. He never mentioned what had happened a few hours earlier, so I did. Neither Jane nor Mike seemed the least bit surprised. I never mentioned Peter's birthday. I hoped Jane remembered and would send him a card.

We were soon back on the road heading for December second and Peter's surprise birthday party. Meantime, Thanksgiving was at hand. Although we didn't make it home Thanksgiving Eve, instead of reading about it, I told Peter the history. He'd never heard about it before and thought it was interesting.

"You know, Peter, I think you and I have an awful lot to be thankful for."

"I know, Jake. Almost every night before I go to sleep, I thank God for you."

I looked at him. "You do?"

"Yeah. Sometimes I fall asleep too fast, but most nights I thank him."

"You know what? I do the same thing. And when you were having those terrible nightmares, I was praying for both of us."

"You were?"

"I sure was. I guess God is still answering our prayers, isn't he? How about sleeping down on my bunk tonight and we can say our prayers together." That night I put his bag next to mine and we both crawled in, happy, contented and thankful for each other.

On the evening of December 1st, Peter and I sat in the passenger seat talking for a good half-hour. I did not once bring up his birthday. He didn't either, though he dropped several hints. One was in the form of a question: "Do you know what tomorrow is?"

As soon as I said yes, he became all smiles, for the moment: "It's Sunday, December 2nd."

"Anything else?" He asked hopefully.

I thought for a while before concluding, "I can't think of anything except we're going home." He looked so disappointed, I thought he was going to cry. He didn't need presents or gifts, a party or a birthday cake. But he wanted to hear from the most important person in the world, "Happy Birthday, Peter." It would have to wait for tomorrow.

I knew he'd never outright inform me. I knew all of this, and it was killing me. Betty had no idea what she was asking of me when she told me to pretend I forgot.

The Gift

When it was time for him to go to sleep, he couldn't. This whole thing was tearing him apart inside and as a result, it was tearing me up, too. He was usually asleep within minutes but tonight it took a good thirty. It took me quite a while also because in one respect, I felt guilty. However I knew I'd be vindicated once he realized we had planned to surprise him.

The next morning I woke up at six to find Peter already up and dressed. "Good grief, Kiddo, this is one of the first times ever you got up before me. What's the special occasion?"

I could see he was already disappointed. He was hoping I'd remember this morning, but I didn't. "Oh, I don't know. It's just a nice day." I guess one reason I wanted to wish him a happy birthday was I really wanted to be the first in his entire life to do so. Who could blame me? But to spill the beans would make it disappointing later for the others.

Outside, the early-morning sky was clear and full of bright stars. "Well it sure looks like it's going to be a nice day. I guess we might as well get going." I got up and dressed. After I fired up the truck, I said, "Oh wait a minute, I forget something."

His eyes brightened as he looked hopeful, "You did?"

"Yeah, I almost forgot my coffee. I have to pee anyway and you probably do too, right?"

"Yeah, I guess," he said. I knew he was on the verge of tears again, but I pretended not to notice. It was sad and funny at the same time. I was having a hard time keeping a straight face. I helped him out of the truck. We walked into the truck stop, took care of business and went for my coffee. He walked slowly. His head was bowed as if he were carrying all the problems of the world on his shoulders. Well, he was – with respect to his little world.

"Well, let's get going. We'll get rid of this load and head for home." Being Sunday, it was just a drop and hook. We drove to Erie in silence, dropped the loaded trailer, picked up an empty and had breakfast. Not much was said between us.

We didn't make it home for church. Betty didn't go that morning either. She was busy preparing for Peter's surprise birthday party.

When we got to the truck stop, I called Betty to let her know we were in. Since it was winter, I couldn't park at the curb in front of the house because of the snow removal law. About ten minutes later, she showed up, causing Peter to brighten up immediately. He was surely hoping that she, at least, would remember; of course, she didn't.

In fact, she seemed annoyed. "Look you guys, I'm really busy today. I'm baking things for a party I'm going to later. When we get home, why don't you take my car and go over to the mall. You can have lunch over there. Just be back by 1:30. I need the car at two."

"Is Uncle Jerry home?" Peter asked in a thin voice so weak that we could hardly hear him.

"No, he's on the road today." Jerry was the only other person who knew today was his birthday and he was gone. Just like before, nobody cared.

We dropped off our stuff at the house and headed for the mall. Peter was so lifeless he wasn't interested in even looking out the car windows. We had lunch but he barely touched his food. We got home at 1:30. Betty said, "Jake, would you come into the living room for a minute? Oh I suppose you can come in too, Peter."

"No, that's okay," Peter said as he sat down on a chair in the kitchen. I silently waved to Randy, Connie and the girls. Then I returned to Peter.

"Peter, you look awful tired. Why don't you and I go up and take a nap for a while?"

"I don't want to take a nap." He snapped back, the tear he'd been struggling to hold back since last night, slowly worked its way down his right cheek. I picked him up anyway. For the first time, he struggled against me. Thank God this was all about to end. He put his head down on my shoulder. In a tearful voice he asked, "Jake, don't you know what today…"

As I walked into the living room with him, he was interrupted with "Happy birthday, Peter."

In unbridled ecstasy he jerked around in my arms. A spectacular ray of sunshine filled the room as he let loose with one of his most beautiful smiles ever. I wiped away his tears, and put him down. He ran over and gave Jerry, Randy and Connie a big hug. He even gave the girls a half-hearted hug before turning to me. "Ja-a-a-ke!" but he never had a chance to finish.

His back to the dining room, two people walked out and said, "Happy birthday, Peter". He turned around and found Bill and Danny standing there. He rushed over and gave both a hug. I noticed Danny got him turned around so his back was once again to the dining room.

He looked at me, hands on his hips, and in disgust exclaimed again, "Ja-a-a-ke," now another voice wished him a happy birthday. He turned around and there was the very charming Mrs. Pryor. He ran to her and gave her a hug. As she wished him a happy birthday, she gradually ushered him in my direction.

Again Peter stood there, hands on his hips, and again said, "Jake, did…" but again he never had a chance to finish. He again heard someone from behind him wish him a happy birthday. He turned around and yelled, "Hank!" as though he were across the street. He charged across the room to give him a hug. Hank was flabbergasted. Back in Spokane he was unable to touch Peter and at the terminal in Ohio, Hank never tried.

I looked at him and said, "What in heaven's name are you doing here?"

"Well it's not to see you." Everybody laughed. "It's to see my trucking buddy, Peter. I wouldn't miss his birthday for all the tea in China." By this time, Hank had Peter most of the way back to me, once again keeping his back to the dining room. Peter obviously had not caught on to the little staging maneuver taking place. But I wondered who was next.

Again he looked at me, hands on his hips, more disgusted than ever and said, "Jake, did you..." but once again before he could finish, from behind him a female voice wished him a happy birthday. He spun in total surprise. "Jane," he squealed and charged across the room and into Jane's waiting arms. How neat of Betty to arrange these repeated surprises for Peter, but how did she do it? Jane put him down and he ran into the dining room, but that was it. He then walked back into the living room, now on the far side from me. He put his hands back on his hips and said, "Jake, did you know about this all the time?"

"I knew about the party, but I didn't know Mrs. Pryor, Hank or Jane were going to be here."

"So you didn't really forget it was my birthday after all?" He let his arms slide to his side.

I dropped to my knees knowing what was coming. "Kiddo, I would never forget your birthday." With that he charged across the room and into my arms, never slowing down. Both of us went over. I held him and ran my hands across his back. We both shared tears of joy. Everybody stood by in silence.

As we sat up, Betty said, "Peter, would you come here for a minute?" Until then he hadn't noticed the sheet-covered mound she was standing to the side of, beneath the front window. He stood and helped me up. Together, hand in hand, we walked to the mound. Betty removed the sheet exposing an assortment of neatly wrapped presents. I knelt down next to him, put my arm around his shoulders and in a quiet, loving tone said, "Happy birthday, Little One."

I finally got to wish him a happy birthday alone and we both felt it, as if we were alone in the room. Our mutual smiles conveyed deep understanding and heart-felt gratitude. His tears reformed as he threw himself into my arms. "I knew you wouldn't forget, Jake." Now he turned to the presents with a look of total amazement. "For me?" he asked, and plopped on the floor in front of them. This was almost too much. All he'd wanted was someone to wish him a happy birthday. And now all this.

I put my arm around his shoulder, pulled him close, kissed him on his head and said, "For the best little co-driver ever, Peter Stevenson."

"Should I open them?" he asked weakly.

"Sure," I said. "It says who each gift is from."

He carefully read the tag on each gift then tore into it. He got a couple of Tonka trucks, which were too big to take with us, but would be fun at the house. He got a heavy winter jacket, heavy boots, long underwear and heavy moose hide mittens with fur lining. Danny gave him a small but high-quality pocketknife, and I gave him a digital watch (which Betty had to pick out for me). She had just the right number of links taken out of the band.

Hank gave him a company jacket with his name on the front. "Wow, it's just like yours, Jake." It fit – a good call on Hank's part.

After opening all of them, Mrs. Pryor presented him with another surprise. She handed him a bag full of birthday cards from every child in her class. Each child had made his or her own special card. Peter was smiling and at times laughing as he opened and read every one. He showed me two. The first was from Jamie. It read, "How does it feel to be seven, Little Brother? Happy birthday! Your big brother, Jamie."

The second one after the message said, "Love, Tammy." I kept my promise. I didn't tease him anymore, yet.

Peter grew solemn. "Everybody's been so nice to me." Tears filled his eyes again. "Thank you everybody. Thank you, Jake. I love you so much." I gave him a hug.

Finally Betty said, "Come on, everybody. Let's go out to the dining room." Sitting on the table was a large birthday cake with seven candles. I lifted him up so he could read the blue frosting writing: "To our special friend. Happy birthday, Peter." His eyes were as big as manhole covers. The candles were burning as we sang happy birthday. After making a wish, he blew the candles out. Then we dug in.

During the meal everybody commented on how nice Peter's haircut looked. Peter ate it up.

"Betty, how did you manage to contact all of these friends?" I asked.

"Because of you camping with Bill and Danny, I called and asked if they'd be interested.

"Sue would be here but she had to work.

"I knew Mrs. Pryor would want to be here to represent the class. As for Hank and Jane, I called Jason. He was wonderful. He knew you two spent some time with Hank in Spoken, so Jason got to Hank for me."

Hank added, "Thanks to Jason, he arranged a trip for me to the area."

"Hank reminded Jason of Jane, George and Mike in Basin. Jason didn't know their last names but knew the name of the saloon. I alerted them."

Jane said, "Peter, Mike, George and Tasha sent their love. They just couldn't get away from business. I knew all about this two weeks ago when you were in Butte, but I had to keep my mouth zipped."

Everybody laughed as we dug into our cake. Upon finishing his, Peter climbed up on my lap while I juggled my coffee and the last of my cake. "Betty," I began, "I can't thank you enough but do you have any idea what you put me through? Last night Peter started asking me such questions as, 'Do you know what tomorrow is?' I could only answer, 'Yeah, Sunday, December 2nd.'"

This filled the room with even more hilarity. I went on, "Then this morning, for the first time since the camping trip, he was up and dressed before me. He was so excited, it was unbelievable. But after a bit he grew disappointed. I thought I was going to cry before he could. I felt miserable."

He looked at me. "You did?"

"Oh, Peter, you wouldn't believe. My disappointment may have exceeded your misery."

"Well you sure didn't show it," he said sarcastically.

"Hey, Funny Tummy," I said stroking his neck, "I couldn't. If I had, I'd have messed up the fun we had surprising you."

"This was really great! Thanks again, everybody."

Just then the phone rang. Betty got it. It was for Peter.

"For me?" he said excitedly. She handed him the phone. "Hello," he said hesitantly. It was George, Mike and Tasha calling to wish Peter a happy birthday.

Peter was on cloud nine as he talked with each of them, entertaining the rest of us in the process. At the end of the conversation, he asked if they wanted to talk to Jane but then giggled, said okay and hung up.

Jane looked at him and asked disappointedly, "They didn't want to talk to me?"

He giggled again and said, "No. Mike said it isn't your birthday."

That brought the house down with laughter.

We spent the next two hours sitting around talking and playing with Peter and his Tonka toys. In time, Peter told Hank, Jane and Mrs. Pryor about our fishing trip.

Then he volunteered to tell them about his week in school. Mrs. Pryor brought a lot of color and credibility to his account.

He brought several other things up but never once mentioned his rescue on the mountain. It didn't surprise me so I looked around to find the girls in another room watching television. They knew Peter as only a little boy. I wanted to keep it that way. While explaining the incident, Jerry and Hank, both veteran truckers themselves, leaned forward in the telling.

"Why didn't you tell us about this, Peter?" Jerry asked.

"I don't know. It really wasn't anything."

"What? What do you mean it wasn't anything? You saved Jake's life and that wasn't something?" Jerry exclaimed.

Peter turned bright red with embarrassment. "I didn't mean it that way." He looked to me for help.

I motioned with my finger, then lifted him up on my lap. "While this young lad is immodest when it comes to his body – and some of us can attest to that, he's very modest when it comes to his exploits. Peter is no bragger. Out there on I-90

The Gift

when the air hose broke, he simply moved to save me. I'd been watching out for him but I learned that day that he had been watching out for me. This just happened to be my first crisis and near death accident with him on board."

Peter spouted proudly, "Jake and me, we're a team."

Everybody cooed at that.

"Well, Peter, I know you have your hands full keeping Jake's sorry hide out of trouble," Hank jokingly stated. We all laughed.

While they were fascinated about our Jim Bridger encounter, I deliberately did not mention our up close and personal view of the 9-11 tragedy.

It was finally time to eat the meal Betty had prepared – hot dogs, hamburgers, baked beans and potato salad. After dinner Bill, Danny, Randy, Connie and the girls said goodbye. Jane and Hank were both leaving the next day, so they were staying in the guest rooms. The remaining seven of us sat around and chewed the fat for quite a while. Once we all got Peter talking about his newfound fishing skills; he went on non-stop for the next half-hour.

"I have a situation I have to tell all of you," I said. "In July, shortly after we left you Hank, Peter had a bout with constipation." Peter shot a glance at Mrs. Pryor.

"Jake," Peter said in a pleading manner, "please don't tell that."

"Okay, Kiddo. Let me just say that we drove a few days with the windows down."

Everybody got a kick out of that, including Peter.

Out of respect, I moved on to something else. "You have all seen the pictures I took of Peter on my first visit to Slippery Gulch. I never told you, but from the beginning – behind the tattered clothes and grimy body, behind the profound sadness in his eyes, I saw hope. A small flame of hope burning there. Well, Peter's hopes have come true, and today is a wonderful celebration of that hope fulfilled.

"And he is filling out too. Jane, both you and Hank saw Peter with little or no clothes on those first two days after he left Slippery Gulch. I'm sure you remember." They both nodded. I put Peter on the floor and asked him to remove his shirt so they could observe how filled out he'd become.

"Give us a muscle, Kiddo." He flexed his muscles in a muscleman form, turning this way and that, causing smiles all around.

"Peter, give me ten push-ups." He gave me ten good ones. As he did, I pointed out the muscles in his back, arms and shoulders. "When he first started these, there was little muscle tone. Now give us some sit-ups." His frontal muscle formation was obvious. "His calves and thighs are showing the same kind of development."

I had him stand up straight. "Remember his twig-like ribs? The point is, he's filled out nicely everywhere but he's still slender. However that's in his genes." I looked at Jane. "I think you recall weighing him in Basin."

Jane put in, "Yes, a mere thirty pounds. He was pathetically all skin and bones."

"Well, he still weighs the same."

The others thought I was kidding them.

I continued. "I pointed all this out to an examining doctor a few months ago – again, after showing him the pictures of Peter. I asked for an explanation. He was at a loss. He was having trouble believing that he was examining what had been a ghost, now turned rehabilitated little boy. He used a term, corporeal body, in a feeble attempt to explain Peter. He declared him an absolute miracle."

All were staring at Peter. Finally Mrs. Pryor, looking at her unusual student said, "Peter is one of the strongest

The Gift

children in my class and is in the best shape by far." She continued to scan his body. "Now I can see why."

Jane picked it up from there. "Peter, you're beautiful. I remember how pathetic you were as you tried on the clothes. But you have filled out so beautifully. You look some eight to ten pounds heavier."

Hank agreed.

"I know, but he isn't."

Jane changed the subject. "Peter, when did you start wearing underpants?" The band of his underpants was showing above his long pants.

He giggled. "I had to wear them when I went to school. Jake said they had a rule. But I saw in the boys' locker room that all the guys were wearing underpants. So underpants are cool. And I just wanted to be cool, too. Right Mrs. Pryor?"

"This is all new to me, Peter. If you say so," she chortled.

Everybody got a laugh out of that exchange.

Peter came back with, "I have on Superman underpants," and quickly lowered his long pants to show them off, proclaiming that he also had Batman, Spiderman, Mickey Mouse, Donald Duck and Goofy underpants.

The boy could not help but be entertaining to the rest of us. Nothing on the TV could surpass this little guy for pure amusement – and amazement.

When the laughter faded and Peter raised his pants, Hank put in, "Personally, Peter, I like my Green Hornet underpants the best."

"Who's the Green Hornet?"

"He's my favorite super hero. You want to see them?"

"Sure," Peter responded.

Hank stood up and started to unbuckle his belt. We all laughed. "That's okay, Hank," I said. "We'll take your word for it." Hank sat down appearing rejected. Peter chuckled.

It was 9:00 P.M. Peter was still going strong but I knew he could not last much longer.

Mrs. Pryor, being sensitive to the energy level of little ones, spoke. "Well, this has been a memorable evening, but I must excuse myself. Thank you so much for including me. I am a Johnny-come-lately into Peter's unique world. My students will want to know everything that went on here, so I'd better go home and take some notes before I forget anything."

Peter said, "Mrs. Pryor, thanks for coming. Tell Jamie and Tammy..." The wheels were turning. "Mrs. Pryor, could Jake and I come to school sometime tomorrow so I could thank all the kids myself?"

Mrs. Pryor looked at Peter and smiled. "Peter, I think that's an excellent idea. The children would love to see both of you again. Could you be there at 2:30?"

I looked at Mrs. Pryor. I hadn't thought about this but suspected she had. "That will be fine. We'll park the car in the side lot."

"Perfect! I won't tell them your coming. It will be your surprise, Peter." He was thrilled.

"Would you do me a special favor, since I'm so special?" Peter asked.

"I know what you're concerned about. My lips are sealed tight, just like Mr. Winter's windows are on a normal day."

Peter smiled and stretched his arms up behind my neck. I looked at her with pain in my bachelor heart. "Mrs. Pryor, please, call me Jake."

She beamed. "If you prefer. Thank you, Jake. And please, call me Grace."

I showed her to the doorway and helped her on with her jacket. As I did, she remarked, "Jake, you are such a gentleman. Peter is so fortunate to have you as a male role model and his grandpa. You are both blessed. And while Peter may not be able to appreciate that, and put it into words, you are a blessing to him. I only wish more fathers these days were similarly devoted to their sons in the little things that go far beyond their little muscles and their miniature athletic fields."

I thanked her. And after I let her out, I watched her walk to her car by the curb. A little fantasy came over me – that she and I met years ago, back when we were nearly the same age and both on some college campus. That was Mrs. Jake Winters going down the long walk to her car tonight. She was leaving to go home to Jake who would have the coffee on, eager to hear how her evening went.

It's a strange thing: A person watches the years go by without paying much attention. Then something comes along and for the first time, he regrets how old he's grown. And how he might have done some things differently.

It dawned on me, then, as she pulled away from the curb, that had I married a girl named Grace, I would not now be the answer to a dying little boy's prayer a century ago.

Peter always enjoyed being the center of attention, but gradually his energy ran thin. At ten he fell asleep. The small group talked for another hour, but finally the excitement and emotions took their toll on all of us. We said our goodnights and headed to our respective rooms, bringing a wonderful and successful day for Peter to a close.

CHAPTER TWENTY-SEVEN

Over coffee the next morning we heard the upstairs toilet flush. A minute later Peter staggered into the kitchen, rubbed his eyes and smiled slightly. "Well, if it isn't our birthday boy," I lifted him onto my lap. "You're not tired are you?"

"Yeah, Jake, I'm real tired. I'm going to need an awful lot of help waking up this morning," he said crossing his arms on the table and laying his head on them.

"A nap will definitely be in order for this afternoon, Kiddo." I replied.

I rubbed my hands up and down his sides. "Peter, both Hank and Jane have to leave this morning."

He looked at both of them. "You do? Why?"

"Unlike the old geezer, I have to work for a living," Hank said. "I'm darn glad I was here for your birthday, though. And very likely I'll see you on the road again, sooner or later."

"I'm glad you were here too, Hank. And thanks for the jacket. It's really cool."

"Peter," Jane said, "I have to be at the airport by 11:00. I have to get back to Basin. You understand how George and Mike can't get along without me."

Peter giggled as he sat up straight and stretched his arms behind my neck. "They can't get along without you like I can't get along without Jake."

I rubbed my hands up and down his rib cage. "Hey, kiddo, don't forget, I can't get along without you either."

He smiled. "Can you help me wake up now?" I did – until he was short of breath.

Everyone there but Jane had witnessed our tradition. I told her we'd been doing this every morning since Basin.

"That poor boy. Jake, you should be ashamed of yourself."

Peter giggled. "Jane, I love it when he tickles me."

"You two are good for each other. I can see some changes in Jake. Thought I didn't know him that well. Do you see that, too, Betty?"

"Well, yes, I guess I do. But I've known Jake a lot longer than you. I think I see a certain playfulness coming out that I haven't seen since his college days."

"Well, Jake. What happened after college that you lost your playfulness?"

"Two things. Public school bureaucracy and the demands of the increasingly regulated trucking industry. So I'm happier with Peter on board."

"And safer!" Jerry shot back. "Peter, do you know any other ghosts like you that might like to ride with me?"

Peter and the rest of us had a good chuckle over that thought.

"Peter," I began, "why don't you go get dressed and then come back down for breakfast. After we feed the old coot Hank over there, we'll take him back to his truck."

"Hey, Grandpa, watch it. You're Hank's same age I bet." With that, Peter ran off.

While he was upstairs, Jane confessed, "You know Jake, when you two left Basin months ago, I really didn't think you'd even make it to Spokane. I knew Peter was excited, but I wasn't sure about you at all."

"To be honest, I had my own doubts, Jane."

Peter returned to my lap. I looked at Jane. "How could I get along without this kid, Jane? He's mine now."

He pushed back from me and said, "You're mine too, Jake."

"Well Kiddo, lets get some food into your belly. Then we'll take the ugly one over to his truck and get rid of him."

Peter chuckled but didn't move. Something was up.

I said, "Well?"

After a long moment he sat up and winced like he was having trouble phrasing his thoughts. "Jake, is it true that people come from dust?"

I thought, Uh-oh, I wonder where this is going. "Well, that's what the Bible tells us."

"Is it also true that when people die, they go back to dust?"

"Yeah, I guess it is, Kiddo." Everybody was poised for Peter's next words. "Why do you ask, Kiddo?"

He slid off my lap, took my hand and said, "Jake, come upstairs with me, quick."

"Why? What's up?"

Looking dead serious he said, "I was just sitting on the floor tying my sneakers when I happened to looked under your bed. Jake, I think somebody's either coming or going."

The five of us were laughing so hard we had tears in our eyes. Peter was hurt and embarrassed but mostly annoyed with all of us. When we quieted down he said, "Did I say something stupid?"

"Peter, you never say anything stupid unless you're fooling around. Don't worry, Kiddo, it's the wrong kind of dust. You *are* a thinker though. Most kids wouldn't make the connection. I'll tell you something else, Peter. Not too many weeks ago, if we five had laughed at you half as hard as we just did, you would have run from the room in tears. Even though I was laughing, I could see you weren't even close to tears. You've come a long way, Funny Face. What do you think, you ready to eat?"

The Gift

He gave me a big smile and climbed into his higher chair. After breakfast, we took Hank over to his truck.

"Hank, thanks an awful lot for showing up for Peter's birthday."

"My pleasure! Peter, you are one neat kid. My only disappointment is that I can't tell everybody I have coffee with, all about you."

Peter smiled like the sunrise itself. "Thanks Hank, and thanks again for my neat jacket."

Hank put his thumbs up in reply. I know his voice was caught.

We couldn't wait to wave Hank off, for we had to take Jane to the airport.

Peter had seen a few airports from a distance, but this one he was going to see firsthand. We parked and walked to the terminal with Jane. People, taxi cabs, limousines, shuttle buses and security were everyplace.

Inside because of security, we weren't able to go everyplace, but he could see what an airport looked like. We were able to see how people got their luggage. We could look out a window and see a couple of airplanes close up. Peter could see how much larger they were than Sam's.

Finally, it was time to exchange thanks and say our good-byes. I gave her a hug and kiss then she picked up Peter, gave him a hug and a kiss and said, "You take care of Jake, and be a good boy, okay?

She smiled and waved as she went through security.

On the way home, Peter asked why they looked in Jane's purse.

I tried to explain how things were going to be different in America since airplanes in control of terrorists took down the Twin Towers.

I wanted to get off the subject. I knew it bred nightmares. "Hey, this afternoon we visit your friends at school." It worked.

That afternoon Peter and I drove to school by car. We parked in the regular parking lot out of sight of Peter's classmates. Mr. Stewart was expecting and met us at the door and escorted us to Peter's room. He knocked and Grace came to the door.

With a smile she said quietly, "Hi, Peter. Just a minute. Children, we have two very special guests. Would you like to meet them?"

She opened the door to a chorus of yeses. I walked in behind Peter. I'm sure the roar would have registered five on the Richter scale. Control went out the window as Peter and I walked in. Peter was swamped.

At one point, Jamie came up to me. With a bigger smile than usual, minus one tooth on the bottom, we greeted and shook hands.

"I missed my little brother, Mr. Winters. I had a nightmare last month." He motioned for me down to his level. "I dreamed you lost your brakes out west on a mountain road in a snow storm. I woke up screaming and crying."

My all-familiar chill returned to my spine. I was shocked. I looked at him. "Jamie, do you remember exactly what night that was?"

"Yeah. It was two weeks ago this morning at 6:30. When mommy and daddy came in, I told them what my dream was. I said a prayer for both of you. Did it really happen, Mr. Winters?"

The Gift

The chill continued. "It was close, Jamie. I started to lose air pressure going down a long, steep hill in a snowstorm. But we made it or we wouldn't be here now."

"I know. Peter was under the trailer wasn't he?"

More chills! "We'll talk about it someday. Thank you very much for praying. We'll plan to have you over sometime during the Christmas vacation."

That generated a huge smile. "Okay!" He rejoined the rest of the kids.

Grace approached, knowing. "I wanted to see if Jamie would bring it up today, so I kept it to myself last night at the party."

"The time was a perfect match, if you count the time zone difference."

"And Peter was under the trailer?"

I nodded, deep in thought. "He knows Peter is different. I'm going to have to tell him."

"I think you're right. I'm sure he'll handle it fine. Jamie's very intelligent and perceptive. Besides Peter, he's my best and brightest student. He told me he stayed overnight with you and Peter the last time you were home. He had a great time."

"He's a nice kid. Peter picks good friends and perhaps closer friends than what he realizes. Jamie thinks highly of Peter."

Grace agreed with me. "I've got news for you. Jamie worships you, too. From what he told me, you're very much like his grandfather."

Just then it was dismissal time. The class formed a line and passed Peter and me saying good-bye. Jamie whispered something in his ear then Peter looked at me, smiled and said, "Okay, Jamie!"

When Tammy came by she gave Peter another peck on the cheek. They both looked at me and blushed. She came to me next. I took her hand, winked and said, "Tammy, you don't like my grandson, do you?"

She giggled and exposed her own missing front tooth. She looked back at Peter and they both blushed again.

Finally all the children were gone so it was just Grace, Peter and me. "Well, Peter, I think you had quite a birthday," Grace said.

"Yeah! It was great. It really was special but Jamie and everybody else thinks I'm seven. Jamie even asked why my teeth haven't started growing back. What should I do?"

Both Grace and I looked at each other. "I don't know. We'll think about it."

That evening during our talk, I started by asking what he thought about yesterday. His eyes lit up. "It was great!" He thought for a minute. "It didn't start out very good though. I really thought you forgot. I was so disappointed I even thought about going back to Slippery Gulch, but then I remembered I promised you I'd never do that."

"Yeah, I know. I really felt rotten. I really wanted to be the first one ever to wish you a happy birthday."

"I know. I did too but it was okay. Why did Betty send us over to the mall?"

"Everybody was coming in and we couldn't be here. Hank and Jane were already here."

He looked at me surprised. "They were?"

"Yes. Jerry was too. Jane helped Betty bake your cake. In fact the party Betty was talking about when she picked us up was yours."

"It was? Jane did? Did you know they were here all the time?"

"No. I knew Jerry was here and I knew Bill and Danny were coming, but I didn't know about the rest."

"I finally had my very own birthday party."

"And what a party it was. Did you enjoy today?"

"Yeah. It was neat seeing all the kids again. But what do I say to them next time?"

"I've been thinking about that. I think we, or you say you have a condition that doesn't allow you to grow. Actually that's not a lie. You do."

He chuckled. "Yeah, I guess I do. Okay, I'll try that next time."

"That sure was a pretty card you got from Tammy yesterday, especially the way she signed it, love. I didn't know it was getting this serious. Then the way she kissed you on the cheek today. Man, I think she's really hooked."

Peter was bright red and no longer smiling. I turned him toward me. "I overdid it, didn't I?"

He put his head down. "A little but that's okay."

"No. I promised you I wouldn't and I did. I'm sorry."

"You also promised you wouldn't tease me in front of anybody else and you haven't. Thanks, but Jake, isn't it kind of hard to tell when you've gone too far until you have?"

I chuckled. "Yeah. I guess it is but I'll try to pay closer attention to it next time."

I hesitated. "Peter, I'm going to change the subject. Jamie knows something's going on. He had a bad nightmare two weeks ago." I explained it to him. Peter was shocked. I also told him about the conversation Jamie and I had the last time we were home.

"The next time we're home we'll have him over for a sleepover again. Depending on how it goes, we may have to tell him."

Peter was excited. "Jamie whispered in my ear that we were going to get together, but do you really think we should tell him?"

"As I said, we'll see how it goes. He's a smart kid. In fact he's almost as smart as you. He knows something's up.

"Hey, the next time we come home it's going to be Christmas, then you might even get a visit from Santa Claus."

"What's Christmas and who's Santa Claus?"

I would have been shocked if Santa Claus had visited him, but I thought he would have at least heard of him. The same with Christmas! I explained both to him and although he was not too excited about either one, he was curious and had a lot of questions.

After answering his questions, instead of being excited, he was sad. I wasn't expecting his reaction. "What's wrong?"

"He'd never visit me."

"Why do you say that?"

"He never did before and he must have known where I was. Now he doesn't."

"He knew where you were before and I'm sure he knew you were a good kid, but Slippery Gulch was such a terrible town, he may have been afraid to go there. I don't know for sure but I would guess he knows where you are now. He's not afraid to come here. He came here when I was a little boy."

Suddenly his eyes were huge. "He did? Do you think he will find me?"

"Look Kiddo, I don't want to build your hopes up too high, because there's always a chance he won't, but I kind of think he will. I just can't say that for sure. Hey, I've got an idea." I lifted him off my lap and handed him a pad and pen. "Let's help him out. How about writing a letter and letting him know where you will be."

If possible his eyes grew even larger. "I can do that?"

"Sure. There's no guarantee he'll get it, but it's about the only thing we can do."

He wrote, "Dear Santa, I'll be at Jake Winter's house for Christmas." That part I suggested, but he added, "If you find me, I'd be very happy, but if you can't, I'll understand. Love, Peter Stevenson." What a kid! "How do we mail it?"

"It has to be mailed in a very special way. Come with me." We walked downstairs and to the fireplace. I explained to Betty and Jerry what Peter had done, then I took out my lighter.

"You're going to burn it?" he asked in horror.

"Yep. That's the way it's done with Santa Claus." He was skeptical and looked to Betty and Jerry for confirmation. They both nodded. I lit it and we watched it go up in smoke.

"Are you sure that's going to work?" he asked more skeptically than ever.

"No, but that's the way it used to work. That's all we can do. We'll just have to wait until Christmas morning and see if he found you."

"How will we know if he did?"

"Trust me, you'll know." What a Christmas this will be.

"Does he ring the doorbell?"

"No. He doesn't want to wake anybody, so he comes down the chimney." He looked at me as if I were nuts. He crawled into the fireplace among the partially burnt logs and looked up. Then he stood up. His feet and legs were covered with soot. Betty, Jerry and I were trying to keep a straight face. He couldn't see a thing, so he felt around the chimney. Sitting down again he turned toward us. He was covered with soot. "You've got to be kidding."

We couldn't hold back the laughter. I carried him carefully into the bathroom. "Not only that, he comes down the chimney and never gets dirty." I lifted him so he could see himself in the mirror.

He laughed at himself. "How can he do that?"

"It's the magic of Santa Claus," Jerry said.

"How about taking a bath?"

"Do I have to?"

"No, but if you don't, you'll have to sleep standing up tonight." He chuckled then agreed. I carried him up to the bathroom. "How about a shower, Kiddo? I think it will work better." He agreed. Once dry, he put on his new bottoms then we returned to the family room.

"Did you bring down your pajamas?" Betty asked. "I'll throw them in the wash tonight." Peter and I looked at each other. Neither one of us thought about that. She looked at both of us. "Typical men. Peter, run up and get them for me." He was off my lap and on his way up the stairs like a shot. A few seconds later he was back on my lap.

After thinking for a moment he asked, "Jake, what happens if Santa doesn't find me?"

"You'll still have a good Christmas Kiddo, because we'll all be here with you."

"But it would be better if Santa Claus finds me?"

"Oh, yeah. No doubt about it," I volunteered.

He looked to Betty for confirmation. "Jake is right," she said.

"Is there anything else I can do to let him know where I am?"

"I don't think so. All you can do now is hope," I said. He was really worried, but none of us were.

CHAPTER TWENTY-EIGHT

He wandered into the kitchen at 7:30 the next morning. After waking him he said, "Jake, I think I had a visitor last night."

Betty and Jerry looked at me. "You mean a ghost?" I asked.

He thought for a minute. "I think so. I think it was a woman. She touched my forehead. I tried to sit up but I couldn't. I couldn't even open my eyes."

"Any idea who it could have been?"

"I think so. She was nice like Aunt Betty. I knew she loved me right away. Jake, I think it was my mother."

Jerry and Betty looked at me in shock. "Do you have any idea why she was here?"

"I think so. I think she was making sure I was okay. I think she likes you."

"Why do you say that?"

"I'm still here, aren't I?"

I couldn't argue with his logic. I wasn't sure if it was a visit, a very pleasant dream or just wishful thinking. We all sat there deep in thought. I finally broke the trance. "Why don't you run up and get dressed?"

While he was gone, Betty asked, "Do you think he really had a visitor last night?"

"With Peter, anything's possible; but I don't know what to make of this."

I wanted to change the subject for now. "I've noticed neither one of you ever refer to Peter as Kiddo."

"We won't either," Betty assured me. "We noticed that Kiddo, Funny Face, Little One and a few others are affectionate names that you use. Those belong to the two of you, Jake."

"Okay. Thanks for that. I guess I'd not thought it through, as you two have."

Just then Peter came bounding back into the room. "Well, Kiddo, I've got to take a shower before we leave. You're lucky. You took yours last night. Give me ten minutes, okay?"

After rinsing my hair, I stepped back and my foot landed on the soap now on the floor. I went down hard. Instantly, Peter was beside me with terror in his eyes. "Jake, are you okay?"

"I think so." He lifted me up with little effort on my part. I felt his miraculous strength. This was incredible. I knew I'd be sore later. Then I noticed the door was still closed and locked. Drying I said, "Peter, how did you get in here?"

"You know. I heard you fall and I was scared, Jake. I had to make sure you were okay."

I looked at him with renewed awe. "Thanks, Kiddo. I appreciate your concern."

After getting dressed, we both joined Betty and Jerry for breakfast. As we walked in, Betty asked if I was okay. I assured her I was. "I've never seen anything like it, Jake. You fell and Peter instantly vanished. You've got quite a caring little buddy here, Jake."

Before I had a chance to reply, Peter said, "And I've got a caring big buddy. We watch out for each other."

"You sure do. Together you two make quite a team," Jerry stated.

After eating, we said good-bye to Betty and Jerry, thanking them for being such gracious hosts to us and to our friends. Betty didn't know it, but I phoned in a beautiful flower arrangement to be delivered after the senders were long gone.

I had not always been such a thoughtful brother. There was to be no note attached. So I doubted she'd guess the originator of the gesture. If and when she ever brought it up, I would pass the credit to Peter's supernatural powers. (It would be Peter's and my secret intrigue.)

We picked up our load, destined for the Bronx. The security going across the George Washington Bridge was understandably intense.

The load was to be delivered at 6:00 that evening. The next morning we would pick up a load going to Salt Lake. When we got to the warehouse, it was dark. I wanted Peter to stay in the truck but he refused. We took the paperwork inside and were told to back into dock 19.

I stopped at the truck to get our gloves, then we walked to the rear of the trailer. Suddenly three thugs were on us. I got punched hard in the stomach and went down. Everything turned gray fog. I tried to feel for Peter, but he was not there. I heard one of them say, "Hey, it's a kid."

"So what?" another said. I heard him say, "Give me your wallet or I'm going to blow the brat's brains all over the lot."

My eyes cleared to see Peter suspended three feet in the air by a fist full of his shirt. In the other fist was a pistol, now pressed to his forehead. He was barely conscious. What had they done to him?

I came to my knees slowly, stalling for time. "Better put him down. You have no idea what you're dealing with."

They started laughing. "Yeah. Right." Peter smiled slightly with tear-filled eyes. I knew I had his attention.

"He's a fun-loving ghost, but when he gets mad, watch out. Sure glad I'm not in your shoes." Their laughter increased. Suddenly, Peter disappeared. The thug was left holding air.

"Hey, what happened? Where'd he go?"

"I tried to warn you." Peter was visible only to me, so what happened next was a complete mystery to them. The thug's gun went flying in one direction while he went flying in another, landing hard and unmoving. The other two had seen enough and took off running, but neither made it very far. They were both picked up and slammed hard into a wall. Then Peter drifted back to me and lay down on his back crying. In his ghostly form, there was no pain but now he was a mortal again.

I knelt down next to him. "You got punched in the stomach, too?" Holding his stomach he nodded. I checked for broken ribs. Two were tender and may have been cracked. "Let's get you into the truck, then I'll put the truck in the dock."

As I was assisting him he asked if I was okay. I assured him I was. After putting the truck in the dock, I checked on the thugs. The closest one was just coming around. He asked where the ghost was. "He's drifting over your head. He's not very happy, but for now, I'm holding him back. I'd suggest you and your friends get out of here while you still can." He wasted no time in gathering up his cohorts in crime and splitting.

Then I checked on Peter. He was in severe pain. There wasn't a thing I could do. At least he wasn't bleeding from the mouth. No damage to his lungs! "Jake, I'm sorry. I should have known they were back there."

"How could you? Look, you taught those punks a real lesson tonight and saved me again. You'll be okay in the morning, right?"

"Yeah, but it sure hurts now."

The Gift

"Yeah, I can imagine. Why don't you change into your ghostly form until tomorrow morning?"

"And not be able to be touched or held by you? No way! Besides that would be cheating."

I smiled. "As soon as we get unloaded, we'll go back to New Jersey and spend the night. You're sleeping next to me tonight." I finally got a hint of a smile. I brought his sleeping bag down on my bunk, helped him into his PJ's then to bed.

By the time we got back to New Jersey, it was after 9:00. Peter was still awake and very sore. I rubbed his ribs gently. He was asleep in seconds.

The next morning I was up by six. While Peter slept, I ducked in for coffee. We were in the dock when he woke up. I was sitting in front reading when he called my name.

"Hi there, Funny Face. How do you feel this morning?"

"Okay, but I have to pee, bad." I made use of the urine bottle. I decided not to mention the night before unless he brought it up. He didn't. Apparently because neither of us was hurt, it was no big deal.

"Let's go see how they're doing on our load." I climbed out of the truck and he jumped into my arms.

The woman in shipping looked up with a smile. "I didn't realize you had a co-driver."

Peter smiled. "He's short but he's good," I said. "How's my trailer coming?"

She called the dock. "Give them another fifteen or twenty minutes. Say, is this your son or grandson?"

"Grandson."

"He's a little darling."

We soon had our bills and were on our way to Salt Lake. As we drove north on the New Jersey Turnpike heading for I-80, we once again had a good view of Manhattan. The Twin Towers were gone. Recent painful memories came rushing back for both of us. As Peter continued to stare out his window, his tiny shoulders jumped in wracking sobs. I let him cry on without a word.

Finally I said, "Kiddo, would you sleep next to me tonight? I think we'd both sleep better."

He turned to me. Through tears he smiled and said, "Thanks, Jake."

Before we were out of Pennsylvania, we were treated to heavy snow. Peter was incredible. He was able to see things no human could possibly see. For example, in heavy snow where visibility was down to a quarter of a mile, he was telling me about vehicles on the right shoulder a half-mile ahead. He would tell me whether they were small or large in size, such as a bus or truck. That was the help I needed.

We ran into a similar situation going through Ohio. I soon became the proverbial front door because I was always able to move along with some certainty and tell the other truckers where danger areas were located. (In truckers terms, the head truck in a group is the front door, the rear is the back door and those in the middle – the rocking chair.) I rarely drive in a pack because there is too much dangerous tailgating. Fortunately, with Peter's help, our group was moving responsibly and confidently.

West of Cleveland, Peter said, "Jake, slow down. A car just spun out. He's turned around and coming back towards us." I switched on the four-way flashers, got on the CB and told everybody to back it down.

"It just spun again, Jake. It went up against the guardrail on my side. Oh, it bounced off and went into the guardrail on your side. It's not moving. Someone inside is hurt."

"Can I pull off to help?"

"There's not enough room."

The Gift

I got on the CB and relayed the information to everybody. Somebody said, "I've got the back door. I'll pull off and check it out."

"No," I said. "There's not enough room to pull off safely. You'd be rear-ended. I'm calling 911 right now." Turns out that the accident was a mile ahead of us, yet Peter saw it all.

As we were going by the car, one trucker asked, "Man, how did you see that, front door?"

"I didn't. My six-year-old grandson next to me did. His eyesight and intuition are incredible. When he warns me, I listen."

"Hey, buddy, anytime you want to adopt him out, just let me know. He can ride in my truck anytime," one of the truckers said. Several others chimed in as well.

I looked at him. "You're a hit, sight unseen."

One of the truckers asked, "Can you let your grandson talk for a minute?"

I looked at Peter. He nodded. "Sure, here he is."

"Hi," he said shyly.

"Hi, son. What's your name?" the trucker asked in a southern drawl.

"Peter."

"Well, Peter, I want to thank you for all of us truckers in this convoy. You possibly saved a lot of lives back there. You're our hero."

"I am?" he asked sincerely.

Another trucker came on and confirmed the same. One by one, everyone in the line took his or her turn thanking him. Peter was in seventh heaven.

It was 8:45. He was tired and fading fast. He thanked everybody and handed the mike back to me.

"I hate to tell you this guys, but there's a service plaza coming up in two miles. I'm pulling off. Peter and I are going in for hot chocolate. Then he's going to bed. That will be it for me tonight. In this snow, I'm not going on without help."

As it turned out, six of them pulled off with us. The other three thanked Peter again. Each of the six asked if we'd mind if they came in with us. They all wanted to meet their little hero. Of the six, four were teams and three of them were husband and wife teams.

We were easy to spot. Within five minutes we had a couple of tables pushed together with all twelve of us. Before being seated, each driver shook Peter's and my hand. It developed that several said they weren't proceeding without Peter's help.

At 9:00 I excused ourselves. "Even little heroes have to get their sleep." I rose and picked Peter up. Every one of the drivers stood, shook his hand and thanked Peter again. His hair was ruffled more than once. By the time we got to the truck, he was asleep. One of the couples walked out with us. The man held Peter while I climbed into my truck. As he handed Peter up me, he said, "Buddy, we'll never forget this. I feel like one of the wise men being guided safely through the night." He looked at Peter as if he were looking at baby Jesus. "Problem is, we can't tell anybody. They'd think we're nuts."

That night he had a serious nightmare. I quickly moved to the front seat with Peter on my lap. I held a towel in the right place, just in case. After he settled down, he woke up. He was shaken but dry. The dream was about 9-11. Seeing Manhattan yesterday did a number on him.

Through pools of tears in his batting eyes, he said, "Why did it happen, Jake?"

I thought out my answer. "You know about hate, Little One. This is about hate on a worldwide scale. Unfortunately, it could happen again, but you and I and everybody we love will be safe. Let's go back to bed."

"Can I sleep with you tomorrow night, too?"

"You bet. If you feel you need to."

He slept with me for the next five nights, but no return nightmares after the first two. He slept in his Pull-Ups all five nights, but remained dry throughout. I had one nightmare and remained dry as well.

The next morning was clear. We didn't have any more snow until Wyoming. At Sidney, Nebraska, we stopped at Cabela's, a huge sporting goods store. They have a fantastic display of stuffed animals, ranging from ground squirrels to brown bears, plus some amazing aquariums. In one tank, Peter pointed out a muskie. Quickly he noted it was not nearly as big as the one I caught. He spotted one in a glass showcase. It was larger than mine. Peter diplomatically kept quiet about the fact. One aquarium had several large and smallmouth bass. I pointed out that none were as large as his.

While walking through the camping section, he spotted a tent. "Hey, this one looks just like yours."

"It is. This is where I bought it." We also looked at the sleeping bags. Peter noted the many different bags for children. But he examined one closely before moving on, asking, "Can I keep using your bag, Jake?"

"Sure! As long as you need it." Little did he know that the last time we were home, I ordered from Cabala's catalog, the exact bag that he had just looked at. Come Christmas morning, he'd find it under the tree, from Santa Claus. What a Christmas this was going to be!

Once we got to Salt Lake, we delivered the load and headed for the yard. Peter had to turn invisible and stay in the truck while I went in to see Jason.

"When's your next break?"

"Jake, good to see you. I get a half an hour in about ten minutes."

"Great! I'll see you out in the truck."

"How was the birthday party?"

"It was Peter's party. I'll let him tell you. While I'm thinking about it, thanks for helping to get Jane and Hank there right on time."

A few minutes later, Jason walked to the truck carrying a medium sized paper bag. I figured it was his lunch. Peter was sitting on my lap invisible to Jason until he closed the door. They greeted one another with big smiles. Peter told him about the big party.

Jason listened with great interest and amusement over Peter's animated gestures.

"I feel like I was there, Peter. Listen, I've got to get back to work. But here's my birthday present for you."

"Thanks, Jason." Peter tore into the wrapping.

"A model of the Babes. Wow, this is neat. Thanks!"

On each side of the hood was painted my truck number. On the driver's door was Jake, and on the passenger door was Peter. It was a huge hit with both of us. "How did you paint the numbers and names so clearly?" I asked.

It had become a family project: His wife was the artist who did it.

"So with your birthday behind you, I bet you're looking forward to Christmas and Santa Claus."

Peter hung his head wistfully. "I didn't know about Santa Claus in Slippery Gulch. He didn't know about me then and I don't think he'll know who I am and where I am now, either."

"Did you write a letter to him?"

"Yeah, then Jake had me burn it in the fireplace," he said with skepticism.

"That's the way you do it. Always worked for me."

Peter's eyes lit up. Just hearing this confirmation helped. "It did?"

"Sure did! All the kids I knew did it that way."

"Really," he said excitedly.

"You bet. I can't say for sure, but I'd be willing to bet he knows where you are. In fact, I bet he's watching right now to make sure you're a good boy." Peter looked in all directions. Jason looked concerned for a minute. Hesitantly he asked, "Have you been a good boy?"

"Pretty good, I think." He looked at me for reassurance.

"Except for a couple of minor instances, he's been real good." Peter half smiled in some relief.

"Were they little boy instances or more serious situations?" Jason asked of me.

"Little boy instances – mostly a result of not listening."

Jason wiped his brow. "Phew! I know from experience, Santa overlooks little boy instances like that. He did in my case. How about you, Jake?"

"Same thing."

"He makes allowances for little boys. He doesn't have to for girls. I suppose that's because he remembers when he was a little boy himself once. He understands little boys. I think you're safe, Peter."

Peter let loose with an audible sigh of relief.

"Well, I've got to get back to work and get you guys a load. Both of you have a real good Christmas and a happy New Year."

We both wished him the same and thanked him.

After Jason got out, Peter asked what a New Year was. By the time I explained it and answered more questions than

I ever dreamed surrounding those two simple words, Jason had our load. We were on our way to Denver.

For the next two weeks, Peter's mood changed as often as the weather. It had to do with Christmas and Santa. At times he was depressed, sure that Santa didn't know who or where he was. At other times, Peter was so excited, he couldn't sit still and had a problem sleeping.

He had another bout with constipation. I'm sure it was as much a result of his mood swings as anything else. I gave him four days as the doctor suggested before we moved into a motel. The enema came in handy. He didn't like it, but he appreciated the results. So did I!

As we drove around the country, Peter loved spotting evidences of the coming season everywhere. About a week before Christmas, we stopped at a mall in Topeka, Kansas. Once inside we started walking. "What are you going to buy?" he asked.

"Not a thing, Kiddo."

He looked at me confused. "Why are we here then?"

"You'll see." Suddenly, there he was. Peter saw him at the same time I did. His eyes lit up like Christmas Tree lights. "Is that really Santa Claus?"

I sat on a bench with him on my lap. "No, it's not, Kiddo. Santa's so busy this time of year, he doesn't have the time to see all the children in the world. So he sends out some of his helpers so he can get all the orders. That's what those kids are doing when they sit on his lap. They're telling him what they want for Christmas."

"They tell him and he tells the real Santa. I got it."

"Would you like to sit on that Santa's lap?" Peter thought about this for a while. I don't think the issue was whether he wanted to or not, but what he wanted for Christmas. Finally he nodded and we immediately got in line.

The longer we waited, the more antsy he became. He was very nervous.

He asked to be picked up. In a quiet voice, he asked, "Jake, is he nice?"

"He's very nice, Kiddo."

"What if he laughs at me for what I ask for?"

"I promise you, he won't."

Finally it was his turn. I put him down and ruffled his hair. He walked up and was lifted onto the helper's lap. I couldn't hear the conversation but at one point, Peter pointed at me. They both looked at me. Suddenly a chill went down my spine. I'd seen many Santa's before but I felt this one was different. As he looked my way he smiled slightly, then he winked. As he did, there appeared to be a twinkle in his right eye. It must have been a reflection from the ceiling lights. It had to have been a reflection, didn't it? But then, why the chill?

After a brief confab, Santa put Peter down. As he moved toward me, Santa looked at me one more time. There was the hint of a smile on his face and he winked again. The chill returned as Peter took my hand.

As we walked to a fast food place, he said, "You were right. He was nice."

I was tempted to ask him what he asked for, but didn't. If and when he wanted me to know, he'd tell me. Neither one of us said a word during lunch or for the first half-hour back on the road. He was deep in thought. I decided it best to keep my mouth shut. Finally he said, "Jake, if I tell you what I asked for, do you think Santa Claus will be mad at me?"

"No, I know he won't."

He thought for a moment as I pulled into a rest area. I knew this was going to be lap-sitting time.

After coming on my lap, he said, "I asked Santa to let me stay with you forever." He then looked at me to see my reaction, hoping he hadn't made a mistake.

Wow! I knew he hadn't asked Santa for a toy or anything like that, but this I was not prepared for. I didn't know what to say. When I didn't say anything he said, "Do you think that was a stupid thing to ask for?"

I was choked up. It wasn't a stupid thing to ask for, but I didn't know how to answer him. I didn't know what was going to happen at his funeral; I didn't think he did either. Then again, maybe he did and maybe that's why he asked Santa for help. "Peter, it wasn't a stupid thing at all. But it may be a long time before you find out if Santa can grant you your wish."

"Why?"

"Forever is a long time."

He thought about this. "Maybe I should have asked him for something easier."

"Maybe, but what you asked for came right from your heart."

"Jake, do you want me to stay with you forever?"

I was fighting my emotions. "I'd love that, Kiddo, but there is one problem."

Suddenly he was worried. His lower lip started to quiver. "What?"

"I just wish there was a way you could wake up in the morning and not be so darn ugly." With that I dug into his ribs. Needless to say, his lower lip was no longer quivering.

CHAPTER TWENTY-NINE

A week before Christmas, I bought three special books for Peter, *Frosty the Snowman*, *The Night Before Christmas*, and *Rudolf The Red-Nosed Reindeer*. He loved them all but *The Night Before Christmas* was his favorite. We read at least one every night and often two. It didn't make any difference to either one of us that we read them over and over again. He had lots of questions.

The Night Before Christmas was read first. Peter sat on my lap ready to be read to, but suddenly the memories came flooding back. I remembered my childhood Christmases with my folks, both now dead. The memories were grand and numerous but my immediate memories were of the book in front of me now. I sat on my mother's lap, wide-eyed, waiting to hear the story of Christmas I knew by heart. That made little difference. I was sitting on the lap of one of the two people in the world I loved more than anyone else. Now Peter was sitting on the lap of the one person he loved more than anyone else in the world. I smiled at the memories and the thought. It never occurred to me how much I could miss something I never had or thought about before.

Suddenly I realized Peter had said something and was waiting for an answer. "I'm sorry, Kiddo. What did you say?"

"I asked if you were okay."

"I'm fine. I was remembering being read to as a child your age by my parents. Are you ready?"

His smile was sad. "I wish I had those memories, Jake." Suddenly his smile brightened. "But now I have you." If possible he moved a little closer. "I'm ready."

"I never thought I'd ever have anybody to read this to." I ruffled his hair. "Now I have you. I'm ready too."

As I opened the book, his eyes enlarged to the size of silver dollars. His mind was on the miracle of Santa Claus and the marvel of Christmas Eve. At one point, I asked if he'd like to read for a while. He put his arm around my neck, looked at me and shook his head. His eyes twinkled in wonderment. When finished he asked, "Jake, do you think he'll find me?"

"I sure hope so, Kiddo."

One night after reading Rudolf, I sang the song to him. He had memorized the whole book. He asked if we could sing it together. Oh boy! I didn't want to discourage him, but Peter was tone deaf. We tried it together. I was shocked. Except for a couple of notes, he was right on tune. How can that be? If a person is born tone deaf, how can he suddenly develop that ability without a lot of practice and hard work? His speaking voice was unusually high so his singing voice was a high soprano. I also noticed his words were crystal clear.

I suggested we sing it again. This time he was on tune through the entire song. Not only that, I detected a slight vibrato. However, he did have a slight whistle now and then because of missing his front teeth. That was cute.

I then taught him *Frosty The Snowman*. His abilities were improving with every note. "Peter, you told me you couldn't sing."

"I didn't think I could. I never tried it. Do I sound okay?"

"You have a fantastic voice. And it's improving with every song." It was one more thing I didn't understand. Suddenly I came up with an idea, one I would have to discuss with Betty and Jerry once we were home.

His voice was so high, I wondered just how high he could go comfortably.

As he learned more songs, we sang more together. There was one he never joined in. I knew he knew the words so I finally asked him why. "That song's special. That's your song to me, Jake." The song was *Santa Claus Is Coming To Town*. He never tired of it.

Several times a day he'd ask if he'd been a good boy. One day he asked me if I thought Santa was mad at him for peeing on me.

"I doubt it, after all, you didn't pee on him." He chuckled as we continued our trip.

Later that day, a song was announced in advance on the radio, so I taped it. "Peter, I have that special song I sing for you. This can be your special song for me. I've loved this song since I was your age." It wasn't a beautiful song, but it was cute and when sung by Peter, very fitting. It was, *All I Want for Christmas is my Two Front Teeth*. Like him, I never tired of hearing it. He even had the whistle in the right places.

East of St. Louis by about 20 miles, I left I-64 and headed east on U.S. 50. We had a load that delivered the next morning in Salem, Illinois, a small town on I-57 about 50 miles south of Effingham. As we were slowing for the town of Lebanon, Peter saw an unusually shaped pile of snow. He questioned what it was. "It's a snowman, Kiddo. Kids make them by rolling huge snowballs and piling them on top of each other."

"Cool! Could we make one when we get home?"

I promised him we would. I decided to stop in Lebanon, one of the quaintest towns in the Midwest. For dinner, we stopped in a little place called Dr. J's. Upon walking in, Peter stopped dead in his tracks. To the right of the door was a piano. It was playing a ragtime song but no one was sitting at the bench. The keys were being depressed without fingers pushing them down. Peter's eyes were huge. He stared at the piano then at me. "Jake, that thing's playing but no one's there...not even anybody like me." He looked back to the piano then at me again. "How can it do that?"

"It's a player piano, Kiddo," I said chuckling. Picking him up so he could see it better, we walked closer. I pointed out a coin slot. "Someone must have put in some change just before we came in. It plays all by itself."

"Awesome! How long will it play?"

"I don't know, but when it runs out, I'll give you a coin to put in." Thanks to Peter and my change, it was playing during our entire dinner.

After dinner we ate some of the most delicious ice cream I'd ever eaten. The place transported me back to my earliest childhood when everything dated back another 40, or 50 years. Peter and I couldn't take our eyes off the beautiful bevy of high school girls that served everybody. Then outside, I could hardly get Peter away from the windows full of old Christmas decorations and antique toys.

After we left there, we went shopping for Betty, Jerry, Connie, Randy and the girls. It was hard to climb back into the Babes and push on.

We delivered the next morning in Salem then moved on to Effingham to pick up a load going to Erie, Pa. From there it was home for Christmas and New Year's.

I taught him several more songs. His memory constantly amazed me. There were many on the radio that I recorded. That way we could sing along with them until we knew them by heart. One I had him learn well. I replayed it several times when he announced he had it.

"Do you think you can sing it on your own?"

The Gift

"Sure!" He did. Even over the noise of the engine, I could understand every word perfectly. Sung by this little angel, *The Little Drummer Boy* never sounded more beautiful.

"Peter, do you think you could sing that song in front of a group of people?"

"I don't know. How many?"

"Maybe one hundred."

"One hundred? Where?"

"At church on Christmas Eve."

"I don't know. Would they laugh at me?"

"I guarantee you, they wouldn't. You have a fantastic voice. They'll love you."

"Would I have to stand up front where the minister stands?"

"Yes. I'll tell you what. When we get home, I'd like you to sing it for Betty and Jerry. We'll have Betty play the piano. We'll see what they think and then you can decide, okay?"

Suddenly, another idea hit me so hard I wondered where it came from. "Hey, how about singing it for the truckers this afternoon. We'll see what they think."

His eyes brightened. "How?"

"On the CB, right now!"

He was excited. He didn't have to stand in front of anyone. I picked up the mike and said, "Hey, everybody, I've got a treat for all the drivers on channel 19. *The Little Drummer Boy* sung by my grandson, Peter, who's riding with me."

One driver came back and said, "Don't waste our time, Buddy." Peter was crushed. The tears weren't far away.

But another came back and said, "Hey, let the kid try, after all, it's Christmas." Others mumbled their agreement. One lady said, "That's exactly what I need right now. Go for it, Peter. I've got two boys of my own waitin' for their mamma tonight." The tears that were forming were replaced by an uncertain smile.

I handed the mike to Peter. He hesitated then keyed the mike. When finished, everyone tried to talk at once. They checked themselves and began to take turns. All marveled at the beauty of his voice and wanted him to sing another one. Peter was amazed. "They really like me."

A trucker asked what truck he was in and his age. Peter responded "My grandpa and I are in QZX eastbound and I'm six."

Then he sang, *All I Want For Christmas Is My Two Front Teeth*, with the same results. Again, chatter was instantaneous! The same woman finally made it through the chatter. "If you're six, I reckon that's exactly what you want for Christmas."

Other drivers asked to talk to Peter. He was a bit overwhelmed, but his newfound confidence saw him through.

The original wet blanket came on and apologized. "Damn, I ain't done heard such pretty singin' in years. Keep at it boy. Give us some more."

Peter came back with *Rudolf The Red-Nosed Reindeer* followed by *Frosty The Snowman*.

I began to notice something: The trucks in front of us were slowing down to match our speed, and trucks behind us were slowing down so as not to pass us. Within a short few minutes we found ourselves in the middle of a sizable convoy. I marveled at what was happening around us. Meanwhile, Peter moved to more serious songs. He sang *I'll Be Home for Christmas*.

The number of trucks in the convoy increased. As I rounded a curve I noticed two empty low-boys that were equipped with multiple yellow flashing lights that had been turned on. All the trucks in the convoy, one by one, turned their headlights and their blinking hazard lights on. The speed of the convoy slowed to 50 MPH. The size of the convoy continued to grow.

Peter sang *Away in a Manger*. As he was doing so, a state trooper slowed as he went by to smile and wave. As he sped up, he put his flashing red lights on. He pulled to the front of the convoy to make himself our official parade marshal. Never in my wildest…well, what should I have expected, given the nature of my teammate. Now I noticed that the trucks traveling south were flashing their lights at us.

Peter keyed the mike. "These next two songs are especially for us truckers." He sang *Home Sweet Home* and *There's No Place Like Home For The Holidays*. Those two songs touched me as I knew it would touch most of the drivers around us. As Peter went through his litany of songs, I was reminded of his incredible memory. He completed his solo performance with the first verse of *Silent Night*. That's all he knew so far of that grand old hymn. As I listened to him sing it, I was choking up. I had to wipe my eyes to see the road. It was my mother's favorite carol. I'd never heard *Silent Night* sung so beautifully in my entire life. I realized Peter had a way of putting his heart and soul into certain songs.

When he finished he told the truckers he didn't know any more. We both waited for a response but got none. We looked at each other wondering what was wrong. Then he keyed the mike again.

"Drivers, this is Peter. I'd like to say a prayer. Dear God. Please help to get all these truckers home safely for Christmas. Amen."

The CB was silent. "I hope Santa is good to you and your families," Peter continued. "Thanks for letting me sing. It was fun. And Mr. Smokey, thanks for guiding all us truckers through this section of the road. Merry Christmas to all."

As I listened to that Christmas prayer and wish, I could imagine it leaving our truck cab via the CB – soft, innocent and beautiful – and sounding like the voice of an angel to all those listening.

The CB remained silent. I looked in the two side mirrors. Nothing had changed. In the next curve I could see the convoy was still intact with no one jockeying for a better position. All the lights were still on and the trooper was still at the head of the convoy with his lights flashing. What was going on?

Peter looked at me for an explanation, but all I could do was shrug my shoulders.

Finally, a trucker came back to us. "Peter," (He cleared his throat of emotions.) "I can't talk for anybody else but…the gift you just gave me is the best gift I've ever received on the road. I've never heard the voice of an angel before…but I believe I have now." He cleared his throat again of emotion. "You and your grandpa have a wonderful Christmas. I can tell what you gave to all us truckers came right from your heart. For me, you're my Christmas angel…I'm sure Santa Claus is going to be extra special to you this year. God bless you, son. And thanks."

Peter's eyes lit up with a big smile at the mention of Santa Claus. Soon many other truckers responded with their own Christmas greeting and thanks to Peter. Many were verbally struggling with their emotions, including the Illinois State Trooper. Today Peter gave many truckers and one state trooper a Christmas gift they'd never forget. There were a lot of tears of Christmas joy on I-70 in southern Illinois that afternoon.

This individual expression of heart-felt gratitude continued for what seemed five or ten minutes. Frankly I was so suspended outside of time, I can't honestly report how long it went on. It was the closest thing to feeling what eternity must be like that I think I ever felt.

CHAPTER THIRTY

The next day on the way home, I felt that I must talk to Peter about the true meaning of Christmas, why we celebrate it and whose birthday we're celebrating. After talking about Jesus, he seemed a bit confused and finally asked, "Well, what was his last name? Who was this Jesus guy?"

I thought, wow what a great title for a sermon. I told him he was the greatest man that ever lived, and that he was the Son of God. His earthly name was Jesus, son of Joseph. And he was also known as Jesus of Nazareth, the town where he grew up in ancient Israel. I explained that they didn't use last names like Stevenson and Winters back then.

Before I could go on he asked with his little boy innocence, "Jake, was Jesus even greater than you?"

I chuckled silently. His question was asked in sincerity and out of love. If there was ever any doubt in my mind the depth of his love for me, there wasn't anymore. "Yes, Kiddo, Jesus was even greater than me, but you're a nice kid for asking." I spent the next hour talking about the birth and life of Jesus. Peter was fascinated with everything I said. During that time I told him Jesus' mother's name, but right or wrong, I decided not to mention Jesus was born of a virgin. I was certain that would lead to more sensitive questions and I didn't want to deal with them now. When I mentioned Mary, Peter looked at me, surprised. "That was my mother's name."

After allowing time for things to bounce around in both our heads, he asked, "Jake, is he the one that answers our prayers?"

"I believe he is, Little one. It might even be his voice you hear in your head."

The Gift

As we drove along, I thought about Jesus and Peter. There were more similarities than differences between the two. Jesus was born in a stable, while Peter was born in a log cabin. But once Peter escaped from his father, he survived during the colder months by living among the animals in the town stable. Both were born into a hostile world. Both their birthdays are celebrated in December. Both suffered a brutal death, but I wasn't in the mood to go there now. Their mothers shared the same name, but while Jesus' mother lived, Peter's mother died in childbirth.

Jesus' earthly father was strong and Godly, while Peter's father was insane and of the devil. As I thought about it, this was the big difference between the two.

Then I thought of something else. Jesus was born to suffer and to be the savior of mankind. Peter was born and did suffer, but for what purpose? I believe God has a purpose for all of us from conception on. Did God mean for Peter to suffer and if so, for what reason? Why was he granted his final prayer and why is he with me now? Not that I'm complaining, but plenty of other people didn't have their final prayers answered. Why Peter? I looked at my little mysterious passenger. There were so many question and so few answers. Where was this all going?

We arrived home the afternoon of December 23rd, Christmas Sunday. Jerry met us at the truck stop where Peter and I transferred everything we needed from the truck to the car. On the way home we observed many people playing golf on a local course. Out of the blue, Jerry said, "Jake, I think we have a problem."

I looked at him with concern. "Oh! What?"

"It's December 23, sunny and warm. The temperature of Lake Erie is still in the 40's. We haven't had any snow to speak of, this year. I think we're going to get nailed soon."

I'd been so excited about Peter singing with piano accompaniment, I forgot about the weather. I've been a lifelong resident of Buffalo. I knew that the temperature of Lake Erie was critical. The temperature of the lake still being in the 40's in late December was highly unusual and could spell big trouble. If the wind shifted from the south to the northwest and brought in cold, Arctic air across the warm water of the lake, we could expect snow – lots of snow. The only question Jerry and I had was when, and how much.

I turned around and looked at Peter. "I think you're going to have a chance to build a snowman, Kiddo."

He looked out the car window at the sunny day and the green grass. "When?"

I looked at the clear, blue sky. "Soon, I suspect." Peter smiled.

Once home and before we even had a chance to unpack, I asked Betty if she could play the song, *The Little Drummer Boy* on the piano. She knew it well. I asked if she would mind playing it while Peter sang. She was delighted. I could tell that what Betty and Jerry expected to hear was a cute performance from our sweet, untrained Peter. What they got was quite different. When Peter had finished the song, Betty was in tears and Jerry was close. Neither said a word. Peter waited for their reaction but finally reacted in his insecure way. "I knew I couldn't sing."

"Oh, Peter, I'm not crying because you can't sing. I'm crying because I've never heard that song sung so beautifully in my entire life. Your voice is angelic."

"What does that mean?"

"Your voice is like that of an angel. It's beautiful. Peter, your voice is special."

Again, I wondered. He smiled angelically. "Really?"

She smiled back. "Jake, why do I have a feeling you have something in mind?"

"You're right, I do. I would like to have Peter sing this in church Christmas Eve along with another song; *Oh Holy Night.*

"If he sings that song, there won't be a dry eye in the church."

"I know. He doesn't know it yet. How about if we teach it to him right now?"

"Jake, *Oh Holy Night* is far more difficult a song to learn and sing than *The Little Drummer Boy*. It's not a child's song. *The Little Drummer Boy* has a seven or eight note range. *Rudolf The Red Nosed Reindeer* has perhaps a five note range, but *Oh Holy Night* has at least a ten note range. I know two or three notes don't sound like very much, but trust me, it is."

I went up the scale and found I could hit nine notes comfortably; and ten or eleven notes if I had to. I never thought about this before and told Betty so.

"Betty, I could be wrong, but I think he can do it. You don't know this kid's singing ability and memory. A week ago I didn't either. It's incredible! Let's give it a try." Peter was looking between the two of us.

Betty looked at Peter. "Do you want to try it, Peter?"

Smiling, Peter said, "Sure." He was always ready for a challenge.

Betty played it through twice to give Peter the melody. I read through the words with Peter looking on. Betty and I sang it twice. Peter was unbelievably attentive through the whole exercise. "What do you think, Kiddo? You want to hum it a couple of times?"

He agreed. The song started on E above middle C. Shortly into the song it dropped to middle C. That was as low as Peter could go comfortably. Now could he hit the highest note which was high E? But at that point it could go to high G if the singer could reach it. Betty played the E. Peter hit it without a problem. I stopped her. "Try the G Betty." She looked at me as if I were nuts. She played the high G and Peter hit it beautifully and without straining.

Betty looked at Peter, unbelieving. "Jake, this is incredible. He has a twelve-note range without straining. I would never have guessed it."

"And I never thought about it until you just brought it to my attention." I took Peter by the arms. "Peter, you're amazing."

"I am?" He had no idea what the big deal was.

"How about singing it through without interruption, and we'll see what happens." He stumbled on the pronunciation of several words but the note was always perfect. It was going to take a lot of work, but he was showing real promise.

"Hey, I've got an idea." I got Peter's higher chair and had him stand on it. We were at eye level. I directed him. I moved my hands higher on the higher notes. I gave him a strained expression and stood on my tiptoes. He loved it. His words improved each time through. It wasn't perfect but practice would take care of that.

Jerry called the minister and told him what we had in mind. He was skeptical, so Jerry suggested he stop over to the house and hear for himself what Peter could do. An hour later the minister stopped in. I could tell he was trying to cover his annoyance; after all, it was a busy time of year for him. He sat down politely and waited for Betty to play the piano and for Peter to begin.

When they had finished, the minister sat there in stunned disbelief, close to tears. Finally, he said, "That was unbelievable. Do you know any other songs?" Peter nodded. "Please, could you sing it for me?"

Peter stood on the chair with me in front. He sang *Oh Holy Night*. This time the minister could not control his emotions. He looked at Peter. "You have to sing these songs in church tomorrow night." Then he looked at me. "Why do I get a feeling there's more to Peter's story than what you've told me?"

I'd simply told him and a few other members of the congregation that Peter had been an abused child, and that I had temporary custody. I went over an abridged version of Peter's story and had him vanish. Unlike everybody else, he was not the least bit shocked or surprised. "Jake, I don't believe this child is a ghost. I believe he's an angel. No child can have a voice like that." That statement appeared to go over Peter's head. Then he looked directly at Peter. "Will you sing in church tomorrow evening?"

Peter was nervous. He felt trapped and in reality he was. Maybe I wasn't being fair to him, yet I felt this would do wonders for his confidence. "Can Jake come up with me?"

"Absolutely!" the minister replied.

Peter looked at me. I promised him I would. He looked back to the minister. "For the second song, can I stand on a chair with Jake directing me?" Again the minister agreed, as did I. Nervously Peter agreed.

The rest of the day was spent setting up the Christmas tree and other decorations. Peter was thrilled, since the only Christmas trees he'd ever seen were those in windows of homes around the country. Every hour that went by he became more excited, and more nervous. He was anxious to give out his presents. At the same time, I could tell he wasn't expecting to get any. He was nervous about church on Christmas Eve. He still wasn't convinced Santa knew where he was. Now I myself was becoming more excited, for the first time in decades.

That evening after dinner, Peter and Betty practiced both songs again. I didn't think he could improve on *The Little Drummer Boy*, but he did. However, something was missing in *Oh Holy Night*. I went through the song in my head and finally realized what it was. There were places in the song where he should fill his lungs with air and hold a note longer. Betty agreed so Peter sang it again. As we got to those places where he had to take a full breath, I put my hands on my stomach. He took a huge breath and made it through that section. Yet his breathing needed work. He had to take in that breath without making a noise. We still had time.

About the time he would normally start cuddling, he began asking questions. "Do you think Santa Claus really knows where I am? Can reindeer really fly? How? Where are their wings? Is Rudolf really their leader? What if it's snowing tomorrow night? How will he find his way? How does Santa keep track when people move in the summer and there are no tracks?"

We had a fire in the fireplace. If we hadn't, I'm sure he would have checked it out again. The questions continued. "Are we going to have a fire tomorrow night? How can he get down it without getting burned? Leave a treat for him? Will he eat it? Does every little boy and girl leave him a treat? No wonder he's so fat. If I come downstairs tomorrow night, do you think I'd see him? Do you think the people in church will like my singing? What if they don't?" And on and on they went. He was a worrier, a trait he came by honestly the last time he had lived. He'd had lots to worry about.

He finally drifted off about 9:30, much to the relief of the three of us. Of course, most of his questions were probably the same ones we all ask as children. I took that opportunity to call Bill.

"Jake, you're home. How's Peter?"

"He's great and unbelievably excited. As with his birthday, this will be his first Christmas. He had never heard of Christmas or Santa Claus before. Since Santa never visited him before, it's hard for him to believe; so he's keeping his fingers crossed."

"Sounds like fun."

"Let me tell you Bill, this is going to be a Christmas to remember."

He was laughing. "Sounds like you're pretty excited yourself."

At that we both laughed.

"Look, the reason I'm calling: We've got something special going on at church tomorrow night and thought you'd like to know about it."

"Well, I've got my own…"

"I know, but we have a guest singer lined up. This guy has an unbelievable voice. I know you've never heard anything like it."

"What's his name?"

"Actually, you know him. His name is…Peter Stevenson."

"Wait a minute. Do you mean your Peter Stevenson?"

"Exactly!" I explained how I discovered his ability. "Bill, if I didn't know better, I'd say he's been taking voice lessons from the masters. But he's nervous. He's frightened that people will laugh at him."

"He still hasn't gotten over that yet? Hang on a minute." He put the phone down and was back in a minute. "We'll be there. Danny's excited, but not the least bit surprised. See you tomorrow."

About three in the morning, Peter woke me up. "Jake, I have to pee." He was really excited. At least he woke up.

"Do you want me to go with you?"

"Yes, please." I walked with him to the bathroom. When we got back to the bedroom, I was just about to turn off the light when he asked if he could sleep with me for the rest of the night. I smiled and agreed. Suddenly the questions started again. I put my hand over his mouth. "Peter, it's three o'clock in the morning. It's time to sleep, not talk."

He giggled a little. "Sorry." Instantly he was asleep again.

The next morning I was up at six. I was just leaving the room when Peter started to stir. I went back to him and said, "Hey Funny Face, wouldn't you like to sleep a little longer?"

"I can't. Would you wake me up, please?" After waking him, he dressed quickly and looked out the window hoping to see snow. There wasn't any. He was a little disappointed but bounded down the stairs with the energy I surely lacked.

Snow or no snow, he was so excited, he couldn't sit still.

After breakfast we went outdoors and played in our grass-covered back yard. I'm sure he found every muddy area there was to find. When Betty called us, Peter was covered with mud and wet through. At least it was warm outside.

I had him remove his outer clothes in the garage while Betty put a sheet of plastic down on the kitchen floor and newspapers on that. "Now get out of everything else and leave them for Jake to clean later."

I looked at her. "Me?"

She put her hands on her hips. "Yes, you! You're the one responsible for this mess." Peter giggled. Betty whispered something in his ear. Peter was excited again. "Now Jake, carry Peter upstairs and into the shower. Don't let him touch anything."

After his shower I opened the bathroom door to find Betty waiting for us. She took Peter's hand. "I'll take care of him now. You go downstairs and work on his clothes." I thought to myself, Uh-oh, Peter's in big trouble now.

In a few minutes he and Betty were back downstairs and reaching for their coats to go out.

Surprised I asked, "Where are you guys going?"

"None of your business," Betty said. Peter giggled, now part of a Christmas conspiracy and loving it. "We'll be back after lunch."

During lunch, Jerry asked, "What do you think he's going to get you?"

"I don't know but whatever it is, it'll be special."

Before they returned, I walked out and got the mail. Included were a few bills, last minute advertisements and three nearly late Christmas cards. Two were addressed to Betty and Jerry but the third one really got my attention. It was addressed to:

MR. JAKE WINTERS AND PETER

And postmarked Hornell, New York. It was from P. Evanston. I was at a loss. I didn't know anyone by the name of Evanston and I sure didn't know anybody in Hornell. My curiosity was killing me but since it was also addressed to Peter, I decided to let him open it. He had never received mail from anyone so this could be a treat...at least I hoped so.

They returned around 1:30 but only Peter came in. He quickly climbed onto my lap. I asked where Betty was but he didn't know. Then I heard the front door open. "What was that?" I asked acting surprised.

"I didn't hear anything," he said trying to remain straight-faced. Five minutes later, Betty walked into the room and nodded to Peter. With that he got off my lap.

Pretending not to notice, I said, "Peter, you and I are going up to take a nap."

"I don't want to take a nap."

"I know, but you were up late last night and you're going to be up late again tonight. Plus you were up early this morning and you will be again tomorrow. Let's go."

He didn't argue. I had him get into his PJ's, then he crawled in with me. He was soon out like a light. After a bit I went down for a cup of Betty's coffee and a chat.

About forty-five minutes later he walked into the family room rubbing his eyes. I looked at him and said, "Oh no. Don't tell me you need help waking up again?"

He giggled. "Yeah, I do…real bad, Jake," he said climbing onto my lap.

After the laughter subsided, it dawned on me that I'd not mentioned the mystery card. "Peter, I forgot. You got some mail today."

"Me?" He was so excited you'd think Santa had walked in the door. I handed the card to him and he read the address aloud. He looked at it. "This is for both of us, Jake."

"You're right. One problem, I don't know anyone from Hornell, do you?"

"Sure, Darlene."

I looked at him. "Who?"

"You know – Darlene and her mother, Paula."

I was puzzled. "How could it be? We never exchanged last names. I never gave them my address."

The Gift

"You didn't have to, I did. When they were visiting our campsite that night, Darlene asked what your last name was. Then she asked for my address. So I wrote it down for her."

"I didn't know you knew my address back then."

"Sure I knew. You told me." I'd forgotten how keen this kid was. He then looked at me concerned. "Jake, are you mad I did that?"

"Well, I guess not. But I don't want you giving out our address and phone number to just anybody. From now on, check with me first, okay?"

He agreed. "Why don't you open it and see what they say?"

He looked excited. "It's okay if I open it?"

"Sure! It's addressed to you too." As routine as it is for us to open mail, this was a new experience for Peter.

He gingerly began to open the envelope as if the card inside were delicate. On its cover was a bright, cheerful winter scene of pine trees and sleighs. Written in gold were the words, "Christmas is the time to remember God, family and friends." Peter looked at me and smiled angelically, then opened the card. Inside was a Christmas verse and two pieces of folded paper. One written in a child's handwriting said, "To Peter," the other in an adult hand said, "Jake."

Peter read, "'Dear Peter; it was fun meeting and playing with you this summer. You helped me remember what fun it was to have my brother back for a while. Thank you. Thank you for teaching me about fire safety and other things. I hope Santa's nice to you this year. Love, Darlene.'"

I repeated love Darlene. "I hope Tammy doesn't hear about this."

He punched me and blushed. "Jake," he said in disgust.

Betty and Jerry laughed. Betty asked what Darlene meant when she said, "to have my brother back for a while." But I decided to read through my letter first before explaining. I chose to read it silently first, just in case.

I unfolded the letter and held it away from one set of little eyes. "Dear Jake. I hope I'm not offending you by writing this. Apparently, Peter gave Darlene your address without your knowledge. I wanted to thank both you and Peter for a very special day in August. It was the best untimely Christmas present Darlene and I could have received.

"I want to thank you personally for something else. Being able to talk to a mature male did wonders for my heart and spirit. I consider you both angels. Have a wonderful Christmas. And, Peter, I'm sure Santa is going to be extra special to you this year. Perhaps we'll see you both next summer. Love, Paula and Darlene."

It was safe so I read it aloud. When I had finished, Jerry said, "Oh, are they the two beautiful women in the string bikinis you two met while camping last summer?"

Peter blushed, but I said, "Yep, they are.

"Paula, the mother, was beautiful. And Darlene was cute as a button. Peter taught her how to swing out over the lake and dive in. Peter is quite a teacher. But teaching someone that cute is easy, isn't it, Peter?"

Peter blushed more. Then he shot back with, "I didn't know you noticed, Jake, with all the time you spent looking at Paula."

Now it was my time to blush as Betty and Jerry laughed at my expense. "You little peanut." I dug my fingers into his ribs and we were soon all laughing together.

I became serious. "Teddy, Darlene's little brother, was Peter's age. Last February, he died of Leukemia." I went on to explain what Peter did for Paula, Darlene and Teddy.

Both Betty and Jerry sat in silence for several minutes, absorbing and visualizing the emotions of the situation.

Finally Betty asked Peter, "You allowed Teddy to borrow your body for a few minutes?" Peter nodded modestly. "And this youngster spoke to his mother and sister through you?" Again he nodded, somewhat embarrassed.

"Paula and Darlene recognized instantly who was talking to them. Teddy referred to Darlene as 'big sister.' We learned that's what Teddy had always called her."

They both looked at Peter with renewed awe. "Peter, you are amazing," Betty said. Peter again bowed his head and would take no credit. Quietly, he thanked both of them.

After a few minutes of absorbing the whole scene I urged, "It's time for you and Betty to practice again." They went through each song three times. His breathing improved with each try. The occasional whistle was ever present but that was cute. And he was showing his nervousness.

When they finished, he came to me. "Jake, I'm really scared."

"That's not as much fear, Kiddo, as it is nervousness, and being nervous is a good thing." I knew there were old fears trying to get new life, but I wasn't going to acknowledge that to Peter.

He looked at me. "It's okay to be a little nervous?"

"Sure. Some nervousness helps you do a better job. If you weren't nervous, I'd be worried."

"Really?"

"Trust me, Kiddo, you'll do fine tonight, and I'm going to be right up there with you the whole time. In fact, I've got an idea. How about you singing *The Little Drummer Boy* one more time, and I'll stand behind you right now with my hands on your shoulders, just the way I will tonight." He agreed with enthusiasm. That was the encouragement he needed.

When he finished, I said, "How was that?"

"Yeah, that was good. Promise you'll be up there with me tonight?"

"Yep, I promise. How about taking a bath?"

"If you'll go up with me."

I threw him over my shoulder and bounced up the stairs with him laughing and giggling the whole way. I started the water running, while he got undressed. Once in the tub, I sat on the counter waiting to wash his hair. But he just sat there quietly and wouldn't wash. Finally he asked softly if I'd wash him. Normally I'd refuse. But tonight I agreed.

I knelt down next to the tub ready to start, when he started to cry. Through the tears he said, "Jake, would you be disappointed in me if I didn't sing tonight?"

As mean as this may sound, I felt he needed this to build confidence; I wasn't about to let him get out of it. "Yes, I would, Kiddo. And so would Betty, Jerry and the minister, too. I didn't tell you earlier but Sue, Bill and Danny are going to be there tonight. Danny is so excited."

He cried harder. "I just don't think I can do it."

This was serious lap time whether he was wet or not. I lifted him out of the tub, wrapped him in a towel and sat him on my lap. "You're going to get drenched," he sobbed.

I smiled while wiping away his tears. "You're worth it." I pulled the towel around his shoulders. "Peter, remember last summer on the ball diamond? You swung at that ball and fell in the dirt. Everybody was laughing at you. You were in tears and stormed off. You were mad and scared. But you went back to the diamond and got the best hit of the afternoon. You didn't quit. I told you then that you gained temporary control of a huge fear. This is the same fear. I wouldn't make you do this if I weren't sure you could.

"I know you're scared and you have every right to be. But I just remembered a few things. First of all, this isn't Slippery

Gulch. We all love you. Second, you're a cute kid with a beautiful voice. Third, you know both songs well. Fourth, Betty will be playing the piano, and I'll be with you. Any time you want, reach up and take my hand. One more thing: Your worst time is right now. Once you get up there and start singing, you will relax."

"I will? Have you ever done this before?"

"I have sung in front of between 180 and 200 people, but that was around a campfire at a summer camp and quite a bit different from what you're doing. But I was still nervous every time I did it. I did have to give a speech once to about a thousand people."

"A thousand! Wow! Were you nervous?"

"Very! But once I started talking, I was fine. One more thing Kiddo, I know we understand each other, right?" He nodded. "Trust me, I know you're going to do an outstanding job. I haven't been wrong yet, have I?"

He thought about all of this. "Thanks, Jake," He gave me a big hug.

He got off my lap and climbed back into the bathtub.

"Jake, I think I can wash myself now, but could you stay in here anyway?"

As he started washing, he asked, "What do I do if I make a mistake?"

"You continue. If you make a mistake, do you think I'd stop loving you?" He smiled and shook his head. "A few days ago when I introduced you on the CB, one trucker came back and said, 'don't waste our time.' What they were all expecting was a little kid to come on the radio with a high, squeaky voice who couldn't carry a tune or remember the words to the song. What they got was something quite different and beautiful. You caught them by surprise. As a result, the whole convoy heard what may be the closest thing they will ever hear to a real angel. You gave them a Christmas they will never forget. The same thing is going to happen tonight. You have a wonderful gift, Little One. Tonight, you are going to give to many more unsuspecting people and make their Christmas special, too."

"I'll sing the best I can. I want to make you proud of me."

"I already am, Kiddo. Now get your hair wet. When I get finished, your hair is going to shine like we know it can." Later as I sat him on the counter and started using the hair drier and brush, I said, "Wow, is your hair ever going to shine tonight."

He turned around and looked at himself in the mirror. "Gee, it looks good, Jake!"

I picked him up and carried him into our room. "Is it true Betty bought you a suit today?"

"Yep, and shoes and even a tie."

"Man alive, are you going to be handsome tonight! People aren't going to recognize you."

He put on long pants and a shirt, then we went downstairs.

Betty said, "Wow, look at that boy. And his beautiful hair! It fairly glows. Do you feel better?"

"Yeah. Jake helped me a lot."

"He has a way of doing that, doesn't he?" He nodded. "The more I watch you two, the more it seems to me you're good for each other. My little brother's as happy as I've ever seen him. Come on you two, into the family room."

We walked in to find many wrapped gifts on the floor. Peter's eyes lit up. In his concern, he nearly forgot about Christmas. As excited as he was he wanted to give his gifts out first.

Before anyone could respond, Betty opened the drapes and turned on the backyard spotlights. The yard was instantly bathed in light, revealing a light coating of snow and large flakes falling majestically from the heavens. Peter's excitement grew.

Betty drew our attention back to the gifts insisting Peter open some of his first.

He was at the point that he loved mysteries, so she handed him the gift-wrapped Hardy Boys mystery from Jerry. He thanked Jerry with a big hug. After that he opened some neat clothes from Betty, which earned her several hugs. And there were more books and toys.

I can't tell you, dear reader, what this boy's infectious delight did for us old geezers. On my part, I felt like a child again. Peter's spirit had a way of infecting your own that way.

Some of the books were a little beyond him, enough to challenge him. Some six-year-olds might have been disappointed with such books – and even clothes, which never seemed to impress little boys anyway, but Peter was thrilled with everything. This was his first Christmas.

And a cold shudder went down my spine at that thought. Would this be his last?

In between opening his gifts, Betty let him pass out his, saving his gift for me 'til last.

He came beaming toward me with a present that appeared to be something he wrapped. I'd been complaining about my flashlight for months. It worked fine until I really needed it; then it didn't work at all. I opened the gift, but kept an eye on Peter as I did. He was so excited, as if the gift were for him instead of from him.

"Hey, and a good quality flashlight at that. And small enough to put in my back pocket."

Betty told me later that Peter shopped in several stores for just the right flashlight for me. Finally he found this one in a sports store. I told Betty it must have set her back a pretty good penny. She said the look in Peter's eyes was worth every cent.

Peter beamed as he showed me how to make it work. And how to change the batteries! Interest in his own gifts was eclipsed by his gift to me. He was so proud of himself, he could bust. He was bursting with Christmas spirit.

During dinner we had the TV on, waiting for the weather forecast for Christmas Day. Suddenly a bulletin interrupted the normal broadcast. A high-ranking air force officer was on the screen in front of a globe. He said that an unidentified blip had been seen on the radar screen about five hundred miles off the coast of North America, and heading our way. Because of 9-11, we were all concerned. The officer stated that several jet fighters had been scrambled to intercept.

Peter's eyes were as big as the TV screen now.

The officer said that he was getting a report in his earpiece just then. He was rolling his eyes over the ceiling and nodding. The suspense had Peter on the edge of his seat and leaning way in.

Once the pilots made visual contact with the object, a pilot reported the object was friendly. As they did a fly-by, one of the pilots took a picture. I knew then what the picture was and watched Peter carefully. The picture came on the screen. In the background of the picture was a star-filled sky. The object was a sled being pulled by eight tiny reindeer. Santa could clearly be seen waving to the jets as they flew by.

At that point, Peter's excitement exploded. He jumped out of his seat squealing, jumping up and down and yelling, "It's Santa Claus! He's coming! He's really coming!" He was so excited, he couldn't finish his dinner. What a Christmas this was going to be.

The Gift

When it was time to get ready for church, Santa's excitement was on the back burner.

Normally he was able to dress himself but tonight I had to help him with everything. Tying his tie was the most challenging. To begin with, it was small. Then tying the thing backwards was a real test of nerves – his and mine. I started over five or six times before finally getting it.

I got his jacket on him. Then I stood back and looked. He was a knockout. His suit was navy blue. The shirt was light blue with button-down collars. His tie was red with blue and white stripes. His shirt brought out his blue eyes and his suit was a striking contrast to his blond hair.

We went downstairs. Betty immediately gave him a wolf whistle. "Peter, you're gorgeous," Betty said. She took several pictures of him. (I was a little jealous.) With his toothless smile, I knew all he had to do was stand in front of the congregation and smile. He'd be a winner.

As soon as we got in the church, I checked the program to find out where his song came in the service. He wasn't mentioned. I was worried. Just then the minister appeared.

"Jake, I apologize. The program was already printed, so I wasn't able to put Peter's name in it. His singing will come right here," he said, pointing to the place. I was relieved.

Just then Sue, Bill and Danny walked in and came directly over to us. Sue and Bill shook our hands. Danny went right to Peter, picked him up and gave him a big-brother-little-brother hug. I watched with a flash of jealousy.

Danny put him down and the two of them talked. In a bit I noticed that Peter was in tears. I was about to go to him when Danny knelt down to Peter's level. I had no idea what was going on, but finally Danny had Peter put his hands up and tickled him in the ribs. Peter laughed and my jealousy went nuts. Then Danny wiggled his fingers as if he were tickling him. Peter giggled then nodded his head. Peter was no longer crying. But my jealousy was about out of control. (Was Christmas Eve turning me childish?)

As we were turning to go in, Peter announced he had to pee. I knew it was nerves. Alone in the men's room, I hoped he would say what he and Danny had talked about, but he didn't.

We joined the others in the second pew from the front so Jerry could take pictures. I showed Peter where he was in the program. When the service began, he couldn't sit still.

Finally, it was Peter's time.

"Folks," the minister began, "as many of you know, Jake Winters has temporary custody of a little boy. His name is Peter Stevenson. He is going to sing at least one and possibly two songs for us tonight." He looked at Peter and me then sat down. Peter looked at me with pleading eyes. I took his hand and led him to the front while Betty headed for the piano. I said a prayer I wasn't making a mistake.

The poor kid was scared stiff. I whispered in his ear, "Once you get started, you'll be fine. I'll be right here. I'm very proud of you." I stood behind him with my hands on his shoulders. "Ready?" Hesitantly he nodded. I nodded to Betty and she started the introduction. When his time came to sing, there was nothing.

Betty stopped and waited. I knelt down next to him, put my arm around his waist and said, "You can do this, Little One. I haven't misled you yet. I know you can do this. And remember the most important thing: I love you."

He looked at me and smiled slightly. I then noticed Danny. He was standing. I drew Peter's attention to him. Danny started wiggling his fingers. Peter smiled again. Now I knew what the conversation was about. "I'll sing with you this time when you start, okay?" He nodded, so I motioned for Betty to start again. When it got to the point for him to start singing, I sang. I rubbed a thumb over a rib. It was just enough. He put his right hand on mine then started to sing, weakly. As he relaxed and realized that no one was laughing, he sang with more confidence and strength, so I stopped. He faltered at bit, but I squeezed his hand gently. He regained his confidence, and soon his voice resonated throughout the church. As I looked around the congregation, I could tell they were totally captivated by the beauty of his voice, even the children.

I saw several of the women wiping their eyes. Although *The Little Drummer Boy* is a simple song, Peter's voice ruled. Sue and Bill sat with their mouths open in total amazement. But Danny had a big smile on his face, not the least bit surprised.

When Peter finished the song, no one moved, including the minister. Finally, he rose and faced the congregation: "Folks, would you like to hear another?" Immediately the entire congregation stood up and clapped. Peter jumped into my arms. "See, I was right. That was beautiful and they loved it. Do you want to sing the next one?" He smiled, nodded and gave me a hug. As I put Peter down, the congregation sat while the minister brought us a chair. The platform was one step higher than the main floor where I would be standing. As a result everyone could see him over me.

"Remember your breathing, Kiddo," I said quietly, "and the most important thing to remember, Little One is, I love you." He gave me a huge smile that caused some chuckles among the congregation now to my back.

I nodded to Betty. This time I did not sing at all. *Oh Holy Night* is far more difficult than *The Little Drummer Boy* because of its range and its breathing, but Peter outdid himself. As he got to the highest notes, I stood on my toes and gave him a strained face. When he got to the areas of tricky breathing, I pushed in on my stomach, held my breath and puffed out my cheeks. He would smile slightly and keep singing so very beautifully.

As I watched and listened to Peter sing, I was aware he never sounded so good. I felt his very soul touch me like never before. And even though my back was to them, I knew that his soul was touching the congregation like no one ever has. The beautiful notes were coming right from his heart. The tears were on my cheeks before he reached high G.

When he completed the song, my arms dropped to my side. I found myself staring at him in awe. I haven't heard *Oh Holy Night* sung so beautifully or with such feeling since my father sang it in church two decades ago. I looked beyond Peter to the cross on the wall behind him. Could he be? I wondered to myself. Looking back to Peter, he looked at me, confused. Finally I put up my arms for him. He jumped. I hugged him then ruffled his hair. "That was beautiful, Little One." He wiped the tears from my cheeks and smiled.

When I turned around I found the entire congregation standing. I never heard them move. Most cheeks were as wet as mine had been. I stood there not knowing what to do. It was as if everyone were waiting for something. Peter looked at me, then back at the congregation. Suddenly one person started clapping. Before long, the entire congregation joined in. I wondered if *Oh Holy Night* had ever been applauded in this church before. They didn't applaud my father, but they were expecting an outstanding solo. We finally took our seat. It was only then that the congregation did too.

The minister remained seated for two or three minutes while the congregation remained silent. A baby started to cry. It was only then that he returned to the podium. He looked over the congregation with his wet cheeks. "This will be a

Christmas Eve I will never forget. I believe we have all heard a miracle tonight."

Suddenly I was worried. I was hoping he wasn't going to mention Peter's true status. He looked at Peter. "My boy, you have a God-given gift. Thank you for sharing that gift with all of us tonight." Suddenly the congregation stood and clapped again. Both Peter and I were overwhelmed.

I whispered to Peter, "I told you they'd love you." On my lap again, he stretched his arms up behind my neck and gave me his characteristic reverse hug. Another fear bit the dust. His was being unwrapped a week at a time like a giant Christmas present from God. I bowed my head in a silent prayer of thanks.

At the reception following the service, everybody came up to Peter, shook his hand and congratulated him. Almost everybody asked if he would sing the following Sunday. We both agreed. The service was over at 8:00. Peter was flying high.

While others continued congratulating Peter, the minister pulled me aside. "Jake, I'm more convinced than ever this child is an angel. I'm sure I saw an inordinate, beautiful glow surrounding his head as he sang *Oh Holy Night*."

Suddenly I saw Peter spot Danny.

I quickly asked the minister. "Do you think others saw it?"

"No. At least I haven't heard of any."

"If he is an angel, why wouldn't everybody see what you saw?"

He didn't have an answer.

"See, I was closer to him than anybody. And I am the closest to him personally. So why would I not be the logical one to see it too?" I was having renewed pangs of jealously.

I pressed my case: "Couldn't it have been your imagination or wishful thinking?"

He agreed, but I sensed more to ease my tension than to concur with my thinking.

It was time to leave for home. The only thing my little angel had to concern himself with now was whether Santa Claus – who had been spotted heading this way, would find him.

Sue, Bill and Danny walked us to the car. Again, they marveled at the beauty of Peter's voice. "If you're singing at the next service, Peter," Bill said, "we'll be here."

We wished Merry Christmas back and forth and headed to our respective homes.

All the way home, Betty and Jerry recited what they heard people remark about Peter's singing. He was so pumped by the time we got home, he didn't want to go to bed.

"Jake, when we get home, may we build a snowman?" There was already six inches of snow on the ground.

"It's too late, Kiddo. It's time to go to bed."

"May I stay up and see Santa when he comes?"

"There's a little known fact concerning that, Peter. When some people have tried that move, Santa failed to show up. Apparently, he has no time on Christmas night to make small talk, even with cute little boys like you."

Peter tried other stalls, but I finally ushered him upstairs and into his PJ's, then he was changing, I had to ask. "Peter, you have a beautiful voice, but is it your own or are you using your ghostly powers?"

He looked at me, disappointed. "It's mine Jake, otherwise I'd be cheating. I thought you knew that."

I smiled at him and ruffled his hair. "I thought it was, but Peter, it's so beautiful, I had to ask."

He smiled. "Thanks, Grandpa. I wasn't sure if I could do it, but when you're there for me and with me, I feel like I can do almost anything."

For the first time he wore his pajamas tops on his own. Lying there he said, "Jake, just because Santa's coming this way, doesn't mean he's going to find me, does it?"

"No it doesn't, Kiddo."

The tears started to form. "Peter, I've got an idea. God has answered your prayers more than once. Why don't you try it again?"

"Do you think it would help?"

"I don't know, but I'm sure it wouldn't hurt. You can't pray for every little thing you may want. But this is your first Christmas. I think God will understand."

He and I both knelt on the floor. He reached up and put his hands on the bed and said, "Dear God," then hesitated. I looked at him. His head was bowed and his eyes were closed, deep in thought. "I really wish you could help Santa Claus find me tonight, but if you can't, that's okay. Just let Jake, Aunt Betty and Uncle Jerry have a good Christmas." He paused. "And God, this is the first year Darlene and Paula will be without Teddy. Please be extra caring to them. Amen."

Wow! What other kid would say a prayer like that? "Peter," I said with a tear in my eye, "you're really something. You're always thinking of others. That prayer may be more powerful than what you think."

As we climbed back in bed, he fired off several additional questions. I tackled the first one, but before I finished he was asleep, so I rejoined Betty and Jerry downstairs.

We put presents around the tree and stuffed the stockings with small gifts wrapped in tissue paper, totally different than the wrapping paper used earlier for the gifts. I could hardly wait for morning myself.

At one point during the night, I realized Peter was no longer next to me. I was alarmed at first but then I saw his silhouette at the window. I went over, knelt down next to him and put my arm around his shoulders. "I thought I heard bells, Jake."

I hugged him. "Maybe you did, Kiddo." Every child sooner or later hears bells on Christmas Eve. Some are even lucky enough to see Santa's sleigh and reindeer.

"Can we go down and check?" he said excitedly.

"Nope, we can't take a chance. If he is down there, we'd scare him off. We don't want to do that, do we?"

He shook his head. "When can we go down?"

I looked at my watch. It was a little after one. "Not for a long time yet." I ruffled his hair and carried him back to bed. "Santa has his job to do tonight and we do too. Our job is to sleep." I put my hand on his chest and he was soon back to sleep.

CHAPTER THIRTY-ONE

Morning came early, yet it seemed to come slowly. I was so excited that I felt like a kid. At 5:30, Peter woke me up. He wanted to go right down, but I told him not until six. We had to make sure Santa was gone if in fact he was even here. Besides, 6:00 was the time Betty, Jerry and I agreed on.

At six sharp, Peter was up. He impatiently waited for me to get dressed. Once dressed, I ushered him into the bathroom. While we took care of business, Jerry went down and turned on the Christmas tree lights. The camcorder was set. Jerry yelled to us to come down but sounded disappointed.

Peter picked up on it immediately. He looked at me, eyes already filling with tears. He turned to go back to bed, convinced Santa had passed him by again. I picked him up and carried him downstairs, his head resting on my shoulder with his arms around my neck. My shirt was soon wet. I felt his sobs. I put him on the floor just before entering the family room. Slowly he walked in, head down, sure the room would be empty. When he looked up, he couldn't believe his eyes. Presents surrounded the tree; the stockings were full and the snacks were gone. Jerry said Peter's eyes almost popped out of his head. He started jumping up and down, squealing. He turned around and jumped into my arms. "He was here, Jake, he was really here. I knew I heard bells last night."

I winked at Jerry but he shook his head. He was going to shake bells under our window last night but fell asleep. What then did Peter hear?

"Uncle Jerry, you're as bad as Jake. You sounded so disappointed, I thought sure Santa hadn't come."

"I know. I shouldn't have done that."

"No, it was okay. It was kind of funner that way."

All of the presents under the tree were from Santa Claus and most were for Peter. When he got to the sleeping bag, he said excitedly, "Wow, Jake, I've got my very own sleeping bag and it looks just like the one I saw in that store in Nebraska."

"It could be, Kiddo. There are so many children in the world, Santa gets some stores like Cabala's to help out at Christmas time." He was satisfied with my answer.

In addition, he got a snowsuit, a plastic sled that matched mine, two remote controlled 4x4's, two pairs of dress pants, two sport jackets, two dress shirts to go along with the jackets and two new ties. He was set for his next singing engagement. He also got his very own camera.

Then we went to the stockings. Peter got several new pairs of socks and a brand new set of super hero underwear. He got some snacks and other simple, non-expensive items. But one gift he pulled out of his stocking was a complete surprise to all of us. Betty was the official gift wrapper using tissue paper for all gifts in the stockings. This gift was wrapped in a different type of paper unfamiliar to all of us, and the wrapping was not her style. She looked at both Jerry and me, but neither one of us had a clue. Peter opened it with care then held it up for all to see. Peter looked at it, confused. "Wow, this is neat...but what is it?"

With any other child, it would have been a simple little plastic thing, but with Peter, it wasn't that simple at all. It was a cute, little angel: Its mouth circular as if singing. There were small wings. Its hair was long and golden. It eerily resembled Peter. Above its head was light-colored plastic in the shape of a halo. The halo seemed to take on different colors in the light.

"It's an angel, Peter." Betty bent at the waist to examine it more closely. "It's a precious, beautiful little angel." She noticed a golden string attached. "And a Christmas tree ornament." She stood up and looked at Jerry and me, confused. Jerry and I shrugged our shoulders. None of us knew who it was from or how it got into the house, let alone Peter's stocking.

Peter took it to the tree and carefully hung it from a branch. As his tiny hands left it, the ornament gave off a slight glow.

My familiar back chills were racing. I again looked at Betty. She was rubbing her arms as if in fright. I knew she saw the glow and was experiencing her own chills. I knelt next to Peter and put my hand on the back of his neck. We both stared at the small angel. He said, "It sorta looks like me, Jake."

Did he see the glow, too? "Yeah, it does, Little One." We were silent and transfixed for a long moment by this…this mystery gift.

My thoughts returned to Peter's prayer the night before. Someone must have been listening. Maybe a real angel. I knew Santa would find Peter; after all, Betty, Jerry and I were Santa. But who else found Peter last night? Peter's prayer was beautiful and so typical of him. But how powerful was it? I told Betty and Jerry about it while we were filling the stockings.

Just then I noticed a folded piece of paper sitting under the empty plate where the snacks had been. I looked at it quickly. On the outside it was printed in pencil, "To Peter". I thought to myself, "Nice touch," thinking Jerry or Betty wrote it and put it there last night. I gave it to Peter, since it was for him. He unfolded it and read it aloud. "Dear Peter, I'm sorry you didn't think I visited you in Slippery Gulch, but I never left your side. Now you're with your friend. You want to stay with Jake forever? Time will tell. Keep saying your prayers and be a good boy this year. Remember, I'll be watching. PS. I hope you like the little angel."

It wasn't signed.

Peter's eyes met mine. I didn't know whose were bigger.

What did the writer mean when he said, "I never left your side?" And who was the writer?

I'd told no one of Peter's wish. The Santa Claus in the Kansas mall was the only other person who heard Peter's wish to stay with me forever. I knew Betty's history of a good practical joke.

But then, she could not have known Peter's wish either.

Just as the chills kicked in, Betty said, "Jake, could I talk to you for a few minutes?" I looked at Peter. He was busy with Jerry on the floor installing batteries in the two remote-controlled 4x4's. Betty and I walked into the living room separated from the family room by the kitchen and the front hall.

"Jake, tell me the truth: You came down last night and put that angel in Peter's stocking, didn't you?"

"Betty, I swear to you on a stack of Bibles, I've never seen that angel before."

She was not convinced.

"I know only this: Whoever wrote the note is the same one that gave Peter the gift."

"How do you know?"

I told Betty about our stop in the mall two weeks earlier. And I told her what Peter said he had asked Santa for. "You see Betty, I never told one single person Peter's request. Anyway, that note is not my handwriting. You know I can't write pretty to save my life."

She thought about all of this. "Jake, Peter is a gift to you as you are a gift to him."

"Profound. And true."

"Life itself is a gift to Peter. His voice is a gift to all who heard it last night. Could we be missing the big picture?"

My big sister lost me. "What do you mean?"

"Could this gift be a symbol of the biggest gift of all – that is to both you and Peter?"

"Betty, stop beating around the bush. Just tell me what you're getting at."

She shook her head. "Jake, sometimes you are so thick. Could the gift be a symbol meant for you – of exactly what Peter really is?"

I looked at her, puzzled, then thought I got it. "You mean an angel?" She nodded. I chuckled. "No way! You sentimentalists drive me nuts. Think of his misbehavior around here. Would an angel go running around the house naked?"

She chuckled. "A tiny angel? Why not, Mr. Science Teacher Know-It-All?"

"Hey, sister. You're hitting below the belt. Come off it. Lighten up!"

"I'm serious. You are so smart about everything. Even about how to raise that boy, you who've never been married. I told Jerry, my bachelor brother is doing a better job with Peter than you and I did with our offspring."

"That's wrong. You were younger then. You're comparing me at my age, and all the schools of hard knocks I've been through, with you and Jerry way back when you were learning on the job. Damn it, I watched you guys, and I learned from you two a whole lot of what you say I've always known.

"Here's something else. I taught school and worked in a residential camp. For over twenty years I worked with the products of both good and bad parenting and fatherhood. While kids Peter's age stayed in my cabin for two-week periods, I was able to put into practice the good parenting I witnessed. I could find out what worked for me and what didn't, never figuring I'd be able to put it into long-term practice."

"I'm sorry, Jake. Why is it that something always tries to ruin a perfectly good Christmas family time?"

"Because we're human. We're all sinners. Hell, that's why God gave us Christmas. Life doesn't make sense without it." I put my hand on her shoulder. "I'm sorry I came off with having all the answers. I'm trying to be a father and put everything I know into play. Believe me, Peter is dissolving any illusions of grandeur I ever had about myself. I've been stretched three ways from Sunday with that kiddo of mine.

"Here's something else, Betty. There have been many times during the past six months, when I've said something or acted without thinking. The perfect example is when Peter's hatred of Indians surfaced. We were upset with each other. I sat him on the floor of the family room and gave him a choice; either go to the Indian Reservation with me or go back to Slippery Gulch alone. As soon as I uttered those words, I wished I could take them back, but I couldn't.

"Betty, I was scared to death I was going to lose him. Unlike me, he thought through the situation before acting. He's teaching me a lot, Betty."

"I'm sure he is."

"The latest is, yesterday afternoon and into the evening: Will you believe me when I tell you that I wrestled with being jealous of that...that...whatever it is. I was disgusted when I went to bed...disgusted with me, Jake Winters. Your answer man has no answer for that one. Imagine, me jealous of Peter, a ghost."

"He's an angel, and one day you will agree," she said.

"I'm sorry. I know too much. I've been through too much evidence to the contrary. Betty, you remember how seriously hurt he was when riding his bike with Nathan in September, because he didn't listen. Angels listen, I think. And obey!

And the first time on his bike with me, he got hurt for the same reason.

"Think about our camp-out. He got into trouble. And hurt! More than once for the same reason! And that's not to mention a few times in the truck. Plus he peed on me...more than once. He's had both constipation and diarrhea. Is that a common problem among angels? Does any of this sound like the behavior and character of angels like we see in the Bible?"

She started laughing. "No, I guess not." She paused for a minute. "Are you saying Peter is a holy terror then?"

"Heavens no! Peter's a terrific little boy. He doesn't listen all the time. He's normal...well except for the fact that he's been dead for one hundred years. I wouldn't change him in any way. But an angel? I don't think so."

"I guess you're right, but that brings us back to the reason for this talk," Betty said. "If none of us gave him the angel or wrote the note, who did?"

I sat there thinking. It couldn't have been written by anyone outside of this house, nor was it written by anyone inside.

I thought of Santa Claus; more specifically the man that played the store Santa in the mall in Kansas. Aside from Peter and me, he was the only other person in the world that knew what Peter asked for, for Christmas, until Christmas morning.

Now I wondered. Who was that guy? Or maybe a better question is...what was that guy?

Then I thought of Peter and realized I could ask the same questions of him. Right now, Peter was a fun-loving little boy with the wonderment of Christmas and Santa in his eyes. Last night in church, Peter demonstrated the beauty of his voice to the congregation. While he sang *Oh Holy Night,* the minister reported seeing a glow around his head. Was it a halo? Could it have been a result of an over-active imagination? Wishful thinking? The magic of the Christmas season?

Peter was murdered in 1901. We know that for a fact. His physical body was restored and returned to him one hundred years later, apparently as a result of his final prayer. And I was the answer to his prayer. I know that for sure. But what is he?

Bill Early, while on our camping trip in August, speculated Peter could be a demon disguised as a cute little boy. The ghost of Jim Bridger blew that speculation out of the water. That only left two possibilities; a ghost or an angel. Many people believed him to be an angel. But none of them know Peter as well as me. I was convinced he was a ghost. Peter thought he was too.

In a week we would pass into the year 2002. The ending of the old year marks closure for many people. Would it for me? Would all of my questions then be answered? How could they be? For many people, the new year brings new hopes with new beginnings.

But what would it bring for me? Would it bring the answers to my tons of questions and a continuation of the wonderful six months I'd just experienced? Or would it bring the end to that experience with those questions gone unanswered as a result of Peter being forced back into his grave at the end of his funeral on June 30th? For Peter and me, would it be the beginning or the end?

ABOUT THE AUTHOR

Doug White, author of the Jake Winters series, including **The Load, The Editorial,** and now **The Gift**, is a former school teacher and camp counselor. He drove an 18-wheeler cross-country for thirteen years until 2003 when he turned in his big truck for an RV. A graduate of Massanutten Military Academy in Woodstock, Virginia, and Ashland College (now Ashland University) in Ashland, Ohio, White is JC International Senator #32834. He resides in Orchard Park, New York. In his free time he enjoys camping, canoeing and fishing.